KU-015-774

MARTINI HENRY

SARA CROWE

BLACK SWAN

TRANSWORLD PUBLISHERS
61–63 Uxbridge Road, London W5 5SA
www.penguin.co.uk

Transworld is part of the Penguin Random House group of companies
whose addresses can be found at global.penguinrandomhouse.com

First published in Great Britain in 2016 by Doubleday
an imprint of Transworld Publishers
Black Swan edition published 2016

Copyright © Sara Crowe 2016

Sara Crowe has asserted her right under the Copyright,
Designs and Patents Act 1988 to be identified as the author of this work.

This book is a work of fiction and, except in the case of historical fact, any
resemblance to actual persons living or dead, is purely coincidental.

Every effort has been made to obtain the necessary permissions
with reference to copyright material, both illustrative and quoted. We apologize
for any omissions in this respect and will be pleased to make the appropriate
acknowledgements in any future edition.

A CIP catalogue record for this book
is available from the British Library.

ISBN 9781784160609

Typeset in 10.45/15.3pt ITC Berkeley Old Style Std by
Jouve (UK), Milton Keynes.
Printed and bound by Clays Ltd, Bungay, Suffolk.

Penguin Random House is committed to a sustainable
future for our business, our readers and our planet. This book
is made from Forest Stewardship Council® certified paper.

1 3 5 7 9 10 8 6 4 2

To Sean and to Lizzie

PART ONE

*Pushing the Smallest Boundary
with an Afternoon Drink*

> *Aunt Coral's To Do*
> *Make will*
> *Library (Gardener's Chronicle)*
> *Compost*
> *Cheddar*

Green Place
Clockhouse Lane
Egham
Sat Jan 30 1988
2.35pm

Dear Sue,

I'm sorry I haven't written each day as I promised – I have been rushed off my feet.

This evening my Texan guest Mr Hart will be hosting a talk in the drawing room on the Victorian love affair with gardens. Mrs Bunion has made a paella. (I am sorry to say she was given the wrong brief.)

This is because Mr Hart *was* going to give a talk on Calypso dance but today he spontaneously decided to change it due to our remarkable discoveries.

I should start by explaining that every time I put the radio on lately, they say a new record has been broken, the coldest day, the wettest month, the angriest sky. And the last time it wasn't raining was last Tuesday week. And so in a rare respite from the elements, the Admirals, Mr Hart and Hugh from Chertsey took the opportunity to catch up with some garden To Do. With our new tenants, the male to female ratio in the house is now 5 to 3. This has many things to recommend it! It is the sole reason that Delia has taken to wafting about in the evenings in a silk devoré diva (glamorous name for a housecoat).

Anyway, all five gents were getting stuck in and cutting back the empires of thorns down at the bottom of the meadows, when they inadvertently began to excavate what looked like solid red brick. So they spread out in a line and hacked their way through the undergrowth and found they made contact with bricks and mortar for at least forty feet! Realizing we might be on the brink of discovering a *building*, I swung into action with the Parish Magazine.

Mr Bellamy, from Dew Garden Mechanicals, has been here every day since then in his digger and the site is now cleared right back, to reveal the decrepit remains of two cottages and a large walled garden! If you look down from the right-hand side of Green Place (as you face the drive), the ruins stand about 2 acres away, at the bottom of the sloping meadows.

The old garden walls are ramshackle, crumbly and only part standing, but still clearly form the shape of an extensive oblong stockade. At one entrance, which I believe could have been the main one, a ragged wooden door still survives under an archway. It is tattered, devoid of its key and ironically it is still locked.

My first port of call in terms of research was to put out a feeler for a historian. So I rang the *Egham Echo* to see if they offered a list of experts in the locale and a very nice woman called Jackie County got in touch. She is archivist for the Percival Library in Egham and also tends the record vaults at the *Echo*.

We have already trawled the garden section at the Percival for any information on old local gardens which, alas, did not bear fruit.

But Jackie is undeterred and has been down at the ruins all day with her camera, paving the way for an article she intends to write. She's a doughty lady with a boot full of spaniels and a cookery qualification. Her hunch is, judging by the state of the brickwork at the site, that at some point there has been a fire.

This is really just a quickie as I desperately wanted to find a moment to sit down and tell you the extraordinary news. But having unburdened myself of the telling, I must rush, as this evening's Victorian Flower talk has transformed into a full-scale event and we expect 15 guests, including our old and new tenants. I did ask your father and Ivana, but they have cancelled on account of Ivana's condition.

So, due to the numbers attending, I do understand Mrs Bunion's being upset over what she has described as 'the paella of shame'.

In answer to your concerns about feeling out of your depth with some of your coursework, my advice is that you should persist and hold tight to your values. Fill your mind with knowledge and *never* be embarrassed to ask questions.

In closing I'll just draw your attention to a clipping I have popped in. It was drawn to my attention by Jackie County herself. As I explained, she tends the archives at the *Echo* and so she has her finger on the pulse. Maybe as far as becoming a writer goes this might be a good way to cut your teeth?

All love,

Aunt Coral Xx

Cutting from the *Egham Echo*

Mid-summer Internship Offered (June 15 to September 30 1988)
To assist in our busy Features Office

....

Candidates please send completed questionnaire by February
28 1988

To: Mr Gordoney George
         Egham Echo
         The Tillings
         Quakers Acre
         Egham

We will endeavour to process and respond to all applications by
April 15 1988.

FEATURES INTERNSHIP APPLICATION

....

ABOUT YOU

Name: Sue Bowl

Age: 18

Home: Green Place, Clockhouse Lane, Egham

Nationality: British

Languages: None (except British)

Education: Titford High School

I am currently studying under Benjamin O'Carroll for a
Diploma in Creative Writing at Taverna O'Carroll in
Crete. I am a half scholarship student. I will graduate in
April and I will be available immediately after.

Experience

The Egham Hirsute Group (EHG) Weekly Writers Group
(FM. Founder Member.)

Also, Individual Winner of the Ramblers Association
Gala Short Story Competition in December 1987, whence
I met Mr O'Carroll MBA.

Skills None (except writing)

ABOUT WRITING

What is your approach to writing?

The devil is in the detail.

What do you think recommends you for a career in journalism?

A love of language, a love of people, 24-hour curiosity.

Why would you make a good intern?

I could offer an alien's perspective, edginess, and an easy way with a beverage! I am open, frank, eager and willing.

What would you hope to gain from an internship in the Features Office?

My dream is to live by my pen. My hope would be that an internship with The Echo would give me a major grounding. I would seek to broaden my classical approach, into tough truncated pith.

What kind of writer are you? Can you offer half a page on your style and any aims?

As a writer I think I'm with Emily Bronte, out there shivering on the moors, tapping at the window, a ghostly spectre running away from all the darkness that lies in the misty other world.

My aim is to retain a leaning towards the classical, and to be scrupulously honest. For when I'm faced with a field of blazing flowers, I feel I could burn with joy till I am feverish and then die of the bliss. But I do see that this sort of bent, or at least the expression of it, is not necessarily a restrained enough technique, and my goal is to endeavour to become more sparton about things, to be muted . . . and to *simmer*. To write as it were, almost as if I am constantly on the edge of having an orgasm, but never actually having one.

A LITTLE MORE ABOUT YOU

Best moment: Getting my creative writing scholarship to Taverna O'Carroll.

Worst moment: The sudden loss of my mother.

Favourite things: Nice stationery, tea party clothes, spontaneity.

If you had a lazy old dog what would you call it? Dave.

And a new kitten? Leoncia.

Favourite poem:
'A sight to dream of and not to tell
Shield, shield oh Cristobel'
(Matthew Arnold)

Why?
Because she seems to be hiding her secret dream.

Favourite book:
Jane Eyre by Charlotte Bronte.

Why?

Because she was never really what we might call
'a teenager' and I feel I never was either. Both Jane
Eyre and I have had to grow up fast due to life's blows.

Any mottos?

'Listen with the ears of your heart.'
(Biblical)

THANKS! Gordoney George and the Team

Sue

Taverna O'Carroll, Creative Writing Course
Shabany Bay, Crete

Mon Feb 8 1988 9am
On a pontoon

This seat of learning stands on the beach at Shabany Bay – the brain child of Mr O'Carroll MBA. It boasts three classrooms and four dorms set over Café English.

One of a handful of villas at the peaceful end of Shabany, with crisp white-washed walls enjoying the nautical chique of seaside shutters in blue.

A sweep of terraces and a first-floor veranda regularly buzz with students, and beyond them the mountain road snakes away like a ball of tossed-away string.

Yet surely, it is the shoreline that commands the finest position from which to view the Taverna life. For, what it is to be young! Our elders say we don't know it. But for my friends, from down on the waterfront, I can see what a great blessing that it is.

Note: I think I sound a bit too much like a travel agent.

I'm just back from the letter box having posted off my application to the *Echo*. Although it is such a coo! to be here, I have still been worrying about how I am going to earn after I finish on the course. And so Aunt Coral's clipping winging its way here is as if it is *meant*. But I must try not to get my hopes up too much, as I'm sure there will be lots of candidates. I must stay calm and do as the infamous doctor advised me after mum died, 'try to avoid stress and getting over emotional.' Doctors!

As to the news in Aunt C's letter, much as I am deeply surprised to hear that they have unearthed these ruins, I am also not surprised at all. Because the grounds of Green Place are so vast and there are *empires* of thorns and *swathes* of meadows that sprawl to the side of the house. This is because Aunt Coral believes that some grass should be left to grow long as a treat for the insects. She studied Evolutionary Biology at university, and had a long romance with a botanist. She carved her career out of spiders and venoms; she's a very big fan of wild things.

5pm
On a rock down by the sea

Our first tutorial this morning was something called an Encapsulation exercise. Point A of the task was to learn how to encapsulate *events*.

Mr O'Carroll set us what he calls an exercise of diminishment, which asked the question 'Can you sum up your life in less than 4 paragraphs?'

He read us out an example of his own life's encapsulization, which is used as a bench mark for coursework. Mr O'Carroll has managed to get his whole adulthood into a single sentence. It goes like this:

> *I can recount the entirety of the last three decades under the headings the peccadilloes of all the wives and the misdemeanours of all the sons.*

I think that is absolutely inspirational!

My dorm mate Helen Spring's was also brilliant, pithy and no nonsense, she wrote:

> *Grew up, went to London, stayed three years, came back with a novel.*

It was a bit like a shopping list.

Here below is mine:

My Life in Less than Four Paragraphs.

by Sue Bowl.

I was born to complicated parents in a terraced house, in Titford. My mother and I were close, my father somewhat distant. They'd grown apart by the time I was ten, our horizons shrunk, we ate piecemeal. They treated home like it was just somewhere to get changed and look in the fridge. And in the midst of it all I had my childhood, in a bedroom that was 8 by 8.

But events took a desperate turn when my life was split into before and after, in the same way that Jesus divided the calendar. This was when my mother split my life in two, on the day she ended her own.

This tragic event was little more than a year ago, but my Father has already re-married and furthermore his new wife is expecting a baby.

And I don't really know how I managed to get from those dark days into these brighter ones, but for the fact that I was somewhat rescued by my wonderful, eccentric, extravagant, bohemiam, omnipotent Great Aunt Coral.

I expect the others will be asking me a lot of questions about what happened to mum this evening and suicide is a hard thing to explain.

When I say that my mum died, people assume that it must have been cancer, and I admit that I feel somehow ashamed that it wasn't. But mum was very sensitive and she found living too painful, and I have to argue this point in my head almost constantly so I don't feel that I wasn't enough.

The appearance of dad's current wife Ivana in his life, has made things that much harder. For here is a woman who has spent her youth philandering around Denmark and then, I'm guessing, hacked her way through an ice flow in order to get to England and philander my dad. Now, she has hijacked him, my childhood home, and my mum's position in it. It's a deeply pain-ful situation and an on-going battle to accept.

But, I think as a result of all this, I conjured Aunt Coral into my life. Because I still needed an adult. Someone who could take care of me when I wasn't quite up to the job.

Tues Feb 9 6am
In the dorm

This time of day is a good time for journaling and catching up thoughts, as I'm keen not to neglect that side of things. When I get back home, I want to have an account of life here to treasure. Because I know that over time, the little details will slip away, until I get to the point where I can't remember the names and faces and the places.

I also wanted to complete my notes on point 2 of the Encap-sulation exercise from yesterday. In the afternoon, Mr O'Carroll moved on to instructing us on the pruning and condensing of *characters*.

We had to come up with a character, i.e. Sabrina Weston-Fair, and offer a three-word description for them, i.e. She eats salad.

Mr O'Carroll teaches a technique he calls 'Active' Description, for which he uses a three-word format to focus detail. He is most keen on observations that convey the way people *move* or how they *sound*, and not only the way they *look*. He uses the Active Description method to kick start fleshier work. If three words won't express a certain character, then they can be pushed to a maximum of eleven.

And so he set us a task where we had to try and capture the essence of some of the people in our current day-to-day lives, as opposed to any fiction or to our past, and do so using both his Active Description technique and his Encapsulation method.

Thus I read out the following:

CAST LIST

AT HOME:

Aunt Coral is my Great Aunt, she is very, very dear to me. Without wishing to sound melodramatic, I'd say she was the light of my life. She has all but adopted me and salvaged me, given me sanctuary, hope, and a new life.

Three-word description: Shopaholic Bon Viveur.

Delia is Aunt Coral's lady companion. She is great fun, yet with a dark side.

3-word description: Joyous, frank, o'reverand.

The Admiral is Aunt Coral's main tenant. We know him as *the* Admiral because it distinguishes him from the other two Admirals living in our house. The Admiral's civilian name is Avery Little, his personal motto is 'Avery Little Helps'. I'd say he looks very striking for his years, but he must be over 70 because all his maps are out of date.

Six words in his case: All his maps are out of date.

Admiral Gordon is a full blooded Scotsman and makes an eligible suitor for Delia.

TWD: *Likes his tucker.*

Admiral Ted is a gentleman, a man of caution and cross-words. Polite, thoughtful, hard of hearing and so old-fashioned he is practically pre-electricity.

TWD: *He never runs.*

Mrs Bunion is Aunt Coral's housekeeper. She is a diamond. This is easier to get into a TWD: She never stops.

And last but not least:

IN THE WIDER WORLD:

Joe Falling in love with Joe happened slowly, it wasn't drastic. Or rather, it wasn't drastic for me. He is a mass of inconsistencies, he is awkward, intelligent, nurturing, unfashionable, cheerful, simple and complicated. It is bittersweet to reduce his description to less than an essay, but if forced I would say that Joe is:

Masculine enough to reveal that gingham makes him feel happy.

As I read out my list, I believe some of my fellow students might have been finding me peculiar, coming as most of them do from stable academic family homes. I do hope that, though I haven't been to university, I'm still going to fit in.

Tues Feb 9 1988 11pm
Back in the dorm

During the middling hours of this morning a bank of cloud wrapped itself round the Taverna like a blanket. I thought it was fog when I looked out of the window, but the villas on the opposite side of the bay stood in blazing sun that bleached their canopies white. This is a phenomenon of Shabany caused by the clouds meeting the air and the sea. And as the cloud disappeared, the warming air smelled of perm lotion and later it was revealed why when Cinnamon came down with fresh curls.

Cinnamon Sunday lives upstairs and runs Café English. (NB I have translated all Greek names into English so I can understand them.) Cinnamon mostly wears a washaday housecoat, but her sandals are golden, as are her eyes.

My nights here on the course are spent in a dormitory, so getting up and out in the morning can be hectic. And due to the lack of space in the dorm, I have only the basics with me in my packing. These items were masterminded by Aunt Coral and this is my infantry: Lotions, bikini, sarong, long-legged trousers for bites. A statement cardi for sharp evenings, swish dress for cocktails and talks. Sleeve top, vests and t-shirts, all wash and wear. Formal shorts, knockabout shorts, hill walking boots, socks and plasters. High-heeled shoes, sandals, jelly shoes, one pair flip-flops, and one pair jeans. Aunt Coral said somewhat wistfully that if you can wear jeans you can travel.

She told me once that she'd be too self-conscious to wear jeans herself. Though far from prim, she is remarkably ladylike in her dress sense. I must write and tell her that I have seen plenty of sixtygenarians in jeans here and Mr O'Carroll wears dungies. It sounds like she could do with a pair of them in her wardrobe so that she can muck in with her tenants and get stuck into the extraordinary archaeological discoveries!

But other than my jeans and the tools of my trade – jotters etc. – the only other things I have with me are a couple of precious mementos of my mum, a letter she wrote me, and her picture that I keep tucked away in my case, because I'm still too raw to have it out.

And I brought a picture of Joe that was taken outside Green Place on January 3rd a couple of days before I came here. It sits on the shelf beside my bunk. I think that the pictures that get placed on the shelf beside the bunk in the dorm are a good indication of some sort of love story back home. (One of my room mates, Helen, has a picture of a fat old cat on hers.)

Joe told me early on in our relationship, which only really began properly in December, that when he was younger he had an imaginary girlfriend called Janet Clarke. You'd have thought that coming from his imagination she'd have been called something like Flick Vanderbee or Cecily Summer, but Joe is terribly modest, it's one of the reasons why I like him. I was telling Helen about him last night and she said she thought he might have something that she called 'working class authenticity'. I think that sounds about right.

I just discovered a dried clipping of lesser celandine, which Aunt Coral had also popped in with her ruins newsletter. I nearly missed it because it was wrapped inside a small tatty scrap of paper, and I only just realized it was there when I came to reread. The scrap of paper said she had plucked it from the earth inside the derelict walled garden, as if it was a time capsule.

And what a dear yellow flower the lesser celandine is, with starry petals that worship the sun. It made me think of all the buds that would be freezing in the ditches of England and I feel as near and far as an echo in a land where the nature is so brash. The sun's garish light is so harsh on a lady's skin tone. It highlights imperfection. Plukes, spots and skin are illuminated so you can see straight through to the tapestry of gristles inside.

Strictly speaking it's not hot enough in February for bikinis, shorts or white linen, but we Brits are so deprived of the sun we just can't wait to peel off. I have been here since January 7th when I got straight into a sarong, which made me feel risqué, liberated, and also a tad self-conscious.

Weds Feb 10 1988, 11pm

Students at the Taverna are divided into three groups, Tolstoy, Dickens, and Zola Tutorial Groups (I'm in Zola). The groups are called after great writers Leo Tolstoy, Charles Dickens and Camille Zola. And Mr O'Carroll subdivided Zola today for some buddy work with a partner. (Mine was Helen Spring from my dorm.)

Mr O'C says I can learn a lot from Helen because she has suffered and emulates the Russians. In fact his main note to me on the course so far is that I must learn to be more Russian in my work, so ever since I've been making it my project to be as simmering as I possibly can. Curious that he thinks I have not suffered, I obviously don't look like I have. But then, I don't express myself like a Russian, because I'm too used to cheering myself up.

But Helen has suffered in her childhood and has never had very much money. Back home in the dire times she confessed that the only way she could afford make-up was to go and apply it from the testers at Boots.

If I were to try and summarize with an active description of her I'd say, Helen is the girl you see at the table in the corner of the nightclub smoking and having opinions.

The majority of the other students here are graduates with smart bars of chocolate in their luggage. There's only one other like me who hasn't been to university.

William McVie comes from the Highlands, and thought

that an Oxbridge went over a river. He explained that a traffic jam in the Hebrides is two minis and a ford capri. He's a poet with ruddy cheeks and suffers from infatuation. He's even had a crush on germy Izzy (who chambermaids at Hotel Bunty on the other side of the Bay). William can't get his head round the fact that I live with elderly bohemiams. But he appears to find anyone over the age of 20 embarrassing. I don't think he will age well himself because it will all come as a horrible shock to him. Helen says he is a Puer Eternis (eternal boy). This could be his TWD.

Other than Helen, William and myself, there are two other members in Zola and they are Diane Winterby and Quiz Wilson, a glittering couple from London.

Quiz (Crispin) is Diane's boyfriend, a devilishly good-looking Englishman. He is so at ease in the world he wears dinner dress as though it's his comfy joggers. He looks like Robert Donut. (If your references go back that far.)

And he's a Professor in his own right, of philosophy, from the University of London in Bloomsbury (which is amazing because he is only 28).

And Diane is probably the sharpest cookie in the Taverna – a prodigy in literature and writing, and when I am around her, I confess I feel something a kin to a crush. She's one of those extra-ordinary waif girls; as Aunt Coral might say, 'she'd have to stand in the same place twice to cast a shadow.' She's tall and blonde, and though academic has chosen a 'film-school haircut' (with angles and both long and short bits to style at the front).

Her vocabulary is enormous, with lots of Latin and French. I have kept a record of some of the words she uses: for example, Ingénue, Oeuvre and Bafouillage (which I believe means simply, gibberish). Plus she keeps a jotter entitled 'Apprentissage

Repertoirier' which loosely means List of Learning. TWD: God-dess of Charm.

As a couple she and Quiz have their own unique language too, which can be infectious. It's smattered with French and Franglais, and they brought research books with them packed in joint trunks which are leather and labelled 'Winterby and Wilson' like a firm of city solicitors.

To complete my early observations – or my reverie as it turns out! – I would say that, I believe that in Diane's case, I would have added an 'A' to the end of her name. She certainly gives the impres-sion of being more a Diana than a Diane. In fact the simple letter A can take a girl quite far in the world, Julie-a, Christine-a, Susan-a, Helen-a. I would go as far as to say it is the most aspirational letter in the alphabet.

And expanding on that, if she were to swap her middle A and I over, it would make her a Daine, which conjures a lady from Den-mark, or maybe the son of a shoemaker. At any rate, I'm only recording all this to get into good habits of description. As I men-tioned, Taverna policy encourages observations which are not based on people's looks . . . which brings me back to Quiz.

The handsome devil seems an intense sort of person and sometimes I find intense people can knock the tops off all your emotional scabs. But in Quiz's case he has always taken the trouble to put me back together again if he's taken me apart with enquiries.

We were chatting in Café English this evening over hugely enjoyable cocktails and I expressed my concerns that as I've never been to university and am the youngest here by a long way, I'm not sure I'm going to come up to scratch. By way of reassuring me he mentioned a writer called Blasé Pascal who wrote a book he called simply 'Pensees'. Which means simply, 'Thoughts'. This sort of information drips from Quiz's mouth like honey. I think I can get his TWD down to one – dazzling.

Perhaps it was my being scrupulously honest enough to describe Quiz as dazzling that has caused me to sit up in my bunk and feel so forlorn about missing Joe. Quiz *is* breathtaking, and if I am trying to be scrupulously honest, I confess to my shame I have discovered I am vulnerable to infatuation. But Quiz doesn't have that little thing that Joe has, that indefinable quality.

I can't describe it, but it is something which leads me out of my little dark place. Joe has the ability to do that like no one else. I miss that, I'm not particularly good at doing it for myself. But Joe can blow the cobwebs away with the simplest of pleasures, like a trip to the garden centre, or a spin out on his bike, for something as ordinary as picking up Aunt Coral's prescription.

I suppose what I mean is that he is that lethal combination of maternal and masculine. Maybe that's why I fell for him. He represents everything that I am missing. And if the boot were on the other foot, in my amateur opinion, for Joe I would be one of those girlfriends who is more like his oldest child, for what he craves more than most boys of his age is a family.

He told me his dream in life is a warm house, with lots of kids and an old cat asleep on the stairs. He called it 'a house with more than one type of mustard' and I understand his shorthand. And I feel a little homesick tonight, and not for Titford, my childhood home, or even for the refuge of Green Place, but for the one that hasn't existed yet, maybe the one with the old cat.

Thursday February 11 1988, 11am

In homage to Di I have decided to keep an

Apprentiessiage Repertoiriez

(Word List)

And today the first words on it are

> *Bathos* and *Pathos*

And in homage to Quiz, I've decided to record

Pensees

Here is my first one:

> *A slim woman devours nothing but paperbacks.* SB

Local Guru, the Cretan Professor John Mushrooms, heads up the majority of our tutorials in Zola when Mr O'Carroll is busy with his own personal group Tolstoy.

Professor Mushrooms doesn't approve of too long or difficult a name in a book, because he says it can be jarring to keep coming up against names like, for example *Zolhanriantin*, because it takes so long to think how to pronounce it that you forget where you are in the plot. (This is the main reason why I have translated Greek names to English, as I mentioned.)

His lectures take place in Classroom 6 above Café English, where a buffet's prepared each morning and we are tormented by the smells from lunch.

I have three categories of homework on-going with Professor John: fiction prose, personal reflection, and technical ability. He was telling us earlier today in a talk about marine life that sharks lay their eggs in something called a mermaid's slipper, and though

I believe in mermaids, I'm pretty sure that in this case that is still a part of the shark?

His main note for me so far is that my writing is too middle class. I tried to explain that, actually, I now consider myself to be upper class but without money, or at least upper-slash-middle. And I attempted to describe a bohemiam, which of course is a class in itself, denoting those who've had money but who now live in reduced circumstances and wear bobbly hats, like Aunt Coral and her favourite tenants. I put myself in the upper-class category because Green Place is now my home. And whilst on paper it is amongst the aristocracy of buildings, we have no money to restore it. This is largely due to Aunt Coral's spending.

It is her true nature, as far as price tags are concerned, to make sure she adds zeros to the end of them. She is not one for the sales, thrift, or a bargain. Aunt Coral would head straight for Harrods if she was let off the lead and might well never come back.

Professor Mushrooms set us some further homework today, to be completed by the end of July, 3 months after the course is finished here. It is something which he calls a *long finger* exercise, meaning it will take longer than other written tasks. But Mr O'Carroll and most everybody else refer to this exercise as 'a dissertation'. We will have to present the dissertation for passing before we can be issued with a pass certificate for our Diplomas from the Taverna, so it is the most important part of our coursework. The exercise, in essence, is to research something factual from history and use it as a theme, and then use that theme as a setting for a story with fictional characters in it. At the moment my interest is torn between Russian literature and mermaids.

This is my favourite time of day here, just after five o'clock when lessons are done and I can come down to the beach to sit on a comfortable rock to write. From here I can look back to the Taverna and observe Tolstoy coming out on to the terrace. This last tutorial often goes on until 5.30, because Mr O'Carroll gets carried away. He likes to linger with the group after their session when they break to take coffee and soft fruit.

How glamorous they all look up there, how giddy the fall of their laughter. And the setting of the sparkling sun on the silvery sea only contributes to this spirit of bedazzlement, but then, the air here is somewhat narcotic. Yet, I have that relieved feeling, like when all the politicians go on holiday, and I do feel amazed to have come through such an unfathomably heartbreaking time.

Fiction Prose Sketch

DOONYASHA

by Sue Bowl

"Halt! Who goes there?" said the traveller "Speak Mon, I will brook no nonsense."

"I am Doonyasha," he said

"My Father lost our home in a card game, my mother is always weeping."

"Where do you live?"

"On the Glade," said the boy, "with my Aunt Bettia Pulnietzova. My sister has been sent to London, but I will find her and bring her home. And then I will throw

myself into the gorse and two fingers to
the thorns."

"But why do you stay in the forest
tell me? What ails ye?"

"I'm making plans," he said.

Green Place
Clockhouse Lane
Egham
Weds Feb 3 1988

Dear Sue,

Thank you for your letter and I hope you're taking care of
your verruca.

I write with some news on a couple of matters. Firstly,
that Jackie County has produced some interesting findings
from her initial archive trawl.

She has managed to exhume plans, issued by my Great
Great Grandfather Edmund Garden, dating from 1857 for
the walled garden, which also feature some hand drawings
by the designer Herbert Frank Hotston-Moore. Of the four
walls, one faces due south, while another is shaded by the
Egham chain. The idea being that plants can then be
carefully laid out according to their preferences.

Hotston-Moore's notes suggest that pears be grown
against the warm bricks of the south wall and shade-loving
blackberries and cotoneasters on the north. His garden
design is crowned at the heart with a beautiful Victorian
sundial, the base of which he suggests should be submerged
slightly below ground level, in order that the shadow of the
dial can be seen from great distances within the two-acre
plot. Imagine!

And the old sundial remains well preserved in situ at the very core of our ruins. The Admiral was drawn to it like a magnet, as was my Texan B and B guest, Mr Hart. Mr Bellamy nearly mowed it down in his digger, but fortunately stopped just in time. When it was revealed, the sundial was caked in mud and detritus and its face was a slab of dried earth as hard as stone.

But we knew it must bear an inscription, so the Admiral got into his boiler suit and scrubbed it down, and he got some tracing paper and a wax crayon and did a little rubbing. When he had the imprint on the paper, it read: 'For the Concern of the Rich and the Poor'.

An unusual inscription, but rather beautiful none the less. We used to have one at school that said 'I stand amidst ye lumiere flowers, to show you passing of the hours'.

It's extraordinary what has been unearthed here, and I feel certain much more is to come.

My second piece of news is that I have been in touch with Johnny Look-at-the-Moon, and the Admiral and I have decided to help him fund a trip to Australia to visit his son, Christie. The poor fellow hasn't seen him for some time, due to a lack of funds. Johnny sent his particular love to you and looks forward to seeing you again on his return. Exciting to know that along with a brand-new Grandfather, you have an Uncle Christie!

I do hope all is going well on the course, and that you're managing to keep up with the heavies. And I expect by now you've probably managed to discover the meaning of pathetic fallacy. It isn't at all what you thought.

I must dash now darling, Mr Hart's calling me. We are likely to come close to a frost tonight and he is considering staying up with a blow heater over the dahlias. It's such a shame that what remains of the old glasshouse in the walled garden is in such a state, as it would be a comfortable place for them to over-winter.

I'll finish by saying something heartfelt, which I'm sure I don't do enough in my letters, but without you Green Place is just a huge draughty house, yet with you it is the heart of the world. No pressure!

All love,

Aunt Coral Xx

Sue

Fri Feb 12 1988
Taverna O'Carroll, Dorm 3, Midnight

Pensees: *How pleasing that in today's world,*
people still wave from boats. SB

I'm sitting up wondering whether to tell my new friends about Johnny. But who would *believe* that I have a long-lost Grandfather or an Uncle I didn't even know? They'll think it's the worst kind of attention-seeking. Perhaps I'd best leave the stories of last year to last year. And anyway, Helen and Di are now asleep, and Christine from Dickens, the fourth man in our dorm, is snoring.

I'm in the top bunk, with the curtain pulled away from the window so I can see the night. Helen is beneath me and Diane beside her on the opposite bottom bunk, and next to me the noisy Chris. I'm writing by the light of the mosquito lamp and contemplating throwing a pillow at her. I can't seem to warm to Christine, in spite of sharing a dorm with her. I feel put off by the way she bigs up her marks for assignments. I asked what she got for her life Encapsulation essay and she said she got 'one off an A' (meaning a B).

We got back from a late supper at Crysanthe's Bar just after eleven. I shared the news from Green Place and Di was very knowledgeable.

'Walled gardens were believed to have been transformative,' she explained. 'I love sundial inscriptions. "For the Concern of the Rich and the Poor" is really rare. My favourite is "Festina Lente". It means "Hasten Slowly".'

Helen wasn't really impressed and just said that was easier said than done.

I think a walled garden must be a bit like having a beautiful room outside, with the sundial the equivalent of the fireplace. I just had a fleeting image of Joe leaning on it attractively and chatting.

Quiz joined Helen, Di and I briefly at the bar and whispered to me somewhat privately that he had found out that William suffers from something called proprietism (which means he wants to have sex all the time). Then he explained about a famous actor who suffered from it too and this poor man's symptoms were so bad he was in a permanent state of arousal, even when pottering around the shops, or just trying to do his teeth. So it would make sense of William's behaviour. Though it's terribly sad for him that he doesn't have the looks to aid the condition.

But I'm not a hundred per cent sure if this is one of Quiz's pranks. We had only been here *two* days and he told me that in order to ask for a coffee with milk in Greek, I had to say: 'Ena café malaka paracalo', which actually means 'Can I have a coffee wanker please?', as I found out a couple of days later. I stumbled on the information by accident as soon as I learnt the Greek for milk (which is megala, *not* malaka). Mr O'Carroll put me straight about this when he overheard me ordering in the hotel lounge.

> *Sat Feb 13 1988, 1.30 am*
>
> *(Can't sleep, reading Encyclopaedia)*

Proprietism, or priapism as it's also known, in fact *isn't* a made-up disease. I'm going to give William a wider berth from now on. Poor fellow.

I will have to apologize to Quiz for not believing him and in future look things up *before* I make any judgements. But it is hard to distinguish his japes, which he claims he mastered the art of at boarding school. I imagine, being somewhat of a natural expert, he must have headed the whole *ministry* of schoolboy pranks.

> *2.00 am*
>
> *(still can't sleep)*

I was having a little day dream about getting the internship at the *Echo*. Where's the harm in hoping? Except that it keeps me awake.

There are only two boats on the waterfront tonight, which are both anchored beyond Hotel Bunty's jetty, and the wire from the tops of the sails is gently tapping against the masts in the breeze. I do feel that it's true to say that a person could mistake Shabany for Heaven, but it's also true to say that there is tragedy in paradise.

It comes in the form of a dog who lives at the other end of the Bay. She's a scruffy outside guard dog type, her name is Boobey. She belongs to the priest, Freedom Yogurt Pot. (NB Boobey doesn't mean the same in Greek as it does in English. In Greek it means something like 'Fido' or 'Rover'.) Apparently she is lucky because she does have food and water and a little shade.

But the tragedy is that Boobey is tethered on a chain that only allows her to move a few feet, and in the night she often cries and whimpers. It's a far cry from the treatment of animals at Green Place, where Aunt Coral got Glenn the builder to double-glaze a hen house. And last year Delia found a stray tortoise who was given free run of his own suite.

But the moon shines on here regardless, as bright as a silver coin in the sky. And it casts a sheen across the sea like a ladder to Heaven that quivers when the waves ripple by.

Such moments as these always make me think of mum. Searching moments, where the endless sea and the endless sky meet our endless quest.

It's funny that in my memory she is even now in different outfits, as though in the midst of death she is still choosing what she'll wear each day.

But at last I can feel my eyelids getting sleepy now. It's time to lie down, but I think all this trying to be more Russian appears to be rubbing off on me, for in signing off I find my final thoughts are not of my own mourning, but of Boobey in chains at the gates of Freedom.

Top Flat
53 Lanterner Drive
Egham
Sun Jan 31, 1988

Dear Sue,

Aunt Coral invited me over again on Saturday, she was having one of her party evenings. Everyone is very excited about the excavations as I expect you'll have guessed.

We had dinner and then one of Aunt Coral's new B and B lodgers gave us a talk with a slide show about the Victorian love affair with flower gardens.

When he was done a historian lady got up and read out a newspaper clipping she said she had found in her archives.

It was all about a grizzly fact she had unearthed about the coffin of Aunt Coral's Great Great Grandfather Edmund. Apparently two years after he died it was exhumed, but nobody seems to know why. It's a bit of a ghoulish mystery. (And after that, she led everyone outside to show them where she believes there is an old tunnel running from the house down to the walled garden. You can imagine this was met with some excitement, curiosity and in the case of the Admiral . . . a little concern for the ladies!)

I was sorry I didn't get to meet your dad. Aunt Coral said that he'd cancelled because Ivana wasn't feeling up to it. I did so want to see what he looked like and whether you look like him. So Aunt Coral showed me a photograph – and I was expecting someone much bigger with a lot more hair, not someone so slight and thin up the top. (Now I know where you get your looks from!!!)

Mum's OK, thank you, she's pretty busy with getting the new Bistro shipshape – which hopefully will be up and running by spring. She is also freshening up the café to start the New Year with a bang. So we've all been laid off for a bit.

She *eventually* lent me the money to get a few sweatshirts and leaflets printed up for my new business, which I have now gone firm on as J F G T Ltd (Joe Fry Garden Tidy), which I hope was your favourite as well!!

I'm following mum's basic business principles, which are really simple:

1. Write down what it is you do.
2. Let people know you are doing it.
3. Get someone to recommend you do it to somebody else.

She said I could carry these principles with me throughout my whole entrepreneurial life. The only problem about the winter being so quiet is that I have more time on my hands and I miss you, I can't wait for you to get home. It feels like an eternity till April. I expect that's because it is. I will count every hour till you come. I would go and wait at the airport now if she'd let me. And when you finally come through that gate I will hold you tight and then carry you home, like the Captain of a beautiful ship that's come into a dock that's called lucky.

A kiss X

And always my love

Joe

Sue

I feel so blessed that Joe has written me the most spoiling of soppy letters (and on Snoopy writing paper. It's true, some men really *don't* play games). And it's peppered with exclamation marks. I'm guessing he's anxious I might not be clear when he's joking. He never takes me for granted.

I wrote back and told him that I've always been fascinated by exhumations – there is something truly compelling about them. I wonder what Aunt Coral's Great Great Grandfather had done to deserve such a thing? Maybe it was to do with the way he died, maybe he had been poisoned or something, or maybe he was buried in some sort of scandal and then moved after things settled down. I am sure they must be desperately trying to find out. I hope it wasn't the body snatchers. Goodness knows what secrets Green Place will yield, below the ground and above it. Scratch off a bit of old wallpaper in any room in the house, and underneath you will find . . . layers of *history*.

This afternoon Professor Mushrooms was lecturing on French influences, of which I know only a smidgeon.

'The French have a saying *Amour-propre*, which means *love of the self*. Loosely, it describes people who see in the eyes of their lovers only their own reflection,' he said.

In a moment of disorientation I put my hand up to speak, forgetting that we don't do that here, and that the Professor, unlike Aunt Coral, likes to be called John.

'John, are you attributing *amour-propre* to La Rochefoucauld or Jean-Jacques Rousseau?' Di cut in before me.

'Rousseau,' said the Professor.

'And do you think it renders human beings incapable of being happy?' she asked.

'I do,' he said.

'Sue?'

'I'm sorry, I've forgotten the question,' I said.

'What are your views on La Rochefoucauld?'

'To be honest, I'm not that keen on Belgium chocolate.'

There was little chance I'd out-clever him, though fortunately he managed a smile. At times the conversation is so technical that I feel like I'm driving a deckchair on a motorway in a language I don't understand. At home I would ask a million questions, but here I am learning to hesitate. The EHG (Egham Hirsute Group) was a much safer place to explore unanswered questions about writing, and Aunt Coral's emphasis when she taught us was more romantic than academic.

'And what might make someone with *amour-propre* happiest, a man, or a woman . . . ?'

'A mirror?' I said.

'Good Sue, very good,' said Professor John with a supportive grin.

'Self-love is the greatest gift of all flatterers,' said Helen.

'Very good,' said Professor Mushrooms. 'Quintessential La Rochefoucauld.'

'Now, could anyone please tell me *the difference* between La Rochefoucauld and Rousseau's interpretation of *amour-propre*? And maybe perhaps which other French philosopher has had a crack at this concept?' Professor Mushrooms asked.

'Blasé Pascal?' said Quiz.

'*Cala*,' (Good) said Professor Mushrooms.

'He wrote Pensees,' I said.

'And La Rochefoucauld's self-love,' continued Quiz, 'states that we are the self-love itself, that it is our soul, and of that we are ashamed.'

'That's righ—' said the Professor but Quiz hadn't finished.

'But then, La Rochefoucauld goes on to tell us that *amour-propre* is hungry and blind. But whether it is in our minds, or in our hearts. It infects our purity and makes us enemies of the truth, so much so that we would *kill* if we were able.'

'Thank you Quiz, that is really terrific,' said Professor Mushrooms.

'Any thoughts on that anybody? Anybody? Sue?'

'That's terrible,' I said.

Luckily I was rescued from having to elaborate more by the noise of Dickens and Tolstoy breaking for peanuts.

'How time flies!' said Professor John, 'and so we will need to finish. Please feel free to use the Reading Room for research about *amour-propre*, and look for characters you suggest show tendency to it. *Endaxi?*'

'*Endaxi* John,' we chorused in the style of modern study.

'*Cala*,' he said. 'And goody so, please close your things and I hope you have found it worthing. Good evening everybody. *Calesperasas!*' which is Greek for have a good evening in the plural. The Professor speaks English like a native, but for the odd little quirk.

I followed Helen out on to the veranda into the peace of the sun and turned my face to Heaven in a warm Mediterranean silence. There is just so much to learn, philosophy, rhetoric, hubris, but this evening, on a much lighter note, Zola has booked a table for Happy Hour at Bunty's Hotel.

> **Apprenissiage Repertoirier**
> *Quintissential*
> *Amour-propre*

Sat Feb 13 1988, 11.30pm
Dorm 3, top window bunk, by torchlight

Pensees: *'Some fools on scraps of learning dote,*
And think they grow immortal as they quote.' (Alexander Pope.
Helen put this in a note under my pillow!)

I lost track of the time in writing up the day's lesson and was last to arrive at our table in the alf resco lounge at Buntys. William was sitting next to Helen, he was still wearing his afternoon shorts. This is a phenomena of William for he can't sit comfortably in proper trousers for more than about fifteen minutes, apparently not for any other reason than he prefers casual clothes.

Quiz and Di sat opposite H and W. They had dressed up in black tie and strapless black towelette jumpsuit respectively. William said he liked Di's 'gownless evening straps' and then he was very embarrassed. (Helen's Happy Hour attire was along the same lines as mine, which was a relief.)

'So what actually is a Happy Hour?' I asked for my opening patter, taking up a seat at the head of the table, which was diagonally next to Diane. She hesitated for a second before answering, re-angling a sparkly hair grip.

'It means that the drinks are half price,' she said eventually.

We had a small pause, to allow someone to jump in with a follow-up remark or an opener. I decided that Happy Hour wasn't a good time to chat about being exhumed.

'How do you know so much about *amour-propre*?' I asked, hoping to kick off a good conversation.

'I've been reading Maxime 563,' she said. 'I've got lots of good books with me. I can lend you a copy of Rousseau's *Confessions* if you like.'

'What had he been up to then?' I asked.

'That's just the title of the book,' she said, and her hair grip gave a little magic flash in the flickering candlelight. Quiz produced the smile of a fond Professor amused by a student. If our group were a pack of stray dogs, he would definitely be the alpha, and he called a waiter over with a practised royal wave so that I could order a banana daiquiri, like Di's. When it came it was served with some home-made chippies, also like Di's. But Di hadn't touched hers, for she believes art and hunger to be two opposing forces. I found it very disconcerting for I would have to be dieing to say no to a chip. Shortly after, Quiz excused himself to go and talk to a member of Dickens.

'I'll see you plus tard, Di darling,' he said, as he left.

'Plus tard,' she answered smoothly. I find their language pure silver.

Apart from the mellow background burble of a handful of Happy Hour drinkers, the night was so quiet that we might have been lucky enough to hear the mermaids call in the water. And though the sky was clear tonight there was a nagging wind on the shore that blew straight through the gaps in my sandals. It felt like the breath of a mermaid. But Helen said she thought it was more likely the breath of the banana daiquiri.

It's a long way from here to the velvet hills by the Clockhouse and all the buried treasures of the past. If Green Place could speak, I wonder what story it would tell?

I can just see it now in my mind's eye, as it stands today. I can travel there as fast as lightning . . . as if I am a fly buzzing in through the universe, to see the earth, and then a small island at the top surrounded by the water, then roads, fields, and the B4532, then the lion gateposts and the long drive all the way up to Green Place . . . and then the haven of faded grandeur at the head, ancestral home of the Garden family, with outdoor unheated swimming pool set on the back terrace, overlooking acres of gardens, with 16 bedrooms inside, a cupboard just for carrier bags, and an empty function room that we use just for the post. Green Place, my sanctuary.

And now I can buzz through the passages, spy on Aunt Coral in her pink tassel bed with her initials sewn on her monogrammed linens, CEG, Coral Elizabeth Garden, and her other tenants in their beds sleeping; hover over the Admiral in his suite like a gentleman's club, spot the robin who is a permanent resident of the Admiral's bathroom, then swoop round Aunt Coral's father's collection of Toby jugs filling up with dead flies (more unfortunate than me), then dart past the old nursery, take the first right and then follow the plates along the wall to guide me into the East Wing and Delia in the Trout Suite. Before circumnavigating Admiral Gordon and Admiral Ted in their suites, Sweet William and Snowdrop, snoring . . . and finally speed into the West Wing and alight on my window that looks out over the drive. It's a vision so strong, I can almost hear the tinkle of the Ladies Hand-bell Orchestra coming from the church beyond the Clockhouse, where Aunt Coral's friends the Nanas are proud and polished members.

In truth, though I love it here . . . I really can't wait to get home.

Pensees: *'It's not in the stars to hold our destiny
but in ourselves.'* (William Shakespeare)

Di came out to my rock this morning to tell me she has seen a
book she thought might interest me in the Reading Room. She was
very excited because she said she had found that Mr O'Carroll's
private collection included a number of specialist tales from the
Raj. I felt a little confused, but followed her to investigate will-
ingly, making an educated guess that she must be thinking that
reading on the Raj might offer insight into the history of the
Russian Rajas, and as such be of interest to me if I went with them
for my dissertation.

'Mr O'Carroll's antiquarian section includes some of the original books from Sir William Denison's 1804 to 1871 collection . . .
and also the Marquess of Ripon,' said Di.

'I see,' I said, knowledgeably.

'I don't want to tell you any more yet, or it will spoil the
surprise,' she said.

Di led me down to the basement which is devoted to Mr
O'Carroll's collection. The Reading Room houses everything from
ancient philosophies through to the present day.

Everything is designed for the pleasure of sitting and reading,
and I mean *really* reading. The walls are painted a restful masculine green and there are four leather sofas and little tables in
the middle of the room, with leather coasters to put your
drinks on. Rugs brighten the marble floor and smell of foreign
moth balls. And each wall is *completely* encased in book shelves,
with four ladders on wheels standing by ready to serve the top
shelves.

Di got hold of one and wheeled it to a dark section in the back corner.

She stopped by some shelves labelled 'Empire' and then looked to the section above it labelled 'Raj'. She positioned her ladder very specifically, turned to me and gave me the following instructions.

'Climb up on to the top step and look straight ahead of you at the books *above* the ticket that says Raj.'

'OK,' I said obediently, feeling somewhat out of my depth.

I climbed up. The smell of the dust of the past emanated from between all the old pages.

I reached the top of the ladder, my head in the shadows near the ceiling, and I cast my eye along the books above the Raj. The books were so old that they were wrapped up in brown paper to protect them, their titles written neatly on labels on their sides.

'*Curry and Rice* by George Franklin Atkinson,' I said. '*Gunga Din* by Rudyard Kipling, *Barrack Room Best*, Georges Dinousiere . . . *Indian Summer*, April Swayne-Thomas . . . but these are about India, not Russia,' I said.

'Keep going, keep going,' said Di. 'The Raj has nothing to do with Russia.'

I felt momentarily terribly muddled, but continued with my search.

'*The Campaign in India, The Pass beyond Mutiny, The Pride of the Bengal Lancers, For the Concern of the Rich and the Poor* . . . *For the Concern of the Rich and the Poor.* Oh my goodness!' I said, almost falling off the ladder.

'You better come down, you look a bit precarious up there.'

'May I take it?'

'Of course, that's what we're here for!'

'Mr O'C!' she called. 'We've found it!'

Mr O'Carroll came tapping down the stairs into the Reading Room.

'Wonderful!' he said. 'Which one was it again?'

'*For the Concern of the Rich and the Poor*,' said Di.

'Oh yes, the King of the Paupers,' he said.

'Would it be all right if Sue were to borrow it?' asked Di. 'Her Aunt has discovered a sundial in her garden with the same inscription!'

'Really? How intriguing. Yes, of course. I'll give you some white gloves to wear when you're reading it. It just saves the paper from the heat and oils of the hands. It's not in mint condition I'm afraid, but I believe it may be one of the only few copies in the *world*. I'm sorry that the front cover is missing, but you'll find the author on the index page, and he tells you who he is in the text.'

I examined the label on the spine of the book, and flipped open to the index. 'Limited edition . . . published 1921 by Kali Press in India. Copyright Mr Lawrence Garden all rights reserved.' I gasped. 'Garden is our family name.'

Mr O'Carroll and Di both took sharp intakes of breath. It was quite a moment.

'Thank you so much,' I said. 'I will treasure it.'

You can imagine the next words to come out of my pen this morning were: 'Dear Aunt Coral'!

And such an extraordinary coincidence that I found this book in a library in *Greece*, in a section all about *India*! I mean, what are the *odds*? I skipped breakfast, desiring to get into the pages right away.

But though it says it is by Lawrence Garden, the author turns out to be an orphan who begins his life in a workhouse. Maybe Lawrence Garden found his story and published it . . . only one way to find out. (Here is an extract.)

FOR THE CONCERN OF THE RICH AND THE POOR

Lately I have been gripped by a heartfelt wish to commemorate my old friends. From the sunset years of my life – I think it is safe to remember.

I am looking back to the year of 1857 and to the days I have cautioned to revive and I see I was a boy much smaller than his classmates, grubby and smelly and weak, but my veins were made of steel and my blood flowed with grit and my heart was frozen inside me.

There I stand in my memory, a child in the granite crowds, standing under granite skies, possessed of all the trappings of workhouse existence, desolation, fear, hunger. The place I called 'home' was in a country far from where I now sit, in a land from the past known as England. The only thing they knew about me at the Mead was that I had come from London and so without further ceremony that is what they called me.

As to a surname I had to invent one and I'd heard that Prince Albert had a London tailor and I thought the two words a good fit. These faint flashes back to the beginnings of my existence are among my earliest recollections and I suppose might set my age at about six or seven at the time, though I could have been older or younger. For the truth was I knew not my name, my age or my origin. I could have been anybody, so in a strange sense I was.

I might have been an illegitimate member of the Royal Family put out on to the steps of Buckingham Palace and then somehow lost or stolen. Being born without identification or label (not even one or two names) provided me with an opportunity not offered to many to create for myself a whole life.

But Constance Longtoft who worked in the laundry refuted my claim to the throne, alleging to know that I had been found as a baby outside a corn chandler's in the city. My only surety was that I came from a tribe known as indoor paupers, because that is what they called us at the Mead.

A short while later, I decided on a more moderate account of my early years; that I grew up in an ordinary house, in an ordinary street, in an ordinary suburb. At the time of this particular fabrication, I must have been about seven or eight.

For a mother I created 'Flora', and my hair smelt of her perfume from where she often bent to kiss the top of my head. And for a father? I made him a Lawrence, firm but gentle. He was a policeman and quite high up. It was more realistic than the Royal succession, which naturally I could not quite rule out.

Most prominent in my memory of the staff at the Mead were the good Master, Master Coyer, and, inevitably, the bad Master, Chaplain Cragg. It was widely reported of the Chaplain that 'His mighty improvement in the morals of the poor was testament to his fervent piety' . . . a subject amongst the inmates which was of some bitter debate. He taught us reading, but curiously he never taught us to write. Maybe the inability to sign our own names would mean we would remain forever the underclass.

Mead buildings were sprawling and scattered around two granite exercise yards. The rooms in which we lived were painted sepia and they smelled of the sulphur from the fumigation of our clothes. Beams and archways inside those rooms were carved with biblical words such as Charity, Mercy and Glory, and the highest arch in the Dining Hall bore the message that God is Love. It shone down on us while we devoured our little meals in strict silence. I could not understand why if God loved us so he would put us here like this? Was charity a punishment? And if it was all about the next life, as the

Chaplain Cragg always said, what on earth was the point of this one?

Word list

Sir William Dennison

Marquis of Ripon

(NB *I am finding 'Apprentissiage Repertoirier' takes too long to write and also spell.*)

Sue

I read for a long time last night, no easy task with a 3,000-page tome. I've decided to keep a notebook of extracts from it for Aunt Coral, even if they take me years to select!

The hero in *For the Concern of the Rich and the Poor* is an orphan boy called London Taylor who didn't even know how old he was when he was handed in to a workhouse. So far, it's about his suffering there and of course I'm curious to know how it develops, to see if it's anything to do with Green Place. I can't imagine how it must feel not to be able to write. And I find it galling that in Victorian times people were imprisoned for being poor. I wonder if this is what a pauper means, a poor person.

It gives me an awful perspective on my silly day-to-day problems such as lack of intellectual ability or boy trouble. When this poor boy was so alone in the world he had to invent his parents. But I feel, to use a Diane word, that this 'resonates' with me, because I have that in common with him. In that I somehow attracted Aunt Coral into my life out of the sheer force of my need.

But all is still here at the moment, except for two ships on the horizon that look like caterpillars crawling along the sea. And the sea has turned almost teal blue, offset with French navy pockets. After the tide has gone out the sky is mirrored in the leftover sea-water that remains in pools on the sand. It looks like there are two skies, one where it should be, and one upside down on the beach. It makes me wonder if there *is* an unseen world, a world only visible when there's enough water? But maybe it is just that I so want there to be some sort of spirit world, even if it might take the rain to be able to see it. I realize that my theory is not on a par with the philosophy of mathematics! Pascal, Rousseau and Bowl on the spiritual nature of rain!

But I'd better get up now, and make myself presentable for the new day, for I wake in the morning to the cark of the hungry gull, and I rise with a thirst for knowledge, but the days come and go as suddenly as the ships passing by in the night.

Sat Feb 20 1988
On the Rocks at 7.00pm

Pensees: *Is there such a thing as a spare moment?* SB

I received a modest Valentine's card today from Joe, which gave me a bit of a lift. The picture on it shows a boy and girl whizzing off on a motorbike, like we do when we go for a spin. I'm glad Joe didn't try and conceal his identity, he's got such a nice way of signing off.

Dear Sue,
I hope all on the course is going well, I am thinking of you, and imagining you on your mermaid's rock writing down all your particular thoughts. Don't forget any.

If you are the writer and the poet, could I be the subject?
(Joke!)

A kiss X

And always my love

Joe

(PS I got you the new smaller helmet in the cherry.)

I read it here on my rock, because I wanted to be private – and when I looked up I noticed that the tree lights were still on in the trees around the beach café like stars on a cloudy day.

On Sunday Quiz gave Diane three dozen red roses, which are difficult to get hold of on the islands, so he had them shipped from the mainland. They are now all over our dormitory.

As a guest at the hotel, Quiz has been issued a booklet of tickets for free swims in Bunty's open-air pool, and last night he invited Zola to join him for a swim early this morning before class. (Perhaps I should point out that Diane prefers to be 'real' by staying at the Taverna.)

Anyway, I'm using the term Bunty's open-air pool loosely, for basically it only means that there is a netted-off area for the jelly fish.

'We get these net pools in Barbados,' said Quiz, while he sat on the jetty beside me. He put coconut oil all over his bare skin which smelt disturbingly nice.

'Barbados?' I asked.

'My Dad lives there,' he said.

'Wow, it must be amazing,' I said.

'Not really, it's just like Weybridge but hotter.'

I knew he was being sophisticated, though I couldn't really confess to understand exactly what he meant. He lit a cigarette casually and looked out to the shimmering horizon.

'How are you getting on with Doonyasha?' he asked. 'Have you pegged out a plot yet?'

'No, I haven't, actually I find the plotting part quite difficult,' I admitted.

'But at least you can be in charge,' said Quiz. 'You can make people up, you can cast them, dress them, feed them, hear what they say, watch them grow up, give them birthdays, broken limbs, choose partners for them, choose what they do, how much they get paid, whether or not they have children. You can kill them off and then bring them back to life in flashbacks, you can make their lives jump about all over the place, to the future and back to the past. You are the god of your story, you add the violins,' he said, before stubbing his cigarette out and jumping into the water with panache.

I can just see him in an old movie star's private collection of black-and-white photos, putting his hand up to the camera while sitting on the beach, wearing one of those all-in-one swimsuits with shorts.

Without doubt Quiz is very inspirational and I just want to take notes while he is talking. I'm sure that just being around people like him and Di will increase my chances of sharpening my intelligence for an internship.

As for stripping off and jumping in the sea myself . . . I have been wishing that I came from the time of Victorian swimming huts. They had some ideas right!

But is it amour-propre that drives me to hide myself? Is it because I want to preserve a vain illusion that can never be shattered in clothes?

It's a shame, because my white bikini looks such a dream garment when it's inside my case. But when I put it *on*, for all I know, my bottom might be as big and as bright as the moon, and when

I get in the water I can sense that those behind me are having opinions.

William won't go in because he is frightened of the fish. I tried to reassure him. But he is nervous about wildlife, and preferred to remain on the jetty writing poetry about his feelings. He is a very excitable person and rarely finishes one sentence before he starts another. He says that he comes from a long line of emotionally constipated Scots, which is why he can only express himself in poetry.

He claimed he'd been chucked out of boarding school 'for women', but, considering that it was an all boys' boarding school, nobody believes him.

And he had a crush on Di again last night, which seemed to have abated by this morning, but it looked like he had woken up with one on Helen.

I don't think he has got that awful disease that Quiz was teasing about; I think William's just one of those poor boys who keeps trying to get off with everyone, and we must all be very caring.

Eventually I managed a swim, with the artful use of my towel, and afterwards I went up to the vending machine in Bunty's reception for a Sprite to settle my tummy. I've got a particularly brainy tutorial later this afternoon and often it's all I can do to try and make sure the whole morning isn't written off in tackling nerves. Sometimes I don't think I'll be able to make it as a writer and I just want to run away and grow raspberries. So I just lay quietly and read for a while, while I forced my mind on to other things.

FOR THE CONCERN OF THE RICH AND THE POOR

Before I came to the Mead I have no memories at all. Those days are half-begun lines in a sketch that was never complete . . . a rumour here, an invention there, a piece of longing. An angel must have saved me as a baby, maybe more than one angel, more than once. This I deduced from the additional information (supplied by Matron Cole) that I was already talking when I entered the Mead. This would have put my age then at about three or four when I arrived, though I could have been older or younger.

St Edward's Mead Workhouse was an extensive red-brick empire, lying in the west of England. It stood deep in the countryside, and a penny post from the town of Bristol. But in those days, for all I knew, I might have gone through the gates, down the lane and dropped off the edge of the world.

The only place I'd heard of, apart from Bristol and London, was Germany, which Ward One boys believed to be a town just down the road. It was said that Germany had hostelries, shops and abundant markets, and if you could get to Germany you'd find a good living.

In my early days at the Mead, I was lucky enough to be put to work mending shoes, but luxury is a relative thing in a workhouse. We stood up to work in the cobbler's room and the window ledges sloped downwards so that we could not rest on them during the long afternoons.

As for our mornings, they were dedicated to the other great labour of childhood, to learning. And my story really began in the middle of my sixth or so winter at the workhouse, when I first saw Harry Benson. It was during one of the Chaplain's early morning lessons, and I must have been around nine. It was a day much like any other, except Chaplain Cragg was giving his rule summary because there was a new boy in our class.

'My life's work lies in the reformation of the cadger, the punishment of persistent idlers, and in the moral improvement of the poor,' said Chaplain Cragg. He had a shrill voice, almost operatic in its tenor, and a crooked and frightful resting sneer.

'To the impotent poor, the old and infirm, I extend the hand of Charity. Here at the Mead we insist on discipline, we conduct ourselves in silence and we pray for forgiveness from our sins. The punishment for stupidity is caning, you'll get half rations if you're idle, time in solitary for cheek, or some of your privileges withheld. Running away whilst wearing your Union uniform constitutes theft and is punishable by caning with the salted rod – in my experience, an excellent deterrent if ever there was one. This is Harold Benson,' he went on. 'He's a homeless from Yorkshire. Lucky for you, isn't it, Benson, that Jesus makes a friend of the poor.'

'Then it seems to me that Jesus must have ditched his old friends and made new ones,' said Harold Benson, with a fearless tone of dissent.

'What?' said the Chaplain, greatly abashed. 'Have you not absorbed what I have said about insolence? I shall have to teach you some manners. When I want an answer from a cadger, I shall ask for one. Is that understood?'

'Understood, but in the light of *your* manners you'd be lucky to get one,' replied Harold Benson defiantly.

There were gasps from classmates all around me. The Chaplain did not speak but fixed Harold Benson in his glare. I shuddered. I don't know how he dared speak up to the Chaplain, but I do know that I admired his rebellion. Could it be possible for a boy to be born without a sense of trepidation?

Chaplain Cragg made no utterance but silently picked up his cane from the side of his desk, and flexed it to check for its bounce. Then he went on with his lesson, tapping it on his desk from time to time, making sure he did not conceal his intended menace.

I can't have been alone in fearing for the consequences of Harold Benson's hutspur, or wondering how he kept his composure for the remainder of the lesson while knowing he was not to be spared the rod. But I happened to be staring into his top pocket at something shining and brown causing a small bump to protrude.

There was something about him, something I could not put my finger on. Courage, certainly, but also a power, or a fiery righteousness, perhaps? He was stocky and rosy of cheek. He was older than myself; he might have been around twelve.

Unfortunately, at the same time as my mind wandered, fate dictated that the Chaplain should ask me a question. He got my attention by rapping me over the knuckles with his cane. It gave me such a shock and such pain that it took my breath away, and appeared to make the Chaplain's frozen sneer crack open further and wider with thinly veiled delight.

'Class dismissed,' then said the Chaplain, adding, 'Not you, new boy.'

He closed and locked the door after the last boy trooped out. We did not see Harold Benson again for the rest of the week.

Word list
Cadger
Penny post

Sue

So far there is no indication in *For the Concern of the Rich and the Poor* of a connection with Green Place, but it is a very long book and I have so little time for reading at the moment that it could well be still ahead of me. And I do so want to approach it as an academic and *really* read it, with my gloves on and everything, so I don't miss anything. (I'm ashamed to admit, that even if I weren't busy, I might just qualify as the world's slowest reader, because often I get into bed, open a book and then immediately fall asleep.)

I am appalled at the corporal punishments they inflicted on the inmates of the workhouse, appalled that they called people inmates.

It's funny that I can't share any of this with Joe, in the moment. I wonder how he is? I miss the day-to-day knowledge of him, what he had for lunch, if he slept well, if he had any travel disruption, that sort of thing. The silly little things that are the corn meal of a day-to-day relationship, and without them the ties that bind us are as fragile as lace. Oh dear, I seem to be becoming more Victorian and not more Russian in my writing, but then I am spending a large part of my days in 1857.

But back in 1988 – and before I left for the Taverna – Joe took me on a date for a picnic at the Percival Library. Perhaps he thought being amongst all the books would make us more intellectual!

He brought two cheese sandwiches in foil and two Fantas concealed in his bag and we hid them on our laps and romanced. I remember we had to whisper because we were in the library.

'I want to put Paris at your feet,' he said. 'I want to take you to little restaurants.'

'I wish I could get inside your head,' he continued. 'I love all your little ideas.'

'You wouldn't want to be in my head,' I replied to him. 'I have seventeenth-century servants giving birth in the moonlight, and jolly farmer's wives running out to wave tea towels at passing trains. At any given time I have a world of fiction running parallel with my reality . . . maybe I am insane,' I said, perhaps a little too enigmatically.

'I don't think you're insane, but you're very complicated,' he answered. 'You're like a beautiful alien and you make me feel very alive.'

Before we left the library, I asked him he if fancied a trip to the coast because I wanted to go and think about sea metaphors ahead of some pre-Taverna coursework.

And so we went. It was the day before I left for Crete, and I sat by a beach hut and wrote metaphors, while Joe watched a seaside orchestra playing just along the Prom. Afterwards, I watched as he went for a walk along the beach and left his footprints in the wet sand. But it sprang back up immediately to conceal that his prints were ever there.

I found out last night that Professor Mushrooms is not a real Professor, and that he is only as old as Helen and William (26). Mr O'Carroll has bestowed the title of Professor on him, but his Professorship only relates to the Taverna.

In his lecture today Proff John asked if anyone would be willing to read out their essays on the differences in international style, and like a fool I spoke up.

It was momentarily like being back at the Egham Hirsute Writing Group as I stood up to read my piece, although my voice was possessed by a recent soprano that was a stranger on my palate. In my essay I had tried to take on board my main note on the course which was about being more Russian. Here it is:

```
When faced with a broken heart an English
heroine, such as you'd find in a Bronte
or an Austen, might suffer a prolonged
fever or chill, from which she eventu-
ally recovers and survives to marry a
Captain. But a Russian heroine, such as
you'd find in a Tolstoy or a Nabakov, will
die of her broken heart, and will prob-
ably have had the added complication of
being married already, and so her guilt
hastens her end. And when the illicit
love is discovered, the heroine's mother
will slowly wither and die of her compli-
cated losses, losses so deep that they
are never outwardly expressed, but turn
```

```
inward to self-destruction. And the seeds
of sorrow will be sewn on the relatives
for they must bear the legacy — resulting
in fragility and over-spending for gen-
erations to follow.
```

Room 6 was silent for a moment and then the Professor spoke.

'Very well done, Sue, you have come a long way. This is very good work and I have two notes for you. 1: Brava that in your thinking you extend to the effect of a character's suffering on their relatives; and 2: I have noticed that in nearly all of your pieces you have an affinity with the matriarch, always you have the figure in the background.'

His comment shot through me like an arrow for it was so insightful. He seemed to have put his finger on something which I thought no longer defined me, the core of my three-word description: 'Lost Her Mum'.

Dying is *her* three-word description now, the last thing she ever did; it's what she is known for. 'Buddleia Bowl died'. I can't express how much that hurts when she used to be known for her dancing.

11pm

After class broke I sat on the veranda with some of my salon just as usual, pushing the smallest boundary with an afternoon drink. Cinnamon Sunday was pouring refreshing ouzo when I noticed Quiz looking at me intently, as though I had a mystery illness.

'You're very young to have lost your mother, you know. Is it just you and your Dad now?'

'Actually no, it's just me and my Aunt. My Dad has already remarried and Ivana, his current wife, is pregnant,' I said, with a hint of sarcasm.

'That was fast,' said Quiz, heading straight to the heart of the matter.

'What's your stepmother like?' he asked.

'Please don't call her that,' I said.

'Ah,' he said, gently stabilizing my emotional scab. 'It sounds like her title should be prefaced by "wicked".'

'That's right,' I said. 'But my dad seems to enjoy her.' I added this to compensate for the struggle going on beneath what I hoped was my smooth surface. I struggle to accept Ivana, I struggle not to hate her.

'Will you excuse me, darling?' said Quiz. 'I've got an appointment with Mr O'Carroll to discuss Proust. Would you like to come and listen?'

'I'd love to but I've got to finish an essay for the morning,' I answered.

'What's the title?' he asked.

'What is an unreliable narrator?'

'What do you think it is?' Quiz queried.

'A narrator who's afraid of commitment?'

'Not quite,' said Quiz. 'It's a narrator who, for some reason, has an unreliable world view. I'll see you plus tard then,' he said as he left.

'Plus tard,' I replied, quietly. And even if the subject of our conversation had been Ivana, Quiz makes me feel terribly interesting.

HERE ARE MY TWD'S FOR DAD AND IVANA, AS AN EXERCISE IN RESTRAINT:

Dad: Pale, grumpy and lost

Ivana (last year would have been): Appears like bad wind

(This year I know I must try to be generous): Slightly too orange

I'm in bed again now, listening to the tunes coming from the nostrils of Christine. I would love to drag my blanket and pillow outside and sleep on the beach under the stars. But this isn't legal on Shabany Beach, though interestingly you *can* go topless on a Saturday. (It sounds like someone's got mixed priorities!)

Here is another extract taken from my reading this evening. If nothing else, my reading on Victorian times might prove to be my specialist subject.

FOR THE CONCERN OF THE RICH AND THE POOR

'Harry Benson, but my friends call me Cheeser,' said the star of the north in the exercise yard before classes.

'Why do they call you that? Because you smell of cheese?' asked Scrapheap.

'Because you like mice?' asked Fogey.

'Because you like conkers?' I said.

'Now here's a man who knows his chestnuts,' said Cheeser with a confident smile. He drew out the brown bump I had seen poking out of his top pocket a week before. It was a small, hard chestnut, dark brown with dryness, shrivelled and tied to the end of a shoelace. He held it up and spun it so we could see it in the light. It was carved with his initials, HB.

'And what you see here is the unbeaten niner of the north. This chestnut is a real old laggie, and it is so rock hard that its knock would smash a rival conker to smithereens.'

By late August, the conkers on Chaplain Cragg's tree were ripe for the plucking; some had already fallen with their cases temptingly split to reveal the conkery bounty inside.

The heroic Cheeser decided upon achieving their collection by climbing over the fence and crawling to the trees to harvest them, whilst the Ward One boys created a decoy (of Fogey performing a fainting fit) in the yard during our five minutes' free time before class.

And after he returned, panting, and wet through with perspiration, Cheeser spent the whole of the first lesson with chestnuts in his socks, in his shoes, under his collar, in his pockets and he had a capful under his jacket.

History was generally taken by Mr Coyer, but he was called away that day, so unfortunately Chaplain Cragg stepped in.

'I have come to give you the lesson that Mr Coyer has been unable to,' he began. 'He has however lent me his books. So, I believe you have been looking at great monuments from around the globe, and so let us continue today where Mr Coyer left off with . . . the Taj Mahal of India,' he said.

He held up a picture of the Taj Mahal from Mr Coyer's book. The page was loose so he took it out separately and waved it about for us all to see.

'Benson, what is this a picture of?' said Chaplain Cragg. 'Do I have your attention?'

'The Taj Mahal,' said Cheeser. 'The Taj Mahal, sir.'

'I consider it a blatant example of exoticism, when you consider by contrast the wealth of elegance you will find in our own Buckingham Palace,' Chaplain Cragg said, still holding aloft the Taj Mahal.

'Buckingham Palace is the principal Royal residence of Queen Victoria,' he warbled. 'Allow me to depict for you the fine marble arch, state rooms in gilt, the grand staircase, the great ballroom . . .'

But as he steered us towards the Queen's vanilla elegance, I beheld the Taj Mahal, mesmerized by the celestial white slopes and shimmering curves and the Palace's reflection, which was perfected in a mirror of water in front of it. That picture, a mere reflection itself of the reality, sowed a seed of desire in my heart. Perhaps, at first, it was no more than a desire for the sun.

'Is it a long way from Germany?' I asked Cheeser after class, with a very inaccurate map in my head.

'It's hundreds of miles and over many more seas – it's very far from Germany!' he laughed. 'If you were to walk to India, it might take you your whole life.'

Green Place
Clockhouse Lane
Egham
Sun Feb 21 1988

Dear Sue,

Such wonderful news about the book! And such a coincidence that you have found it. Do you think Mr O'Carroll will allow you to keep it? You can offer him some money for it and I will write you a cheque at once. It is all most intriguing as I am not aware of a Lawrence Garden on any of our family trees. Maybe he is from a different line. Do hurry up and find out – but 3,000 pages!

I like the fact that you are recording shorter extracts from it. (I hope you have a nice jotter in which to record them.) In those days they used to paraphrase and catchey up all the time, exactly like they did in the theatre in case you missed the beginning, or nipped out to get a drink. And they certainly loved lots of description and acres of characterization; perhaps the fashion for cutting to the chase had not yet begun. So I do understand that though you say it is a wonderful book, finding any relevant information pertaining to Green Place in it is a bit like mining!

Talking of which, Jackie has been fiselling around in the

world of vaults again for the last few days like a woman possessed. She has spent so much time underground that I observed her skin had a pallor.

But she has now gone back to 1857, literally digging up the dead, and she has the beginnings of the tale which relates to the garden and cottages we've found. As you know my Great Great Grandmother Ellen bought Green Place in 1840 out of the proceeds of her large inheritance. She and her husband Edmund (my Great Great Grandfather, the one who was exhumed) had four sons, one of whom was my Great Grandfather, Benedict. He was the eldest and so he inherited. (Please see family tree . . . !)

Sadly Ellen died young and made a widower out of Edmund. But he went on to marry again, the last of the three Miss Parkes. And old maid Rose Anna Parkes, resident then of our neighbouring property Netherby, surprised her family when at 39 she accepted Edmund Garden's proposal of marriage (he was probably by then in his sixties). I am desperate to know more as you can imagine, but sadly this is as far as Jackie has got at the moment with a quick trawl in the archives at St Catherine's House, where they keep records of all the birth, marriage and death certificates for everyone. However, a deep dredge at the land registry office has brought up the deeds to the cottages, which are on parchment and open out to half the size of the kitchen table!

The documents show that the decayed structures of the garden and cottages we have found have in fact existed since 1618! It looks as though the cottages were reinstated by Edmund Garden at the same time as he commissioned Hotston-Moore to revamp the garden around 1856.

'Roselyne' Cottage lay on the right side and 'Edenthorpe' on the left, and curiously Rose Anna Garden (née Parkes's) name appears to have been added to the deeds in relation to Roselyne (Jackie conjectures this must have been at some point after Edmund died). We are wondering why the name of the Lady of the house should appear on a document relating to a *gardener's* cottage? Lady Chatterley springs to mind! Jackie says we must be patient, as she truly believes it's possible to talk to the dead via books and letters and documents, and so we will have our answers soon. I find it slightly ghoulish and also rather exciting.

I hope you can follow my family tree, I know it's not very professional! I had to stick two pieces of paper together to fit in the names of all the poor dead children. There are still one or two gaps I'm not quite certain about. But where I have any more information on anybody or anything, I have jotted them in as well. A few years before my grandmother Carolina was born, there was one other child of Benedict and his wife Adelaide, a boy who survived beyond babyhood, though it seems not much further sadly. I put a little star by him on the tree as he would have been living at the time of your book. (Jackie explained that this poor little chap appears to have died in a fire.)

In more light-hearted news, Mr Hart has called me to his bathroom three times now, to remove a spider, which I did by putting it out of his bathroom window. He has quite a bad aversion to them. But three nights running, each time he went up to his suite, there was a large garden spider in his basin, and he believed it was the same spider coming back again time after time. So, the third time that the spider came back, I *didn't* put it out the window, but took it down the drive to confuse it.

I can't be certain, but I think Mr Hart was a little upset that he wouldn't have a reason to call me up to his bathroom any more. I even wondered, vainly, if it might be he who was putting the spider back, as a device in order to be alone with me. Delia says I am deluded.

Hope all's well with the boffins, darling.

All love

Aunt Coral Xx

Sue

Thurs March 17 1988
Dorm 3

Pensees: *Mermaids under the age of 14 are not allowed to moon bathe on the surface after midnight without an adult.*
(From the laws of Mermina)

Rose Anna Parkes, what a beautiful name. She sounds graceful and loyal and noble. Rose Anna, it's a fragile yet pensive name, a name for a redhead . . . I wonder if I've cast her right? And the little boy Aunt C *'d on her family tree was called Frittie. Green Place must have so many ghosts.

But in my reading in *For the Concern of the Rich and the Poor*, I think a real connection to the house has finally come in! In the exercise yard at the Mead, London Taylor met a gentleman called Alfred Elms, who was passing through the Mead as a vagrant. Alfred saved London from a thrashing by speaking up for him and when they got talking Alfred explained that he was only in the Mead for a short time, because he was tramping his way through *to Surrey* to a new job, as a gardener *at a big house with a walled garden!* Obviously I'm hoping that the big house turns out to be Green Place and that Alfred somehow invites London Taylor to go with him. For just as destiny swept me to the gates of Green Place a little over a year ago, it looks possible that the same thing could have happened to London a hundred and twenty years before me! It is as if it is all somehow *ordained*.

Before I came to the Taverna I was barely aware there are two 5 o'clocks in the day. But this is the only real time I have for studying, and so I have also been studying the Laws of Mermina (the mermaid kingdom), as potential fodder for my dissertation. I discovered the information in a *German magazine* I found in the Reading Room! (I know I'm still supposed to be studying amour-propre but I do find it such a bleak concept.)

I hope my love for Joe isn't unconscious love for myself. It took me all last year to catch up with the way he feels about me and now, in the light of my coursework, I am worried that I'm more in love with him loving me than I am in love with himself. If that were to turn out to be the case then Joe would deserve much better.

Diane believes that it takes at least three years to get to know a person, so Joe and I have got a fair way to go yet. Maybe one day we will be like Quiz and Di and have our own couple language, secret to us and born of our hybrid moments.

But for now, we're at the other end of things, at the very beginning of our story. When I left in January I only really knew the starter facts about Joe, his age (18 also), and the ages of his siblings (2 older brothers, 1 younger sister), his favourite numbers (7, 11), colours (hyacinth and tomato), and groups (Pink Floyd, Mike and the Mechanics). I've since learned more intimate things such as – he can't keep a blister plaster on his foot in bed at night, and that he leaves little piles of loose change on the kitchen table. And slowly slowly through our letters I am building up more of a picture of him, i.e. he prefers curly brackets to plain ones and he has graduated from using too many !!!s to putting the word 'joke' in brackets after he's written something, presumably because he still worries I might not get his humour and be offended. And it is an interesting fact that humour sometimes doesn't come off a page the same way as it comes out of a mouth.

But I feel by turns touched and a bit irritated by his telling me when he is joking.

Still, Joe can't hide his feelings anyway; he is as easy to read as a school book. To summarize with an active description of Joe, as a purely technical exercise, I'd say that in the middle of the night when all the lights are out, I feel that I know who he is.

Thurs March 17, 11pm
In dorm

Pensees: *'Once more unto the beach dear friends!'*
(Battle cry, saying.)

I was just indulging a day dream where I was a writer of articles expressing my opinions about things, after my roaring success as an intern, God willing. I'd be attending debates and functions with a wardrobe to give an impression. I'd have to take part in formal dinners and use words such as ombudsman and plinth. I'd need to use hubris and rhetoric, and learn trumping and badinage for when people were trying to score points off me. I'd learn to drive and travel to new cities and contrast them. And in the mornings I'd read the papers and inform myself over coffee. And that'd be aside from my full-length book work. There's so much to do!

But before the moon sets, I want to achieve today's extraction from *For the Concern of the Rich and the Poor*, which I intend to send to Aunt Coral tomorrow, because I know she will be so excited. I am the literary dentist! Extract ahoy!

FOR THE CONCERN OF THE RICH AND THE POOR

I crept inside the casuals ward and found a long room in fetid darkness, where about twenty vagrants had slung their hammocks for the night. They used the Mead as a pit stop as they tramped from place to place. Vagrants then were a different tribe from paupers. They roamed the great outdoors and were free spirits, storytellers, rustics, who kept their own hours and could make a bed out of nothing. I aspired to becoming a vagrant when I grew up. At the time I had unusual perspectives.

Their hammocks were hung on meat hooks which were dangling from an iron bar that ran one end of the room to the other, and in the middle of the room was a central bar to which the bottom ends of the slings were attached.

'I've come to see Mr Elms,' I said.

'He's somewhere in the middle,' said Tramp Major. 'Best be quick.'

Recognizing Alfred again under the clashing swords of moonbeams was difficult, when the only distinguishing mark that might protrude above his blanket was his bushy black beard and most of the casuals had one of those. I nervously reached the side of the person I thought might be him and I shook gently on his shoulder, not realizing that in so doing I would jostle the entire row. A disgruntled line of vagrants proceeded to swing to and fro in their slings; there was much foul cursing and huffing. The owner of the shoulder I shook on sat up with a start.

'Sling your hook!' he growled.

'Mr Alfred Elms?' I called out shakily. 'Are you in here?'

'Down here,' came a whisper from further down the row.

'What do you want, boy?' asked Alfred Elms when I reached his side. 'Should you be in here?'

'My name is London Taylor, sir', I said, 'and I wanted to thank you for speaking up for me. I hope you haven't been punished for it. That's what I wanted to say.'

'Wait,' said Alfred. 'How old are you?'

'I'm about nine. How old are you?' I asked him. I thought he looked about sixty.

'I'm twenty-seven,' he said.

Once engaged in a conversation I decided to take matters further.

'But, sir, I don't understand, why would you risk your own skin to save mine? You don't even know me.'

'Why should I need to know you? I'd say you must have forgotten that you are a child,' he said gently. 'I couldn't stand by and see an innocent get a thrashing, it wouldn't be right. How long have you been here?'

'All my life.'

'And have you any relatives?'

'No, I'm afraid not. At least, not that I know of. I have nothing and no one.'

'I'm so sorry,' said Alfred. 'I'm sorry for you, little man.'

'What about you, sir? Where are your people? When will you be gone?'

'Well I was moving on in the morning, but now I'm staying a day longer to pay my dues with a free day's work in the Chaplain's garden. But you needn't have worried that they would punish a big fellow like me, not when the Chaplain wants a labourer. I have no people now either; my wife and my son are no more. But, when I take up my new position, I'll have a cottage and garden and thirty acres to tend. It's a new start for me.'

'It sounds beautiful,' I said.

'I'm properly trained,' said Alfred proudly. 'I advertised,' he added. 'The Master at the big house picked me out because I'm apprenticed with the glasshouse. He wants all sorts does Mr Garden, and all to be home grown.'

'His name is Garden?' I said.

'Yes indeed, Mr Benedict Garden, but it would have been better if I had been the Mr Garden, wouldn't it? Ah well, he's got the land, but I've got the green fingers,' sighed Alfred. He stretched out his hands. 'I carry the soil under these nails,' he said. 'The good earth is in my hands.'

'Hssst,' called Tramp Major. 'Hurry up down there.'

'I wish you luck, Mr Elms, and thank you,' I told him.

'A pleasure, Mr London Taylor,' he said.

Word list

Fetid

Tramp Major

Sue

Thurs March 17th. 11pm
In the dorm

Pensees: *A woman may never know the intentions of a bashful man unless she gets squiffy enough to ask him.* SB

I've been thinking about home all day. Perhaps it was because I could hear Cinnamon's radio tuned to the World Service telling me that this is London, which is incongruous and yet familiar when I am in the depths of Greece.

This evening, I expect the residents of Green Place will have had drinks at 6 and dinner at 8 as usual. And Aunt Coral will have been a wonderful host, because she really *enjoys* her tenants. But in spite of the day-to-day sociability of life there, Green Place residents are of an age where people aren't necessarily *conscious* for 12 hours in a day, for naps are included in the routine. When the Nanas – Georgette, Print and Taffeta – come for drinks, they often enjoy a quick snooze.

Last year when the Admiral's ex-navy friends, Admiral Gordon and Admiral Ted, moved in, Aunt Coral commissioned a painter to do a little gentle watercolour of everyone. In it, the group are positioned outside the front door with Green Place as the setting behind them. All the Admirals are in their uniforms, standing chivalrously behind Aunt Coral and Delia, who are seated modestly on a bench with a tartan throw over it, in the dying afternoon light. She and Delia are dressed in dove grey suits and lace-up shoes; they look like they have just settled on the bench after picking flowers from the rose beds. They have cups of tea in their hands poured from a Wedgwood teapot, set on a table beside them with cucumber sandwiches and a white tablecloth.

And of course as a result of *that* watercolour, Aunt Coral commissioned another, which is of herself and the Admiral having dinner together.

In that one, she and the Admiral are dressed in evening clothes, he's in a dickie bow, and they are sitting facing each other, leaning over a sticky toffee pudding with two spoons. (Mrs Bunion is pottering around in the background, because it proved too difficult in the end to get her to sit down for long enough to get her likeness.)

It's funny that, having gone to all that trouble, Aunt Coral then hung both paintings in downstairs lavatories. She said there is no better place to hang a picture than in the toilet . . . because it will get much closer *attention*.

I'm guessing tonight that they will have all sat and chatted by the fire in the drawing room. For really, what else is there to do on quiet evenings, but sit in nice lamplight, eat nourishing food and set the world to rights? The question I believe Aunt Coral asks herself is how can I make life as nice as possible for the next few hours? It's a good question to ask yourself.

Aunt Coral sees Joe's love for me as a precious treasure and a gift and a joy. I said she might well turn out to have the same with the Admiral but she said that sadly she gave up that kind of love ages ago around the same time as she gave up wearing no sleeves.

As I explained, the Admiral is Aunt C's special friend, and she enjoys having special feelings for him. In many ways they behave like a couple, though they definitely one hundred per cent *aren't* one.

And although she sometimes complains that, after three years of living together and still no move for a romance, the Admiral might be what she calls 'a big girl's blouse', she is in fact quite happy with their friendship. (I'm not too sure if by big girl's blouse she means that the Admiral is afraid of commitment or, rather more irrevocably, if he would prefer to have a relationship with another Admiral.)

I might sum up by saying that Aunt C is an outsider who sometimes longs to join in. For although she is all the things that society regards as relatively unimportant, i.e. old and a woman, yet she is the most ordinarily contented person I have ever met, not to mention the most fun-loving.

She advocates the viewing of life always looking ahead, never looking back and *never* down. I thought this was very profound until she added that this is because, after a certain age, looking down isn't *advisable*.

Fri March 18 1988
Airport

I booked a private session on a pedallo at lunchtime because I wanted to write a piece about mermaids. I thought if I went off on my own I'd be more likely to catch sight of one. I was far out beyond Bunty's jetty when I saw Mr O'Carroll waving at me from the beach, so I pedalled back in swiftly to see what was up.

My anxiety level increased tenfold as I approached the shore because I noticed he had come in his car which was parked by Crysanthe's, so obviously something was wrong and time was of the essence.

He tried his utmost to be reassuring to me, but owing to my history with disastrous news, such as when the police gave me the news about mum, you can imagine my state of mind. Once it has happened, you do worry.

'Your Dad told me to tell you there is nothing for you to worry about, but he needs to talk to you as soon as poss,' said Mr O'C, breathlessly.

'Is he all right?' I asked.

'Yes, he's fine, hop in,' he said.

He drove me back around the bay to the Taverna where I immediately rang my Dad.

'Dad.'

'Darling, is somebody with you? I've got some news.'

'Mr O'Carroll's here. What's happened?'

'Ivana went into labour, but there've been complications.'

'Is she all right?'

'Ivana's all right, but you have a baby brother who's arrived in the world a bit soon. There's no pressure, Sue, but I wanted to tell you, in case you wanted to come home and meet him . . . that is . . . I wanted to tell you, you have a brother and his name is Pierre.'

I felt a strange fire inside that couldn't quite ignite. How ironic that someone so fragile should have such a magnificent name.

'Of course I want to come home,' I said. It was a decision that was made out of the clearest instinct, for it sounded as though there may not be another chance to meet my brother again.

'Ring me as soon as you know your flight. I'll be there to meet you,' said Dad.

We said goodbye and I sat down on an easy chair with red poppies painted on it.

Mr O'Carroll dropped everything and offered to take me to the ferry himself. Cinnamon swung into action too and made me a cup of tea with some sugar, which is the universal treatment for shock.

I went in haste to pack my small remembrances and other few bits and bobs. Christine from Dickens came into the dorm and asked me what had happened. She seemed sympathetic at first and grew quiet for some moments.

'Before you go, would you mind critiquing a piece of comedy I've written?' she asked.

'Do you have *any* idea how far down my list that is?' I said, just managing to hold my manners.

'No,' she replied.

'It's . . . about *seventh*,' I said. It was absolutely galling and not surprisingly I was thrown.

And unfortunately I didn't have time to say plus tard myself to my core members of Zola. I bet they will wonder where I've got to. H, D and Q were out on an organized trip to a monastery and W was squirrelled away somewhere on a date with a needy barmaid.

I will miss Shabany, and the sea and having cocktails and learning philosophy. I will miss the sight of the seagulls when they float like boats on the waves. And as for missing the final 3 weeks, perhaps it may even be for the best? I wonder if I might be more of a thinker than a writer. After all, thanks to Quiz, I feel drawn to Blasé Pascal who has already triggered so many pensees.

But I think most of all I will miss being part of a group who all live to write. It has been nice to be part of a salon that is more my own sort of age. I'll miss Helen, who is a patchwork quilt writer – she writes piecemeal and then fills in the gaps. I'll miss her solidarity, her common sense and no nonsense and her ability to be caustic. I'll miss Diane, who can hold an entire plot in her head, and loves to research in the British Library. I'll miss her film-school haircut, her strapless black towelette jumpsuit, her chips. I'll miss tortured William who's so desperate to be in a couple. He pegs his plots out on a poetic washing line, but then he gets distracted like a puppy. He says he's going to write one of those stories with fog, like Jekyll and Hyde or Frankenstein. I bet he does it. And I'll miss fragrant Quiz, who likes to write notes on the beach while he smokes. The sophisticate lounge lizard at such masterful ease in the world. I wonder if he will disappear into London and become dead to me? I wonder if I will ever see him or Di again? I wonder if I will ever see any of them?

Already they seem to be part of the past, but as Aunt Coral says, 'You can't take everybody with you.'

Mr O'Carroll drove like a gangster over the mountain road. His car was extremely plush.

'I will send on a work sheet for you, so you can complete the course,' he said.

'Thank you,' I replied.

'There have been one or two students who've had to leave early before, so no harm done. You won't miss too much, don't worry. You can send back your dissertation for marking as soon as you've finished it – there is no major hurry, as long as it is by the end of July, and I will ask Professor Mushrooms to find you when he comes to London in the summer. As soon as he has passed your dissertation, then I can issue your certificate!'

'Thank you Mr O'Carroll,' I said because there were no other words to express my gratitude.

'It's a pleasure. You're going to be a great writer one day, never give up.'

'Thank you Mr O'Carroll,' I said, wishing I knew a greater selection of words meaning thanks.

I suddenly remembered that I had packed *For the Concern of the Rich and the Poor* in my case.

'Oh Mr O'Carroll,' I said suddenly. 'I'm sorry, I've still got your book.'

'What's that?' he asked without taking his eyes off the road.

'Your book, I very nearly went off with it, it's in my suitcase.'

'You can borrow it if you like, as long as you promise to keep it safe for me. That way I'll have the perfect excuse to visit you if I need to look at it again,' he said generously.

'Thank you, that's so kind. Aunt Coral will be delighted.'

'And I do hope your little brother will be all right. We will be thinking of you,' he added.

He screeched to a halt by the ferry with little time to spare, and I got out of the car and grabbed my case from the back seat as we said farewell. I had a feeling of silent significance when I turned to walk away from my teacher. I thought it'd be the last time I heard his voice, but he called after me out of his window.

'Don't forget to be more Russian!'

FOR THE CONCERN OF THE RICH AND THE POOR

It was the first week of September and those of us left greatly anticipated Cheeser's first conker battle with his niner, which was to be fought that morning in the yard against the winning cheeser from Ward Six.

Cheeser stepped up and stood opposite Eric Needle, his opponent.

Needle won the toss and took the first swipe and made contact with the niner at first strike.

At the first cry of 'snags', which also came from Needle, he was about to take a second swing at the niner as Cheeser held it straight down for him. Both were steadying themselves for the swipe when suddenly the duel was duped.

Bully boy Adam Detail seized his moment and tore the niner clean out of Cheeser's hand.

'Cheeser,' he cried, speeding towards the fence. 'Fetch!'

He hurled the niner over the fence where it was lost in the depths of the long grass billowing in the Chaplain's field.

'Bastaaard!' yelled Cheeser, running after it, but Detail's lackeys held him back.

'I'll get it, I saw where it went! Quick, help me over,' I hollered at Fogey impulsively.

It all happened in an instant.

And as I made my decision to retrieve the niner for Cheeser, the boy who I was before that morning ceased to exist and in his place stood a warrior.

Fogey hoisted me on to his shoulders, and I perched sideways at the top of the fence and swiftly dropped over, losing a shoe as I did. And I ran into that forbidden field with my pulse racing and my heart pounding, before the monitors noticed, or any of the Masters could stop me. I knew that I would be flogged as soon as I turned myself in, for running away whilst wearing my uniform. The Chaplain liked to dissuade runaways with the threat of his salted cane, but even the thought of that didn't stop me.

So I dropped to the ground so as to hide my position in the long grass, with a thimbleful of military instinct, hoping I could get back before the Chaplain could come.

'Governor! Chaplain! Matron!' yelled the Details. 'There's a thief in the field!'

But I remained resolute, flat in the long grass, and crawled along on my elbows dragging my legs behind me. In this way my other shoe was also lost to a hungry stone. I could see nothing but blades of tall grass patched with leaves obscuring my view. Finding a conker in the field, even one tied to a red shoelace, was like trying to find a needle in a haystack, but if only I could get into the vicinity of where I knew it landed, I felt I at least had a chance. But I was going to be much quicker if I stood up and ran.

'Look!' cried Detail as soon as I got up. 'There he is!'

It was a tactical error made out of the heat of the moment, but I was so focused on finding the niner that I was blinded by determination.

Then Chaplain Cragg arrived, followed by Matron Cole. I knew I'd be for it.

'Halt! Thief! Stay where you are!'

I can only suggest that my mind was no longer in charge, because my body made the next decision. I did not stay where I was but dropped down again and wriggled further into the likely niner territory, in a blaze of disobedience.

'How dare you!' cried the Chaplain.

I could see the men in the yard through the slats in the fence. My inner script was racing.

'Maybe I should turn myself in?'

'No, not without the niner.'

'I'll be flogged, I could die.'

'It cannot be worse than living.'

'It's only a chestnut on a shoelace. He can make another.'

'No, Cheeser could never replicate the niner – it is the thing that defines him and gives his life hope. I have to find it. If it is the last thing I do before I die.'

'London Taylor! Stop, thief!' sang the Chaplain, his arms waving wildly, giving out orders to minions enjoying the scene.

I rolled on to my side to catch my breath and rested for a moment. I thought the game was up, but in a dewy thicket I spotted, in my eye line, the niner. How small and plain it looked, that hard shrivelled little trophy of power, threaded on to a dog-eared shoelace; but there it was, my prize, the symbol of the spirit of Cheeser.

'I've got it,' I shouted to Cheeser. 'I've got the niner!' I don't know if he could hear me.

I stood up and took a step towards him holding it aloft, but as I did, Cheeser's whole demeanour changed. He ran to the gates at the entrance to the Mead, which was the preferred way into the field, and he stood on the bottom rung where I could see him better. He shook his head, he held up the palm of his hand, he signalled frantically for me to turn and run the other way. He punched the air, he willed me, commanded me, begged me not to come back.

I was now into a scenario which I was totally unprepared for, that of unplanned escape, the seizing of my freedom, and all delivered by an opportune moment of good intent.

I held up the niner again. 'I've got it,' I croaked through unwelcome nine-year-old tears. Cheeser bolted the gates. I guessed he was trying to buy me more time.

'London, don't be afraid!' he shouted.

He punched his fist in the air, he thrust his arm forward. I beheld his image and drew one last breath before I cut my strings with the Mead. Then, turning on my heel, I thrust my own fist forward and cried like a mighty warrior,

'To Germany!'

And then I ran, as fast as ever I could.

Sue

18 March 1988

Airport

And so he has escaped! And is embarking on a big adventure. It was very courageous of London to make an escape when he didn't even have any shoes on.

As the ferry pulled away from the Cretan quayside, I turned to face the future, but indulged a sharp recollection of school mornings in Titford, and two old gossips who used to wait at the bus stop across the road from our house. On fine days when I looked out from my window, I remember the sun danced over their glasses. And vainly I wondered what they would say if they could see me on this ship now?

'Got herself a scholarship, thinks she knows all about Russia.'

'Now she's after an internship.'

'She's not even been to college, she'll never get it.'

The ferry horn honked as it set sail and my bus stop ladies were gone again. I hope I can prove them wrong.

My ferry crossing to mainland Greece lasted three hours. I paced the decks a lot of the time, remembering my way round by two dogs that were travelling, a spaniel on D deck and a Jack Russell with a family.

There was a shop by the cafeteria, where I bought a ship's jotter and a matching pen with a ferry at one end in a sliding display. I remembered the first note I wrote on Day 1 at the Taverna, 'A writer never leaves the house without a pad and pen', so it seemed appropriate.

I passed some more time on a fruit machine that was beside a 1950s boy figurine with his eyes closed. He was wearing blue shorts, white blouse, socks and sandals and holding out a coin box for the blind. These old shipping lines must have chugged to and fro for decades, from the islands to the mainland and back again, leaving trails of foam in the water like noughts and crosses on the Med.

Back out on deck, I looked down off the side of the ferry and counted the fish swimming back and forth. I don't know why but the counting put me back in mind of something that Quiz once said about using flashbacks and flash-forwards in your writing.

I have always wanted to be patient enough to use the immortal words, exclusively on loan to God and authors, *'three years later'*. And if it were three years later, I should hope that Pierre would be celebrating his third birthday, and I'd be with Joe and settled back at Green Place.

After disembarking at the quayside at the Port of Piraeus, I managed to get a taxi straight to the airport. There was a photo of Jesus hanging from the rearview mirror. I watched it swinging from side to side.

Sitting in the back in the roasting heat, I could see the tops of a thousand cars ahead that were sparkling in the sun like a sea. They flowed up a big hill in the distance, as far as the horizon. It looked like I could just climb on to the top of the taxi and the shimmering roofs would ferry me back to grey little England.

PART TWO

Is It Too Early for a Sherry?

PART TWO

Sue

Pensees: *International airspace. A lawless place, above borders and free from time and taxes.* SB

Three weeks later, Fri April 8th 1988

I wanted to be able to write '*three weeks later*' and still be telling the truth. So I have indulged a little break from writing, so I could have the luxury of filling in the gap.

In spite of being obviously very worried about Pierre, for the remainder of the journey home I still had that lovely feeling you get whenever you've been away somewhere – that is, the feeling of excitement about coming back.

Heathrow was fog-bound and my flight was diverted to Manchester for landing at 2am. Four hours later I was on the first train to London at 5.47am.

I felt suddenly foreign in my pink canvas trousers (bought at the supermarket in Shabany) and floppy T-shirt tied with a knot, crammed in as I was with smart, shower-fresh commuters.

Rain ran sideways along the train windows like tears, and collected in the shapes of shaky tadpoles swimming across the glass. And pylons stretched over the fields for miles; they looked like rows of Morris dancers holding out their wires shoulder to shoulder.

I felt inspired at the prospect of seeing Joe again and I decided to use up the last few pictures in my camera on the passing spectacular views. But sadly, I got a series of close-ups of the woman in the window seat's picnic.

Dad was waiting by the ticket office at Kings X and he looked like he hadn't slept for days. There was so much to say that kicking off was difficult, and once we were on the road he had to concentrate, for there was the rain and the traffic to deal with, let alone a premature son.

'How is Pierre?'

'He's alive,' said Dad, with a trembly voice while we were held up at a long red light. All his usual defences and pleasantries had been stripped away by anxiety and lack of sleep. He was a raw version of himself that I had not acquainted.

'He's in an incubator, he needs a lot of support,' he continued.

'Does he look like you?' I asked, for want of a safe question, but it opened a flood gate for Dad.

'I've only seen him open his eyes once, when the lights went dim for a moment, but I was there, I was the first thing he saw, and he looked through me like a hundred-year-old man. He's unfamiliar, he's a stranger and yet I *recognize* him, Sue. As soon as I saw him, a voice in my mind said "Oh *there* you are" and I knew I would do anything to protect him. It was the same with you. How was your course?' he asked with a flash of day-to-day small talk.

'Great, thank you,' I replied, though under the circumstances it seemed of little consequence.

Being back in England is like being put in a shoe box with the lid on, it's dark and grey and misty and small and silver and cold. At least, that was the impression that Surrey gave as we drove through. We passed a random duck on a woodland puddle in the gloam of the wintry morning, and a terrace of houses slightly illuminated on a hill, their windows like eyes hungry for light. A row of chimney pots was reaching up to the sky for air like stretched-out fingers and cauliflower-shaped banks of cloud were reflected in the car windows.

We parked up at the Titford hospital car park and, once inside, we took the lift up to the sixth floor. I followed Dad to a viewing place behind a glass wall beyond which was a room for the incubators. Dad pointed to number three and I saw Pierre for the very first time.

He was lying on his back with his arms up, in a clear incubator with a top on it. He *did* look like a tired, elderly Buddha. The incubator had holes in the side for the staff to put their hands in to nurse him. They watch over him for even a whisker out of place. We are not allowed to touch him for fear of introducing the cold, for he can't keep his temperature stable because he isn't even fat enough to shiver.

There were three white patches on his tummy attached to wires that were monitoring his life signs. He had a feeding tube in his nose, and at times he has oxygen to help him breathe. (He is suffering from something called Apnoea, which means his heart intermittently stops.)

It seems a miracle to think that Pierre could one day become a grown man. That over time his velveteen hands might wear the barnacles of old age like Dad's.

Ivana was in a private room along the corridor from him. She was sitting up in a narrow bed facing picture windows with a view over Titford. She looked very pale.

'How do you feel?' I asked her, standing at the bottom of her bed.

'Like I've had a baby cut out of me,' she replied dramatically.

She looked fragile and exhausted and a nurse was regularly checking her.

It was the first time I had seen Ivana without her tan on and her usual blonde roots were grey. But even so, she was wearing a droopy silk ribbon in her hair. She is never off duty for effort.

I glanced at her notes, which said that she was a geriatric mother. She can't have been too happy with that! She told me of all the tests she had for Pierre before he was born because of her age. Tests for his heart, his brain, his lungs, his spine, and after all this she joked, 'We had no warning he was going to be ginger.'

Had he been born ten years ago he probably would not have survived. Most likely he would have been put straight into Ivana's arms for a few precious seconds, the time it takes for a feather to fall to the ground.

But at this precise moment, even as I write this, Pierre lies in his incubator, hanging on to the threads of life supplied by all the machines. And as soon as he is allowed out in the cold, he will need the basics of survival, like a hat.

And this is the first that I know of him, the little Buddha asleep in the box.

TWD for Pierre: Hundred-year-old soul.

A little while later, at about 3pm, I caught a taxi back home to Green Place and blinding low sunbeams pierced through the windows, shimmering through the dripping trees. The sun's benign appearance was proof that Spring was on the way *in*.

I glided past a brightly lit boutique full of bridal wear as I passed by in the taxi, with as many white gowns as I had just seen crops in a passing field. First thing on my To Do when I got home was telephone Joe.

FOR THE CONCERN OF THE RICH AND THE POOR

Shortly after my escape from the Mead, I had shed my incriminating uniform in favour of a stolen doll's garments which, in my hour of great need, were the only items I could muster. I took them from a giant doll that belonged to a girl I spotted on my travels. A girl, I thought, who looked wealthy enough for her doll to have a change of clothes. And on my feet I wore the boots of a much older lady, taken from her doorstep as I happened to pass by.

I tied the niner round my neck like a mascot, and I made a pledge that one day I would return it to Cheeser so that he might make it a tenner. And so I went on my way, the very image, I believed, of a modern Victorian urchin.

And I did not stop running until the land itself ran out, and my path led me all the way down to the sea. No one ever told me it was a pool of water so infinite I could not tell if it ever ended. Could it be God was a tailor? Throwing out a roll of silk which he had been spinning out of the sky?

But the triumph of my escape was only fleeting as soon it began to grow dark. The night was quiet and very still. I passed no other but danced on, my shadow walking ahead. And at tea time the sinking sun was my plate, hay my loaf, and the stars my salt and pepper. I had no cane to avoid, no cobbler's toil, no cruel Master, but on the other hand, no food, no shelter, no bed.

So I made my first camp at the edge of a small wood, on a mattress of pine needles, with a sweep of them for a pillow. I could hear the forlorn thump of chestnuts as they fell to the ground somewhere not far off and winced, for I knew that Cheeser would have been beaten six ways from Sunday. I clasped the niner to my heart and shed noisy tears.

The wood grew darker and the clouds heavy and the distant sea turned grey as the grave. All was hushed but for my shivering and the rain hissing in the trees, and eventually the night shrouded my little life.

And as I lay and screwed my eyes tight against my tears, the words of a kind stranger flowed back to me. And the last thing I remember thinking before I fell to fitful sleep was, I wonder which way is Old Egham?

Aunt Coral's To Do

(on the Butterfly Table in the hall)

Make will

Badger the gardener

Knightsbridge 4.30pm

Sue

Fri April 8th 1988
(Later the same evening)

The Admiral and one of the B and B guests, Hugh from Chertsey, were in the drawing room at 4.00 with bitter lemons and a bowl of Mini Cheddars between them.

'Welcome home Sue!' said the Admiral, brushing my cheeks with a tobacco pipey kiss. 'Can I twist your arm for a biscuit?'

'I am a bit peckish, thank you,' I said, as the language of Green Place came flooding back to me.

'You look so well!' said the Admiral. 'We've been very cooped up.'

My heart leapt when I heard the familiar step and smelt lilies wafting down the staircase. I expected to see Aunt Coral thriving when she entered the room, followed by another new lodger. But what a shock I got when I saw her – she was ashen of cheek and pink of eye. She gave me the lightest little featherweight cuddle, and I returned it with a fierce winter-scorning kiss.

'Welcome home Sue,' she said. 'It's so good to see you! You've got a suntan! How wonderful, don't you look lovely. Is it too early for a sherry?' she asked.

Mrs Bunion joined in and patted me, as though I had just scored a goal.

'Welcome home dear,' she said, proffering a bowl of peanuts.

'Thank you!' I said.

'Dry or sweet?' asked Mrs Bunion.

'Sweet please,' said Aunt C. 'Make it a double and save your legs.'

'How is Pierre?' she enquired, glowing at me, and pulling her cardi closer round her shoulders. Sometimes I wonder why she doesn't just put it on properly.

'He's hanging in tight, he's been asleep all afternoon,' I replied.

'Sleep is very good,' said Aunt Coral.

'This is Mr Hart,' she moved on with introductions to her guests. 'He's from Houston in Texas.'

'Hi Sue, I've heard a lot about you,' said Mr Hart.

'And this is Hugh from Chertsey,' said Aunt Coral, before adding, 'who is a third-generation postman.'

I guessed she must have had her reasons to big him up.

'Young Hugh can lay claim to an aristocratic ancestry,' said Aunt Coral.

'What a curse in life expectations can be,' exclaimed Hugh dismally.

'We've just had a room reshuffle. I've put you back into Pearl's room,' Aunt C told me. 'Unfortunately the wind has blown all this rain straight into the old bricks on the main chimneys, and rainwater is now galloping down the walls in the central suites.'

'What we need is a prolonged spell of dry weather and warm winds to blow everything dry,' said the Admiral, suddenly animated by the topic of the weather. The Westminster chimes from the mantel clock chimed out their familiar percussive ding to mark the half hour.

What a shame, the rain damage now adds to the catalogue of disasters that have recently needed attention. The B and B side of things is the latest plan to replenish the Green Place coffers, after the containment of dry rot and refurbishments of two new suites that swallowed up all the funds of last year.

'Where's everyone *else*?' I asked. 'Delia and Admiral Gordon and Admiral Ted? Are they napping?'

'No, no, they're not here tonight,' said Aunt C.

'They have gone away,' chorused the Admiral. 'To Aberdeenshire.'

Aunt C's new B and B guests appeared a little awkward. I sensed there was something afoot.

'I've got another fascinating discovery from Jackie County to show you,' said Aunt Coral in a swift change of subject. And a hush descended on the residents as she read aloud.

'What I have here is a Sotheby's catalogue from March 22nd 1856 and circled is a listing for a "Shipwreck Pearl Necklace",' she said, holding it up. 'This piece was bought at auction by my Great Great Grandfather Edmund.'

'Was he the one who was exhumed?' asked Hugh.

'Yes, dear,' replied Aunt Coral. 'Jackie County believes that he must have bought the pearls as a wedding present for his second wife, Rose Anna.'

'Fascinating,' said the Admiral.

'But what is even more exciting is that these are not just any old baubles, these are rare Tahitian natural black pearls, quite precious, and two whole strands. Jackie is suggesting that we organize an in-depth search of the grounds in case they should turn out to be still on the premises.'

'Does she mean digging?' enquired the Admiral.

'Not immediately, just a little gentle poke about,' said Aunt C.

'Obviously digging would be a last resort because it will make such a mess. We need to exhaust other avenues.'

I was listening, imagining us all out in the garden in our pyjamas looking for pearls, but my mind wandered, the way it does after you've had a long journey, and I have a niggling anxiety over the presence of 'Knightsbridge 4.30pm' on Aunt Coral's To Do (which I noticed when I passed it in the hall). One might have thought that the presence of 'Make Will' on the list would be cause for worry, but that has been on her list for years. It has been there ever since I came to Green Place, and it has always been at the top.

But she does sometimes go to see a very expensive doctor in Knightsbridge and, with her looking so pale, I am concerned.

But then again, since I lost mum I've lost all my confidence in everyone else's ability to stay alive. I must remember that, and not badger Aunt Coral about it.

After supper I went to ring Joe to let him know I was home. Mrs Fry answered and told me Joe had gone Euro-railing with the girls from the Toastie and that she would tell him I called.

It was a *huge* shock. And I feel so disappointed, particularly as I had no idea he was going. But I told myself in all fairness he wasn't expecting me back for another month.

I'm now in my bed in Aunt Coral's mother's old suite, Pearl's room. It's been a very long day. One of those days that feels like months, or maybe even years, and I've travelled hundreds of miles. I've left the curtains and the window open because I want to get up very early and potter about unpacking.

It's so peaceful here in Pearl's room at night. A school of geese have just flown over gently honking a tune. Their wings sounded like the old hinges on an old creaky door. I wonder if they will fly over Pierre?

In closing for tonight I will add that I can just see the crescent moon rising, illuminating Joe's photo. It looks like the little white teeth in the smile of a clown.

FOR THE CONCERN OF THE RICH AND THE POOR

And so one velocipede, three coaches, one rag-and-bone cart, one omnibus and two trains later I arrived at my destination.

'Can you tell me which way is it to Mr Garden's residence?' I asked a stranger, for the third time before striking lucky.

'But of course, young lady . . .' replied a man in a top hat. Then he told me: 'Turn to the left, and then to the right, and then pass straight through Old Egham. Cross the stream and walk down towards Fern Common, until the road becomes Clockhouse Lane. Green Place is the last before the end residence, you can't miss it. The entrance is through two stone pillars with lions on the top.'

But by the time I got there it was well past a respectable person's bedtime. I hovered beneath the iron gates, which were chained up tight for the night.

I had no right to enter, nor any smooth talk to explain my situation, I was too tired after my long journey, and anyway who would care to answer the call of an urchin at the gate in a storm?

And so I took a reluctant decision to make camp where I was for the night and wait till the morning to make my overture.

'At least I can see progress,' I shivered, outside the gates. 'Pauper, vagrant, urchin, I'm already two notches up from two days ago. At this rate by Sunday I'll be a gentleman.'

All I had to do was be patient, wait till morning and throw myself at Alfred Elms' feet. How could anyone with a heart resist?

Sue

Tues April 12 1988, 600am

Pensees: *'Beware every phrase that has tomorrow in it.'*
(An ancient Greek)

But everything was *so* very different when I got up on that morning after I got home from Greece, almost three weeks ago now. Indeed *nothing* was as I expected.

The biggest shock of all was that Admiral Ted has *passed away*. Aunt Coral did not tell me when it actually happened, because she did not want me to feel I should come home from Greece, and when I did get home, she didn't want to tell me straight away, because she thought it would all be a bit much on top of Pierre.

So I rose to discover Admiral Ted was actually gone. His suite, Snowdrop, in the West Wing was all empty and cleaned and echoey. His death as sudden on the one hand as Pierre's birth was on the other.

And Admiral Gordon was rigid with grief according to Aunt Coral, and so Delia took him on a trip to see his Nanny in Aberdeenshire, where they have more or less ended up staying.

I miss hearing Ad Ted's small rustlings about the place. He liked pottery and was collecting thumb pots which he kept in bubble wrap in an old suite. I miss his interest in everyone, his presence, and his daredevil cross purposes, because he had such bad hearing on account of his tittinus.

And his parting has totally knocked the stuffing out of the Egham Hirsute Group and they have not held a writing group since he died. He was watching the cricket on the Common and he went in his sleep. A fitting end for such a gentle fellow.

In further unexpectedness, Joe got in touch two days *after* I spoke to Mrs Fry. (He did not even get the message until then.) Ironically, he said he'd gone Euro-railing because he was missing me and because he didn't have any work on because Mrs Fry closed the Toastie for refurbishment.

And since he left, he has been further delayed because Charlie (another friend from the Toastie) broke her leg and he did not feel he could leave her alone in a Sicilian hospital (the other girls in their Euro-railing group had to come home for school and things like that). Apparently Charlie slipped on a ham sandwich and so the doctors are calling it a 'ham sandwich fracture'. I can't tell you how many times I have had to explain that when people have asked me when is he coming home.

I spent 17 years without Joe so I don't really understand why a few more weeks is proving to be so hard? But while he is away, I feel a bit like a Kenyan rose – I don't open and I don't smell. The trouble is I was *expecting* to see him.

I have been to the hospital each day, but I've not yet seen Pierre open his eyes. He seems to have decided to sleep through the drama of his early days, until he is strong enough to open them.

Plus, there is no word yet on whether I have qualified for an interview for the *Echo* internship and it seems ages since I sent off my application. I wish they would just let me know if I haven't got an interview, because disappointment is far easier to deal with than hope. You know exactly what you're dealing with, with disappointment, but the sky is the limit with hope. I am trying hard to modify my hopes in an effort to save myself from disappointment.

Furthermore, I had to persuade Aunt Coral to ask her new B and B guests to leave, because she got so carried away with giving them nice bath soaps etc. that every time she sold a room she made a small loss. She has absolutely no head for business. The Admiral says Aunt C can't help herself but behave like it's always Christmas. She's had the Nanas here *every night* for three-course dinners. It's a mercy they've gone off on the QE2.

So, in summing up the last three weeks: due to all the unexpected, unforeseen circumstances, it has been a very discombobulating time. Life seems determined to go down a different path than the one I was expecting and I feel very unsettled.

I have thrown myself into writing some exploratory scenes on the seabed as an idea for my dissertation, which, due to my head being all over the place, I feel somewhat dubious about. I shall keep it to one side, in case it may prove worth tidging.

A Russian Mermaid fusion idea for dissertation

THE EMPEROR'S SLIPPERS
by Sue Bowl

'At the bottom of the ocean lie the slippers where the Emperor's children are born. That is how the old story goes.

But if you are born outside the slipper, you cannot gain entry to the Coral Palace. To be born outside the slipper means that you are an outcast and you must live on the sand. That is the way of things, we must accept it,' said Aunt Bettia Pulnietzova.

'What if you can find someone born within the slipper to take pity on you? To invite you inside the slipper?' said Doonyasha, with spirit.

'You hope to marry into the slipper? You speak of Lady Emily De Tue?' said Aunt Bettia pickling grass.

'Pish! I will go to her, and I will tell her that we have lost everything, what harm can it do?'

'You know she is a mermaid?'

'So what?'

'Be quiet bluffer!' railed Aunt Bettia. 'Tisk, tisk. Oh Doonyasha! Such notions! For how will you impress the Emperor? And . . . what, in the name of Heaven, is that dog doing in here? How on earth will we feed him?'

'He can share my food Aunt Bettia,' cried Doonyasha.

'Ha! Kind hearted! Just like your mother, Teyvarya Andropopolov. Why, I should have thought it prudence that you should share your food!'

'Piccolo Aunt Bettia, always so sudden! How she flies up!'

'So what will you call him, Lucky?' said Aunt Bettia.

'No! He is Sacha Lukvario of The Cut.'

Tues April 12
Mid-morning in the drawing room

I keep coming back to the image of Joe and Charlie together. I don't like to think of them languishing in Sicily, but I do understand why he feels he can't leave her, at least until she is able to hobble. And ironically, his sweet kind nature is all the more reason to cherish him.

But what worries me is that Charlie is a bit of a vulture. She plays poker and drinks whisky mac. (TWD!)

Or rather, perhaps I should say she is what Aileen Edgeley, my childhood friend from Titford, calls a *Jackie-friend*. A *Jackie-friend* is one of those girls you see in the photo-love stories inside *Jackie* magazine, the one who steals your boyfriend, sleeps with him, and then goes off with somebody else.

But even more worrying is that Charlie manages to be so nice about it. She'd allow anyone to spend time with her boyfriends and she has boyfriends all over the world. She is just dangerously free. Compared to, say, someone like Delia's daughter, Loudolle, who is a straightforward vulture.

I can't even *begin* to explain Loudolle's gruesome depths. But I have a TWD for Aileen. First one to get bosoms.

Here is a further extract from London upon *his* arrival at Green Place, by way of distracting myself from thoughts of Joe and Charlie.

FOR THE CONCERN OF THE RICH AND THE POOR

'Excuse me please, I've come to see Mr Elms,' I said. My voice was so small I had to shout to be heard through the gates.

'Who shall I say is asking for him?' enquired a man who appeared on the other side of them, early in the morning.

'My name is London Taylor.'

He looked askance at me in my bedraggled doll's dress. 'Have you an appointment?'

'Yes, I have,' I said, shuddering, for I am not a natural-born liar.

'Mr Elms is out by the Hermitage. I will send a message, wait here.'

'So,' said the man when he returned, 'Mr Elms can see you at noon. He asked me to take you to his cottage where you may wait for him more comfortably. Come and stand this side for a moment, I must first take receipt of some parcels for Madam Garden.'

He opened up the great gates to admit me, and we set off up the long drive to the big house. My eyes circumnavigated every acre of splendour, and in terms of looking, did five miles to every one of his.

'I'm Sowerbutt,' he said, 'Estate Steward. What is your business with Mr Elms?'

'It is a personal matter,' I stuttered, '. . . a matter of a personal matter.'

Sowerbutt had a heavy frame but a broad stride that made it difficult for me to keep up with him as we marched up the drive.

And as we approached the top, the big house came into view, pale cream, almost alabaster in colour. Its front flanks were basking peacefully as they dried out in the clear morning air, reigning over the glossy treetops below us, sparkling in the sun.

We walked on straight past the big house. The chimneys were smoking, the windows glinting; a back door opened and out came the smell of cooking. I caught glimpses of black and white uniforms through the windows, suggesting a fleet of maids scurrying inside.

But we pressed on to the other side of the house, past the stables, past fine horses being groomed in a cobbled courtyard. On and on we went, till I wondered if we should ever reach Alfred Elms' cottage.

Then deep into the gardens to the side of the house and down through wide meadows we tramped further, till the green lawns fell away to join a gentle slope, and at the bottom stood two cottages in front of a walled garden.

'This is Edenthorpe,' said Sowerbutt. 'Please wait here. Mr Elms will be back for his lunch. I must go now. Call for Walderon if you need assistance.'

He gestured towards the next-door cottage, wherein I presumed was the owner of that name. There was a wooden plaque on the door carved with the cottage name: Roselyne. My eye was drawn up by a piece of curtain fluttering out of an upstairs window, then a small white hand appeared and gently shook it to straighten it out. I expected a lady might be beyond at her dressing table, with powder and hairbrush to hand. But when I collected my thoughts I realized that the upstairs window of a gardener's cottage was a curious place to see such a lily-white, ladylike hand.

A second later, a lady's face at the window confirmed my suspicious curiosity. Her skin was as pale as the moon, her features framed by wispy red hair and a high collar of solid black at her neck. Her eyes were misty, and her expression far away. She moved away from the window as soon as she saw she'd been spotted, and out of politeness I pretended not to have seen her.

Reverently I diverted my gaze and made a study of Alfred Elms' cottage.

Like Roselyne, Edenthorpe was built on to the outer wall of the garden and when I peered in I thought I could make out a window inside at the back, looking out on to flower beds that lay in the walled garden beyond it.

The front of Alfred's cottage bore a similar wooden plaque engraved with its name, 'Edenthorpe', and a sherbet-pink climber with tear-shaped drops was growing all around its name. And beneath its twisted boughs, just above the front door handle, a bronze lucky-horseshoe door knocker suggested to my sense of destiny that I had come to the right place.

> **Word List**
> *Hermitage*
> *Circumnavigated*

Aunt Coral's To Do

Make will

Sash window wedges

Soup Spoons

Badger the gardener

Sue

The above extract took place here 120 years ago in 1858, according to my book. So effectively today I *could* write '*120 years later*' and *still* be telling the truth!

2pm

Pierre was declared out of danger last night and will soon be moved to a normal ward. I was so relieved that after an early visit with him I went and treated myself to a strapless black towellette jumpsuit and a film-school haircut like Di's. Unfortunately the hairstyle doesn't *work* as well on my wavy hair and the film-school angles spring up into extra short tufts, so I'm going to need products to keep my fringe down. But Aunt C has told me not to worry, because I'm not the first person to have to survive a pudding bowl or a mullet.

(I think she was trying to cheer me up.)

6pm

I wasn't expecting to see Quiz and Di again, so you can understand how mortified I was this afternoon when, having got home from the course and finding themselves in the area, they decided to look me up a mere 3 days after finishing at the Taverna.

I cannot *describe* to you how ashamed I felt when I opened the door to them dressed *identically* to Di and sporting the exact same haircut. It was one of the most embarrassing experiences of my *life*.

'Surprise!' they both said in unison. There was a truly awful moment as they stood on the threshold of Green Place.

'Hi!' I said. 'It's *such* a shock to see you!!'

'Wow – you look great,' said Di, clearly electing to ignore the elephant in the room. 'What an AMAZING house.'

Quiz bent down and gave me a hug, and I blushed from head to toe.

He looked handsome, tall, floppy of suit, clipperty of shoe, and fragrant of scarf. And Di was effortlessly chic in her jumpsuit and black flatties with gold buckle.

'I like your hair,' said Quiz mischievously.

'How is your Aunt?' asked Di earnestly, appealing with her eyes to Quiz for a change of subject.

'She is well thank you,' I laughed, as though she had said something terribly funny.

I showed them into the drawing room. Mrs Bunion came in and I hosted.

'This is Mrs Bunion,' I said. 'Quiz and Di from my course.'

'Hello!' they both said cheerfully.

'Good afternoon,' said Mrs Bunion. Her eyes flicked between my jumpsuit and Diane's.

'Would you like some coffee?' she offered.

'Ooh yes please,' I said.

'Creamer?'

'Yes please,' I said, cringing.

'I'll light the fire,' she said, and she did so, with considerable modesty and skill.

'What's that noise?' asked Di, referring to the high-pitch tweeting that emanates from the wall behind the fireplace.

'We have a choir of soprano pipistrelles living inside the wall,' I tittered.

When Mrs Bunion came back with the filtiere, she had changed into a clean pinny. Aunt Coral was out of the house for the day, which meant I could talk about her freely. Usually when I have visitors, I *know* she listens in.

'Aunt Coral told me in her letters that she had been economizing,' I kicked off bravely, 'but I get home and find she's been offering her visitors four different grades of pillow!'

'For goodness sake!' said Di. 'And your little brother? I do hope he was all right?'

'Pierre is doing well now, thank you,' I said, 'but he has only just come off all his supports.'

'Is your Aunt here?' asked Quiz. 'I've never met a real chatelaine.'

'No, in a freak move she is out shopping,' I said. 'She's had a lot to do of late. She's been very busy with the ruins that were found under the thorns. And she *was* taking in B and B guests as well as the Admiral.'

'The Admiral?' said Quiz. 'Of course, I forgot you have an Admiral living here.'

'In our heyday we had three Admirals living here . . . we had *the* Admiral, Admiral Gordon and Admiral Ted, but very unfortunately Admiral Ted has recently passed away. I only knew him for a year, but I am really sad about it.'

'I'm so sorry,' said Di.

'Thank you, there has been a lot of change of late,' I said

sadly. 'But did I tell you I've applied for an internship at the local paper?'

'Good luck, darling,' said Di.

'Thanks, it'd be a grand job.'

'Would they *pay* you?' asked Quiz with a wink.

'Is that Joe?' asked Diane, looking at a photo of him on the mantelpiece. 'I think he looks like the young Renato Salvatori.'

'I'd say he looks like I should give him a nice tip when he clears away my pasta,' said Quiz.

'Honestly!' said Di.

'Would you like to see our ruins? See what you can make of them?' I asked.

'That would be lovely,' said Di.

I nipped into the cloakroom while they finished their coffee, and got straight into a jacket of mercy. Then I found a kirby grip of compassion in the pocket and worked it in round the back, to re-arrange my copycat hair.

On the way out to go to the ruins, Quiz's eye was caught for a second by Aunt Coral's To Do list, which was featured in a sunbeam in its usual place on the Butterfly Table in the hall.

'Make will? On a To Do?' he said with some amusement.

'I know! But that's been on her list since she was about 30!' I said.

'Who's she going to leave it all to – her children?' he asked.

'She doesn't have any children, there's just me,' I replied.

'You're her only relative?' he asked me.

'Yes, I am now that there's no mum.'

'Of course, I'm so sorry darling,' he said, with great charm.

We wandered out into the grounds. Quiz drifted behind us, taking it all in, and I walked ahead with Di. The wispy spring sunshine bounced off her gold buckles. She looked so beautiful, thin, knowledgeable and elegant.

I showed them through the old meadows down the slopes to the side of Green Place, to the walled garden and cottages.

'And the ruins of the cottages are now the homes to periwinkle, ground elder, moss, ivy, nettles and absolutely rampant blackberries,' I pattered. 'The Admiral has begun the business of piling up the loose bricks, in an effort to reinstate the garden walls, because Aunt Coral was so excited to see what it might have looked like.'

'How beautiful,' said Di. 'There must have been paths meandering all over here.'

'Yes, and that's the old sundial in the middle,' I said.

'Look,' said Di. 'You can still see the divisions where the rooms must have been in the cottages.' She pointed to a scraggly line of stones.

'In *For the Concern of the Rich and the Poor*, I'm up to the part where the little boy arrives and knocks on the door of this cottage, Edenthorpe. It's where we're standing right now,' I said.

'Gosh, how *relevant*,' said Di. 'How old was the boy?'

'He must have been about 9 or 10 when he got here in 1858,' I said grandly.

'The tops of the bricks are all charred – looks like there's been a fire,' said Quiz.

'Do you know what happened?'

'No. Aunt Coral has a historian friend who is trying to find out. But I don't think even Aunt Coral's *father* knew any of this was here, it is a complete revelation. I'm going as fast as I can to see if the book will shed any light, but you know, he's coming at it from the writer's perspective.'

'Oh darling I know exactly what you mean,' said Di. 'I bet he likes to recap and linger over his longuese! I'm so sorry, but we'll have to dash off in a minute,' she said, glancing at her watch. 'I've got a research appointment for my dissertation.'

We walked back up to their car.

'These are some notes that Professor Mushrooms sent you to help you with yours,' said Quiz, handing me a folder from the top of the dashboard. 'How is it coming along?'

'Not well,' I said. 'I am blocked. It's probably all the worry.'

'I'm sure it'll all come good,' said Quiz. 'But if you need help just you give a call. Prof M is coming over himself in July, so he'll talk to you about it once he has marked it, as promised. We'll have to have a full Zola reunion.'

'Bye darling, look forward to seeing you sometime in the near plus tard,' said Di, kissing me on the lips.

'Bye darling, plus tard,' said Quiz, also coming in for a smacker.

'Plus tard, à bientot,' I said faintly, feeling a little shaken. I watched them zoom off down the drive in their porch, and I felt somewhat lacking in my own personality.

REMINDER

Deadline for dissertation, July 30.

I must stop swinging about between Russians and Mermaids and commit to both in The Emperor's Slippers.

Word List
Chatelaine.
Longuese.
Sowerbutt!

FOR THE CONCERN OF THE RICH AND THE POOR

At twelve noon I saw the figure of Alfred Elms approach, carrying his spade over his shoulder. I wasted no time when he came nearer.

'Please sir, please,' I began, dropping to the ground and embracing his feet. 'I have come to throw myself on your mercy.'

'You mean you have walked here by yourself from the workhouse by Bristol?'

'Yes, I have.'

'Good grief child, please release my feet and I will fetch you a glass of water. What can I give you, some food? Or perhaps some warm or more appropriate clothes?' he said.

'These clothes belonged to a giant doll I stripped at the seaside,' I said in agonies. 'I couldn't wander about in my uniform, they'd have taken me back.'

'You do make a convincing little girl,' smiled Alfred.

I got to my feet and remained facing him with my head bowed in humility.

'Please, please, I have come to throw myself on your mercy, I don't know how else to put it.'

'I think I understand,' said Alfred. 'And I pity your position, I do, I really do,' he added gently. 'But I'm afraid, my poor fellow, this is not my decision to make. You must understand that everything you see here, even I myself, are the possessions of Benedict Garden. And he could evict me at a moment's notice if he found that I harboured . . . a fugitive. He is not someone to be trifled with, nor is his wife Madam Adelaide. We will need to be canny about this and put the case before Sowerbutt.'

It took most of the afternoon for Alfred to persuade Sowerbutt to let me stay. As Estate Steward, it was his job to hire or fire servants. He was reluctant at first, but came round in the end and employed me as Alfred's apprentice, largely due to his great affection for him.

And so, many hours later and greatly relieved, I stood with Alfred in the small back room upstairs at Edenthorpe.

'Is this where I should sleep?' I asked him.

'Yes,' he replied. 'Just move aside the seedlings.'

'Aren't there any other boys sleeping in here too?'

'No, there's just you.'

'There's so much space in my bed!' I marvelled. 'So this is how a gardener sleeps!'

But I woke that first night to the sound of wretched deep sobbing coming through the wall, and I wondered if it was made by the owner of the lily-white hand I had seen at the window of Roselyne. It troubled me; I felt I should not be able to hear something so private. Instinctively I reached out and put my hand up to my side of the wall to comfort her before I drifted off to sleep.

And when the sun rose the next morning, I looked out of the window and I realized I was an eagle standing guard over the garden. I threw it open, and was intoxicated by the scent of the rain and jasmine and figs.

There were thirty acres of grounds to tend to, in which Sowerbutt took charge of the rougher parts, but the formal gardens, lawns, glasshouses and the entire walled garden were Alfred's work alone. I tried to help as much as I could, to repay the great debt I owed him.

Alfred used one of extravagant Master Benedict's most new-fangled purchases, called a wheel-driven grass cutter, and I ran behind collecting the stray clumps, with green knees, green fingers, green cheeks, and my neck perfumed with grass.

Deeds out on the dining table.   A sketch from the past.

The Echo Vaults
Archivist J. County. 45723. April 2 1988
Subject Roselyne–Edenthorpe
Green Place
Egham

Feb 1 1857
This deed of enlargement made on the fourteenth day
of February One Thousand Eight Hundred and Fifty Seven, by
Edmund Garden, hereby grants permission for the re-erection
of two former dwellings with the addition of a walled garden.
The same as be put up at no less than five feet from the
most westerly boundary with the neighbouring five acre
plot at 'Netherby'. The tenure is to remain as leasehold for
the term of two thousand years from April 1618 (as
before) and the yearly ground rent is one shilling and
one good capon.

*Note from Jackie County: NB one shilling is equivalent to about five
pence today.*

18 Jan 1858
This indenture, to which the deeds of the foregoing indenture
refer, is for the registry of one pair of cottages by Mr Benedict
Garden, upon completion of works begun by his late father
Mr Edmund Garden, *Edenthorpe* and *Roselyne* in title, both
recently and well re-constructed of brick and tile. Each
cottage containing, kitchen, washhouse with copper, and two
bedrooms over, having separate lean-to wood houses and

private closets, in the respective occupations of Alfred Elms,
gardener, and Rose Anna Garden (widow) for the tenancy
agreed at three shillings a year at parochial rates,
aside the peppercorn rent as stated.
The above stand in a plot of garden ground, with each
dwelling having a well of spring water and a rainwater
tank for their supply.

This indenture signed this day 18 Jan 1858 by
Charles Penfold Draughtsman for the Parish of Fern Common
Benedict Garden   of Green Place
Alfred Elms   of 'Edenthorpe'
James Gallion power of attorney for Mrs Rose
Anna Garden of 'Roselyne'

Sue

Pensees: *When the doorbell goes, hide.* SB

'Morning all,' said the Admiral breezily, taking up his seat at the dining table for breakfast, plumping out the paper and pouring himself out a cup of hot, malty tea. He tapped his teaspoon against Aunt Coral's zingy porcelain cup so hard it sounded like he was ringing a gong. I heard it from all the way up in Pearl's room, echoing in the big empty house! It's like an alarm clock.

'For some years now the Admiral has been able to spend very many hours of most days doing his crossword and reading the paper with utter joy and no guilt,' said Aunt Coral, regarding him fondly.

She looked out of the dining room windows and crafted a significant sigh.

'After all the greyness of winter I can just see in the orchard the tease of a fluffy pink tree,' she said. 'I feel I've become obsessed with the very meaning of the word shade. Shade,' she said luxuriantly, 'it means that *somewhere* there will be sun.'

The Admiral seemed to bask in her croquettish poetry. I wonder if he thinks all English ladies are like this.

Mrs Bunion came in to potter about.

'Ah Pat, thank you,' said Aunt Coral. 'You know Jackie County is coming? I expect she'll be ravenous – could you put up a tray ready in the drawing room?'

'Yes of course,' said Mrs Bunion, collecting stray dishes briskly together on her tray, her new purchase of some navy Scholls click-clacking professionally as she tidied. She exited the drawing room trailing a scent of scrambled eggs and furniture polish.

'I do wish Badger would get back to me,' said Aunt C. 'I wanted to ask him if he might find time to work on the walled garden for me this summer.'

'Good luck with that,' said the Admiral sympathetically, for Badger the gardener is known for his unreliability. (A world away from Alfred Elms!)

The Admiral soon excused himself from any further early conversation, to morning pursuits in an armchair, and Aunt Coral and I went into the drawing room, which was flooded with spring-morning shafts of light, spinning with dust.

Aunt Coral got stuck into a pile of post on a silver tray, working her way through each item with a letter knife that made a satisfying ripping sound.

But as she opened each letter, the sound was followed by a sigh that I know to be associated with the misery of a pile of fresh bills.

'I've been meaning to ask you,' I launched in, hoping to offer some hope, 'what you might do about Admiral Ted's suite? Do you think you will look for another permanent lodger to bring in some funds?'

'Yes, of course I will, I'll have to. I know we need the money, but out of loyalty I don't feel quite ready to, yet,' she said. 'At any rate we might discover these Shipwreck Pearls or some such, mightn't we?'

I finally met the infamous Jackie County – who was just as Aunt Coral described. She's the sort of old girl who might have been the first to fly a Spitfire during the war, or parachute into enemy territory on a secret mission.

She was wearing *a cape* and comfort shoes, which Aunt Coral wouldn't be seen dead in. But there was a random glamour to her make-up, from her no-nonsense short red nails to her taupey half-moon crayoned eyebrows. Her hair was sculpted into water waves held in place by a fine net and finished with a kirby grip at the front, like a schoolgirl's. I have noticed that some ladies stick with one hair style all the way through life. (But for my part, I will definitely *not* be sticking with my mullet, as I am now in the process of a *very* long grow.)

Jackie's arrival was set to the background of the spaniels barking inside her car, which I would suggest as her theme tune. Either that or the sort of music that accompanies a hippopotamus on a nature programme, because she is built like a little barrel (TWD!).

'Let them out, let them out,' said Aunt Coral, when we went out to see the dogs.

'Oh thank you,' said Jackie. 'Come on boys.'

She opened the boot and two brown-and-white Springer spaniels ran off into the grounds as though they were late for appointments. Jackie County stretched herself after her car journey and lingered for a moment looking at the ground towards the side of Green Place.

'Everything all right?' asked Aunt C.

'Yes, yes,' replied Jackie. 'I just wondered if you'd considered my proposition?'

'What's that?' I asked.

'About a little investigative digging,' replied Aunt Coral, cautiously.

'In lewe of finding the Shipwreck Pearls,' clarified Jackie. 'Nothing fancy, people do it all the time when they want to check their drains.'

'I am absolutely considering it,' said Aunt Coral. 'But not till we have completed a thorough search of the house and gardens ourselves. And I don't want to launch into a dig while the meadows are full of columbine, not to mention the small matter of the expense! Shall we go in?' she finished warmly. 'This is my niece Sue,' she continued, 'who discovered *For the Concern of the Rich and the Poor.*'

'Ah yes, clever girl,' replied Jackie as she introduced herself. 'Jackie County.'

'How do you do, Mrs County?'

'Please call me Jackie,' she said.

Afterwards we went into the drawing room and Jackie got out her papers to explain things. She rustled through the bundle of dusty documents, and it occurred to me that the past has a smell.

'Now then,' she began, 'the thing that most pricked my curiosity was, of course, why was your Great Great Grandfather Edmund Garden's coffin exhumed two years after he died?'

'And did you find out?' asked Aunt C.

'I'm afraid not, though one can make some assumptions. In these cases, in my experience, it is often because something was not conclusive about the cause of death, or there was a dispute over the burial site, or something to do with the burial itself,' said Jackie. 'But I believe in order to find out one has to go right back to the beginning. And so I asked myself, apropos the deeds we've found, why would your Great Great Grandfather Edmund's second wife, Rose Anna, be living in a gardener's cottage so soon after his death?'

'The author in my book talks about a lady living next door, and it must have been Rose Anna, because the deeds on the dining room table confirm it!' I piped up. 'But the author in my book hasn't met her, up to where I've read, he has only heard her crying through the wall. How strange – I'm ahead of him!'

'I don't wonder Rose Anna was crying,' said Jackie, 'because when Edmund died, she would have been left in a very vulnerable position, particularly as she wasn't Benedict's mother. I expect you've heard about "Primo-Geniture"? It's the tradition of leaving your estate to the eldest surviving *male* relative.'

'Thank goodness I never had a brother,' said Aunt Coral.

'Why didn't she go back to her own family?' I asked.

'I'm afraid that's harder to piece together. Suffice it to say, things weren't really the same in those days. Benedict would have probably got his hands on Rose Anna's dowry and whatever money she may have had. The men held all the cards.'

'How chilling. It's like robbery, or a cruel science fiction,' I said.

'Yes,' tutted Jackie, 'so the poor lady was left, completely alone in the world, and at a time when she couldn't just go out and get a job. So thus she was left at the mercy of Benedict and his wife Adelaide.'

'Do you mean Benedict forced her to move into Roselyne cottage? Turfed her out of Green Place?' I asked.

'It seems so. And if I were asked to choose between the workhouse, the asylum or a gardener's cottage, I know what I would prefer,' said Jackie.

Aunt Coral and I were in shock.

'I feel rather horrified to be descended from him,' said Aunt Coral.

'I don't wonder,' said Jackie. 'I am sorry.'

'Might I read *For the Concern of the Rich and the Poor* after you?' she asked, breaking a small silence that intervened between us.

'Yes of course, but after Aunt Coral,' I answered eventually.

'And the Admiral,' added Aunt Coral.

'By the way,' Jackie continued, 'I hear you have applied for the Features Internship at the *Echo*. Very well done. You know they received hundreds of applications, so I will put in a little word for you!'

'Thank you so much. That would be really kind of you,' I said.

A short while later I left them to chat and wandered down to the ruins, feeling a bit giddy at the thought of Jackie County putting a word in for me at the *Echo*. I can't wait to tell Joe.

I walked down past the meadow at the bottom of the big slope to the garden and cottages. And the old walls were alive with little insects and creatures moving. I think I saw a fox's tail slinking away. Proof that, though derelict, these buildings have not stood empty.

And I thought of London Taylor, and Alfred the gardener, and Madam Rose Anna here, amongst the vestiges of such decayed beauty. And I felt their presence so strongly, I could almost touch them.

I shall have to take an extract now or I shall die of symbolism.

FOR THE CONCERN OF THE RICH AND THE POOR

The pale lady of Roselyne cottage did not come out until my first Sunday evening at Edenthorpe, when she and a second lady exited to go to church.

The clanking of the gate next door drew my attention and I looked out to see a tightly corseted figure shrouded in the weeds of full mourning, with a heavy weeping veil, weeper's cuffs, and not an inch of flesh uncovered, and another lady likewise attired offering her arm to support the first.

'Who are they?' I asked Alfred. 'Why do they wait until twilight on a Sunday to go out?'

He was in his armchair, resting in front of the hearth, and I remained at the table flipping the picture pages of one of his botanical books.

'The first is the widow Rose Anna Garden,' he said. 'She is Master Benedict's father's second wife. She is in deep mourning and I believe has been for the past year . . . and the other, Sowerbutt tells me, is known as Walderon. She is Madam Rose Anna's old habit.'

'What do you mean by that?'

'Her nursery maid – it is a term of a big house. I should think that they have been together for a long time.'

'But why do they mourn here in seclusion? Is Roselyne a retreat for the grief-stricken?'

'I don't know why they have withdrawn to Roselyne, I suspect because Master Benedict's wife would not tolerate there being two Mistresses at the big house. But it's not my place to wonder. I do know that the lady looks too young to me to devote the rest of her life to grieving. She can't be much more than forty.'

'Is her heart broken?'

'I think so.'

'Will it mend?'

'Who can say?'

'Charity is not a good thing,' I said.

'But better than destitution,' said Alfred. 'The lady lives in genteel poverty of the purse and of the heart. But I can sympathize with her position, for we each of us have our ghosts.' He cast a glance to a sepia photograph of his lost wife and son. And I tried clumsily to divert his attention.

'I have seen a ghost in the window up at the big house,' I told him. 'Yesterday and today and last week. In fact, he is always there looking out when I pass by in the morning. He startled me the first time I saw him. He presses his face right up against the window, he writes letters in his breath.'

'That's not a ghost,' said Alfred. 'That is Master Benedict and Madam Adelaide's son. He lives up in that old nursery. He probably fancies he sees a playmate – maybe he was trying to get your attention.'

Sue

Fri April 15 1988

Pensees: *The best way to get straight hair is to sleep in a hat.* SB

After a few months or years without use, the bathrooms in the East Wing get a sort of snow in them, which Aunt Coral thinks might be old bath salts crystallizing and turning to powder.

I've decided I'm going to target one bathroom a week for use, to keep the water flowing through the pipes, and prevent the snow building up.

When you turn the tap on in the Avocado bathroom, at the furthest end of the East Wing, it takes about ten minutes for the water to arrive in the taps. At about five o'clock this afternoon, I was just sitting on the edge of the bath, waiting for the water to come out, when I heard the telephone ring in the hall.

'Sue!' called the Admiral. 'Telephone!'

Hastily I turned the tap back off, just as the pipes honked into action and a few drops of water banged out. I ran all the way back through the East Wing and downstairs, anticipating it might be Joe calling long distance.

'Hi Sue, it's Quiz.'

'Oh, hello,' I said with surprise.

'Are you OK?'

'Yes, yes I'm fine thank you. Sorry, just ran all the way down to the phone – I was up in the bathroom!'

'Is this a good time?'

'Yes, yes of course, how are you, how's Di?' I chatted.

'We're fine, thanks darling for asking. Listen, the reason I'm calling is I have been asked to step in and cover a research post at Surrey University, and I need to find somewhere to stay from the beginning of May. I was wondering if your Aunt Coral was taking in any more lodgers? It's going to be a bit full on during the weeks and I don't really fancy the commute.'

'I can ask her,' I said. 'Congratulations!'

'Look, we're at my mother's at the moment in the West Country. We could look in on you on our way back to London and then your Aunt can put a face to the name. We could be with you in a couple of hours or so?'

5 minutes later

'What time are they coming?' asked Aunt Coral. 'Are you sure I shouldn't get something out of the freezer?'

'No, no, they're not coming for a meal. Quiz just said that they were on their way home from his mother's house and that they'd look in on their way back. I'm so sorry, I was thrown. I didn't look at the time.'

'It doesn't matter,' said Aunt Coral. 'We'll just have to be come-as-you-find-us.'

Unfortunately, Mrs Bunion had the night off so that she could go to the cinema, and so Aunt Coral pottered about setting the scene and tidying and polishing the hall floor to give a nice impression. She removed some dead-smelling flowers from a vase and she sent the Admiral up for a bath. Then she herself went upstairs to change into a being-caught-at-home outfit.

And about two and a half hours later, by which time Aunt C had swept the floor, laid the dining room table with mini pizzas, crisps and biscuits, I heard a car pull up outside. I was in the drawing room with the Admiral in our intellectuals-at-home positions, as desired by the exacting excitement standards of Aunt C.

By the time I heard the car doors slam Aunt Coral was already waiting in the hall. And by the time the doorbell rang she was already opening the front door to them. I think since Delia and the new B and B guests left she is somewhat starved of her fun. She likes her home to be a bit like a sea port with lots of people coming and going, very much in keeping with her omnipotent joie de vivre.

'Hello! Welcome back to Green Place,' she said. 'I'm Sue's Aunt Coral.'

'Hello,' said Di. 'It's so good to meet you.'

'How do you do,' said Quiz. 'Quiz, Crispin Wilson. This is my girlfriend Diane.'

'Come in, come in, Sue's told me so much about you. Would you like something to pick at?'

'Thank you, we're fine actually, we had a late lunch before we left my mother's,' replied Quiz.

'Please come through,' said Aunt Coral. 'I'm sorry the house is such a mess,' she added, casually leading them over the absolutely sparkling floor.

As per her instructions, when they walked into the drawing room I was relaxing in there with the Admiral, I with my white gloves on reading *For the Concern of the Rich and the Poor*, the Admiral with the *Financial Times* and his pipe . . . we must have looked a bit like one of Aunt Coral's watercolours. I do feel perhaps to complete the image I should have had a pipe too. I must remember to give Aunt C my feedback.

'Rear Admiral Avery John Little,' said Aunt Coral, making formal introductions.

'Quiz and Diane from Sue's course.'

'Hello there,' said the Admiral, heading straight towards the drinks cabinet. 'Can I get you a sundowner?'

'Thank you,' said Di. 'I'll have a dirty Martini please.'

'Coming right up!' said the Admiral, leaving the room momentarily, I think to go and check what she meant.

'Just a tonic water for me thanks,' said Quiz.

It was starting to get dark outside but through the windows I spotted the last couple of birds flying home to their weary nests. The soprano pipistrelles piped up in the wall and we settled around the weak early-evening fire. The Admiral reappeared with a jar of olives to dirty Di's martini with some brine.

'How is your mother?' I asked.

'She's fine, thanks darling for asking,' replied Quiz.

'Where does your mother live?' asked Aunt Coral.

'Westover – it's a little market town just south of Bath,' said Quiz.

'Is she on her own?' asked Aunt Coral.

'Yes, she is. My Father lives in Barbados,' said Quiz.

'Good heavens!' said Aunt C. 'What do you do?' she went on, gently interrogating him. 'Sue tells me you're a PhD.'

'That's right, I'm an Associate Professor of Philosophy at UCL,' said Quiz.

'A young Professor,' she said, giggling.

'And Di's assistant to Timothy Magdelen, in classics at the British Library,' I said. 'It's a really big job.' But I could tell Aunt Coral was finding Quiz too swoony to be socially balanced.

'Keeps me off the street,' said Di.

'Sue tells me you were hoping to find somewhere to live that is nearer the University of Surrey?' said Aunt Coral.

'Yes, I've been asked to troubleshoot the Philosophy Department next term. There's been a to-do with the current posting. They'd like me to start next month as interlocutor for the Debating Society and I've been given the green light from London as it's considered pro bono. The idea is to develop a strategy for updating and motivating the module,' said Quiz.

'I see,' said Aunt Coral gravely. 'You know the University of Surrey is in Guildford not in Egham, don't you?' she added, knowledgeably.

'Oh yes, thank you, I do. I think it's about 30 minutes by car,' replied Quiz. 'Please don't feel you have to decide now – just give me a buzz when you've had time to think about it. I just thought, as we were passing, it would be a good opportunity for us to meet.'

He gave her the most winning smile and for a moment she grew girlish and inundated everybody with repeated requests for mini pizza, to which Quiz eventually caved in. Di had a polite half biscuit, but I saw her discreetly slipping the unfinished half into a tissue which she put in her bag. The Admiral watched her doing this and he looked totally *baffled*.

But as I suspected, Aunt Coral was very taken with them and decided to show Admiral Ted's suite spontaneously. I went up with them to be adhesive. (In many ways, it seemed that Quiz was knocking on an open door.)

'Snowdrop is spacious, and recently decorated,' gestured Aunt Coral, 'but it does get bitterly cold in the winter, and you have to hunt around the other end of the wing if you want to find a warmer bathroom.'

'But it's beautiful,' said Quiz, looking through the tall bay window out over the dark grounds, with the twinkly lights from Clockhouse Lane sparkling beyond the tops of the trees. 'I wouldn't mind being cold in here, it's absolutely stirring, isn't it Sue?'

I murmured agreement but couldn't flesh out an answer. I was too busy imagining all Quiz's *things* in the room: his text books and notepads, personalized trunks, his *aftershave*. It's a stunning Chanel one, Pour Monsieur – For Mister. A trademark scent in keeping with his effortless chique.

I noticed that the clock in Admiral Ted's suite still had a black velvet cover on it, a silent reminder of his quiet little death. Mrs Bunion also stopped the clock when he died, as a mark of respect.

Aunt C led the viewing party back down to the drawing room, guiding by the light of her torch – because one of the Admiral's 'I'll do it tomorrow' jobs is to replenish our stocks of light bulbs.

The night fell quiet again after Quiz and Di left. The only noises were the spitting and crackling of the fire in the drawing room, the lullaby of the bats in the wall and the sucking of the Admiral on his pipe.

'I'm afraid that Professor Quiz looks like Robert Donat,' said Aunt Coral, as she settled back into her chair in the drawing room.

'Why do you say *afraid*?' I asked.

'I suppose what I mean is, are you sure it's *wise* he comes to live here?' she whispered, for we were in front of the Admiral. 'A boy like him probably has a trail of broken hearts behind him.'

'Just because he is good looking doesn't mean he leaves a trail of destruction. And he isn't a boy, he's a man,' I said.

'Exactly,' she said.

'I thought you liked him?'

'I do, he's absolutely charming. It's just a feeling, and I'm not thinking of myself but of you, darling Sue.'

'Oh no! No, Quiz loves Di and I love Joe, and I love Di too. Anyway, Di is his equal; he wouldn't be interested in someone like me, even if there was no Joe, which there is,' I said forcefully. 'And he'll be home soon. Anyway, they're different from us. They notice sort of academic things. Quiz said tonight he finds my sorrow beautiful.'

She said nothing in reply but gave me one of her special looks that says 'Sweet Child you have so much to learn'.

'And don't look at me like that. I know what you're thinking. You think plutonic friendship is impossible.'

'What you don't understand my darling is that I've got cardigans older than you,' said Aunt Coral.

'What are you girls talking about?' asked the Admiral, looking up.

'We were just saying that in terms of loyalty to Admiral Ted, we think we feel ready to let his suite,' said Aunt Coral. 'And it seems fortuitous that Sue's young Professor needs a room, just when we had begun to think about finding someone.'

'No doubt Ted would have wanted us to keep the wolf from the door,' said the Admiral.

'And I'm sure Delia will have no complaints! So is everyone agreed?' asked Aunt C.

'I agree that he should come,' said the Admiral. 'He seems a very charismatic fellow.'

'Agreed, yes he is very charismatic,' I said.

'They both are,' I added.

> **Word List**
> *Interlocutor*
> *Pro Bono*
> *Module*

When I came to sit down this morning, I had not long settled into an easy chair in the drawing room to obsess in private for a moment as to why I haven't heard any news about the internship yet, when the doorbell went and, curiously, neither Aunt Coral nor the Admiral got up to get it. My only clue that there was something afoot was a covert look that passed between them. And when Mrs Bunion didn't come to answer the door either, I got up to go.

'Woo hoo!' said Joe, standing framed in the doorway.

'Oh my goodness!' I said.

He lifted me up off the ground and spun me, in a way I have always wanted to be spun. It was a fleeting moment that spirited away faster than a bird flying out of a tree.

'Congratulations on Pierre,' he said, kissing me on both cheeks as though it was *I* who has had the baby. 'How is your father?'

'Fine, thank you.'

'And your stepmother?'

'She's fine.'

'How is Aunt Coral?'

'She's fine too, and she didn't tell me you were coming!'

'I'm a surprise,' he said.

Aunt Coral and the Admiral remained in the drawing room

for a couple of minutes before they burst into the hall to say hello to him. It was obviously 'a plan'.

I took Joe into the conservatory where we had some powerful embraces over largely ignored cups of tea.

He was dressed in his gardening clothes because he said he was due at a job at 10am. He looked in equal parts hunk and trainspotter. It's a style that I find quite lethal.

'I'm so sorry about Admiral Ted,' he said.

'I know, we miss him.'

'And I'm so sorry I wasn't here when you got back,' said Joe. 'Honestly, what a terrible mix-up.'

'Is Charlie OK now?'

'Her mother arrived from New Zealand to take care of her, so I got on the first train home,' he said.

'And how's everyone?' I asked him.

'Sandy's OK – got chucked by his girlfriend and has had a symbolic haircut. Yours looks different,' he said, looking puzzled. 'It looks very . . . swish.'

'It's a film-school haircut. They've got them in London,' I said. 'I'm afraid I can't do very much with it. Your hair looks different too.'

'Charlie changed my side parting for me. I've had lots of comments,' he said. 'And Mary-Margaret's OK,' he continued. 'She's started listening to Radio 1.'

'They grow up so fast,' I said.

'And Icarus has got a part-time job working as a pirate on Treasure Island at the theme park. They're looking for more people actually, so he's going to put a word in for me.'

'How's your mum?'

'Chugging along, trying to get everything ready as usual. How is everything here?' he asked.

'We have a Professor moving into Admiral Ted's suite at the end of the month,' I said. 'He's someone I met on my course.'

'Aunt C will love that,' said Joe. 'She likes an old man in a gown! What are you doing later? I could pick you up and take you out for dinner if you're free? I'm off to see a new client in Addlestone – they're so wealthy that they have a separate toilet for the gardener!'

Inspiration at Last! Could I be unblocking? Fleshing out of my Fusion Idea for dissertation:

The Emperor's Slippers (continued)

'I have written the Emperor a play. It's a post-apocalyptic three hander set in a coastal community. I intend it for the amphitheatre at Roon, the one with the famous rake,' said Doonyasha.

'Doonyasha! You can't play tragedy on a slope,' said Aleksandr.

'Try telling that to Petrovia.'

'You mean she wants to do it?'

'Actresses eh? There's no telling.'

'Ach Gizzards!'

'I know . . . I need a vodka!'

'But that's all very well, but how can you write a play at such a time as this?' said Aleksandr.

'Must you bring me par terre?' said

Doonyasha. 'You mean because of Aunt Bettia don't you?'

'But why did they take her? Was she a member of the circle?'

'Was she bollocks. It's because of that Serge, coming round here thinking he might just pop by. They have arrested every single person who knows him. She has been taken to a labour camp in Siberia, she'll be 86 by the time she gets out.'

'Then there is hope. And she may be re united with Serge! Late love, Doonyasha, the love of remembrance, a love made even sweeter in the light of departing.'

'First love, last love, love that is hidden, love that cannot hide, this will be the subject of my play,' cried Doonyasha. 'And I know. She loves him. It is simple.'

'Love love.'

'Love love love.'

Aunt Coral's To Do

Make will

Small flowers that bite

Knightsbridge 4.30

There it was again, Knightsbridge 4.30. Though I'm trying not to be, I am a little concerned. Because if I tie this 4.30 appointment together with the fact that Aunt Coral has always wanted to see those small flowers that bite (in Buenos Aries I believe). But wherever they are in the world, I know it's one of the 'things she wants to do before it's too late'.

Thank goodness Joe is back and could make discreet enquiries on my behalf, and according to Mrs Bunion, Aunt C and the Admiral are just going to Harrods. Maybe they sell the flowers there? Maybe that's her latest extravagance?

We went to the Triple Hatrick in Egham for a celebratory dinner last night and Joe ordered us a bottle of carafe. This little slip was followed up when we were in the deli in Egham this morning and he asked for a bag of tapas. I don't know quite why, but I so love all his little gaffs.

He had to fill out a form because Mrs Fry has moved them to a new doctors. (I should explain that he has now started working at the theme park at the weekends.) And so where the form said *Occupation*, he put *Pirate*, and where it said *Place of Work* he put *Treasure Island*. I would love to have been a fly on the wall when it was processed!

And it's due to Joe's being back that I have been really busy, and this in spite of the fact that I still have no job and no word of the internship. The reason I've been *so* rushed is due to enhanced need for personal grooming. I let myself go a little bit while Joe was away and now I've got to get myself back again. But it all takes so much time that I wish I had someone to do it all for me. Someone to do my teeth for me while I shower and someone to paint my toes while I pensee. Honestly, I don't know how anyone ever has *time* to *work*!

But I'm keeping everything crossed for word on the internship, as I would be over the moon if life spun the other way around, and I was so rushed due to *work,* that I didn't have *time* to personal groom.

3pm

Di just rang and asked if I would like to go to Pimlico for supper on Wednesday, as a thank you for the letting of Quiz's suite. (Though he's not actually moving in until May.)

I explained that Joe was back, and she extended her invitation, but unfortunately he can't come anyway, because he has signed up on a turf course for the next three Weds nights. He's keen to start building his skills.

Mon April 18

Pensees about Pierre: *It must be so nice to be a baby. Just sleep, eat and cry when you want something. And when you grow up and become a child, it will be like waking from a beautiful dream you can't remember.* SB

At long last Pierre was allowed to go home. So I went to Titford to see them this afternoon. Dad and Ivana are taking Pierre to meet his Nana in Denmark tomorrow, where they plan to stay for a little while and Dad has taken an extended leave from work. It does feel strange to think of them travelling about as this little new family. I feel attached and yet totally separate, which doesn't make any sense. Anyway, it made it all the more important that I managed to get my visit in today.

I felt a confusing sense of conflict about going back to Titford, disorientating, strange sort of feelings, battling away inside. Strange, because though Pierre is a relative of mine, he is not a relative of my mum's. And disorientating because when I go to Titford I still have to remind myself that I am not going to see her.

I feel joy, relief, affection for him, gladness that he has made it, coupled with the bitter reflection that he only lives in that house because my mother is never coming back.

So I hopped on a train, and when I got to Addison Drive I stood outside number 42 for a while, trying to gather these thoughts.

Maybe it would have been easier if Dad and Ivana had just remained a couple, but they became a family so quickly, it rubbed salt in an open wound. I do understand why they wanted Pierre, in fact I understand why they needed him, it's just that it's too soon, too sudden and mum's death was too unexpected. I am still haunted by the what ifs and I wonders, such as I wonder if mum and dad's marriage might have survived if they'd just had a slightly bigger house? This of course leads on to my thinking, that if the marriage had been saved, there would have been no need for mum to fall in love with Mr Edgely or Dad to fall for Ivana, and mum would still be alive. But Pierre would never have been born and he is so very tender. It's like a cruel game of chess.

So the sight of Pierre's cot in my old bedroom, which is now the nursery, was very strange. Dad at least seems to understand that this is hard for me. He spoke to me in gentle whispers and left reverential pauses before he agreed with Ivana on how lovely things are. But sadly within seconds of seeing Ivana she always presses my buttons. She said she wants to hack about the house (and therefore obliterate all the old traces of my childhood and mum's existence), and that of course makes me feel angry and want to kill her and piss on her grave and then of course I feel terribly guilty.

So I focus on how very dear Pierre is, just in himself, and

marvel that the whole house is now covered in tiny white baby grows like snowflakes, and socks the size of petals. But Pierre is still full of sleep. Ivana put dreamcatchers above his cot, all around the nursery, above the window and above the door. 'Will he need that many?' asked Dad. She really doesn't want him to suffer one bad second.

And just as he was wired up at the hospital, Pierre's nursery is now wired with all the signs of his life: his mobile spins, his monitor light flashes, his lamp projects stars on to the ceiling. They all pulse and flash and beep to show the whirlwind of his new life.

He has firmly established his residency in my bedroom, and is also firmly embedded in my thoughts. Every day, everywhere I go, I never forget about him, even though having a brother is still a new concept. He just lives in the secret back places of my mind, quietly growing.

I'm going to buy him a hat that I've seen in the window of John Anthony Gordon in Egham, and while his hair is still so scant he can make hats his trademark. For what formal wear does he own just yet? Perhaps one pair of booties, one tiny pair of jeans? Aunt Coral told me with some excitement last night that 'Delia has knitted'.

When I got back to Green Place I took an extract. Whoever it was that abandoned London Taylor when he was a baby must have been truly desperate. It comes home to me in the light of Pierre. But look where London ended up. You could say he landed on his feet.

FOR THE CONCERN OF THE RICH AND THE POOR

The walled garden itself was mainly used to grow the Garden family's food, but it did contain a cut flower garden and a scented garden amongst the other earthy delights. Over two acres there spread kitchen and herb garden, rockery and vinery, and these carved between meandering paths by herbaceous borders thirty feet deep with flowers! Up the walls themselves climbed a jungle of creepers, which I later learnt were firethorns, honeysuckle and cotoneasters.

'There are two entrances to the garden, one on either side of the long walls,' explained Alfred as he showed me. 'On the south side you enter by this door straight under the Apple Arch. There is something always in fruit, first the early eaters, then the crab apples, then the cookers.'

We passed under a rooftop bulging with fruit. Truly a sight for the hungry eyes of a boy from the Mead.

'And on the cottage side you enter through this door at the meadow end. The servants go to and fro through a tunnel just nearby that goes all the way into the big house. It comes out a few feet from the garden. The cook sends down for delicacies every day.

'I lock up tight at night,' he moved on, 'to keep everything safe from the hands of thieves, and the jaws and paws of animals. These walls give the garden shelter from the wind and frosts of winter. It's always much warmer inside.'

There were even cavities built into the walls of the garden where Alfred lit fires to keep the fruit trees warm, and others which he left empty to encourage the bees to come and make honey, close by the source of heat.

Having been weaned on bread and skilly I could not identify the abundance of fruit, so Alfred pointed out pears, peaches, plums, apples and figs, which were growing up against the warm bricks on the south facing wall, and cherry trees whose branches were trained out and displayed in a technique called fanning.

Alfred had set aside a special plot where he made an arbour, screened off to make an owl walk fringed by a small tree grove. And at the end of it he grew violets and a wall flower he called a bee flower. I knew the name of nothing, but the pleasure of all.

But at the centre of everything, fruits, herbs, flowers and food, there was a sundial, with a green stone face, and the shadow of the dial fell on an inscription which read, 'For the Concern of the Rich and the Poor'.

'It means that I, the sun, rise every day for the concern of the rich and the poor,' said Alfred. 'Or for that matter, I, the sun, am truly egalitarian.'

Sue

It's getting hard to put my book down, the garden sounds *so* beautiful. It is eerie to look at it today – now that it is a ghost of itself, all dry and empty, when clearly then it was bursting with life.

But *still* no word from the *Echo*, and day two of another new week . . . so Joe suggested I go along to the Toastie today and see if they are hiring staff for the new Bistro, as a Plan B. I have only £10.73 to last me until Christmas, and I do realize that much as I can't think of anything better than to be paid to work around writing, Plan Bs are often what life is all about.

Joe warned me that the Toastie was closed, but told me to nip in and have a word with his mother. And when I got there, that was what I discovered: *three* signs up in the window saying Closed Closed Closed! Perhaps Mrs Fry thought people wouldn't understand it the first time. She is the Shrew of Egham (TWD).

I looked in and saw a group of men in boiler suits and then I heard a familiar voice behind me.

'Hi Sue.'

'Hi Icarus!' I said. It was vicariously like being with Joe again to stand beside his brother. But he looked different than I remember him, thinner and paler, and he had a big spot on the end of his nose. I can't believe that last year I found him so attractive I almost had to be hospitalized. I still feel rather embarrassed. It's because he is so much like a cheeky Fairground Boy. (TWD)

'Were you looking for Joe?' he asked. 'He's out at Addlestone, jet-hosing a patio.'

'No, no, I know, actually I just came to see your mum, to ask if she was taking on any staff at the new Bistro.'

'Mum's had a problem today with a delay on the licence for the Bistro, so she's getting this place rewired while it all goes through. She's hanging fire on taking on waiting staff, because she doesn't know exactly when we will be opening. Why don't you give us a call, or pop back in two weeks?' he said fluently. 'I'll put you on the list.'

'Cheers mate. I'll do that,' I said, a little self-consciously.

'Is Loudolle here at the moment? I haven't heard from her,' asked Icarus. As I mentioned, Loudolle is Delia's daughter. She is at finishing school in Colorado, but she was going out with Icarus in her holidays, last I heard.

'No, she's at college. I expect she won't be over again until the summer,' I said, somewhat witheringly, for Loudolle and I have . . . history. To encapsulate it, I'd say she was my nemesis.

'Thanks Sue, I'll see you later. Your hair looks snazzy,' said Icarus, giving me a killer wink.

'Cheers a lot,' I said, noting inside myself that in spite of being over him, I still used the language of cool. But it is a miracle that in under a year I have gone from having a ruinous crush on him, to talking to the spot on his nose.

Though I'd rather forget about her, I feel I ought to come up with a TWD for Loudolle. It's hard to limit a description of her to 3 words, because she is just so ghastly. But I think my best effort would be to get it down to *seven* – in that Loudolle 'always thinks the phone is for her'.

But for all that happened last year, time really is the greatest healer . . . time, and Joe.

Tues April 19th eve
Postbag! Mrs Bunion put this in the Sun Room, so I missed it before I went out! An informal note from the *Echo*:

Hi Sue,

Thank you for your application to the *Echo*'s internship programme.

We'd like to invite you to come and interview with Gordoney George at 1.40 on Thurs 28 April at the Shilling Street Hotel in Egham.

Yours sincerely

Lucy Johnson-James

Aunt Coral's To Do

Make Will

Fence oil

Neighbours

Badger Badger

Pensees: *The moment between sleeping and waking is the make believe time of day.* SB

I dreamt we were all living here together at the same time, London and Alfred and all of us. I dreamt that time was arranged quite differently, and there was nothing to divide us into the people of then and now.

London was sitting outside Edenthorpe, he waved as I walked by, and Alfred was by the sundial in the garden, wiping the sweat from his brow. But then Aunt Coral appeared at the window in Roselyne cottage; she was wearing black, just like Rose Anna at the window, and she was deathly pale. I sensed she was not alive any more and I woke up in a cold sweat, and it took me a few horrendous moments to make sure I had been dreaming.

It went on to be a poke-yourself-in-the-eye-with-your-sunglasses type of morning. For obvious reasons I felt stressed. But I spent the morning at least peacefully, pottering in my suite followed by a walk down to the ruins. The robin that sometimes begs at the kitchen door of Green Place was drinking from a pool of water on the sundial, his breast looking very red against the green and grey of all the old stone. Of all the birds in the air, perhaps the robin is the most solitary. This is something that Joe said while he lent on the sundial and chatted, and I got the shivers for I remembered I *imagined* him once doing that.

And this afternoon at about 3.00 he ran me up to Pimlico on his bike and he came up to Quiz and Di's flat to say a quick hello, before heading off to his turf seminar in Croydon.

He seemed a bit thunderstruck when he first met Quiz, and I believe it's because Quiz is not the old man in a gown that Joe was expecting. However, Joe did manage to hold it together and engage in some polite banter before he left. He is ever the gent.

Quiz and Di live in a fifth-floor Pimlico flat, with a little gold plaque outside their door. It is engraved with their solicitor esque trademark Winterby and Wilson – and Di has top billing.

The living room at 5C Lupus Street has a balcony with River Thames glimpses. There is a galley kitchen and three bedrooms, their room – the Master – which was very untidy, then a small tiny double, and then there's a walk-in cupboard in the 'vestibule', which is also used as bedroom three.

Di made supper of pasta with pesto and then didn't eat any herself. They have a log burner by the dining table, which I sat next to during the meal. It was so hot that I would have had to have been practically nudey to enjoy it. And the kitchen is really dirty. I am guessing they are both too busy to have time for cleaning. Over supper I showed them 'The Emperor's Slippers' to get their feedback. Di told me she thought it would fit into the genre of literary nonsense. I am unclear at the moment as to whether she was being cruel to be kind.

After dinner we went and sat effortlessly on the soft furnishings in the living room while Di prepared some coffee.

'Di tells me you've got an interview for the internship,' said Quiz. 'They'd have to be barmy not to choose you, and I bet there were *hundreds* of applicants.'

'Thanks,' I said. 'Everyone's been so kind.'

'Did you go firm on your dissertation subject yet?' he asked.

'I think probably just the Russians, but I'm still attracted to mermaids.'

'Well, if I were choosing between the Russians and mermaids, I would choose the Russians because there is infinitely more information on them,' said Quiz.

'What are you doing yours on?' I asked, doubtfully.

'The History of Civil Aviation or the East India Company, I can't decide either.'

He flashed his invigorating smile, a smile that said none of it really *matters*.

'Thank you so much for persuading your Aunt to take on another lodger,' he said.

'Oh I didn't have to persuade her – she thought it was a brilliant idea.'

Di came in with some coffee and chocolates.

'Darling, Craig and Angela just rang to say please could we come and do the quiz.'

'I forgot about that. It's just a quiz at the pub – you wouldn't mind would you Sue?' said Quiz.

'No of course not,' I said. 'Will we be in teams?'

I sat at a table in between Quiz and Di and opposite their couple friends Craig and Angela.

Craig and Angela got tipsy and let Quiz and Di answer *everything*. It was clear that with Winterby and Wilson on our team we would definitely win.

'Question number one. Who wrote *Beau Geste*?' said the Quizmaster into a microphone.

'Percival Christopher Wren,' whispered Di, as she wrote down our team's answer.

'Question number two. Can you tell me the name of another book by the same author whose title also begins with Beau?'

'*Beau Sabreur*,' said Quiz, writing it down.

'Question number three. What was the infamous Russian Rasputin's Christian name?'

'This is one for Sue,' said Quiz.

'Was it Ra-Ra?' I said.

'Grigori,' said Diane.

'Question number four. From these six pictures of famous old ladies, please give the name of the woman in the top left, and I will accept either popular name.'

The pictures were of old ladies in nineteenth-century costume.

'Do you think we'd get away with Granny?' I said.

'Florence Nightingale,' said Di.

'Question number five. What is a Dower house?'

'It's where you put your mother,' said Quiz.

'Number six. What was Italy known as in 1830?'

'The Kingdom of Italy,' said Di.

Di is like an encyclopaedia, she knows almost everything and she has an incredible memory for dates. The only questions that she struggled with were the popular culture ones – and she explained that this was because when she was growing up she and her brothers were not allowed to watch ITV.

But, as you can imagine, in spite of Di not knowing the answers to any of the more piffling questions, team Winterby and Wilson easily won.

Afterwards we all hurried back to the fifth-floor Pimlico flat for a nightcap, by now under stormy skies. After a cheeky espresso (Di's nightcap, which is made of coffee with a touch of grappa in it), I began to think about getting myself back to Egham.

I was heading into bedroom two to collect my handbag from the bed where I had left it, but Quiz stopped me urgently.

'Don't go in there darling. Craig and Angela went in there to make love,' he said.

'I'm so sorry. What time is it?' I said, appalled.

'It's midnight, darling. I better run you home.'

'I can't let you do that.'

'I insist. Look, it's pouring, you look very tired, and I like driving at night,' said Quiz. 'Just . . . wait a minute and then we can go in and get your things. Here, you can borrow this if you like,' he said, handing me his windcheater. 'Di darling, I'm just going to pop Sue home,' he called.

'OK darling, see you plus tard,' she called. 'Plus tard, Sue darling.'

Once we got on the road Quiz's big gold watch glinted in the lamplight and flashed sparks of amber light when he crunched through the gears. But he drove the car so smoothly it felt like we were flying.

'Do you want some music?' he asked. 'I've got Dizzy Gillespie, Miles Davis, Acker Bilk.'

'I like Acker Bilk,' I said, recognizing the name from Aunt Coral's collection.

'"Stranger On the Shore", I love this one,' he said. 'I think he wrote it for his daughter Jenny.'

We passed through the streets of London to the rich, mellow tune of the clarinet, as we cruised along gently through the shadowy suburbs on the way out of town, till the roads became fringed by nothing but the dark, dark trees gliding past my window.

'Stranger On the Shore' begins as almost a smooch, but when the clarinet goes all high and sweet, I can't help but get tears in my eyes, I think for no other reason than life is sometimes so beautiful.

'I want to get driving lessons soon,' I chatted, to prevent myself from slipping into the blues. 'But I've got to save up a bit of money first!'

'We'll need to get you selling some of your work,' he said. 'I expect the internship will be just pocket money.'

'And I haven't got it yet!' I said.

The journey was so swift that I must admit I was a little disappointed when we got back to Green Place. I thought it would take ages, but it only took just under an hour. Green Place towered over us in the darkness like a hillside – all the lights were off.

'Night, and thank you very much for bringing me home.'

'Night darling, keep in touch. Plus tard,' he said.

'Plus tard,' I said quietly.

'And see you at the beginning of May,' he said.

I wondered if he would lean over and give me an inappropriate sort of kiss, like he did when he came out to visit that day with Di, but he didn't; maybe because Di wasn't there this time, it would have been one notch too much. And if I'm being scrupulously honest, I feel both relieved and a little disappointed that he didn't, because when he kisses in *that* way, it makes me feel embarrassed, excited and also a little confused. For I feel I only have one forever, but I imagine someone like Quiz might have quite a few, if that makes any sense.

It took a long time for the dark grounds to fall quiet again after his porch drove away and I realized that this is the first time that I have had an older plutonic friend.

The hiss and tap of the rain as it landed on the hedge sounded like the sweep of the brush on some symbols, like a band of percussive raindrops, or like 'rain jazz', I thought.

On the Butterfly Table in the hall there was a note from the Admiral saying that:

Joe rang to say goodnight

And on my bedside table now:

> **Word List**
> *Ennui*
> *Dizzy Gillespie*
> *Literary nonsense*

I have put 'The Emperor's Slippers' to one side, and am now searching for a better idea for my dissertation.

Sat April 23 1988

Pensees: *Doctors must have their appointments, window cleaners appear.* SB

> ## Aunt Coral's To Do
> Make Will
>
> Undersheets
>
> Roast
>
> Avery
>
> Knightsbridge 4.30

Knightsbridge 4.30 *again*? I don't know why Aunt Coral hasn't just written down where she is going. She is very open as we all know, even to the point of putting Make Will on her To Do, or Sort Briefs under the nose of the Admiral. I must remain calm, as there is probably some innocent explanation. But I do hope she is all right, and as soon as I get a private moment I am going to ask her.

She has decided to put the deeds, along with a new family tree that Jackie is assembling, out on the table in the White Room. The White Room is one of the many reception rooms downstairs that have been overlooked in favour of warmer climbs. She has been up in an attic all morning tracking down the family portraits, as she now believes that with Jackie's work we can fit some names to the faces within those old frames. This afternoon, Mrs Bunion will be dusting and polishing them and tomorrow the Admiral will hang them in the White Room, and thus Aunt Coral will have created a dedicated space for the past. The idea is that the portraits will hang there respectfully, along with those others we have yet to name.

There isn't one of Madam Rose Anna or obviously Alfred Elms or London Taylor sadly. But in *For the Concern*, Alfred says of Rose Anna that he has never seen a lady 'so buttoned up', with her weeper's cuffs and her high necklines and her weeping veil. He says that underneath it she was pale and red-headed and buttoned up to the elbow on each of the cuffs. NB weeper's cuffs were worn for exactly the reason you might expect . . . to wipe away tears. Walderon probably dressed in mourning too out of respect for her Mistress – apparently many maids did that, to show solidarity.

Alfred was tall and very dark, and London says, 'of a rangy, athletic build'. And London himself was very small with blonde hair that grew in ringlets, but for a bald patch round the back of his head, from repetitive wearing of his cap and most likely malnutrition.

But there are proper portraits of some of the Garden family from the 1860s, those wealthy enough to commission painters. There is a vast oil painting of Benedict and Adelaide posed together, but there is no image of the son, who Alfred and London mention, in the picture.

Here is a further illuminating little extract. I feel I should say that, at the time this extract was written, there was a party going on at Green Place, as Alfred is about to explain. London had probably been here now almost a year.

FOR THE CONCERN OF THE RICH AND THE POOR

Nov 1st 1858

'Have you heard about Queen Victoria's proclamation?' I asked Alfred, when he came home with a box of frost-bitten onions. 'Sowerbutt was talking about it and I didn't like to ask if the Queen was unwell.'

'Well yes I have, and it's all right, it is good news – it means that the Queen is the new ruler of India. Master Benedict is hosting a great banquet for his brother Thomas, who is blazing a trail for her Majesty's government with a Civil Service posting to Allahabad. They are expecting a great number of guests, carriages are not called until dawn.'

Later the same evening, I begged to accompany Alfred out on his rounds to tuck in the peas and fill up the boiler in the glasshouse and stoke up the fires in the walls. When we returned to Edenthorpe, Alfred made us hot milk and we sat up a while to thaw out.

At about half past midnight we heard a knock next door and, to our surprise, visitors were admitted to Roselyne.

There were voices and growls and murmurs, and then we heard sobs which were quickly subdued amid bumps and the scuffles and scrapes of chairs. But it all so pricked our curiosity that Alfred agreed I should put my ear up to the wall.

'They sound like men,' I said.

'What are they saying?'

'I can't make it out. But I think the lady is in great distress.'

'Do you think we should intervene?' said Alfred, pacing the floor.

'I don't know,' I replied, as the voices from Roselyne grew louder.

'Where are they?' came a hoarse cry from the other side of the wall, and afterward a rasping cigar cough.

'Master Benedict,' hissed Alfred.

'You will never find them, never,' came the voice of the lady. 'I would rather die than give them up.'

'Tell me where they are, I say!' shouted the man.

'Never! You should have asked your Father before it was too late,' screamed the lady.

'Calm down, both of you,' said a second man's voice. 'We must settle the matter peacefully.'

'You whore!' yelled Master Benedict.

'What's a whore?' I asked Alfred.

'Shhh,' he said.

Then the door of Roselyne opened and slammed shut with violence, followed by heavy footsteps crunching back to the big house, shattering the cover of ice.

I rushed to the front window to see what I could see, but could only make out two shadowy figures walking back to the big house, dressed in the top hats and black evening cloaks of gentlemen.

It does make you wonder if something was buried along with Edmund Garden, doesn't it? And it makes *me* wonder if it was the Shipwreck Pearls.

Sue

I took the opportunity of the Admiral going to his club to find a moment alone with Aunt Coral and ask her about her 4.30 appointments. We were in the kitchen and she was actually updating her To Do, which mercifully gave me an opener.

'I noticed you keep having four thirty appointments in Knightsbridge,' I said. 'Everything's all right isn't it?'

'Oh yes,' she replied. 'But why do you ask?'

'I just thought you might be going to see that doctor and not wanting to worry me,' I said.

'Oh good gracious no! Four thirty is the time that they reduce the French pastries for sale in the Food Hall,' she said.

Though obviously I'm very relieved about this, my mind has already moved on to the next problem. Because I don't recall *seeing* any evidence of French pastries being brought back to Green Place.

At 5pm, Aunt C and I returned from Gladys's Tea Rooms in Egham to find a note from Jackie County marked urgent.

Dear Coral

As you know because of the various mentions of Sotheby's in Valentine Garden's letters, if you remember, he was Benedict's youngest brother.

I did ask my friend Cyril if I might be allowed access to his Sotheby's archive again to see if I could fish out anything more. Now, we all know that the Shipwreck Pearls Edmund Garden bought at auction before he died in 1857 were worth a decent sum. BUT when I dug deeper into the listings of exotic jewels recorded at that time – I discovered it is not the pearls but the clasp of the shipwreck piece that is the real draw. It comprises a large hand-cut diamond called the 'Star of the South' and this is where it gets interesting. Please see clipping:

> The Star of the South is a jewel of near perfect clarity, pure white, eighteen carats, honed by the process of bruting. The jewel has been placed in a lathe with another diamond in it to rub against it. It is a diamond cut by a diamond, and then it has been further polished in diamond powder, applied to the polisher's wheel. The whole process taking possibly up to two years. The overall effect is a stone so delicate, multi-faceted and sparkling, it is said to resemble the southern star Sigma Octantis on a moonlit night, producing a shimmer against the skin of near perfect lustre.

It is my opinion that the time has come to persuade you to let me DIG.

I promise I will be careful and tidy, I understand your concerns about all the mess and damage to plants at ground level. And so I've studied the plans at the buildings archive and as you know, I'm VERY interested in that old tunnel you have running out from under your kitchen.

I think it would have made the most obvious hiding place. You see, normally when jewels have a name, it's usually not very difficult to discover what happened to them. They are invariably listed somewhere for insurance purposes, but I can't find any paper trail on these.

In the light of this, or should I say the dazzle!, do you think I might target just one little spot for excavation direct into the tunnel? Maybe at the old garden end? My archaeologist could come and dig a little hole and initially just put a camera down and take a peek. There'll be no charge, unless, that is, we find something! I have asked him to pop some literature and photographs through your door of similar domestic excavations. Have a read and a look at the pictures and let me know what you think.

Very exciting and oh what possibilities!

All my best

Jackie

'Goodness me,' said Aunt Coral, when she'd finished reading, with an expression that I can only describe as her jewellery face. She looked suddenly animated and cocked her head to one side, the way Jackie's dogs do whenever she puts her hand to her pocket.

Word List:
Lathe
Bruting

Mon April 25 1988, 9am

Pensees: *One person's stand-out star-dust type is another person's pain in the arse.* SB

Going for a hot chocolate in the garden centre this morning with Joe and then we are going on a little trip to the hardware store, because he needs some ten-inch screws. I am somewhat disproportionately excited.

It seems Joe isn't altogether relaxed about Quiz moving in at the weekend. Ever since they met on the threshold of the fifth-floor Pimlico flat Joe seems to have taken against him.

So the prospect of Quiz's imminent arrival somewhat overshadowed our hot milky drinks. Joe said he thinks Quiz is the type of person who calls you darling because he can't remember your name. I did try to explain it's more likely because Quiz is just so charismatic.

After we got back, I found Aunt Coral up in the East Wing long passage. She was going through the dressing-up box. She had been foraging for the Shipwreck Pearls and the Star of the South all morning in the 'East Wing attic left four'.

'You never know,' said Aunt Coral. 'I'm just checking that the Star of the South necklace hasn't got muddled with the dressing-up.'

She pulled out an orange velvet cape made out of a curtain and some ladies' white Victorian boots. And then out came a chest with all sorts of jewels that resembled pirates' treasure.

'It's all paste,' said Aunt C, 'but we used to think they were real.'

She told me that when they were little, her and her younger sister Cameo had hours of fun pretending to be various icons from history. The orange curtain apparently belonged to Queen Elizabeth the first and the white ladies' Victorian boots to Dick Turpin. I love the way that children aren't fussy.

I looked out of the window and down the lawns at the side of Green Place where Jackie suggests target digging.

'Why would they have needed a *tunnel* for the servants to go to and fro from the garden? Why didn't they just walk down the meadow?' I asked.

'It was to hide the servants, so they wouldn't spoil the Master's view, a bit like an awful sort of tradesman's entrance. I'm afraid some Victorians were terribly snobbish,' said Aunt Coral.

'But how can Jackie tell if the tunnel isn't all filled in again, and . . . why does she feel so sure that these jewels might still be on the premises? They could be anywhere in the world couldn't they?'

'Well,' Aunt Coral piped up again. 'That is true, but I think checking might be sensible. But then again, the photographs of other sites that the archaeologist provided are rather overwhelming. It seems what Jackie means by "dig a little hole" is that the garden should be turned upside down.'

'And even if a diamond did prove to be down there, wouldn't it have perished in the damp and dark?' I asked.

'That's just it,' replied Aunt Coral. 'Diamonds are one of the strongest and most durable substances on *earth*. A stone like this could well survive a century of darkness and damp. As a matter of fact, *light* would have more of an adverse effect on it. That's why I feel so conflicted.'

10pm

Aunt C went on to have a bit of a de-clutter, as a result of the routelling in the attic. She has assembled a large pile of jumble in the Sun Room destined for the charity shop, including the old telephone from the hall, which the Admiral retrieved because he said it should be given straight to a museum.

Sue

> **Aunt Coral's To Do**
> Make will
> Undersheets
> Roast
> Avery
> Egham 1.40

The 1.40 on Aunt C's To Do today referred to my appointment time as per the PA slip for the interview with Mr Gordoney George for the *Echo*, which took place at the Shilling Street Hotel in Egham.

There were several other candidates sitting on the sofas in the reception area, all nervously waiting for their appointments like me. I locked eyes with one of them; it was obviously going to be a fierce contest. She was whippet thin with slippery dark hair and her vibes were so strong I felt she inwardly spat at me. It made me feel so smirched I had to go to the ladies and take deep breaths.

When my name was called by a lady with a clipboard, I followed her into the Penny Farthing restaurant to join Mr Gordoney George at a table by the window, where he was conducting his interviews over coffee, tea or soft drinks. To say I was nervous was rather an understatement, but I still get excited about going to hotels – because of things like hotel cups of tea, little sachets of things, interesting free biscuits, and Gideons.

My first impressions of Gordoney George were of a tall, well-built man in his fifties, in a light blue casual suit, worn over a white T-shirt with incongruous tennis pumps. He has a gap in his front teeth and a nicotine-stained right index finger. He has that frequent-visitor-to-campsites look, long silvery hair, a peanut tan, and a pot belly. (I'm using Mr O'Carroll's active Description method.)

Gordoney put his hand through his long locks, a style on an older man that Aileen Edgeley calls 'honey and roses'. To be scrupulously honest though, I'd say it looks a bit wiggy, as though he has got his hair on back to front.

'Welcome, Miss,' he looked at his name sheet, 'is that Bowl?'

'Yes, that's right,' I replied.

'As in pudding?' he asked.

'Yes, that's right,' I said, sombrely.

'So, thank you for coming in,' he said, sipping his tea and swallowing a burp.

'It's such a pleasure,' I said and then regretted it because it sounded too pushy and transparent.

'So, first of all, would you call yourself an ideas person?' he asked.

'Oh yes, definitely,' I said.

'I see,' he said. 'Is there anything you'd like to ask me? Sometimes I find the most illuminating things about candidates are their questions.'

'Would I get the chance to write articles along with my intern work?'

'The six million dollar question,' he replied. 'You could of course submit, but you'd need to be prepared to get knocked back. So, it says here on your application that you have just completed a sabbatical in creative writing under Benjamin O'Carroll at Taverna O'Carroll in Greece.'

'That's right. Actually I had to come home early, because my brother was born prematurely.'

'I see. And what was it you say you learnt on the course?' he said, picking up my application form. '*To hold back, simmer, and be muted? To write as if you are constantly on the edge of having an . . . mm.*'

I deeply regretted my frankness.

'To be honest, my main note was to try and be more Russian, so that's how I want to progress.'

'More Russian,' said Gordoney, jotting down a few notes in a reporter's notebook. 'And how do you do that? Wear a big coat?' he asked.

'But also,' I hesitated, unsure if he was joking, 'I think that you have to try and write about the heart and soul of things, about guilt, death, greed and things that are doomed. Coming from a place like Titford, I have always tended to dwell on the positives – as a means of providing relief.'

'Interesting. Well, thanks very much Miss Bowl, I think that's all for now. A pleasure to meet you and we'll let you know by the beginning of next week.'

After I got back to Green Place I wondered how I would survive the next few days in agonizing anticipation. How do you carry on as normal when your every passing moment seems so significant? You know, will this be the last Thursday afternoon I will ever sit in the drawing room and not be an intern, sort of thing?

I distracted myself by taking an extract. After almost a year at
Edenthorpe, London Taylor *still* hasn't met Rose Anna, because she
is still in deep mourning and as a result she rarely ventures out.
But they seem to be getting to know each other in spite of this.

FOR THE CONCERN OF THE RICH AND THE POOR

To Mr Alfred Elms' Valet
Edenthorpe
Green Place
Egham
Sept 26th 1858

To the little man next door,
Thank you for the enchanting gift of baked apples.
    We enjoyed them very much.
    And you are right, ten to ten on a summer evening is
the time that the fox comes out. We could set our watches
by him. Thank you very much for pointing it out.
    Yours sincerely
    Madam Rose Anna Garden

To Alfred Elms' Apprentice
Edenthorpe
Green Place
Egham
Oct 2nd 1858

Dear Mr Elms' Apprentice,
Thank you for the delightful chestnuts. No, I must
confess that I have never played them.
    A very kind thought.
    Yours sincerely
    Madam Rose Anna Garden

To Mr London Taylor
Edenthorpe
Green Place
Egham
Oct 23rd 1858

Dear Mr Taylor,
Thank you for the interesting stone, which I have added
to the collection. You do seem to have a very good eye
for small overlooked things.
Yours sincerely
Madam Rose Anna Garden

To Mr London Taylor
Edenthorpe
Green Place
Egham
November 1st 1858

Dear Mr Taylor
Thank you for the beautiful garland of mimosa and
milkweed.
I think it looks like the studded choker of a mystic
Indian Princess, very much in keeping with today's
news. I hope you and Mr Elms are well, he never seems
to stop working. I am sorry you have had no luck in
luring the little boy at the big house down to the owl
walk to show him the beloved creatures that are keeping
us all awake. I believe he is not allowed to mix with
anybody. His parents fear he might catch cold, and his
mother, Madam Adelaide, is very strict on this matter.
Sadly she has already lost two sons before him, both of
them in their infancy.

Poor fellow, I'm sure he would have loved to meet you in more ideal circumstances. And so Alfred is correct, the child is not a ghost, but a little boy and his name is Frittie.

With my best wishes for your health and happiness.

Yours sincerely

Madam Rose Anna Garden

To Mr London Taylor
Edenthorpe
Green Place
Egham
December 23rd 1858

Dear Mr Taylor

Thank you very much for the plum pudding. It is a personal favourite of Walderon's – I practically had to wrestle it from her hands.

Wishing you both a Merry Christmas and a Happy New Year.

Yours sincerely,

Madam Rose Anna Garden

To Mr London Taylor
Edenthorpe
Green Place
Egham
January 1st 1859

Dear London,

Walderon tells me that Alfred was saying that you have been wondering why Queen Victoria has been so much in the headlines lately, and by way of thanks for the poinsettia, I am sending through a copy of today's

Illustrated London News. Its front page has all the details about Queen Victoria's proclamation (which was made on November the 1st) and read out in every territory to almost every Indian citizen. We are living in fascinating times.

In addition I am sending one of my favourite books on the country itself for you to look at; I do hope you haven't read it. *Wanderings of a Pilgrim in Search of the Picturesque* by Fanny Parkes, with illustrations.

With my best wishes to you both for a prosperous New Year and heartfelt thanks for the poinsettia.

Yours sincerely,
Madam Rose Anna Garden

Sue

May 2 1988

Here is my first rejection letter.

May 2 1988

Sue hi,

Thank you very much for coming in to meet Gordoney.
He felt it was a close call. But ultimately he decided to go
another way with the position, purely because he feels that
the paper would benefit from a candidate with some
experience already.

Wishing you all good luck in the future.

Yours sincerely,

Lucy Johnson-James

PART THREE

Hold the Bottle by the Dimple

Sue

Going from 'Hi Sue', to 'Sue hi' feels like the work equivalent of 'It's not you it's me'.

How do you *get* experience, if you have to *have* experience to *get* it?

Aunt Coral is very concerned about me, and I can't do anything remotely off colour, like miss drinks at 6, or skip breakfast. If I do, I know that she will pounce and shower me with support. But apart from being so bitterly disappointed I just feel so utterly *embarrassed.*

Joe swung into action immediately, the minute it became necessary to activate my Plan B, and he has asked Icarus to arrange a position for me at the new Bistro, where I start on Friday. Aunt Coral says that there are some jobs you do for your soul and some for the bank. And unfortunately this will be one for the bank.

Joe couldn't have been more understanding, and when I went up to bed last night I discovered that he had written several silver-lining post notes and put them up for me to read, at strategic sights of doom. Such as the ceiling above my pillow, and the mid-point of the window sill, which lies below where I look into the middle distance.

By *not* being an intern, I will have my days free for improving my more classical writing and working on my dissertation without other pressures.

By *not* being an intern, I can spend more time with Joe.

By *not* being an intern, I will be able to meet lots of interesting diners at work, and get a flattering new uniform and tips.

By *not* being an intern, I can wholeheartedly embrace Plan B.

Fri 6th May

The Lanterner Bistro is the vision of Joe's mother, Mrs Pam Fry. A project that has been *years* in the pipe work. It is the second of her two brain children, and the sister establishment to the hugely successful Egham Toastie on which Mrs Fry cut her teeth.

It lies in a quiet street in the town centre, a two-minute walk from the shopper's car park to the north of Quaker's Acre.

Before it was a Bistro, it was a Pancake House, and before it was a Pancake House it was a Pram Shop. Before that it was a private residence, but now it has been knocked through to create a spacious restaurant, with twenty tables downstairs and ten more upstairs laid out on a galleried landing.

Mrs Fry heads up a team of six waiting staff. Icarus and Joe only work week nights because they are pirating at the weekends. (Joe has three jobs on the go at the moment.) He is especially good at being a wine waiter, and pours customers' wine beautifully. With one arm behind his back, he pours with the other, holding the bottle by the dimple, as he's been asked to by Mrs Fry.

Tonight I was sent to serve upstairs on the gallery where I had a bird's-eye view of everything. And when I felt pangs of disappointment about the internship, I played a naming game for the diners.

Mr Belgravia was sitting at Table 7 and Mr Knightsbridge took Table 8. They both appeared to be bachelors. Then there was the Comptessa who wore a stole and dripped with jewellery; I thought she could have been a spy. She was joined for dinner by a streaky woman with a good appetite and BBC hair. I wondered why Mrs Fry didn't match-make the ladies with the gents, it seemed like a missed opportunity, but then life's not a novel. (If it was perhaps I would have got the internship.)

Charlie was waiting downstairs; she still has quite a limp. Joe waited downstairs also, so he saw more of her tonight than he did of me. I am trying to open my heart and be magnanimous about this . . . to be modern and unbothered and Russian, but obviously I don't feel like that. I feel old-fashioned and bothered and British.

And the last of the waiting staff in the Lanterner team is Posiedon Rodriguez, who happens to be one of Aunt Coral's prodigies. Posiedon is the daughter of a magician, whose parents Aunt Coral struck up a friendship with when she went to London last year. (Mr and Mrs Rodriguez became members of Aunt C's salon, and joined in with the EHG writing group.)

Posiedon is a girl of six feet two, who smells a bit like a rabbit hutch and has been told she must wear deodorant. She wanted to be a model but she has never got far because she has an awful gate. I find her terribly striking.

She wears an expression on her face all the time that says: 'How did I get here?' And so that's what I might offer as her TWD.

She reminds me of myself a year ago, obsessed with getting a boyfriend. She says she is determined to be in a relationship by Christmas. She is very open about it, even with the customers.

But the pulse of the Bistro, as with any such place, is of course the kitchen. And there, at its *heart*, lies the Italian chef, Beniamino Mimo. Mrs Fry took a shrewd business decision when she made Beniamino her partner.

Apparently, he is thirty years old, self-taught, and provides cuisine which is Italian with traces of French bistro fusion. He is exuberant, tempestuous and vibrant, and he swung out of the kitchen at the end of tonight and walked through the Bistro patting everyone. I felt I could spot a mile off that Posiedon is already becoming infatuated with him and may be imaging herself having Italian babies. After dessert, she asked him if he was married and he said that he has no interest in it, as if it was something he'd do in the shed.

Sat 7th May

Pensees: *I am a woman of simple tastes. I do not want my pasta to be amazing.* SB

Quiz moved in today! And Admiral Ted's old suite is now home to his trunks and dreamy items. Mrs Bunion removed the black velvet cover from the clock and got it ticking again, and Snowdrop has officially come back to life. Aunt C left a large floral arrangement for Quiz to find on his dressing chest, which he was delighted by. There is a feeling of great excitement amongst the residents to welcome such a glamorous tenant. When I left Greece, I thought I would never see Quiz again, and yet here he is under my roof.

And after I got back from the Bistro tonight, he gave me a wonderful thank-you present over nightcaps in the drawing room.

'Apparently it looks very good worn over a nightie. I am guessing being a young lady you'll know what this means,' he offered.

I tore open the tissue paper to reveal a super trendy coat.

Di has been having a clear-out in her wardrobe and wanted to donate a fabulous snazzy coat. It is one of those military-style ones, long, grey and trampy with coin buttons and deep pockets. I put it straight on and swished.

'Di thinks it's the sort of coat that scantily clad female vampires wear in horror films when they climb out of their coffins,' said Quiz elegantly. 'But I thought it would make you look more Russian.'

I'm not normally aware of the Westminster chimes of the mantel clock that sits on the fireplace any more – over time you become immune to them – but as they chimed into sixteen-ding action to mark the passing of the hour of midnight, for some reason they seemed very loud.

Sun 8 May

Even though this is a job for the bank, there are still some highlights. Aunt Coral and the Admiral came in to dine this evening. The Admiral has got a slight beard on the go and Aunt Coral is really enjoying his snowy whiskers. She was thriving for hours after their meal because Beniamino called her Senyorina. And Beniamino in his turn was thriving because Aunt Coral asked him to repeat the word vanilla so many times, she loved the way he said it in his accent so much. This came about when she asked him what were the ingredients to his crème anglaise. As I walked past their table, all I could hear was 'Van-ee-lah! Van-ee-lah! Van-ee-lah!'

And Quiz also came in, and insisted on sitting at one of *my* tables at the front of the gallery! He was every inch the most debonair customer. Posiedon nearly dropped her soups.

But I have to say the *best* thing to have come out of *not* being an intern . . . apart from the fact that I can spend more time with Joe, is that I have finally been inspired with a new idea for my dissertation.

The story that came to me is about a young intern in Moscow. It fuses my emotional disappointment, my Taverna coursework and my life. And the brilliant thing about Quiz living at Green Place is that he can critique it as I go along.

I left my work on his desk up in Snowdrop in the late afternoon yesterday and he put the noted work back for me outside Pearl's room this morning. I will now leave my corrected version out for him later, and on we will go.

'Jenvaria Andropopolov Rentski'

OR 'JENNY GETS A CHANCE'
by Sue Bowl

Jenny Strausse Cliffton was born on the Ul Lenivka Strasse in Moscow, a hundred yards from the Bridge of Kisses and a stone's throw from the Pushkin Museum. Her mother was an Anglo-French composer Virginie Cliffton who went mad in exile. Her Father was the Oligarch Sebastian Strausse-Yuirikov, a close family friend of the Tsar. They counted amongst their circle, artisans and poets, members of the Imperial dynasty, and in happier times before the revolution, Gawky himself. Jenny kept her Oligarchical past a secret, particularly when she found employment as an intern.

Notes for Sue on Jenvaria Andropolov Rentski, with love from Quiz

1 Maxim Gorky.
2 Is the title Russian or gobbledy gook?
3 Ul already means road.
4 Remember to be more Russian, make sure it isn't all too nice. Is the piece sexy enough? Has it got *legs*?

(rewrite for Quiz notes)

'Dzjhenia Pulyucheyer a Shans'

OR 'JENNY GETS A CHANCE'
by Sue Bowl

Jenny Strausse Cliffton was born on the Ul Lenivka in Moscow, a hundred yards from the bridge of kisses and a stones throw from the Pushkin museum. Her mother was the Anglo French composer Virginie Cliffton who went mad in exile and died. Her murdered Father was the Oligarch Sebastian Strausse-Yurikov, a close family friend of the Tzar.

He counted among his circle artisans poets, members of the Imperial dynasty, and in happier times, before the revolution, Gorky himself. There were many parties, many lovers, but not enough days to love them.

Jenny kept her Oligarchical past a secret, particularly when she found employment as an intern.

Aunt Coral's To Do

Make will

Hamster muesli for Delia

Steam clean tapestry

Sue

I love this time before anybody else has surfaced, it's the truly secret part of the morning. The only sounds are the tickings of the clock, and animals scurrying away up pipes and down drains. I watch the light grow pale under the curtains and these days I make pensees.

I'm having to get up earlier and earlier to catch the secret hour, because Mrs Bunion has started to arrive *so early*. Aunt Coral says it's because old ladies need less sleep; she makes her sound like a fable. But I know the real reason she gets here earlier is that Quiz requested breakfast up in his room, a special privilege he seems to have negotiated by the bribery of his pure charm.

Here at home, it is the early bird who catches the hot water, and we have to stagger our bath times. Separating the slots is the only way to guarantee the water will be hot and not lukewarm or 'just with the edge taken off', which is the Admiral's preferred temperature (which means that it's actually cold).

If I am up before Mrs Bunion gets here, it takes me about 40 minutes to open the house up, to free all the doors, draw back the curtains, air the rooms and unbolt things. At this sort of time there is only the soft purr of the fridge in the kitchen and the deep roar of the boiler down in the laundry to accompany my steps, which are joined when the boiler's timer clicks itself on and water starts gurgling in the pipes.

By the time I get back upstairs into the furthest suites of the West Wing, the boiler's drone becomes a distant hum from its original roar several feet below, and the overall effect is of a ship, sailing along, HMS *Green Place*, across the centuries, down the generations.

I have just now indulged in a silky, silent bath where I lay in the steaming bubbles and read the labels on Aunt Coral's bottles, gently letting the world seep in a little. 'This product contains no parabulalabalems.'

After my bath I settled down to write, but with the first tweet from the earliest bird, I know the secret hour is almost over. Soon the rest of the world will be awake and the morning will truly be broken.

And there now . . . there's the tap of a shoe, the closing of a door and the sweet smell of oaty porridge and pretty soon Mrs Bunion will fire up the hoover.

Weds May 25

Joe was very worried this morning because he said he found Quiz outside Aunt Coral's room at 6am. He said he felt uneasy about it, because Quiz looked as though he'd been fingering the miniatures on the landing shelves.

He asked Quiz if he was lost and Quiz said yes he was, and explained that he was looking for *my* room. So I can understand why Joe got the wrong end of the stick! But as for fingering the miniatures, I think Joe has got an in-built hostility to Quiz and as such looks for reasons to find fault with him.

So *I* explained that it wasn't what Joe *thought* and that Quiz would have just been leaving me my critiqued homework, because we've got this new system in play for 'Jenny Gets a Chance' and it's all quite innocent, which in all honesty is only a little true. Because Quiz does have a vibrant effect on me, and I can't help but admire him. And Joe knows, as I do, that admiration is something I have never really done before without it turning into full-blown love. But then, Joe has never been in the picture before, and I have never admired a man with a girlfriend, so I'm sure that this time it's going to be safe.

But it's clear to me now that Joe is obviously very insecure about Quiz and I do understand how that feels. I used to feel devastated all the time last year when Loudolle was around and I was in love with Icarus. Reading that back, I do sound rather fickle, but I'm just trying to be scrupulously honest.

Here is a diversion.

FOR THE CONCERN OF THE RICH AND THE POOR

I kept Madam Rose Anna's letters pressed together in Alfred's heavy botanical book, the incongruous and proud owner of a real lady's correspondence. Something about her manner suggested to me, that though we still had not met in person, we would not remain strangers forever.

On cold nights I remained beside the fire with the book about India she had lent me, The *Wanderings of a Pilgrim* by Fanny Parkes.

I had forgotten about the mythical town of Germany, thrown it over for something better, upgraded to a dream land where the sun was warm enough to melt all the horseshoes in the Cavalry, a place of desert and spice. Maybe I just liked having dreams?

But my passion for India grew so intense that I imagined that the mist curling over the meadows in the mornings didn't come from the fires of the big house, but from incense burning in a china-blue temple, and that the climbers entwined around the trellis over the bench outside Edenthorpe were in fact the exotic gates at the Port of Bombay. And at sunset I found the amber glow of lamplight reflected in a pool of ice on the sundial, to be tipped with the ruby and gold of a Maha Raja's crown. And the wisteria branches twined round each other outside the big house became an elephant's trunk, and their grey crooked boughs, the elephant's knees.

My dream was strong and it grew fierce like a disease. Sometimes I was so enraptured that I imagined anything with curved sides and a pointed top looked like the bottle-shaped domes of the Taj Mahal.

It all amused Alfred so much that he cut the yew hedge into the contours of the domes of the Palace of the Royal Pavilion at Brighton, which he copied from a picture postcard.

When we sat once again at our dinner table at Edenthorpe, Alfred said he had made some sensitive enquiries from Sowerbutt as to the wellbeing of our widow neighbour.

'He says Master Benedict is greatly in debt and apparently he is trying to force Madam Rose Anna to give him a treasure which if sold would go six times past clearing them, and setting his credit back to rights.'

'Good gracious!' I exclaimed, in the thrall of the best gossip at Edenthorpe.

Aunt Coral's To Do

Make will

Avery's Singlet

Knightsbridge 4.30

Sue

Mon May 30 1988

This morning I was helping Mrs Bunion dust the portraits in the White Room, for the tops of them seem to attract it.

'It looks like Jackie must have been in,' I said.

'Oh yes dear, she left some notes and a chart,' said Mrs Bunion.

The chart Mrs Bunion referred to turned out to be a new updated family tree, which lay on the table next to Aunt C's old one, which was opened out on the table like a nautical map, with lots of boxes and arrows on it.

'Mrs Bunion,' I asked carefully, toying with the family tree, 'do you happen to know if Aunt Coral and the Admiral are going to Knightsbridge to buy pastries?'

'Yes dear, it must be Harrods again because the Admiral is driving her in the Bentley,' replied Mrs Bunion.

'It's just that I haven't seen any evidence of pastries being brought back from London and into the house. I wondered if she might be going to visit that doctor?' I said.

'No, I expect it's because they will have been eating the pastries before they get home,' suggested Mrs Bunion helpfully.

I distracted myself by looking at the family trees after she left the room, somewhat reassured by her. I read over some of Jackie's notes:

Benedict's wife, Adelaide Garden, had two sons before Frittie (one a year after another), who both died in their infancy. They were christened, Augustin and Plato. Benedict's youngest brother Valentine Garden's letters state that Plato was called after the philosopher who believed that this world is not the real world, it is only a reflection of the better world that is to come.

They are buried in the church just on the other side of Clockhouse Lane. At that time Clockhouse Lane lay in a parish that used to be called Fern Common. This should be corroborated in Sue's book.

Copies of death certificates:

Augustin Garden   stillborn 1846
Plato Garden   b. 1847 – d. 1848, cause of death
                         unknown
Frederick 'Frittie' Garden b. 1850 – d. May 12 1861, cause of
                         death Fire

Adelaide went on to have one last child, after Frittie, a late daughter Carolina in 1875. Carolina survived to adulthood and went on to have three children herself – twin girls, Mercy and Veritay, and three years later Aunt Coral's father, Evelyn, in 1898, which brings us up to the present date.

Rose Anna's letter confirms that at the time London lived here, Adelaide had one surviving son called Frittie. He must have been nine years old by 1859 and tragically, according to the death certificate, it appears that by 1861 he had passed away.

I feel struck that I, here, now, in 1988, know that Frittie is going to die. It feels somewhat chilling, when I assume from my reading that he must have been the boy in the window whom London thought was a ghost.

Poor Adelaide was so concerned that Frittie would not live to see adulthood that she kept him locked up most of the time in the Old Nursery with a fleet of nurses and nannies. Though it's awful, I can understand it, when history tells me she had already lost two sons.

And everything, absolutely everything has a history, even Clockhouse Lane, even places like Croydon and Crawley. Even rooms within houses, even the dust within rooms.

FOR THE CONCERN OF THE RICH AND THE POOR

In the middle of the night a howling wind got up and Alfred leapt from his bed and rushed into the garden. I followed.

The late frosts had already destroyed every bud, and withered every climber, leaving the garden without any protection to divert the angry wind trapped screaming within its walls.

The gale tore up vegetables, uprooted their netting, overturned the arches for the runner beans and smashed the roses to the ground, and it swept the remaining fruits and flowers from the trees in a savage fury.

Alfred turned hither and thither in a state of total confusion. He tried to walk into the wind but could hardly move against the force.

'Leave it, Alfred! Leave it!' I cried out. 'We'll have to come back in the morning. We can't hold the fruits on the trees or keep the flowers on their stems.'

And as I stood there, yelling at the top of my lungs to try and make him see sense, a glass panel from the roof of the glasshouse blew out and shattered.

'Look out!' cried Alfred.

The next thing I remember is when I awoke, there was a lady watching over me.

'I'm so glad you're alive,' said the pale creature at my bedside.

'I am?' I said.

'We heard the wind, the shatter of glass, and looked out through our window. We saw you were carried in the arms of Mr Elms but he struggled to kick open the garden door, so we rushed around to pull it open from the outside.'

'Who are you?' I asked.

'I am your neighbour,' she said.

I drew a sharp intake of breath.

'You are here!' I said.

'You are right, I should have come and introduced myself sooner, I have become far too much of a recluse. I am the lady of the letters – my name is Rose Anna, as you know.'

'I've been longing to meet you!'

When she moved she rustled because the black crepe gown she wore was so stiff, and her every inch was shrouded in deep black, the colour of all spiritual darkness. On her bosom she wore a silver pin, shaped like an arrow and dove. She laid her soft, cool hand on my forehead just as a mother might, and I nearly died where I lay in my bed from the bliss. She was so beautiful, serious, calm and intense. And my prayer was offered immediately.

'Don't leave me,' I said.

She came often after that, fresh as a flower on a misty grave in gowns of less severe black, something she called 'slightening the mourning'. I hope I am not being presumptuous to say it, but I think I brought the sun out for her. And when she and Alfred and I all sat together and visited at his table, it felt as though they were a curious manifestation of my parents, each in love with their ghosts, but each happy for me to fill the void that was left by them. And I, fed on imaginings and reared on hope, consumed their love, like the starving child I was when I dreamt them up.

Sue

So London got his parents, not the Lawrence and Flora he imagined specifically, but the wonderful Alfred and Madam Rose Anna.

They say that nature abhors a vacuum, but unfortunately there has to *be* a vacuum before nature can fill it. The vacuum that mum left in my life has been filled by Aunt Coral, but it was a sudden and terrible gap and I wouldn't wish it on anybody. Amazing that London didn't actually meet Rose Anna for over a year, when she was living right next door to him ... talk about private!

But in some ways, these days, I actually feel worse about my mum, not better. Because much as I am getting more accustomed to her not being here any longer, at the same time I miss her more and more, because I haven't seen her for so long, and the two feelings run simultaneously and cancel each other out, or maybe I should say they negate each other, as Quiz might put it.

And all that I feel anyway is hidden away and private, it's unexpressed, which makes it all the more lonely.

I might be lucky and catch a glimpse of her, in the faces of

Johnny Look-at-the-Moon or Aunt Coral, but all that is left of Mum now is her image in my memory, and this is only accessible by me, a truly private view. Joe understands. He lost his dad when he was young, so he has a ghost with him too.

Tomorrow I expect I will go back to keeping it all hidden, but for now I want to indulge, to talk about her, think about her, remember her, and love her.

HISTORICAL FACTLET

Tornado: I looked this up in the encyclopaedia and apparently it is a phenomena that wind can get trapped between the walls of a walled garden and cause a tornado effect. This is why they grew climbers along the tops of the walls, to encourage the wind to skim off the top.

To quote Alfred in *For the Concern of the Rich and the Poor*, the same principal applies to the glasshouse. If you leave a window open, the wind can get *in* but it can't get *out*. Alfred says it took two panes of glass to blow out before he realized he was the master of his own disaster. (I must remember to tell Joe.)

Arrow and Dove pin: The arrow and dove pin that Victorians wore was symbolic of resurrection to Heaven. The arrow was the knife of heartbreak and the dove was the promise of a better world to come.

Sat June 4

Pensees: *Laugh a lot hoover a little.* SB

Dad rang long distance (from Denmark) this morning and told me that Pierre is doing very well. 'He is very content to sit under someone's legs and chew things,' said Dad, 'and he is trying to pull himself up with his stomach muscles, which of course he can't, yet.'

Apparently he still has a wobbly head as well, but that is normal for a baby his age. His legs however are a different story, they are sturdy and raring to go. Dad says one of his favourite pastimes is bouncing. (Pierre's that is.) It must be wonderful to be a baby, to be aware of nothing else other than that you want to *bounce*. There may be death and darkness on the one side of life, but on the other there is ridiculous light!

5pm

Joe came to collect me in the car this afternoon to go to the Lanterner. (He has the weekend off the pirates.) It was raining and all the gutters at Green Place were splashing with water, as were the roads. I got so carried away with romantic notions about us driving together . . . that I forgot a very regrettable factor. Because he is still a learner driver, his mother has to be sitting in the car.

So I got in the back of the little blue fiat, behind Mrs Fry, whom I deduced must have just come from the hairdressers, because the back of her head had been painted in fresh copper stripes.

She sat nervously in squeaky tan boots, with one hand on the hand brake and the other hand on the passenger door handle and gave jumpy instructions.

'Mirror signal manoeuvre, mirror signal manoeuvre, second gear, steady, mind the lady. Why are you driving so slowly?' she asked him.

'I'm driving at a romantic speed,' replied Joe.

He looked in his rearview mirror to smile at me and hit the kerb. Then he stalled, and they both got out of the car and for a moment I thought they were going to quarrel, but she ran around to the driver side with a carrier bag over her hair and Joe reluctantly came round to the passenger side and got in.

'The hub caps didn't even come *off*,' said Joe.

'I cannot sit with you until you have mastered the art of driving down the middle. You know very well that I'm a catastrophist,' said Mrs Fry.

She clipped on her seat belt and moved the car off with condescending proficiency.

'I don't know what you have been doing during your lessons,' she said.

'Trying to get my confidence back after you've been sitting with me,' replied Joe through gritted teeth. He finds it difficult to be disrespectful to his mother, it is just the way he is made.

When we got to the Lanterner, we went into the butler's pantry to get changed and Mrs Fry went off to do table plans, clacketing around the Lanterner importantly.

'She acts like she's in her own mini-series,' whispered Joe. 'We'd have been better on the bike,' he added dismally. 'I'll ask Icarus to ride it in, so we don't have to go home with her.'

'Definitely,' I said, putting my arm around him and offering a little respect.

'I'm so sorry your mum's so ... self-absorbed,' I said tactfully.

'I find it hard to forgive her sometimes,' said Joe.

'I know, forgiveness is a negotiation,' I replied.

'Who told you to say that?' asked Joe.

'How did you know I wasn't quoting myself?'

'I know you!' he answered. He has shockingly adept antennae. Of course it was something Quiz said about forgiveness, and I thought it was terribly clever. Naturally, I did not tell Joe that.

If I had been waiting downstairs at the Lanterner I might have had a chance to look at the big book of bookings and see that Table 10 tonight was booked out to the *Egham Echo*!

I hoped Gordoney George wouldn't recognize me, but when they arrived he looked at me in the way people do when they recognize you but can't quite place you.

I took a couple of deep breaths and went about my business on the gallery. Table 10 is right in the middle downstairs; it's *the* table to see and be seen at, and fortunately it is one of Posiedon's. Gordoney settled down with a dapper little man, with listening eyes and a perfumed coat.

They were joined by the whippet-thin girl with slippery hair from the interview. She has an absolutely crazy little bob almost up to her nose. She must have landed the job, because she was just so next level.

My heart sank when she arrived, and I hid behind a plate of food. It was a great relief when Quiz came in for his supper and sat at my table up in the gallery in his usual spot.

'Who is the man down in the middle who you keep looking at?' he asked when I served him his starter.

'He's the Features Editor at the *Echo*.'

'The man you met at your interview?'

'Yes, I'm not sure if he recognized me.'

'I'm sorry. That must be hard for you,' he said.

'I recognize the girl from my interview too. She must have got the job.'

'Damn her,' said Quiz. 'Well, if I were you I'd talk to your colleagues downstairs, find out who they all are and put some names to the faces.'

'But why, what's the point?' I said. 'I just want them to "gobble and go".'

'I've got an idea for you,' said Quiz.

'OK,' I said, intrigued. 'I'll ask Posiedon to do some digging.'

'Good girl,' he said, breaking a little bread into his olive oil and biting into it with fiendishly Hollywood teeth.

I put out a feeler to Posiedon, who gathered some information, and before dessert she filled me in at the back of the gallery, in front of Mrs Fry's hand-painted belanterned mural.

'The bald man is Rueben York,' she whispered. 'He is the *Echo*'s sub-editor. He ordered the pork and is a widower with three sons. The girl is Cinema Nixon. She is the intern and a rawist – she wouldn't eat anything on the menu, so Beniamino did her some nuts. And the man with the long hair is Gordoney, divorced with one dog. He had the sandwich. Oh and they were having an intelligent conversation about the miners' strike, if that's of any help,' she said.

'Good work!' I said.

I fed the information back to Quiz when I served him his gateaux.

'She's called Cinema Nixon,' I said. 'No wonder she got the job.'

'She's probably called something far more ordinary in real life,' said Quiz.

'Like Sue Bowl,' I said. 'And I wouldn't be able to contribute anything to a conversation about the miners' strike, because I'd be too ashamed to say I don't know anything about it.'

'I expect that's because you were up a tree at the time, weren't you darling?' said Quiz. 'Listen, why don't you be bold and submit an article with the editor's bill, prove that you're not just a scullion?' He winked at me with an inspirational wink that could have shorted the lights.

'But they rejected me, I'd feel too humiliated, and I haven't got anything with me.'

'But you'd be like a girl in a French film,' Quiz urged me. 'You're even set to music! Why don't you nip into the ladies and write something?'

'But that's insane!' I said.

'Nobody in the history of the world, sane or otherwise, ever got on by doing nothing.'

'But I'll need to get someone else to place it. I don't have the *nerve*.'

'Will Posiedon take a bribe?'

'She'd do it for a date,' I said. 'She's not interested in money.'

'I can bring her some students,' suggested Quiz.

'OK, you're on. I'll do it for you. Have you got pen and paper?'

I moved towards the ladies to try and write the speediest article ever.

For the attention of
Mr Gordoney George

THE SANDWICH
by Susannah Parkes

For as long as I can remember, the great moments in my life have been accompanied by a sandwich. Childhood beach holidays laying on a rug, tucked in a nook between the sand dunes, cheese sandwich nestling in foil at my side, slowly grilling in the sun. I can hear the tune of a boy patting his bucket with his spade as he makes a sandcastle, and smell the briny air and the windmills flying round against the placid roar of the sea.

And in more mundane times, I recall those sandwiches that had been left in my school bag all day were all the better for an added twist of satchel and books.

So a salute to sandwiches everywhere, from the special occasion baguette, to the dainty cucumber classic, to the polite bridge roll, to the exotic open sandwich, via the club sandwich and on to the humble bap. Voila the food of life! *Et viva, la pain de la vie*! Long live *le camping, le parking et aussi peut etre le sandwich*!

Susannah Parkes

Afterwards I slipped the article to Posiedon and asked her to place it under Gordoney's bill when requested. In return I promised Quiz would introduce her to some eligible students. She was only too happy to oblige.

At the end of the night, Posiedon rolled the cheese out and Beniamino swung out to do his rounds. 'Have a good next time,' he said to departing diners as they finished. I watched as Gordoney picked up his bill and put my article in his pocket. He looked around at the staff with amusement. His eye alighted on Posiedon and he winked.

After the *Echo* team left, Mrs Fry wearily turned the closed sign in the window. She went into her office to totty up the takings and I joined Quiz at his table for the briefest minute.

'I'm going now darling, do you want a lift?' asked Quiz, twiddling his car keys.

'It's OK, thank you, Joe is going to bring me back on the bike.' I waved to Joe from the gallery.

'Well, take care,' he said, arising. He kissed me on the lips in that way which is *almost* French, and when I returned downstairs I was not altogether surprised to find Joe looking put out.

We got changed in silence, and went out to find Joe's bike, where Icarus had left it at the roadside. Joe was stony-faced.

'Please tell me what's the matter?' I said. 'I know you're upset about something.'

'He kissed you,' replied Joe uncomfortably.

'That's just his way. Di does it too. It's French.'

'I know,' said Joe. 'And why is he in here on a Saturday anyway? Doesn't he *ever* go and see his girlfriend?'

'I think you're reacting out of proportion to what actually happened,' I said.

'Maybe,' he said, 'but I don't know. I look up to the gallery and I see you whispering with him. I get back from Sicily and . . . he *moves in* to Green Place, and you're *leaving notes* for each other over your homework, then he gives you *instructions* and you follow them. He's just so . . . relentlessly smart Alec. Why do you like him so much?'

'Why are you asking when it's clear you *don't* like him?' I rankled.

'I'm asking because I like you, and I know what's important to you,' said Joe.

I thought he'd finished but he piped up again.

'And why are you wearing that ridiculous coat?'

'It's not ridiculous.'

'It's June.'

He stopped talking again for a moment and all of a sudden seemed panicked.

'You can't wear that on the bike Sue, it'll get caught up.'

'Well can't I tuck it under?'

'It's so long on you, it'll be dangerous,' said Joe.

'Toot toot,' said Quiz, pulling up in his car. 'Is there a problem?'

'No,' said Joe.

'Yes,' I said simultaneously. 'I can't wear my coat on the bike. I'll have to take it off and I might be chilly.'

'Well hop in the car and I'll drive you back to Green Place,' said Quiz.

The night was dark and starry and Quiz's engine was running. I could not choose what to do. Whatever decision I made was going to be a fraught one.

'It's just so huge on you,' said Joe eventually. 'You better go in the car and I'll follow on the bike.'

'Come on then, hop in,' said Quiz, revving his engine.

I felt like a different person when I got into Quiz's car. Maybe it's because I don't really belong there. Or rather, perhaps, it's just that it felt a bit like trying on a different life. Di's life, of fast cars and books and fashion; a life of art and classicists and libraries and confidence, and brilliant men friends who like living life off piste.

In the wing mirror, I caught sight of Joe following on the bike behind us, like a shadow. Quiz put on the Acker Bilk and we drove home.

> **Word List**
> *Scullion*
> *Destiny*

FOR THE CONCERN OF THE RICH AND THE POOR

Standing under an elder tree on Midsummer's Eve is said to guarantee a sighting of fairies. So, when Alfred and Sowerbutt went to light fires in the fields, to ward off evil on the day when the earth turns her back on the sun, I went into Alfred's wood in the hopes I would catch a flicker of the winged creatures.

Alfred's wood was a secret pass I had thought only frequented by gardeners. But I was not alone for soon I heard the snap of a twig behind me and, turning, I was shocked to see the boy I had seen so often at the window of the big house.

'Shhh!' he urged me urgently. 'Please don't betray me.'

'I won't,' I said, trying to reassure him, for he was so nervous that he jumped every time there was a rustle in the trees. I wondered if he wasn't a ghost then he might have been a fairy. He was so pale and luminous his skin glowed. And he gulped his words out amidst gasps and hiccups and a fearful shivery little stammer.

'The air out here is so sweet and light,' he said, and he sat down for a moment – no, not sat, I recall, he almost fell.

'What is your name?' I asked.

'I'm Frittie, and you?'

'London.'

'I've never heard of a London.' He shivered. 'I'm cold,' he said.

'On a warm summer's evening?' I asked him.

'It's the first time I've been out in a while, I'm n . . . not used to it,' he said.

I offered him my waistcoat which he accepted with grace. He looked small and porridgy in it, as if instead of flesh he were made out of steam, and though we must have both been about nine or ten, my waistcoat looked more like an adult's on him. As he spoke I noticed in between his hiccups and gulps that he had a vibrant chuckle that got out occasionally and I thought if he was given the chance he'd make a spirited little fellow.

So I asked him where he was going and how he got out of the big house. He seemed strangely relieved that I knew all about him.

'I got out of the nursery under the skirts of Fat Nanny,' he puffed. 'I remained under her dress, walking like a crab, without making contact with her, so as she'd notice. She wears a stiff petticoat, with bones the same as mine, so it wasn't that difficult.'

'But how did you get out from under her dress without being spotted?' I asked him.

'That was easy,' the boy replied. 'When I could smell she was in the kitchen, I crept out from under her dress and slipped away into the servants' tunnel and ran deep into the depths of the garden. It's a plan I have had months in the making. Fat Nanny always goes for her supper in the kitchen at the same time, and she stays for a moment alone there.'

'That's very clever, I am full of admiration and respect,' I said. 'I've seen you at your window often this past year. I began to wonder if you ever got out. But how did you get under her skirts without her knowing?' I exclaimed. Naturally escapology was, and still is, a subject very close to my heart.

'The difficulty I had was in tricking her into believing

I was in my bed in the Old Nursery. But it wasn't me she said goodnight to, it was a pile of my pillows and clothes. I crept out of bed and swapped myself for my double while her back was turned. I have been building my courage to try it.'

'But won't they be wondering where you are? Hadn't you best get back?' I asked him.

'I'm not going back,' he said.

Sue

Aunt Coral's To Do
Decanter
Dry Biscuits
Blue tac.

Something seems different about Aunt Coral's To Do, but I can't put my finger on what.

PART FOUR

Rum for a Pony

I Coral Elizabeth Garden of Green Place, Clockhouse Lane, Egham, being of sound mind, do bequeath all my estate both real and personal, and all my worldly goods, and any residue remaining from my estate after debtors and funeral expenses, to my great niece Miss Susan Olivia Bowl of Green Place, Clockhouse Lane, Egham, absolutely. This is my last will and testament and revokes all former wills. The term 'my estate' to include any chattel or item discovered on, or under, my property, clearly delineated in the attached plans.

I appoint as my executor Miss Delia Shoot of Eaglehurst Hall, Aberdeenshire.

Signed in the Presence of Rear Admiral Avery John Little of Green Place, Clockhouse Lane, Egham, on this day, May 30th, Nineteen Hundred and Eighty Eight.

Sue

The reading of Aunt Coral's will took place at the offices of Mr Perry in Knightsbridge at 4.30pm yesterday. The will is being kept in a strong room there, and she has been making trips up to town to finesse it. Finally, the 4.30 Knightsbridge piece of the jigsaw fell into place.

There is absolutely nothing wrong with Aunt Coral, she has assured me. She explained that it was Admiral Ted's sudden passing that prompted her into action, because he was a man of a similar age.

Yesterday began when Aunt C asked me if I'd like to go to London with herself and the Admiral. Her suggestion was tea at the Ritz.

I had absolutely no idea that it was a rouse until we arrived at her solicitor's. It was a total *shock*. In fact I've had no suspicions at all, because I'd stopped seeing Make Will on her To Do list a long time ago. Make Will has remained at the top of the To Do ever since I arrived at Green Place in 1987, and I believe it was there many years before that.

We were seated on solicitoresque furnishings opposite Mr

Perry the solicitor's desk. The Admiral got out a bottle of champagne and three glasses he'd brought with him in his dilly bag, and he popped the cork and poured out. And then Aunt Coral took my hand in hers and composed herself to speak.

'All this time I feel that I have been waiting for the right person to hand on the baton to,' she said.

There was a profound hush. I felt choked.

'I feel so unprepared for this moment,' I said.

'But what I am leading to,' she continued, 'is a thing for which I am lost for words, and so in place of them I would like to raise a toast . . . to my heiress.'

'To Sue,' said the Admiral respectfully and then Mr Perry stepped into the room and bowed his head.

Well, that was me in pieces for the rest of the afternoon. Sometimes I wish Aunt Coral were more pedestrian. This was the handing over of her baton. And I take it with open arms.

Mr Perry, a portly gent of a certain age, tiptoed solemnly across the deep blue carpet to join us. I noticed he was wearing slippers. I thought perhaps it was a professional decision he'd made in order to be reverend and discreet.

He sat at his desk and with great clarity he read out Aunt Coral's will. I couldn't contain a small gasp when he mentioned Aunt Coral's 'funeral expenses' and when he got to the phrase about her leaving everything 'to my great niece Miss Susan Olivia Bowl absolutely', I whispered, 'You have *already* given me everything absolutely.'

The formality of the will was followed by a reading of a long catalogue, on which are listed all Aunt Coral's antiques, bank accounts, shareholdings, rainy-day sticks and stones – and finally, overshadowing debtors. There is a little caveat Aunt C has recently added, that anything found on or under the boundaries of Green

Place, is to be considered my property too. This is in the event that Aunt Coral agrees to a dig.

And in true Aunt Coralian style, there was one final bitter-sweet coda to the proceedings, when she asked the Admiral if he wouldn't mind leaving the room. I felt some trepidation as to what was coming next, but was very soon relieved to learn the content of her special request. Aunt Coral normally lies about her age by three years (in truth she is sixty-eight, but I have no guarantee she's isn't fibbing), but whatever the truth, she just wanted to make sure that the same timeline applies to her headstone. I don't believe there are any lengths she won't go to, in trying to retain her mystique.

After we got back from Knightsbridge, we had more champagne in the drawing room and the Admiral congratulated me warmly.

'You'll have rum for a pony here,' he said.

'Is that what you give them traditionally?' I asked.

'No, "room", not "rum",' he laughed. 'It's what agents might say on their particulars.'

Later, I went up with Aunt Coral to her suite, to find a small private moment alone with her. The sight of her sitting at her dressing table putting her hairpins into their porcelain pot made me feel choked.

For I don't think I will ever get to grips with the vanishing of people. I want to hang on to everybody, nail them to me, so that they can't disappear into the mist.

I sat beside her at her dressing table and talked to her reflection in the mirror.

'Thank you so much,' I said, 'but I don't know what I would ever do without you.'

'Precious treasure,' she replied gently.

But before I could slip into that little dark place, where my sorrows and losses fester, Aunt Coral managed to lift the mood again by telling me that porcelain is very overlooked.

Before turning in, I rang Joe to tell him the news. (He's been away all day at Addlestone.) He said he felt overwhelmed. We agreed such moments in life are of a peculiarly reverend tragedy. I don't know how I'm ever going to begin to deserve such a very great honour.

Weds June 8 1988

'Dzjennia A Puluchayer Shans'

OR 'JENNY GETS A CHANCE'
by Sue Bowl

(part two for Quiz notes)
Monday morning and the torrents of rain that fell on the street overnight, had reactivated all of the ca-ca in the bird-poo, made it seeping and green again. Oh, it was such a mess. Jenny was late into the office because of the traffic on the Ulrika Strasse. One of the problems of living in a small bed-sit outside Brune.

At the office Sabrina addressed Maxim pertly, 'Draw that poof there near to the fire and let us begin,' she said. 'Put something like Mon 5th at the busy Moscow

paper *Fthor-Neek Gazeta*, so called
because it came out on a Tuesday,'
dictated Sabrina. She looked so cool and
crisp in her dauphinois mint floatey tea
dress.

And upon her entrance, she disdainfully
passed the late Jenny some paperwork,
which she dully filed.

'Sorry I'm late Sabrina,' said Jenny.

'Businesses don't run themselves,' she
replied tersely.

Tough Cookie Editor Sabrina Weston
Fair was not known to tolerate lateness!

Maxim would read out his eulogy on
the wet garden, Jenny would not get the
chance. He began:

'The silver wet grass in the morning
is drenched with pearly dew. Autumn came
in overnight, born on a storm that swept
the sorrow in with it. Now the dusty
heads of the time flowers will not
withstand the dying breaths of an old
man. All glory for the fecund gorse, that
peach scents the Moscow fog.'

Part Two notes for Sue from Quiz:

1 The Ulrika Strasse?
2 Brune? Might this be an opportunity for one of your
atmospheric gobbled-gook words? Something that evokes old
Russia?

3 An English Lady Editor? (Wasn't she the one who likes salad?)

4 Do they have an open fire in their office?

5 Do you mean it was a diaphanous mint tea dress, meaning it was see-through? Dauphinois is a type of potato. Perhaps Sabrina should be more unkempt? Maybe a smoker?
A lack of grooming perhaps? Very Russian.

6 Duly filed.

7 The late Jenny, is she dead?

8 Gorse is not often found in cities. Maybe some fog? Or what about Pushkin's Moscow spires? Or some culinary gloom?

9 Why don't you come up to my suite after you finish work tomorrow and we can collaborate. I heard your good news and I wanted to offer my congratulations.
X Quiz

(Rewrite for Quiz notes)

'Dzjennia A Puluchayer Shans'

OR 'JENNY GETS A CHANCE'
by Sue Bowl

Monday morning and the torrents of rain that fell on the street overnight had reactivated all of the ca-ca in the bird poo. Made it seeping and green again. Oh it was such a mess. Jenny was late for the *Fthor-Neek* because of the traffic on Ul Natalia. One of the problems of living in a bed-sit beyond the border out at Rimtalyikikirikov.

At the office Sabrina addressed Maxim pertly. 'Draw up that chair and let us begin,' she said. 'Keep on your coat if you're cold. Now put something like Mon 5th at the busy Moscow paper *Fthor-Neek Gazeta*, so called because it comes out on a Tuesday,' dictated Sabrina. She looked strained, she drew on her reefa and ran her hands through her tumbling dank hair.

And on her entrance she disdainfully she handed Jenny some paperwork, which she duly filed.

'Sorry I'm late Sabrina,' said Jenny.

'Businesses don't run themselves,' she replied tersely.

Tough Cookie Editor Sabrina Weston Fair was not one to tolerate lateness!

Maxim would read out his eulogy on the wet garden, Jenny would not get the chance. He began:

The silver wet grass in the morning is drenched with pearly dew. The Autumn came in overnight, born on a storm that swept the sorrow in with it. Now the dusty heads of the time flowers will not withstand the dying breaths of an old man.

All glory to the fecund fog that curls round these Moscow Spires.

Thanks Quiz and hope to see you tomorrow.

With my love from

Sue X

Word List

Culinary gloom.

Diaphanous

Thurs June 9

Meanwhile in a nursery somewhere in Titford,

newly back from Denmark

Pierre chews his blanket. I spent a few hours with him this afternoon on a light visit from Egham. He is going through a phase of pinching noses – he is a delight and has earned himself the title Naughty Pierre. Funny he might one day grow up to become an accountant, play squash, live in Wimbledon, give up nose pinching and conform. I was just imagining what I'd put on Pierre's first ever CV: bouncing, gurgling, looking, chewing his toe.

He is now almost three months old, he can smile and hold his head up. He has a complete ring of hair in a line around his head. Dad calls him Friar Tuck.

Dad and Ivana are doing well, and Pierre is suffering no ill effects of his prematurity other than the fact that the paediatrician thinks he is certain to need strong glasses, but we'll have to wait and see. They are looking into a curious sideways look that Pierre often gives, as though he finds you very suspicious. The doctors say it's likely just because babies have to learn how to use their eyes, as well as try and make sense of what they are looking at, so it's possibly just Pierre's baby bewilderment.

Pensees: *Life is short, eat your dessert first.* SB

I went to Quiz's suite to collaborate last night. I did feel like perhaps I shouldn't, but I rang Joe first thing this morning to check he was all right.

Though, as absolutely nothing inappropriate took place, I can't really explain why I did that.

When I got up to Snowdrop, Quiz had candles going and soft music playing and his suite was an intelligent mess. We did some work on Jenny and then had a brilliant talk.

You know how things go in a talk when you're moving seamlessly from subject to subject. We covered philosophy, history, mermaids, the East India Company, if we believed in a soul. Quiz was telling about 'the Shamans' who believe that when you go through trauma in your life, a bit of your soul can detach itself and run away because it feels too sad to go on. That's why in this philosophy it is believed that many people feel like they are searching for themselves. But a Shaman can enter into the spiritual realm and go and retrieve those lost parts of the soul and bring them back to the person who has lost them. This can be done while a person is dreaming.

This idea has seemed to unlock something, because I thought I knew who I was before mum died, but I only knew who I was in relation to her. And when my anchor went, it was as though I went spinning off into infinity with her, and then splintered off into little bits searching for who I was before it happened. Maybe I left part of my soul behind and I need someone to go and get it for me.

Word List
In fera dig
Potemkin Village
Raskolnikov
Oblamov by Goncharov.
Punt. (This is Latin for full stop.)

Sun June 12, 2.00am

Pensees: *Old Money means it has now run out.* SB

Of course, as is the way of things in this life, becoming an heiress is a wonderful thing but it doesn't come without baggage. The foremost concern being how on earth will I fund Green Place, when day to day I live hand to mouth. Aunt Coral says she would never ever blame me, and she would totally understand if I chose to sell. The problem is it would break my heart to do that, because Green Place is a magical place of sanctuary and leaving is unimaginable.

Joe suggested I write down my concerns so we can begin to chip away at them together. He said it always helps me when I pour something out on paper and he is absolutely right.

The last thing I want to sound is ungrateful for the very many blessings in my life, but my major concerns are that I, the prospective Chatelaine of Green Place (a 16-bedroom Queen Anne Mansion) currently have savings of £4.11. It's unlikely I will be able to support such a house from my earnings as a waitress and as for my prospects, at the moment, they are rather few. So if I can't end up selling some of my work somehow, the only way I'll be able to manage is if I find a valuable family heirloom knocking around the house. In short, I feel as fiscally capable as one of the mice in the pipes.

Sun June 12 6am

I took this extract up in the Old Nursery early this morning, and the Old Nursery is the sort of room where you enter and feel like someone is watching you. But it isn't a bad watchfulness, it is more of a searching. I think Green Place might have a little ghost.

I sat by the window to write this, where the little boy Frittie must have sat.

FOR THE CONCERN OF THE RICH AND THE POOR

I felt it incumbent on me to persuade Frittie that he would be better off waiting until he was older before running away. He didn't take much persuasion. The lightest shower of summer rain was enough to turn him blue with shivers and that night he made his way back to the big house, via his secret entrance, and engineered somehow his way back to his gilded cage.

I saw him many times after that; whenever he could make an escape he came. The adult residents of Roselyne and Edenthorpe knew about his visits, and Walderon sometimes baked for him. As a result he grew chubbier, and his pallor diminished. Over the following two years, between 1859 and 1861, he became an expert at getting out and the tunnel became like his own private exit and entrance.

He employed a trusted ally in the tweenie (between-stairs maid), who covered occasionally for his absence, and in this way he got to see the owl walk and sit in the garden without ruffling his mother's feathers. Once he even took a siesta under the tickling sweeps of a willow and went away very content.

I showed him my room at Edenthorpe. He asked where were all my toys! So I showed him my niner, and he was so taken with it, that we found him a conker and he carved it with his initials, FEG: Frederick Edmund Garden.

Two years passed and at the cottages we became like a tribe, or a family: the widow, the old habit, the gardener, and the boy.

Some nights I woke up to the sound of fierce banging on the door of Roselyne, but try as he would Master Benedict could not get Madam Rose Anna to reveal the hiding place of her treasure . . . and by 1861 he had given up. She obliged him to find another way to pay for his extravagance by making small economies, such as cutting his members of male staff (because he couldn't afford their taxes).

Two years passed, my legs grew longer, or my breeches shorter, and my voice dropped into my boots. I grew stouter and sturdier and pounds heavier, due to Walderon's old habit of cooking! I got a farmer's tan. My hair darkened and thickened, my bald patch grew in, my ringlets were lost forever, which caused weeping from Madam Rose Anna, and she begged that she may cut and keep a lock of my hair for posterity. Alfred believed that she was lonely for her own children and so found great happiness in my company.

She flourished, dressed in less morbid fabrics, with perhaps a little more jewellery or sheen to her cloth. She laid aside her weeping veil, and eventually even dispensed with her weeper's cuffs (the long garments so particular to her unique identity).

Two years passed, and if my schoolwork suffered, I received an education in the garden. 'Save the soot from the chimneys, onions love it, maggots don't' . . . 'spray the roses with a little arsenic and water, or the ticket collectors will come' (caterpillars) . . . 'The privy contents make an excellent fertilizer and the parsnips will love your bath water' . . . Alfred had a trick for everything and everyone in his care! In the summer he smelt of sunshine, and in winter he smelt of frost.

He worked like a Trojan, in spite of the development of a particularly loathsome and persistent cough. In my memory I have pictures of Alfred out there in every season, plagued at times by his coughing fits. He thought it was probably as a result of being out all day in the dampness – England is a very damp country.

But toil he did through the passing seasons of 1859 and 1860 . . . I remember him amongst the white heads of the snowdrops like the silent bells of mid-winter, or tending to lawns peppered with silver lilac crocuses in the spring, or digging before a palace of hawthorns, his tools strewn with a scattering of magnolia petals. Each summer began when the feather-light fins of the sycamore lit up in the sunset and ended when the fins turned to sails and spun down to their autumn rest. And when the earth turned to face the winter, I turned for dreaming to the India in Madam Rose Anna's books.

Alfred planted an Indian Tuberose under the south wall in the garden, in honour of my abiding passion. And late in each August it materialized into incomparable flowers.

I told him that their mere presence brought to my senses the strong notion of my dream land, and that they transformed every grey squirrel that spied on me into an extravagant lizard. Alfred explained that the distant hills we could see at the back of the garden told tales of their grandfather hills, the Himalayas. He suggested I refer to one of my picture books to see if I could spot a likeness and I scoured the pages for the proof.

But in the silent part of each night that fell in those years between 1859 and 1861, I lay like a professor amongst the seedlings, and I still remembered Harry Benson, 'Cheeser'. He was the reason I came to be here, he lit the fire in me. I wondered where he was, and if perhaps by now he had many champion conkers in his gallery.

On Sundays I wore the niner round my neck, but otherwise it lay in my drawer like a symbol of courage. I hadn't lost sight of the plan to return it to him, though it seemed more of a distant chance.

Sue

This morning Aunt C left a note from Jackie County out on the table in the White Room:

> I found a police report from December 1860 stating that a thief had been spotted pilfering cuttings from the walled garden in the small hours of the night. Please see below a statement that was signed by the butler Mr Edgehill. The pilfering of cuttings was considered a criminal offence, though the thief remained unidentified.
>
> Jackie

I wonder if it might have been Frittie? He first met London in 1859; maybe he sneaked down to the garden at night? But if the garden was kept locked, surely the thief must have *known* where to find the key?

Aunt C sloped off after breakfast for what she said was an urgent appointment with the Admiral, but actually I now know it was with Glenn Miller the builder. Because I found out from Mrs

Bunion that she has commissioned Glenn to build an *Orangery* at the back of the morning room.

The morning room is a large, sunny sitting room rarely ever used, nestling first left off the hall. Sometimes Mrs Bunion puts the post in there, by way of giving it a function. (Therefore it is occasionally referred to as the Post Office.)

To fund the Orangery Aunt C says she is using a small donation Admiral Ted kindly left her in his will. Her vision for his legacy is that the Orangery will act as a sort of look-out over the walled garden, because its position overlooks the meadows with a sweeping view out to the ruins. She woke up with the idea as a welcome-home for Delia, who will be arriving in July, and Glenn is already on board.

I had thought that Aunt Coral has been trying to reign in her spending, but she says that the Orangery is something she has always wanted. And it's so good to see her thriving with perfect health, I don't want to rain on her parade.

On the other hand, there are so many rooms not in use at Green Place and she goes and builds another one. Yet I know in her own peculiar way she is at least *conscious* of pulling in her belt.

I can just see them all in the Orangery – the Admiral in a smoking jacket, Aunt C and Delia adjusting their turbans, Admiral Gordon in a paisley dressing gown, while a young red-headed man with a squint plays the piano for them during drinks.

Perhaps Quiz will join them occasionally, flanked by the Nanas. Perhaps it's not such a bad idea!

FOR THE CONCERN OF THE RICH AND THE POOR

One evening in the first month of 1861 I was just about to lock up the garden for Alfred when I noticed Madam Rose Anna at the end of the apple arch. Occasionally she wandered alone in the garden, I think it gave her solace, yet it was odd to see her there so late.

'Hello, I'm about to lock up,' I said. 'Would you like me to wait?'

'No, no, I . . .' she hesitated. 'I was worried, I feel I must tell you, because last night I saw Alfred in the garden after midnight, and I was concerned that he will be punished if he gets caught taking cuttings,' she said.

I was a little stricken, but I trusted I could confide in her.

'He has had to start moonlighting in the sale of clippings, because it is the only way he can afford to buy some medicine he needs,' I said.

'What does he need medicine for?'

'His cough,' I said.

'Has it got worse?' she asked.

'Much worse,' I replied.

'Has he seen a doctor?'

'No,' I replied, 'not yet.'

'Then he should see Doctor Marshall at once, there is no sense in waiting. If Edmund had seen him sooner, he might have still been alive today.'

'Was it very quick?'

'Very,' she said. 'He left it much too late . . .' She began to tell the story she had told me many times before, but each time in the telling it grew shorter and easier to bear.

'I was so happy when he asked me to marry him. He was so very kind to me. I had long given myself up as an old maid,' she said. 'I thought that at last my life was come, but for me there was only a year between bride and widow.'

'I'm very sorry. Truly,' I said.

After locking up I returned the key to its hiding place in a hollow inside the trunk of the old oak tree, thrusting my hand down inside it into the insecty darkness.

'You're very brave,' said Rose Anna. 'What a good hiding place.'

Good grief, I am slightly ahead of the story again! Of course it was *Alfred* who was the thief who was spotted on Mr Edgehill's statement. Who else could it have been?

But the *first* thing I did after reading this was not to read on, but to go and see if I could find the old oak tree by the walled garden, to see if the key to the garden door was still in the same hollow. AND IT WAS!!

I ran to get Aunt C and the Admiral and we tried it in the lock. The old door creaked and swung open and a hundred moths flew out from where they had been hiding between the door and the frame.

After locking and unlocking it and opening and closing the door a few times, we decided to return the key to the hollow, as a homage to the past. There is something sacred about finding something that somebody left a century ago. We are walking on the same ground as London and Alfred, and we are using the same key, and maybe London was the last person to touch it. In this way, he might have *passed* it to me!

But suddenly Aunt Coral had a change of colour, and without further explanation bolted off up to Green Place to get the mini hover.

She returned to the oak tree a short while later and vacuumed inside the hollow, to see if she could suck up the Star of the South. And when she'd finished, she emptied the contents of the hoover bag and we dissected them. But all that was there was one dead spider, one stag beetle and one half of a pine cone.

But as a result of this rush of excitement Aunt Coral telephoned Jackie and told her she may now approach the matter of digging, softly, softly.

Pensees: *A true lady-killer has a devil-may-care attitude, even in fancy dress.* SB

Joe arrived for a late supper as we planned, straight from Treasure Island. He looked ridiculously rugged in his costume, moody and tanned and frisky.

It must have been top of Aunt C's To Do to seek Joe out, because after her routine cocktails with the Admiral, she postponed their supper and came and joined me and Joe in the conservatory, where I'd prepared a light-hearted picnic.

She tottered in and perched beside Joe on the rattan sofa. She'd clearly picked up the wrong eye pencil this evening because she had blue eyebrows.

'Dear Joe,' she said tenderly, 'you do look sweet in your little costume.'

'I'm not sure if that's a compliment?' said Joe.

'Dear Joe,' she began again (she gets very fond when she's tipsy), 'I won't keep you long because I know how much you and Sue love to be alone,' (she also gets frank) 'but I have been thinking, long and hard, and I have a proposal for you, something that I'd like you to think about.' (She also feels the need to explain what obvious things mean.)

She padded over to the side of the conservatory, stood at the doors and, pulling her cardigan around her, looked down towards the old garden.

'It would be so nice to restore it,' she said. 'Just imagine how beautiful it would be. But Badger keeps cancelling me, he is so very unreliable . . . I wonder, do you think that you'd have any space in your busy schedule?'

She swept some wisps of her hair back and smudged her blue eyebrows across her forehead in the process. And then she returned to spoon with the Admiral, looking like Picasso had stamped on her face.

Late Pensees on Sunday's events:

When I look back over what I have written today, it makes me believe that some days really are longer than others. This morning feels like it was three days ago. I think this is because it has been such a prodigious day, what with hoovering the trees and what have you.

It says in *For the Concern of the Rich and the Poor* that 'many berries make a hard winter'. Alfred the gardener is just full of little factlets like this. London talks about his hard-working hands and says that his fingers clicked when he splayed out his hands and also that he used to bless the good earth under his nails. There is something about gardeners. (Well for me there is!)

I must remember to tell Joe about the berries as I'm sure he would find it pertinent. Sadly he had to go home tonight, though he did stay till late. He had a driving lesson at the crack of dawn in the morning with one of his male relatives from Staines and he is immensely stressed about anyone seeing him.

Tues June 14th

Pensees: *And on the menu tonight we have a choice of gratinated pies.* SB

Joe swung into action straight away and has already lined up rows of Hessian gardening bags to fill up with weeds. He reckons it will take him the best part of 18 months to get the life of the garden going again and all properly reinstated and several weeks to clear it at first.

Joe seems the same sort of person as Alfred and I have come to the conclusion that the most attractive quality in a man is not big biceps or rogue looks, or even a tously fringe, but kindness. Or maybe I am just a little needy.

Joe started fisselling in the garden this morning almost as soon as it was light. And at breakfast he came in to show us a flower he found called Town Clock. It has four square faces, so obviously that's how it got its name. I read about Town Clock growing in the old garden under the shade of the sundial. London Taylor says that Alfred planted them there as a homage to the passing of time, and here they are 125 years or so later at our breakfast table, tick tock tick tock.

After the Lanterner last night we nipped to a little place Joe knows called the Double Shot and had one of those amazing interesting chats where everything is fascinating and there are no awkward or dull bits, just like the one I had with Quiz. It occurs to me that maybe I am the common denominator, because maybe I just love talking.

Aunt Coral's To Do

Carpenter

Asda

Argos

Sue

Since the night of the sandwich article back at the end of last month, I have had the most lovely day morphia. The days seem to melt together, so that I can't tell one from another and life has been spectacularly routined. I work at the Bistro, I work on my dissertation, 'Jenny Gets a Chance', I potter and pensee.

When I open the window in the morning, I can smell – rather, I inhale the scent of – the warm bark and the sap rising in the trees as they lean and buckle under the weight of their branches, stretching up aching for the sun and the rain. No, perhaps I shouldn't say aching, although it is definitely the way they appear to me, but the more Russian way of putting it would be . . . stretching up, for the touch of the sun and the rain? No, that sounds almost more Victorian . . . no, reaching for the sun and the rain . . . no, just plain reaching.

The wisteria on the front walls of Green Place is so full and leafy, it is like scaffolding. If I look up from underneath it looks like a green and lilac parachute filled up with air, so fulsome and powerful that it might lift the house away from the ground and take it flying.

Right at this moment there are two tall trees to the left of the ruins that blow together in the wind; they look like they're kissing.

And talking of kissing, at work it is Quiz that has set our lives to music. He comes into the Lanterner at least once a week, and as a result I have submitted two more articles to Gordoney.

The second one was inspired by a conversation I overheard between Aunt Coral and the Admiral. He was complaining about the council's lack of attention to the Clockhouse pothole, in spite of his letters and petition. Aunt Coral said she agreed it was frustrating but sadly inevitable in a world where ninety-nine per cent of people are morons.

I felt her comment had great potential for an article on how we see strangers, i.e.: 'Ninety-nine per cent of people are morons, is that a bit harsh?'

Nothing back from Gordoney so far, but Quiz says I must show tenacity.

He has even inspired Mrs Fry, who, as a result of feeling mortified over Quiz's being served with a bottle of corked wine, has decided to send Joe on a sommelier course in France in a couple of weeks' time. This will interfere with his restoration project, but she's insisting he learns more expertise and has lots of strings to his bow.

They have a strange relationship, Joe and his mum, and I can see that in the best possible way she is a bad influence on him. As for Joe, on the one hand I'd say he hates his mother, but on the other I'd say he loves her more than anything else. I know this because he is allowed to be horrible about her but he doesn't like anyone else being. Relationships are never easy.

Joe and Aunt Coral have agreed on terms of £120 per week for his restoration project. He will work from Monday mornings to

Fridays at noon, with Friday afternoons off to go to his other client and Saturdays and Sundays with the pirates. The Admiral has offered to front up Joe's wages as *his* legacy to Green Place. (Now that Admiral Ted has given one, there seems a little gentle competition.) But these days I'm pleased that Aunt C is at least trying to eek out her rents and live on donations from friends like a real society lady. She hasn't bought a handbag this year, as far as I know, and her To Do list shows Argos and Asda as opposed to Harrods and Waitrose.

The first thing Joe has done for the garden was to get a stone mason to come and give his opinion on whether the old bricks from the walls were recyclable. Passable bricks can be sent to a heated warehouse to be baked dry and have their edges cut and made flush.

Added to which he has decided he will need to hire a tractor, so he can churn up the two acres of soil. Imagine London and Alfred doing that with a horse and plough!

Joe says he wants his design to be 'gardenesque'. He is currently trying to come up with a centrepiece to be built around the sundial that will incorporate somewhere to sit. So that when Aunt Coral eventually gets to sit in the garden and everything is growing round her, she will be blown away by the *pleasure*.

FOR THE CONCERN OF THE RICH AND THE POOR

Alfred went downhill so quickly, it was devastating to see. Doctor Marshall diagnosed him with something he thought was akin to potter's rot; he did not think it was consumption. This was in spite of the fact that coughing and fever consumed much of his body in the same way.

'I believe Alfred's difficulty in swallowing and breathing is likely due to inhaling particles of soil or perhaps smoke from his bonfires,' said the Doctor, 'as with a potter at the wheel who inhales so much dust from the clay.'

'Then that sounds encouraging?' said Madam Rose Anna.

'It may be,' said Doctor Marshall. 'But you should prepare yourselves, because we have no way of knowing how much damage there is to the poor fellow's lungs.'

When Master Benedict learnt of Alfred's incapacity we were promptly evicted from Edenthorpe. He did not seek out a new gardener, but put the task on to Sowerbutt's shoulders to save money. For all the residents of Green Place cared, Alfred, sick as he was, could end his days in the workhouse. But Madam Rose Anna stepped in and Alfred took up residence on a daybed downstairs at Roselyne, unbeknownst to the residents of the big house, at least for some time. And I stayed close by his side and ever nearer to my dear widow.

Walderon nursed him tenderly, making him hearty soups and tonics to coat his dry throat. Sowerbutt came to visit and brought him a case of wine. 'Compliments of the butler, Mr Edgehill,' he said.

Alfred kept working in the garden; he just could not bear to be parted from it. He used to sneak out behind the Madams' backs to tend to the roses, or propagate the pineapples . . . and though he coughed and spluttered, his spirits soared the minute he got out into the air.

> **Word List**
> *Potter's rot*
> *Propagate*

Sue

Thurs 16 June 1988, early am

Aunt Coral's Great Grandfather Benedict comes across as a terrible gambler and a show-off in my book. And so cruel to Alfred, because he didn't employ an under-gardener, in order to save money, and then he wasted all he had gambling.

Alfred was paid a pittance for his toil which never ceased. Small wonder he got ill and awful that when he did he was *evicted*.

4.00pm

Jackie's team of archaeological experts arrived at midday to have a scratch around in the grounds, following Aunt C's go-ahead. They were here all afternoon with their cameras. Two men stood in green suits around a small hole at the side of Green Place. They were hovering over a prong-type thing, at the walled garden end of the tunnel, which they had put down into a cavity. And an area of about one foot is now cordoned off with bright yellow tape.

They targetted this spot because after talks with the Admiral, Aunt Coral concluded that it would be best to start looking for the Shipwreck necklace further *away* from the house, so as not to upset any bulbs.

They worked meticulously and also made an intensive search of the formal gardens at the top of the drive, but so far they haven't found anything interesting, other than those bits of broken china people seem to leave behind in the earth. I believe that there must have been many picnics and many quarrels in these gardens over the years and down the generations.

Friday June 17, 7.30am

Mrs Fry actually went away for a night to a health spa, which is unheard of, so I went to stay with Joe at Lanterner Street after work tonight. It was like having our own place, apart from Icarus and Joe's little sister Mary-Margaret being at home.

Everyone was very relieved Mrs Fry was away. Mary-Margaret didn't go to bed till midnight and Icarus watched rubbish telly.

I wrote another article for Gordoney while I was at the flat, about the passing of time. It was inspired when I woke to a peaceful morning as I looked down over the dark summer streets.

At Green Place you forget what it's like to live somewhere normal. Joe's windows look out on to the opposite houses, in a tree-lined quiet road . . . at least it's quiet at such a time before the world is awake, before lamps begin to pop on in the windows, before gradually people surface, come out of their houses and walk down the road to work, as though they are attached by strings to a giant musical box. Open the lid, the clock strikes seven and round we go again, tick tock tick tock.

Pensees of Mary-Margaret (age 11):

I love Bruce Willis unconscious.

Joe has this little-boyish quality, I can just imagine Mrs Fry sending him on many errands when he was younger. Carry Mrs So and So's bag, put the picture up, pump Aunt Anne's tyres, run and get me twenty bensons. Joe is very, I don't know, willing, and not as a result of the slavery of his childhood but because it comes naturally to him to be thoughtful. He offered to post a letter for me this morning, and the letter box is only at the end of his road.

Back at home, and the Admiral had to go to the Isle of Wight on Wednesday and I forgot how Aunt Coral can be very Victorian about these things: take to her bed for four or five hours at a time reading, and then come down looking pale and haunted (she makes me feel quite sensible).

It's funny because even though the Admiral is back now, I haven't actually *seen* him yet, as we keep missing each other in person. So it feels as though the Admiral is a mythical creature, who only exists in noises. He has a very distinct clatter pattern: he is a cupboard slammer, a door banger and a spoon tapper.

Jenny is really coming on and I have high hopes of passing my dissertation. Quiz's notes are the business, but sadly I haven't seen him except at the restaurant for we work at opposite ends of the day. I write, I work, I spend time with Joe in the garden, I bathe by the bottles, I listen for the gong of the Admiral's spoon.

'Dzjhennia a pulchayer shans'

OR 'JENNY GETS A CHANCE'
by Sue Bowl

Maxim was jealous of Robert. Robert the boss, Robert the svengali, Robert the Leader. And when he overheard Robert and Jenny fighting on the balcony, it only fanned the flames.

'Don't flirt with me Robert, it makes me feel so low,' said Jenny.

'Do you think I look like this out of pity? You silly little fool.'

'Please don't lie to me,' said Jenny, fighting, battling, marshalling the tears that would incriminate her Oligarchical past.

Jenny closed her eyes, for they were heavy with the weight of her passion.

'Robert you know how I feel, but Sabrina, she would kill us both if she knew.'

'Jenny Jenny, don't you want to live before you die?' said Robert, shaking her.

'Oh God Robert, I love you. God Help, me I do.'

'Jenny, your smell intoxicates me, Jenny, let's live, let's live.'

'I hope I'm not interrupting anything,' said Maxim Tartly. 'I suppose this is one way to try and get your articles in print,' he said.

'I wonder what Sabrina will think about this when I tell her?'

'I'm peckish,' said Robert, 'are you coming Jenny?'

Quiz notes for Sue on Jenny part five

1 the balcony is a bit sudden, has it just been built?
2 we already know she has an Oligarchical past, don't patronise the reader.
3 Jenny your smell intoxicates me . . . perhaps scent is a more literary choice?
4 Maxim Tartly, omit capital letter.
5 Robert's comment 'I'm peckish' somehow takes away from the drama. But I do see what you are up against in terms of trying to be more Russian while living at Green Place! Why don't you come up to my suite again after you get back from work over the next couple of days and we can go into the matter very fully. X Quiz.

'Dzjhennia a pulchayer shans'

OR 'JENNY GETS A CHANCE'
by Sue Bowl

Maxim was jealous of Robert. Robert the boss, Robert the svengali, Robert the leader. And when he overheard Robert and Jenny fighting in the office, it only fanned the flames.

'Don't flirt with me Robert, it makes me feel so low,' said Jenny.

'Do you think I look like this out of pity? You silly little fool.'

'Please don't lie to me,' said Jenny, fighting, battling, marshalling her secret tears.

She closed her eyes, for they were heavy with the weight of her passion.

'Robert you know how I feel but Sabrina, she would kill us both if she knew.'

'Jenny Jenny, don't you want to live before you die?' said Robert, shaking her.

'Oh God Robert I love you. God Help me I do.'

'Jenny, your scent intoxicates me, Jenny let's live, let's live.'

'I hope I'm not interrupting anything,' said Maxim, tartly. 'I suppose this is one way to try and get your articles in print,' he said.

'I wonder what Sabrina will think about this when I tell her?'

'Damn you,' said Robert. 'I'm *leaving*, are you coming Jenny?'

Thanks Quiz and hope to see you at some point, if I'm not back too late. At brekkie otherwise?

with my love Sue X

Sat June 18, 6.00am

I dare not go to Quiz's suite *again*. It's not that I feel anything for him, but I really really don't want to upset Joe. But I'd go if there was no Joe, which there is, he's on Treasure Island. But does that make me a Jackie-friend to Di?

No, even though there's nothing in our collaboration, except admiration on my part, I shan't go again, of course I shan't. I shall forgo the opportunity to have coco with a literary heavy hitter, for the sake of Joe who I love and treasure, and Di who I admire and adore.

But I wish I *could* go, I mean I wish it didn't *matter* if I did. I wish making the decision wasn't such a *battle*. I wish I was Jean Jaques Rousseau and then I could relax.

11am

I have been pondering Quiz's note about the difference between the words smell and scent. A scent is something you go after, want more of, and a smell is something you try to get away from. He's right, of course, so clever.

I so wish I was involved in word-work rather than waitressing. But you can't have *everything* that you want. At least I am still doing something towards my greater ambition, with 'Jenny Gets a Chance'. But perhaps life would be easier without an ambition, then maybe not to be achieving it wouldn't matter so much. But Joe says he thinks it's a gift to *have* an ambition, because he hasn't got one, apart from working outside, and so that makes him feel drifty.

Sun 19 June 9.50pm

Pensees: *'Ten to ten on a summer evening is the time that the fox comes out.'*

Curiously, I have noticed a fox at that time crossing the front gardens, recently when I've happened to look out. And I remembered Rose Anna's letter to London, where she talks about setting their clocks by the fox, at ten to ten on a summer night. I find it very poignant that the foxes have been here for as long as we have. We are never alone.

Mon 20 June 1988, 8.00am

Aunt Coral and the Admiral have started to go into Egham for their shopping trips *very* early in the mornings, so that they avoid any build-up of traffic. Even to the point of taking pot luck on what shops will be open at that time. I believe that they are trying to recreate the B4532 before there was any traffic on it, so that they can go about their business as if it is still 1950.

I bumped into the Admiral as they were about to set off, when I came down for an early pensee by the pool.

'I have just put your Aunt in the Bentley,' he told me.

He makes her sound like a suitcase.

Aunt Coral's To Do

Lemons

Financial Times

Swizzle sticks (for mixing drinks)

Sue

Pensees: *Apparently is a word not to be taken seriously* SB

Delia and Admiral Gordon have arrived and are summering (Loudolle's not here yet mercifully). Delia and Admiral G are both well, robust, even rugged you might say. Admiral Gordon has been very animated about the effect of the weather on the roads. He has been railing against the injustice of the English parliament and just generally being Celtic.

With Delia back in residence the pool is back in use, as she finds early swims bracing. Aunt Coral and I don't go in unless it is over 80 degrees in the shade.

And did I mention works to the Orangery are nearly *finished*?! Glenn just has the tidging to do and Aunt C has already moved things in. The paint on the woodwork was barely dry before she was excitedly wheeling in palm pots. I am in awe of how fast Glenn has worked, but as he explained, he has been under the *thumb*. He enlisted his sons and his nephews to help and they worked round the clock.

As suspected, Aunt Coral has installed a grand piano and has booked a young man she interviewed, called Eccles, to play for them every night between six and eight. I have to hand it to my imagination because he actually does have red hair and a squint. I wonder if this would qualify as a self-fulfilling prophecy?

The Orangery has the look of a theatre set from a drawing-room comedy: French doors to the garden, a grand piano in a shawl with lots of silver photo frames on it, magazine wracks with *National Geographics* in them and silver bowls from Aunt C's botanical trips laid out on tables all ready to be filled up with Bombay mix.

Aunt Coral has commissioned fashionable banquettes, uphol-stered in crushed red velvet, for relaxed seating adjacent to the windows and Orangery entrance. Cost? I dare not ask. But pru-dence apart, it is a space that is delightful and expansive, if *expensive*. Admiral Ted would have been proud.

And departing from tradition, Aunt C has had a beautiful dance floor laid in the middle, and also retained a nod to an Orangery's historical purpose by installing rows of orange and lemon trees along the traditional masonry fruit wall.

In addition there is a new water feature outside on the terrace. It is a statue of a gothic cherub that stands with his bare bottom facing Egham. He is holding an urn spouting a tinkly fall of water and the first thing you notice when you come round the bend in the drive is his bottom flashing through the trees. Apparently, nobody else seems to have spotted this but me.

Word List
Banquette

FOR THE CONCERN OF THE RICH AND THE POOR

It was now the spring of 1861, I would have been eleven. And a fine morning saw Madam Rose Anna and I take Alfred to promenade in the rose garden. He was unable to walk for long without our support by this point in time, but he still lived to be in the open air, to inhale the scent of his flowers, to catch sight of them, to touch their heads, I recall.

I offered one arm to Alfred and the other to Rose Anna to lean on. And if I was a little on the short side for them, it did not matter, for my arms were just as solid and true as a man three times my age.

As we approached the heady delights of the early rosebuds, Alfred needed to stop and rest on a bench for a little while. Rose Anna placed herself next to him, and a conspiratorial look passed between them. I faced them, kicking stray stones from the path, wishing that we could walk on.

'I am considering a proposal I have had from Benedict's brother Thomas to join him and his family as their resident widow,' said Rose Anna, with a most deliberate effort.

'The brother in India?' I asked her.

'That's right. Do you remember? Benedict gave a party for Thomas some time ago, before he left.'

'Then that is a decision which seems clear cut to me, for what is there to keep you in England?' I told her bravely. 'Don't you agree, Alfred?'

He did not speak, but offered an earnest nod.

'Are there any family members who are likely to come forward and claim you,' asked Rose Anna, 'if you and Alfred have to leave here?'

'No, there is no one,' I said.

'And so, if I were to be travelling to India, loving the image of the country as you do, would there be a chance that you might wish to come with me?' she asked.

'Both of us?' I asked, looking at Alfred dubiously.

'I would hope to join you as soon as I'm better,' said Alfred. 'I'm sure the climate would do me good.'

'And I as your servant?' I asked Rose Anna, to clarify my position.

'No,' she replied, lightly connecting herself to both Alfred and myself by each of our hands. 'No,' she said again, 'as my son.'

I faltered, too stunned to summon my powers of speech, and so Alfred picked up the threads for me.

'I think it's a fine idea. And haven't you been telling me for years that you are already there? That the book is already written!' he said. 'We can't expect to clutter up Roselyne indefinitely, and certainly not in the light of such a wonderful offer,' he spluttered. I patted his back till he had finished and we remained quiet for some time.

'You see,' said Rose Anna eventually, 'being here is like looking back to my old life. I am tied to the place that I love, and yet I can never go back to it.'

'You know what you should do when you feel like that? Run,' I said. 'I would never have come here unless I had . . . And I would be . . .' I looked at Alfred to make sure of my answer. He bid me to go on with an expression of encouragement but I could not finish.

'I can't say how much I would . . . but . . .' my voice trailed away.

'What London is trying to say,' said Alfred, 'is that he would be honoured to go with you.'

He put his arms around me and pulled me down between his shoulders, in a tender embrace that said the words which we could not.

'Thank you, thank you,' whispered Rose Anna, her tone uneven.

As long as I live I will never forget that moment. My head buried in Alfred's chest, hanging on to him for dear life.

Sue

Weds 22 June 1988, 5 am

Doctor Marshall, in *For the Concern*, called Alfred's condition 'Potter's Rot'. Last night after my extraction, I finally found a reference to it in the Medical Encyclopaedia. It said Potter's Rot used to be the broader term for lung disease.

And I have just woken up with a chilling realization. For I remembered Joe telling me that in his gardening studies he read that the life expectancy of a glasshouse man in Victorian times was not much more than thirty, because they used to use insecticide sprays that contained *arsenic*. I wonder if this is what happened to Alfred?

(And he wouldn't have known what was wrong with himself, as we would expect to know nowadays. In those days, you just got ill and you didn't necessarily know what was wrong. Perhaps that's why so many Victorian illnesses were named after their symptoms, such as consumption for tuberculosis, or 'the strangling angel', which was diphtheria.)

But I also wonder if London Taylor became London *Garden* if Madam Rose Anna adopted him after that? And if he did, then I still wonder who the author of the book, *Lawrence* Garden is.

Maybe he is one of the children of the other brother, Thomas, in India? And maybe he wanted to tell London's tale?

Aunt Coral's To Do

Decanter

Dry biscuits

Cocktail umbrellas

Sue

22 June, 6pm

I have the night off work tonight when we will say a warm welcome to the Orangery. Mrs Fry wouldn't give Joe the night off as well – she said she couldn't do without him. But I hope by the time that he gets here, things will still be in full swing.

23 June, 12.30am
The Pianist's debut

Eccles was practising his repertoire on the new piano which is set between two potted palms. Quiz, Delia and the Admirals were up in their suites getting ready for pre-dinner drinks. It was just like the old days at Green Place, apart from dear Admiral Ted. Mrs Bunion was in the kitchen and there was the smell of nourishing food in the hall. I know how she misses the sight of Admiral Ted sauntering down for his dinner. He was such a pleasure to cook for, so effusive and polite.

As it is now June, this evening I chose to wear head-to-toe white. I wore my long white skirt and a light white blouse teamed with white pumps for a casual finish. Aunt Coral's choice was somewhat opposite to mine: dramatic black velvet cocktail dress with sparkles in her hair and lots and lots of perfume. We sat together in the new, echoey Orangery and waited for the others to get down. The room still smells of polyfiller, paint and varnish and the soft furnishings need breaking in.

'I hope, in time, we could use the Orangery for the dancing and the Club for conversation and groups,' said Aunt Coral.

'The Club?' I said.

'The conservatory,' she said. 'I've adapted the name because I've been worrying that to have an Orangery *and* a conservatory isn't quite the thing.'

I begin to see that Aunt C had a master plan when she dreamt the Orangery up. She seems to have advertently or inadvertently created a dedicated party space. And after all my concerns about her health over the past few months, I feel very reassured that her mind is taken up with dancing and parties.

Mrs Bunion entered the new room with a highly polished trolley of dirty martinis and two platters of finger buffet, and as she did so, Eccles went into a spontaneous rendition of 'I'm Just a Girl Who Can't Say No'; it did make her grin. She had made little baked toasts, dipped in cinnamon, sugar, butter, nuts and cream.

'I'm sure this can't be very good for us,' I confided to Aunt C, as I tucked in.

'But it's delicious,' she said, 'so in another way it is.'

Jackie arrived to join us and at the piano Eccles slipped seamlessly into 'Devil Woman', and when Delia arrived he melted his tune into 'Love Story'. And when the Nanas appeared, he sneaked into a jazz delivery of 'Three Little Maids from School'. I'm coming to the conclusion Eccles is a bit of a one.

When the gents emerged, he played the Protestant marching

theme, and when we were all assembled Aunt Coral raised her glass. 'To the Orangery!' she said.

'To the Orangery!' we replied. There was a chinking of glasses and the squeak of Mrs Bunion and her trolley, and the summer moon was visible through the window set faintly between the clouds.

'Better to live one day as a lion in luxury, than a lifetime as a mouse in mediocrity, eh Sue?' said Quiz, regarding Aunt C's lavish choices. 'When she is as old as the hills and sitting in the chimney corner looking back, she won't remember all the bills that she paid, but she will remember the dancing,' he added, before settling himself on to a banquette. I sat down beside him.

'I'm sorry it was so late by the time I got back the other night, I didn't come up to collaborate,' I said. 'I thought you'd be asleep.'

'You mustn't worry about that,' he said. 'Just wake me up.'

Aunt Coral has ears like a fruit bat, for in a heartbeat she and Delia were drawn to sit beside us on the banquette.

'What did you say?' she asked.

'Have you thought about doing interior design professionally?' Quiz chatted.

'Oh what a tremendous *idea*,' exclaimed Aunt Coral.

Within the next few moments of course she and Delia had decided upon converting a suite for a show room for interiors that would be just the job.

'They are so very suggestible but they just don't *see* it,' I whispered to Quiz.

'It must be *hereditary*,' he whispered back, with a certain *emphasis*. His breath was very hot in my ear, and his aftershave smelt very spicy. 'You look sweet tonight,' he said. 'You look like you're going to play tennis in 1920.'

I instantly regretted that I hadn't broken up my white theme with a colour-contrasting belt.

'Picked up anything on those cameras of yours, Jackie?' asked the Admiral.

'No, not at the far end of the tunnel I'm afraid,' answered Jackie. 'I believe in order to find out what lies down there we may have to come further up nearer to the house, trace the path of the old tunnel and follow the footsteps of the past,' she stressed with significance.

FOR THE CONCERN OF THE RICH AND THE POOR

It must have been early April 1861, and Alfred sent me to gather up worms and snails in the garden after a late-afternoon shower.

I delighted in this task and most particularly having been hemmed in all day in the tiny parlour at Roselyne by the foul weather.

But as I approached the oak tree to fetch the key to the garden, I found it had already gone. And investigating at once, I spotted Frittie in the garden, barefoot and in his nightgown, dangling merrily from a branch.

'What are you doing here?' I called, greatly relieved it wasn't a thief.

'This isn't your usual time. How did you get out?' I continued with my questions as I levelled with him.

'I've discovered a ladder,' he said.

He pointed to the wisteria that grew to the side of the big house.

'So you have,' I replied. 'But wasn't that a terrible risk?'

'It gets a bit suffocating up there,' he said, 'sometimes I just have to get out.'

He retained his stammery speech and since I had

known him had developed a repressed, strangled tone, as if he were swallowing his own words. I thought maybe it was because, in all his shut-away days, he had been so left out.

'I had a nightmare and I woke with an urge to escape,' he said, guzzling the cool, damp air.

'What happened?' I asked. We walked along the paths in the garden.

'I dreamt that my nursery had no windows and no door, I was completely entombed,' he said.

'I can't believe you've been sent to bed already!'

'My mother has decided it will increase my chances of good health if I sleep for longer. Fat Nanny says it's "macabre".'

'Well I understand that sleep is good for a person, but I don't understand what she thinks is going to happen if she lets you go out?' I said.

'She thinks I might catch an infection, and since recently I did actually have a cold, along with my earlier bedtime I now have to have my temperature taken all the time.'

'This is getting worse my friend, I am so sorry. It must be very dull up there, day in and day out.'

'But, look at me,' he said emphatically, 'the great thing is, *I got better*!' He whooped and threw himself face down to the ground comically, in passionate frustration.

'I am to be her survivor.' He turned dramatically, wiping the mud off his face. 'I wasn't even allowed to see my Father for a week after he returned from London, in case he had any town air in his lungs!'

'She must love you very much,' I said, with my own particular angle on the matter.

'I suppose so,' said Frittie. 'I've never thought of it like that.'

We turned and saw Alfred at the window and waved

exuberantly. He gave a weak wave back, but managed a smile. A few moments later he knocked on the window and opened it as we hurried over on the garden side of Roselyne, and Alfred passed out a pair of my boots.

'The cold bites, take care,' he said.

'Thank you!' called Frittie.

'What would you like to do?' I asked him.

'I like trotting,' Frittie answered.

'You mean like a horse?' I enquired.

'Of course,' he said, 'what else?'

How funny he looked, a small stallion in his nightgown raging around the garden. At the age of eleven, I felt too grown up for trotting myself, but then I had already got it out of my system. Alfred looked very amused as he watched from the window of Roselyne. It was so good to see him laughing.

'I often dream I am running,' puffed Frittie, now at a gallop, 'very very fast, often downhill, and sometimes I can't stop.'

'How long can you stay?' I called to him.

'Fat Nanny will come to check on me between seven and eight. I didn't leave my double, so I will have to get back.'

'Through the tunnel? Do you need a decoy?'

'No, thank you, no one uses it at this time. And it is safer than my ladder!' he said.

He trotted off up the meadow and disappeared into the tunnel.

'See you next time,' I called after him, for I never knew when he would come back.

'It's all so beautiful, how can you stand it every day?' he called back to me, his voice echoing after him. 'How can you stand it every day, every day, every day?'

Sue

Joe went down to the kitchen at 5am to make me a cup of tea. Everyone had gone to bed last night by the time he arrived, but Eccles stayed late to give Joe a little serenade, for which I joined him on the dance floor. We had a glorious smooch. It is still a wonderful novelty doing this with a boy and not with Aileen Edgeley.

Not surprisingly Joe has now fallen back to sleep for the last hour or so. And I have finally finished off my dissertation 'Jenny Gets a Chance' for sending off to Professor Mushrooms in London. I so hope he likes it. I so hope I pass and get that certificate telling me that I am a certified writing graduate of Taverna O'Carroll, and not just a skivvy.

Mon June 27

The last few days have been all work and no play. Mrs Fry's personal vendetta for my night off!

So bleary-eyed I came down to get the post at about ten o'clock this morning and I noticed Mrs Bunion hadn't yet picked up the letters from the mat. I collected it together and amongst the envelopes were two red L plates. I looked out of the window and Joe was sitting outside in a very old banger.

'Fancy a spin?' he called when he saw me.

'Have you passed your driving test? When did all this happen?' I asked, rushing out.

'This morning,' he said. 'Hop in – where'd you want to go?'

'Um . . . the Business Park at the viewing point?' I suggested (this is a place we first romanced).

'Sure thing,' he said. 'She may be old but she's still a machine that can move us from place to place *while we are sitting down.*' He twiddled a pretend moustache.

'I see the Admiral has taught you the sentimental language of the car,' I said.

'Solid girl,' said Joe. 'She's a beauty. Pop your belty on and let's go!'

Due to his lack of progress with his mother in the passenger seat, unbeknownst to everyone Joe booked a crash course of private lessons. Anyway, he has already applied for his full driving licence and asked me to keep the provisional one for posterity. Passing your test is really a rite of passage. And it's my turn next. I can't be a passenger all my life, people will form opinions.

July 1 1988, 1.00am

Pensees: *'Where there is no endeavour there is no hope.'*
(Jean Jacques Rousseau)

We have been rushed off our feet at the Bistro, particularly since Joe has now left to go away on his wine course. But I have clocked up so many miles on the dessert trolley that I don't have much time to pine!

I have been typing my articles for Gordoney, on a typewriter hidden in the toilet. I did this because I was worried he couldn't read my handwriting, but the method quickly became unsatisfactory, because of the confined space in which I had to type – and the fear of constant interruptions. So far none of my offerings has proved enough to get noticed anyway. So Quiz, God bless him, decided that we need a *strategy* and *tactics*.

'The strategy is to get your work in print, and the tactics are exactly how we're going to go about doing that at the moment, with the benefit of a newspaper editor dining regularly six feet below us,' he said.

And so (cue the music) we developed the plan further with the aid of Posiedon. When Gordoney comes in to dine, she makes gentle enquiries into his interests, she fishes for specific topics, and after informing me of her findings, I go to the typewriter in Quiz's *car*, and run something a little more specific off! Here, I am not threatened by the imminent entrance of Mrs Fry or a diner requiring the lavatory and all I have to deal with are peculiar looks from passers-by. It's been the most exciting writing exercise ever, and unparalleled experience at working to a deadline.

Posiedon covers my tables for me while I'm away, and if Mrs Fry notices my absence, I have dropped precautionary hints of a weak bladder to beef up the plot. To date she has been sympathetic and not suspicious, in fact no one has, except perhaps, before he went away, Joe.

As for Gordoney himself, Quiz's opinion is that he is finding it entertaining. Being hit on with articles certainly hasn't stopped him from coming back!

He asked Posiedon if she were writing them, and she explained that they were being handed in by a stranger outside. And when I look down on Gordoney, he is often watchful of the window. Last

Thursday he came in with his entire team, Rueben York, Cinema Nixon and his two hacks, Overcoat Home and Barry Arabian (we looked them up in the *Echo*).

Quiz told me that these are certain to be pen names, because as hacks they need names with more punch for their scoops. Posiedon confirmed that in real life they are just Robin Home and Barry Smith.

I want *my* pen name to say historical, brainy, mystery, and I think Susannah Parkes tickles the boxes. Plus in a small way I am paying my respects to Madam Rose Anna (Parkes is her maiden name).

And Quiz is a master-plotter! A brilliant gamester at rouses! He puts the logs in the pram and the baby in the wheelbarrow. He puts the violins in the music. I have never met anyone who made me feel that consequences don't really matter. That life is sweet, life is the point, life and learning.

Consequences like humiliation or the wrath of my elders seem to pale beside the possibilities of what could happen if Gordoney *liked* one of my pieces. And consequences don't kill you either, that's the thing.

Perhaps I should mention here for the record that I have noticed that the expectation of Loudolle's summer visit has heralded the sudden flourishing of Icarus. He has started wearing skin-tight trousers and taking an interest in himself and trying to find out what books she's been reading so that he will be able to chat.

I love that time in a relationship where you are still on your best behaviour, where you pretend not to go to the toilet and that you have classical music at night with your tea. Joe and I have got a bit past that now, we have become quite frank with each other.

FOR THE CONCERN OF THE RICH AND THE POOR

But as the days wore on, Alfred faded before our eyes, the colour drained from his cheeks, and his skin sank into his bones. He could no longer get up and go outside. He sat up in his bed for as long as he could, tending to plants that needed his assistance, his strong hands never ceased until everything in their care endured.

But eventually he grew too tired to move and his hands shrank away to become like feathers. The wasting happened within a week.

After that, he lay still and slept a great deal of the time. Madam Rose Anna read to him from *The Ladies Cabinet of Music and Fashion*, which seemed to amuse him very much. Walderon fed and watered and cared for him in every way when he could no longer do for himself.

And I became his link with the world outside, his arms and legs and eyes. I kept a close watch on the life of the garden and brought him a news report each night, and in return he gave me his instructions for the next day. Sowerbutt was very obliging in keeping secret the fact that Alfred and I were still on the premises, but then I have never known a gardener to turn down help!

In the mornings we cut rosemary and lavender and herbs and picked up rose petals and tied them inside Madam Rose Anna's hankies to place under Alfred's nose.

'If you cannot go to the garden, the garden will come to you,' said Walderon.

When the dark day came, I was at the market in Old Egham on a mission to sell seedlings to buy Alfred more medicine. Sowerbutt rode out swiftly on the bounder to fetch me and bring me home. As we drove back in the carriage I could hear the faint sound of a bell ringing.

'Madam Rose Anna has summoned the priest,' said Sowerbutt.

When we entered Roselyne, there were hushed figures, and urgent whispers all around Alfred's day bed. He had been ill for some days, but their presence seemed much too sudden.

Doctor Marshall was there and Madam Rose Anna and Walderon; the priest was waiting outside. The curtains were closed, but the window was open to keep the room cool and shady, and along the top of the mantelpiece and on the table there gently flickered some candles.

Close by his side was Alfred's photograph of his wife and son, Alice and George, waiting to take his hand in the next world.

Sowerbutt took off his hat and stood back in the corner, and I stood sadly amongst the throng and looked upon Alfred's form . . . he hung in that unsteady place just between life and death, in and out of being, every breath a triumph.

Walderon walked to the front door carrying a candle and asked the priest to come in. We all knelt when he entered and after, the cook and the maids from the big house all took their leave. We who remained turned our faces to the wall, so that Alfred had some sanctity for his confession and the last rites.

'Through His holy anointing, and by His holy most tender mercy may the Lord pardon you the sins of your life . . . and the blessing of the Father, the Son and the Holy Ghost be with you and remain with you always.'

The priest crossed Alfred's head with water and made sure he was fit for Heaven and, surprisingly, afterward Alfred rallied enough to eat the final wafer.

'I would like a moment alone with my boy,' said Alfred when he saw me. Madam Rose Anna called the others out and whispered, 'This time is for you.'

Walderon put one last tonic by Alfred's bed, she never gave up hope, then she left the room quietly, taking the priest with her.

'I'll just be outside, if you need me,' said the Doctor.

And then we were alone.

I took off my cap respectfully, and sat as gently as I could on Alfred's bed and took his hand in mine.

'I don't know how to do this,' I said.

'Then let me speak first, I am the adult,' he said softly. He cleared his throat, and tried a few times to take in enough breath to speak, but struggled for some time, until he was ready.

'I thought it was all over for me, but love had the last word . . . London,' he spluttered.

'You saved my life,' I said through fierce deep gulps and sobs.

'Were we not put on the earth to take care of each other? Will you open the curtains, London? I don't want to die in the dark.'

I gladly opened the curtains to let the sun shine in once more.

'Help me,' he said, struggling to sit up. 'I want to look out of the window.'

I helped him up on to his elbows, which was a great effort for us both and he peeped up towards the big house, like a child.

'Beautiful,' he said. 'The grasses in the meadow are all blowing the same way. You know what that means?'

I shook my head.

'They are all pointing home.'

'I love you,' I whispered, pressing my head into the echo of his once strong shoulder.

'And I love you,' he said.

I gently laid him back down again. He was very exhausted from his exertion and we sat quietly together for a few minutes and his breathing hissed and crackled.

After a discreet amount of time, Madam Rose Anna, Walderon and Sowerbutt came back in as gently as their number allowed. There were rustlings and shadows and tears as they assembled. I was not alone in wanting to hold on to a little piece of Alfred as he passed. And by his goodness, he was surely guaranteed ten times over that he would not have to face death alone. We stood, sat and knelt around the bed of our beloved friend and watched for the moment of his departing. There were long moments of anguish before there came a wheezing, a choking and then a strange rattle in his chest. All the while I stroked his hand.

'What are you up to, you sleepy thing, this is no time for tricks,' I said.

He must have drifted away as I said it, for his chest did not rise and fall any more. I looked for the rapture on his face, looked for a reassurance that he had in his gaze the gates of Heaven, but there was nothing to signify it. The only difference between his living and his dying was his stillness and a sad kind of peace.

'He's gone,' I said.

Sue

Fri 8th July 1988

When I woke up this morning my pillow was still damp from where I'd been crying. I don't know how London could ever recover from losing someone as dear as Alfred. But we have to recover, there's no other option. Sometimes I wish time didn't march on and change everything constantly and throw out the old things. I can only conclude that time is a shopaholic.

HISTORICAL FACTLET

Bounder a light, swift-moving horse-drawn carriage

Later

It was the end of the night at the Lanterner and we had reached the wind-down, the time when the music fades, the atmosphere dims and hot clean cutlery chinks in the kitchen draws. The final stray plates were being fielded and scraped as Beniamino swung out to pat his diners.

'Mrs Fry wants to see you in her office,' he told me. 'She says this is urgent.'

So I set an anxious course for the office where Mrs Fry was sitting behind her desk with Posiedon standing opposite.

'Beniamino told me you wanted to see me?'

'Do you know anything about this?' she asked, throwing down a copy of the *Echo* on to her desk.

'About what?' I said, angelically.

'The paper? Look at the column on the top right of the features last page. Please read me the headline.'

'Ninety-nine per cent of people are morons, is that a bit harsh? by Susannah Parkes.'

Posiedon looked at me with a thousand words in her gaze which I returned with ten million and the thrill that I felt seeing my article in print was overwhelmed by fear and dread.

'My article! It's in the paper!' I gasped quietly.

'Yes, and I wondered if it had anything to do with what I caught Posiedon just putting under Mr George's bill,' said Mrs Fry.

She held in her hands this evening's article, entitled 'If sleep were a science fiction premise, nobody would believe it'. (Inspired by my being very tired.)

'Tell me, if you were me and you caught a member of staff passing notes to a valued customer, what would you do?'

I guessed where she was going with her logic.

'It's not Posiedon's fault,' I said. 'She had nothing to do with it. I asked her to do it, to help me, because I so wanted to have a success. Mr George didn't seem to mind – in fact he has seemed quite amused by it,' I waffled.

'Posiedon, you may go,' said Mrs Fry, sternly. Her nose seemed to grow more pointy.

Posiedon left the office and looked back briefly before she closed the door.

'I'm sorry you are about to be shot,' she said with her eyes.

'It's OK, I had it coming,' I replied with mine. I suddenly felt very distant from Joe, far away in France with his study of wine. I'm sure he would have tried to help, I'm sure he would have stuck up for me.

'I'm sorry to have to do this Sue,' Mrs Fry continued, 'but I simply cannot have members of staff taking advantage of customers who have come out for a meal and to relax. My customers don't expect to be badgered for professional reasons when they come here. This is not an employment agency. It's really not on. I have a business to run, and standards to keep up, and the *Echo* have an account here, they come here to relax. I think it would be better for everyone if you were to get your things and go. If I allow you to stay, I will be setting a precedent, and I can't afford to do that.'

'But . . .'

'I'm letting you go,' she said. 'You have taken advantage of your position and I'm very surprised at you. I don't feel I can trust you any more.'

I walked out of the office, through the tables on the ground level, heading straight for the Butler's Pantry. Quiz looked down at me from the gallery and waved.

'What's up?' he mouthed.

'I've been sacked,' I replied, miming slitting my throat.

'See you at the car,' he returned, looking shocked.

I went to the Butler's Pantry and got changed and collected up my things. I had a hug with Posiedon.

'I think you're going to go far and this is just a blip,' she said. 'Thank you for not dumping me in it. She wouldn't have dared sack you if Joe had been here,' she added. 'He's going to be furious.'

'With her or with me?' I said.

'Um . . . both,' she said sympathetically.

'I'll see you soon, it's been great working with you,' I said, hanging up my pinny.

Posiedon handed me a copy of the *Echo* on my way out. It was somewhat overshadowed by my mauling.

'What happened?' asked Quiz when I got in the car.

'She caught Posiedon putting my article with Gordoney's bill, and the rest came out because she was about to blame Posiedon.'

'Well, I know it seems a high price to pay,' he said, 'but congratulations! You did it, you achieved the goal of our strategy. Which article is in the paper?'

'The one about morons.'

'I'm very proud of you, that's a gutsy piece,' he said.

'Thank you, but I'm really worried about what Joe is going to say when he gets home. She made it sound like I was being cruel to the customers by interfering when they were trying to relax and now I feel guilty.'

He put an avuncular arm around me. I felt foolish.

'It's all interpretive isn't it? She should live and let live. When does Joe get back?' he asked.

'Sunday afternoon,' I said.

'Well what you need is to get away for a couple of days, forget about all this trauma and stress. Di and I are going to Westover tomorrow – why don't you come for an impromptu weekend? We'll be leaving around noon.'

The day after I was sacked (Sat July 9th 1988)

Pensees: *Dark horses get lonely.* SB

By the next morning the moron piece was up in pride of place on the kitchen noticeboard. Aunt Coral had rung all her friends and was hosting a coffee morning in its honour. She had crossed out the name Susannah Parkes and written over it Sue Bowl. She disapproves of my name change.

'I understand why you feel upset about the Lanterner,' said Aunt Coral, 'but in the longer term, having two hundred words in print in the *Echo* will do you more good professionally than ten thousand nights at the Lanterner.'

She put my unceremonious dismissal into a life-long perspective for me, as opposed to a here-and-now one, which took the heat out of it, bless her.

Particularly when, as a result of the Orangery, she is at the jumping-off place with her own finances. In my absence, she and the Admiral will be performing one final micro-trawl of the house looking for the diamond and pearl necklace.

Quiz and I were just setting off when Aunt Coral came running out of the house and handed something through the car window to me. It was a sandwich, in spite of the fact that we would be certain to be going out for lunch.

'Take care of her, won't you Quiz? She's very tender.'

'I'm fine, I promise,' I said, unbelievably embarrassed.

She waved and we set off for Westover, down the drive, out on to Clockhouse Lane and on to the B4532.

'Oh, Di rang – and I'm afraid she isn't able to come,' said Quiz. 'Something's come up, a meeting at the library or something. I hope you're not too disappointed.'

In my head it sounded like a triangle had been struck and that I must heed its warning. The sort of triangle you hear in a film when someone gets an *idea*.

'Do you like Stéphane Grappelli?' he asked.

'I'm afraid I don't know him.'

'Here,' he said, passing the cover, 'we'll have a lovely time, I promise.'

He turned to check I was OK and gave me the warmest smile, from which flowed the sincerest comfort and *pleasure*, and as I looked back at him it was like suddenly seeing a face at the window in a house that I thought was empty.

FOR THE CONCERN OF THE RICH AND THE POOR

A couple of hours later Madam Rose Anna brought little touches of superstition to every corner of the house. She stopped the clock and shrouded all the mirrors in black cloth. The date is branded in my memory. May 12 1861.

'It is very dark in here, may I open the curtains a bit?' I said. 'Will it be safe for Alfred if I do?'

'Of course, let in the light,' she said, but before I could we were startled by a violent tap on the door.

'Dear Madam, I am sorry to come back and disturb you, but I have . . . urgent . . . news,' said Sowerbutt.

'What is the matter?'

'Madam Adelaide has heard of Alfred's passing and is very concerned about infection.'

'But the Doctor assured us his illness is not infectious. We would all be ill by now if it was.'

'She has gone mad,' said Sowerbutt, 'mad with the concern for her child, in case any spore or bad air reaches the doors of the big house. The Master is away, and she is threatening to burn the cottages. I can't guarantee she will show restraint. I came quickly to warn you – it would be wise if you were to leave.'

'Now?' said Rose Anna.

'She has gone mad,' Sowerbutt reiterated more urgently. 'She is beyond reason.'

We looked up to the big house, where we could see a row of torches burning.

'Please tell the Mistress we are not leaving until Alfred's body has been respectfully removed, Mr Sowerbutt,' said

Rose Anna. 'She can do what she likes after that, she can burn down the big house too.'

Sowerbutt and his coachmen went swiftly to fetch a carriage to deliver Alfred's body straight to the undertaker, in the cruellest haste. I went with Walderon into the garden to cut some laurel and flowers to put with him.

And we all bowed our heads when they lifted him up and carried him out of the house. They carried him standing up and facing away from the cottage, so his ghost would not look back.

'Why would God take such a man as Alfred and leave such a woman as Madam Garden?' I said. 'I don't understand God, I don't understand him,' I sobbed, desperately.

Rose Anna squeezed my hand to support me, and I returned the gesture, shaking from head to toe, wracked with grief, as if there was an earthquake in my soul.

And after, we frantically got ourselves ready to depart Roselyne. There was barely time to pack anything. I gathered together a couple of books, my cap and the unbeaten niner, which was still the most precious treasure I ever had. I left a brief message with Sowerbutt to give to Frittie, to explain where and why we had gone. I felt so badly for departing without a farewell. I had not seen him since the day I found him wandering in the garden in his nightgown, the same day, fortuitously, that he saw Alfred for the last time. But under the circumstances it would have been impossible to gain access to Frittie and say goodbye in person, as protection of him was the very reason Madam Adelaide was about to destroy our home.

And this done, I took one last look out to the garden.

A robin came to land on the sundial and then fluttered off to rest in a yellow rose tree. His red breast lit up its branches, and I thought he looked like a ruby set in the heart of a crown.

Cheeser led to Alfred and Alfred led to Rose Anna and Rose Anna led the way to India. But if I were to tie the strands of my bootlaces together and climb on to a chestnut that was knotted on to the bottom, I'd say it was the spirit hand of Alfred that flung me from there to here. But I would give it all back in exchange for five minutes more with him.

I wish that I might, now that I am an old fellow, wake up to find that the rest of my life has been a dream, wish that I could find myself back at Edenthorpe, walking down the paths of the flower garden with Alfred, hastening to bend once more to put my eagle eye over some small wonder and give it a name.

A shoelace is the thread of my life, and a chestnut the heart of my story, and love the invisible puppeteer watching in the realm of dreams. Perhaps I was just lucky enough to be the name of Rose Anna's longing, just as India was the name of mine.

Sue

July 9 Sat, noon

I had so much to do before we left this morning, I haven't had a chance to think about this extract until now. But I did wake up with a dreadful thought. What if Frittie had heard the priest's bell and sneaked out to visit Alfred, unbeknownst to his mother? It is too awful to imagine.

Westover looks just like London architecturally except that it's built with blonde stone. If I had to try and encapsulate the essence of Westover, I would say that it's the sort of town that has shoppes and steppes as opposed to steps and shops. Quiz says it's a tight-nit community.

We passed through the town slowly in the car on our arrival, like Sunday drivers, with Quiz pointing out landmarks.

There's a Michelin-starred bistro, where you can't get a table on a Saturday, and a sixteenth-century pub where there's a resident hermit-in-the-corner, with a tankard, white beard and biblical hair. On the high street lies a parade of smart shops where neon is not allowed. Quiz said that Westover's like a sort of mini golf club, and the council rule against the opening of any shops (as opposed to shoppes). Quiz has the ability to make mundane things seem interesting. Rooftops are gabled, chimneys are capped and windows have sashes. The world is full of strange phrases. Sheep contractors, rehabilitation centres, apologia and voluptuaries. And the lay of the land is different to Surrey. There are different, particular types of trees. Quiz actually didn't know the name of them, so he just called them Cézanne-type trees, after the artist.

> **Word List**
> *Voluptuaries*
> *Apologia*

2.00pm

Greylands is Quiz's mother's house, it's full name is Greylands Villa. I was glad, when we got out of the porch, that Mrs Wilson wasn't standing there watching, because the car is so low to the ground, I almost had to lie down to get out.

An old black Labrador ran up to the front door to greet us, displaying some forgetful guarding. He stuck his nose in my nu-nu and then tottered back to lie on a chaise longue under the stairs, where he watches and waits.

'Hello Pilgrim,' said Quiz. 'Good boy. He used to bark at everything, aeroplanes, cats, the moon, but these days he never strays far from his chaise longue except to bite the cleaner.'

'Well as long as it isn't wounding, surely every dog should be allowed just one bite?' I chatted.

'Hello Mother?' Quiz called out, smiling graciously at my joke.

But there was no sign of Mrs Wilson, and so Quiz showed me over the house.

The downstairs rooms at Greylands are painted in colours such as . . . I don't know . . . *elephant's breath,* colours muted and matt, chalks as opposed to pastels. It is a shoes-off house, even on the quarry tiles on the kitchen floor, where I noticed the bin is *scented* and even the washing-up looks nice.

Everywhere else is hush, plush, deep carpeted and almost claustrophobically luxurious.

Quiz carried my bag up to a guest room at the end of a smattering of bedrooms off a long landing.

'This is your room,' he said. 'I hope you like it.'

'I love it,' I said.

'We call it Studio Two,' he said.

'Why?' I asked.

'Because my room's Studio One.'

What lay before me was a room with high ceilings and two long windows dressed in heavy curtains, and at one end there's a glass door which opens on to the top of some steps to the garden, right beside a weir. Quiz put my bag down on one of those baskety Lloyd Loon sofas that I love. I couldn't help myself but take a mental photo of Professor Quiz Wilson carrying *my* bag.

Mrs Wilson herself didn't appear for about twenty-five minutes after that, and when she did, she seemed completely the wrong person for the house. She wore a hip crochet tunic and a pair of shorts and old flip-flops. Her hair has a striking Beethoven patch of white at the front and she has a self-absorbed sort of manner. Her smile is more of a formula for one, and when she looked at me, it was as though she was staring through bullet-proof glass.

Quiz tells me she is an artist and that she has 'photographic standard legs'. (TWD)

'Quiz! You're just in time, I can't turn the tap off in my bathroom. Hello,' she said, as an afterthought.

'Hello, nice to meet you. A pleasure,' I said.

We went down to the kitchen together and had glasses of filtered water from one of those big American fridges that spits ice cubes. I got hit in the eye with one after which I apologized and then felt foolish, for it was obviously not my fault. Mrs Wilson addressed Quiz as if he was 13, which was a bit of an eye opener.

'There are beans in the cupboard and bread in the bin, so get involved,' she said. 'Will you kids excuse me, I've got a nude coming at 6,' and after that she disappeared into some mystery part of the house.

'Come here,' said Quiz. 'I want to show you something.'

I followed, electrified by his life force and the arty vibrancy of his mother.

But he opened the door of the games room.

'Surprise!' said Helen, William and Professor John.

3.30pm (over refreshments in the kitchen)
'I have your dissertation short story checked for you Sue, if you like?' said Professor Mushrooms.

It was strange, that without the Bay of Shabany to put him in context, I thought the Professor looked much more Greek, or possibly even Roman.

'I've been dying to know what you think,' I said, as Professor John got out my Jenny.

'The thing is,' he said, ' "Jenny Gets a Chance" is still too cliché, too prudish. It makes me laugh, but I know it isn't supposed to. I think you need to go back to the drawing board. Throw everything out of the window and start again.'

'Thank you. Oh dear,' I said.

'It's OK, Sue. I know you can get there, but if I tell you that this Jenny is OK as it is, then I'm not helping you to progress.'

'But can you be more specific?' asked Quiz, joining in. 'We have collaborated, so I feel involved.'

'OK, so *specifically* Sue, we don't get a flavour of Russia, though you mention the Moscow spires, culinary gloom and the forest. But what's too slight is your homage to the themes of the great Russians. The darkness under the surface is too . . . much. You hit everything over the head, and you have one too many people dying in the end. In the last five pages we have Maxim dying and then Robert asks what happened to Sabrina and we learn that she died too. You don't need to kill everyone off. It's not a massacre. You have taken to heart a note and gone to extremes with it, and you just need to pull back, or the overall effect can become, ironically, flavourless, beige and silly. Perhaps Maxim *or* Sabrina get ill, and it's touch and go for a while, but then they recover and change as a result of their suffering and so we can have some redemption?'

'I don't agree,' said Quiz. 'I think with a few minor corrections, Jenny is a piece with great élan.'

'Thanks Quiz, but I can take what John says on board,' I said, hanging on by a thread.

'And you're not upset?'

'Oh gosh no, I'm fine,' I said, erecting a smoke screen to hide my disappointment . . . 'What you say makes sense and I will try again.'

'Good girl Sue, don't give up, learn from this. Getting it wrong sometimes can be invaluable.'

'Thank you,' I said wishing he would shut up.

After my talk with Professor Mushrooms I went up to Studio Two to take some time to recover.

In a whole-life context this is a deep blow, when you consider it in the light of my *not* getting the internship and *not* finishing the course at the Taverna and now *not* passing my certificate. I feel humiliated and a bit like they are all laughing at me. But, in my soul, I still feel absolutely determined to improve, so . . . I wrote down this list to remember that I should avoid being: prudish, middle-class, prim, unbalanced, flavourless, beige and silly.

Pretty soon there came a soft tap at my door and Helen appeared and put her head round.

'I came to see if you're OK,' she said. 'Quiz said that John gave you a mauling.'

'I'm OK,' I said quietly, 'thank you.'

She came in and sat on my bed for a minute, mercifully without any *sympathy* showing on her face.

'They can be so boring,' said Helen. 'They're just willie-waving downstairs,' she went on. 'Poor William can't get a word in.'

'Poor William,' I said. 'They can be disgusting.'

'How *are* you anyway?' Helen asked me seriously.

'I'm really OK thanks,' I said.

'Oh, and how's *Di*?' she asked, as if she had just remembered something thrilling.

'She couldn't come, Quiz said something came up at the library,' I said.

'But they've separated – didn't he tell you?' said Helen.

'No, he didn't.' I paused. 'I had no idea.'

'He must be feeling awful about it. Apparently it's over someone else,' said Helen. 'He told John and John told me – oh dear, maybe he shouldn't have. I thought you might have known about it since he's been staying at yours,' she waffled. 'Apparently it's over someone in his inner circle, but we mustn't judge. Did he tell you the other big news, that John and I are together?'

'So that's why it took you so long to get back!' I said.

There was a gentle breeze calling outside, not so much

blowing the treetops as *charming* them, and a plume-shaped leaf spiralled and tapped at the window for a second. It looked like a feather pen quivering.

After Helen left, I remained in Studio Two and gathered my thoughts.

I don't know why I've pushed myself to be here and try to be on a par with such intellectual razzmatazz. I feel tawdry by contrast, a sham and a fool. And yet, Quiz has only to utter words such as 'élan' or 'impromptu' and my craving to join in is overwhelming. I feel a little bewitched.

Later

We spent the remainder of the day in super philosophical talks. After supper, Quiz put on his favourite black-and-white film, *Dead of Night*. And at the end of the evening after everyone had sloped off to bed, I stood for a long, long time at the inside of my bedroom door, not feeling committed to staying in my room. I could hear what I thought might be Mrs Wilson turning in, a tinkly fall of laughter, an unidentified man's voice. I heard Professor John calling softly to Helen, and the sound of a television somewhere, and thuds and squeaks on the ceiling from Quiz above me in Studio One. I felt disturbed, bewildered, somewhere between fearful and curious. I so wanted to ask him why he hadn't told me about Di, and if what he had told me about her not being able to come today because of the library was a smoke screen.

So I just stood there trying to decide whether to go up and see him, wrestling with myself, and terribly tortured that I ought not to because of Joe. That a late-night tête à tête with Quiz, now unattached, would make Joe very unhappy. But I thought it would make it OK if perhaps I could invent some practical premise on which to knock on Quiz's door: I'd heard the dog barking, I couldn't shut my window, there was a spider in my bed. I only wanted to ask him if he was alright, I only wanted to know what had happened. Where was the harm in that?

I climbed the stairs.

'I couldn't shut my window,' I said. 'I'm sorry to bother you, but I didn't want to disturb Helen and the Professor, and William would get the wrong idea . . . so . . .'

My heart was pounding, and my hands were slippery.

'That's all right darling,' he said. 'I'll come down and have a look.'

He had changed into the most fabulous paisley dressing gown; he looked like Noel Coward, or at least like he'd borrowed Noel's dressing gown. We went back down to Studio Two and I realized I had forgotten to set the window open.

'It must have slipped shut,' he said. 'Oh, but it's locked.'

'I'm sorry, I've been rumbled. I made an excuse, because I wanted to talk to you on our own,' I admitted.

He took out a cigarette from his dressing gown pocket.

'You don't need an excuse to talk to me, not ever. Want one?' he asked.

'I don't smoke,' I said. 'Yet,' I added, meaningfully. He unlocked and opened the window and we stood by it while he smoked.

'I just wondered why you didn't tell me about Di.'

'It's out then,' he sighed.

'I'm so sorry, Helen told me. What happened?'

'We've grown apart, that's all. It's complicated but it's all very adult.'

'But why did you tell me something came up at the library?'

'You've got enough on your plate and . . .' He paused. 'And I didn't want to . . . oh God. Is it wrong?'

'Didn't want to what? Is what wrong?'

'You silly little fool, don't you see it?'

'See what?' I asked desperately.

'You're a huge talent and I'm madly in love with you.'

'Am I dreaming?' I said.

'Am I?' he said.

'Are you?' I said.

'You better come here, or we could go on for ever,' he said. 'Dare we be happy?' he asked, kissing me.

'I dare,' I said, kissing him back.

I remember at the time that I said those words, I *knew* that I shouldn't have. I remember everything, the words, the chill of the cold air by the window, the private secret strangeness of a different kiss.

It wasn't that I forgot about Joe: he was in my thoughts at the very same moment as it all happened. But Quiz made it sound like kissing was something we *should* be doing – if *only* we were brave enough to express our true feelings. If only we were courageous enough to *live* – and I do so want to do that. So it was shamingly easy to persuade myself. It didn't mean I loved Joe any less, I love Joe terribly, it just meant that I loved Quiz too and I couldn't help it and I do so know that one day we will all be dead. Maybe it's just all excuses. But Quiz even makes being selfish sound reasonable, like it's *thoughtful* even and somehow more . . . honest.

And so I told myself that maybe I could have just this one little moment to treasure for ever in my memory. No one need ever know about it and it didn't have to go any further.

Sunday July 10

In the secret part of the morning we lay in bed with the curtains closed till just before nine. The faint sound of church bells grew louder when Quiz got up to open the window. He pulled back the two layers of glazing that sealed the sounds of the weir outside. Fresh air seeped in under the heavy linen checked curtains, but there was no breeze to billow them. The sky smelt of clouds and the earth smelt of old rain and flower heads burdened with water. I listened to the gentle swish of car tyres passing nearby at an appropriate speed for a Sunday. And all the time the bells grew more tuneful, before ending their song in a sombre peel of the hour, and then they fell silent – and silence seemed louder than it ever has before.

The noises of someone opening up the locked-up house downstairs drove me out of bed and into the bathroom. I thought of the options like they were part of a multiple-choice puzzle in one of Aunt Coral's magazines . . . would I: A, lie to Joe about this; B, tell the truth; or C, say nothing? And I saw myself circling C in the secret back places of my mind, which is the realm of amour-propre, where nobody else can see, sometimes not even me.

Tuesday July 12

A midsummer night's dream

'Susan Olivia Bowl, it has been alleged that you have gone behind the back of your boyfriend Joe Fry and betrayed him with another man. How do you plead?'

'Guilty, your honour.'

'It has also been alleged that when your Great Aunt showed concern for you, nay, begged you to explain why you had not rsvp'd any of Fry's calls, that you concealed from her the true nature of your reasons. Is this true?'

'It is true, your honour.'

'And is it furthermore true that you not only concealed your reasons but you pretended not to have received any of Mr Fry's messages? That *you even further pretended to have become deaf to the sound of the phone?'*

'I . . .'

'Please answer the question.'

'It is true, your honour.'

'But not content with the charade of deceitful deafness, is it not also true that you went on to pretend your Great Aunt's phone had been . . . disconnected?'

'I, I, I need some water . . .'

'The defendant would like some water. Daphne, would you . . .?'

'Miss Bowl, it has been alleged by my client that you have not returned his phone calls, and that you circled the C in the multiple-choice article on lying, which you thought, being in the secret back places of your mind, that no one else could see. Did you really think you could hide it?'

'I'm sorry, your honour, I never meant to hurt anyone.'

'Susan Olivia Bowl, you have been found guilty of being terribly immoral, extremely selfish, utterly uncaring and concerned with only yourself.'

'Yes, youre Honoure, I am guiltye.'

'Is there anything you would like to say?'

'Only that I am full of remorse.'

'I now pass sentence. Daphne, if you would . . .'

'For the charge of deception and hiding the truth from Mr Fry, I sentence you to a Life of soul searching and torture. And for your deceit about the phone, involving innocent elderly bystanders, you will serve Seven Years of regret. The sentences to run concurrently. All rise!'

'You were dreaming again,' said Quiz.

'It was a nightmare,' I said.

He got up and set about putting on some respectable clothes in order to get back over to his suite and get re-dressed for the day. I picked up my pen and notebook and began to toy with a pensee.

I offered him a line of my seasonal verse, inspired by the height of summer.

'Winter is coming and soon the trees will be stripped bald . . .'

'Bare is better,' he said.

'Will be stripped bare.'

'It's more Russian,' he said. 'Are you still on the rich and the poor?'

'I haven't had much time for reading lately!'

'May I dip in and have a look later?'

'Of course, help yourself, it's fascinating to think of olden Green Place.'

He opened the door and exclaimed as he fell over something on the floor. 'Oh God.'

'What is it?' I called.

'It's my breakfast tray from Mrs Bunion,' he said clattering about noisily.

'You didn't tell her, did you?'

'Of course I didn't. I merely mentioned that I was sorry I hadn't eaten much of it yesterday because by the time I got to it it was cold. I didn't realize she was so clever.'

Thus far the inmates of Green Place have remained in ignorance of the 'situation' in my suite, but I knew it wouldn't be long.

'Now everyone will know except Joe,' I said.

'Then the sooner you tell him the better,' said Quiz. 'Darling, you can't hide in your room for ever. You must try to be a little bit French about these things, let yourself go into free fall, let yourself live.'

But the trouble is I am not very French, just as I am neither particularly Russian.

I was just on my way down the stairs, and from the hall . . . I could hear voices

'Jackie, how lovely to see you,' said the voice of Aunt Coral, clanking and echoey.

When I reached the bottom, Mrs Bunion passed me without the remotest hint of beadiness and for the first time I realized that she is a top-class ally, a world-class secret keeper. *Of course*, someone like Mrs Bunion will have centuries of discretion bred into her.

'Good morning dear,' she said. 'I'm just going to dust the Sun Room.' She pottered off in her Scholls. I never before felt such love for Mrs Bunion. I never before realized what a beautiful person she is. Falling in love with Quiz has woken me up to so many things. And how thoughtful she is to bother to dust the unused empty spaces.

'Would you like some coffee, darling?' asked Aunt Coral.

I jumped.

'Yes thank you, I'd love some.'

'Lovely,' she said, 'do come through, Jackie.'

We went into the White Room and sat around the table with all the historical papers strewn over it. It was a relief to me to be able to listen to Jackie talking about other stories than mine. First and foremost she and Aunt Coral agreed on the digging of a second hole in the continuing search for the Shipwreck Pearl necklace with its jaw-dropping clasp. I don't hold up much hope about finding this, I expect Rose Anna probably took the piece to India with her, although obviously I realize now that she and London did have to pack in a terrible hurry before they left.

But when I told Jackie about the unlikelihood of this, backed up by my reading and extractions from the book, she was still quite adamant that if Rose Anna had taken the necklace to India, then it would have been insured somewhere, and therefore possible to trace.

So this time, vis à vis the search, they are going to target a small area on the surface towards the *middle* of the old tunnel.

'If I drink enough sherry I can get through it,' said Aunt Coral. 'Though I had hoped you wouldn't have to dig in the formal part of the garden. Still, we must speculate to accumulate, just in case.'

'It will be no more invasive than the first hole,' said Jackie. 'And only *slightly* further inside the garden.'

The practical business attended to, Jackie divested herself of a new raft of dusty documents.

'I'm so sorry I had to wait so long for an appointment to get hold of this. These are rather tricky to obtain. It's a report from the London Fire Engine Establishment archive. They were called to Green Place on the night of the fire at your ruins.'

LFEE Report   Green Place   May 12 1861:

Buildings Involved: Roselyne and Edenthorpe Cottages
Type of building: Brick divided by frame Partition
Occupants: None
Origins of Fire: Arson
How was it extinguished: Three teams, buckets, hose streams
Insurance: Marine and General Mutual
Contents: Chattels, soft and hard furnishings
Notes:
Before it was brought under control the fire destroyed most of the cottages and almost three sides of attached walled garden. It also rendered an adjacent tunnel entrance to the main building on the estate impassable. Flames were swept into and through

the tunnel due to the direction of the prevailing wind. The fire progressed towards the kitchen entrance of the main house, but was brought under control just before entry. The confined space in the tunnel enhanced the efficiency of the draw.

No criminal action is advised. This is pending investigation. The fire was started by the Mistress of the house, for the purpose of destroying contagion that had broken out in the fabric and grounds of the cottages and their outbuildings.

LFEE have advised owner to discontinue use of tunnel entrance when re-building. The design and dimensions of the tunnel are ill advised.

We were silent. Eventually Aunt Coral spoke.

'Could you just burn down your own house if you wanted to?' she asked solemnly.

'Buildings were burned down after outbreaks of diphtheria and what have you, sometimes whole villages,' said Jackie.

We had another pause; it was hard to take it all in.

'Interesting isn't it, what the report says about the draw. I have read reports where something as simple as a dumb waiter has drawn flames from kitchen fires straight upstairs and into the rest of the house,' said Jackie.

'Appalling,' managed Aunt Coral. 'What a tragedy.'

Their voices seemed muted to me. I was thinking of Frittie. My eye ran over the family tree on the table to the date of his death, May 12 1861.

Some runaways aren't so lucky.

Tues July 12 at 5pm

When I got up to my suite at 11 o'clock I was surprised to find Joe sitting on my bed waiting.

'I wanted to see you,' he said. 'Aunt Coral said you weren't feeling well and I was worried because you haven't rung me since I got back from France. I've waited in for your call for the last two nights.'

'Yes, I'm so sorry, I haven't been myself,' I said (I couldn't bear to lie to his face).

'I heard what happened and I just wanted to tell you it's OK, I understand,' said Joe.

'Understand?' I gasped.

'I thought I'd better come up and make sure you knew that I'm on your side about the Lanterner,' he said, 'and . . . I can see that you were . . . influenced.'

'Thanks Joe, I do feel bad about it. But I did it off my own bat, Quiz only made a suggestion.'

'Mmm,' he said mistrustfully. 'Listen, I don't think adding articles to restaurant bills was necessarily a good idea, but I don't think you should have been *sacked* for it. And I'm going to have a quiet word with the boss, so you don't have to worry or feel guilty.'

'That's really kind of you.'

'What's this?' he said quietly, glancing towards my 'Jenny Gets a Chance' working papers. '"Jenny Gets a Chance" by Susannah Parkes. Who's Susannah Parkes?'

'That's my pen name.'

'Oh yes, of course it is, I forgot. I'd love to read it, may I?' he asked.

'I'd rather you didn't,' I said.

'Oh, OK,' he replied, easy come, easy go.

Ordinarily I would have snapped up his offer, but I felt very worried about trying to prevent what happened next.

'"Quiz notes for Sue Part 5",' read Joe. '"Why don't you come up to my suite after you finish work tomorrow and we can collaborate".'

He put down my papers.

'Did you go up and visit him in his suite, on your own, late at night?' asked Joe. He looked ashen.

'No, of course not. I didn't go,' I said. 'I knew you would see it the wrong way, when there was absolutely nothing to see.'

'*Was* nothing to see? Do you mean that there's something to see now?' he asked. His antennae are pin sharp.

'Is he the reason you haven't rung me since I've been back?' he asked. He seemed to be piecing it all together without any help from me.

'No of course not, I've had an upset stomach,' I said unconvincingly. 'Professors and students are always collaborating.'

'Mmm-hm,' said Joe sadly. 'I know.'

I saw a dawning cross his face, and he tried to compose himself. I had thought I would be the one who had to struggle to find a way to tell him the truth.

'I don't understand what you see in him Sue – he's *such* a . . . twit,' Joe yelped.

I felt the blood rush to the front of my face and I felt not only guilty for sleeping with Quiz but embarrassed for sleeping with a twit. It was a huge nasty messy *secret* tangle of emotions.

'But a lot of what he says makes so much sense,' I said, 'to me. He's helped me to improve my writing.'

'But you don't have to do everything he tells you. You don't have to write what he tells you to write, or lap everything up like a sponge.'

'Maybe that's what you don't understand about me. I enjoy people, I absorb them.'

'I *do* understand that,' he said, 'I *know* it, but I just wish this time you had fallen under the spell of someone more *decent*.'

'I haven't fallen under anyone's spell, that sounds so pompous.

And he is decent, and anyway, I think I've always had this artist inside me waiting for destiny to bring it out.'

'Bollocks,' said Joe.

'Joe!'

'Boh-aa-locks.'

'I think you'd better go,' I said.

'Why, because of him?'

'No, because of me. I feel confused. I need some time to think.'

'All right then,' said Joe slowly. 'I only came up here to tell you not to worry about mum. But if this is what you really want, then all right, I release you,' he said, shaking.

He went over to the bedside table to retrieve a carrier bag with his Green Place sponge bag and a spare pair of pyjamas in it. There were tears running down his face. And he picked it up and carried it roughly, scrunched and held out to the side, as if it were something he'd just killed on a hunt, hurt and angry and raw.

He walked swiftly out of Pearl's room, and a few minutes later I watched from the window as he went back down to the garden and I was alone again. It was all very sudden. But the history of the world, as with our own small lives, can spin and change on a whim.

FOR THE CONCERN OF THE RICH AND THE POOR

There were loud cheers from the passengers on board our ship the *Ganges* as we sailed up the Bay of Bengal. The night was still, the sea was golden, and the air was as hot as steam in our lungs.

Our voyage took three months, and two more in the planning, and we arrived into the port of Calcutta during the festival of Diwali in October 1861, having left Edenthorpe in the spring. As the sea drifted inland to join the river Hugli, we passed rows of lights floating downstream beside us. It appeared that the river was full of stars.

Disembarkation was a long, lengthy, loud process, somewhat at odds with our smooth passage, involving heckling and calling and filling out papers, amongst throngs of people who were trying to push or shove their way out of long tiresome queues. Rose Anna was suffering, almost faint with the heat, dressed in her heavy black gown, and Walderon swung into action with a bottle of smelling salts. Rose Anna must have been very relieved that she no longer wore her stifling veil and weeper's cuffs in such a raging heat. Mercifully, not long afterwards we were spotted and scooped up by a handsome Indian man, who said he was Thomas Garden's assistant.

'I am the Munshi,' he said. He was greeted by three tired faces looking back at him, still at sea.

We continued our journey overland, by carriage at first, passing through streets that were similarly lit up by the lights of Diwali. The Munshi told us that during Diwali the women and children made patterns with candles to decorate the streets with light.

'The people make prayers to the Goddess of Prosperity, who has come to bring light on the darkest night of the new moon. Lakshmi brings light over darkness, knowledge over ignorance, good over evil, Lakshmi brings hope over despair. I hope this will go some way to helping you in your great hour of loss,' said Munshi.

News that Frittie had vanished on the night we left Edenthorpe reached India before we did. I have preferred to tell myself for all these years that Frittie ran away that night. I hoped he might have carved out a life for himself somewhere, under the same stars that shone for me. And sometimes in my dreams, even now, I see a little silvery-coloured boy standing light as mist on the grass beyond the garden, but always he runs when he sees me. And the wild horses that run with him gallop in silver shoes.

PART FIVE

Martini Henry

Sue

Fri Aug 12 1988

Pensees: *Guilt is the enemy of the cosy.* SB

Quiz has absolutely no patience, he's the sort of person who opens all the doors on the advent calendar at once and then eats all the chocolate at one sitting. And he doesn't like anything half baked, such as gently carbonated water. I have had to update his TWD from dazzling to Won't Tolerate Delays.

And as a lover, there is a *scale* to his romance. It's not small and quiet and everydayish, it's big and dramatic and rare.

His favourite phrase is 'I'm going to make love to you as no man has ever made love to you before.' But he says it in French. (*'Je vais te faire l'amour comme aucun homme n'a jamais.'*) I used to think this was devastating but I have recently come to the conclusion that it is a bit big-headed.

Things have moved on very fast since that weekend in Westover. And the truth is – I lost my head. I haven't written, I haven't eaten, I haven't *slept*. I live, eat and breathe Quiz. I don't know another way to do things.

Joe has been very gallant and understanding, which makes

matters very much worse. Had he been a cad he would have made it nice and easy for me, but he tries to be tender and gentle, in spite of his own feelings. He never even once stopped coming to Green Place to work. Aunt Coral said this was a true testament to his good character, like all the best men in literature.

And as for me, as far as falling in love with Quiz goes, the giddy bit hasn't seemed to last very long. Apart from feeling so terrible about Joe, I feel so terrible about Di. We have not been in touch and it appaules me to know that at the end of the day, for all my morals, deep down I am nothing but a Jackie-friend.

But at the height of the summer while things were still giddy, Quiz and I went to London on a mini-break and stayed at the Ritz. We shopped in Chelsea. And in the evening we went up the river on a cruise aboard Quiz's friend Giles's Gin Palace, and we stood out on deck as we sailed along the Thames and waved to resentful passers-by.

And then, the next evening we went to the Opera. I had never been. But Quiz's romance was even more specific – because the opera was *Rusalka* and Rusalka is a Russian mermaid!

The signs for the Ladies and the Gents lavatories at the Opera were different than I'd ever seen before. The symbolic lady was wearing a ball gown and the symbolic gent was wearing a bow tie. I know that's not the thing you ought to be noticing about opera, but it is something I will always remember.

Quiz likes to speak in French proverbs. He says '*Le seul vrai language au monde est un baiser*', the only true language in the world is a kiss. And then he spontaneously kisses up one of my arms and then down the other. It makes me forget everything.

Even the looks of surprise on Dad and Ivana's faces when Quiz and I went to Titford to visit.

But one smile from Naughty Pierre and the woes of my

complicated relationships fall away from me. And when he sucks his toe, I'm enchanted. Who would have thought that such a wizard could be a person who can't even yet speak?

But Dad and Ivana obviously have opinions about me and Quiz. I have noticed, if you step out of your box, family don't tend to like it, i.e. a boy with a banger is one thing, but a man with a porch is another.

Sun Aug 14

Pensees: *Babies don't judge.*

Yesterday we visited an art gallery in a chapel and Quiz analysed all the paintings for me. He told me some good things to say at exhibitions if I am having to shmutz – from vague things such as 'I feel a presence' to specific things such as 'I like the contrast, but I do feel he could have added more white'. I love his cultured views and all his interesting memberships to things.

But then, quite unexpectedly, after we got back to Greylands, up in Studio One, with the lamps on and the leaves spinning outside and the rain gently tapping the skylights – Quiz *popped the question!* And of course I have accepted! What a whirlwind!

And yet in the secret back places of my mind – this all feels like it's happening to *somebody else.*

FOR THE CONCERN OF THE RICH AND THE POOR

If you had told me on those long icy nights at the Mead that one day I would live in a country where there were thirty-three million gods and not just one, I would never have believed you. Or, that there I would have an Ayah who so worshipped me that she slept across my door to guard me from spirits, I would have said, this really is a strange dream.

If I'd realized that by my absorption into Rose Anna's family I would have mother, brother, sister, guardians, teacher, nanny, I would have fallen to my knees to give thanks. But if you had pointed out to me, as I wandered in my bare feet down the paths of the garden at Edenthorpe, that my Uncle Benedict and Aunt Adelaide were at home in the big house, I would have said, now you really must be joking! News from Green Place filtered into my ears that Frittie's remains still had not been discovered. So there was a chance that he ran away that night. I have always carried that hope.

Ayah called me 'chota Sahib' – little gentleman – or 'sadhu' – old wise man. She treated me as though my status were just as revered as the swarmi on the hill. She had been employed to take care of Thomas and Marcella's son and daughter, Vivien who was three, and Patricia who was five, so I was quite far ahead at eleven.

Ayah was gentle and sweet and sang songs to us. She wore saris that were the colour of peaches.

At first we lived in a visitors' bungalow in the grounds of the Svarga Ghara compound, the grand home of Benedict's brother Thomas Garden. Our bungalow was called 'Gunyah'. It was a mud-brick palace under a high thatched roof. The ceiling of each room was made from a gauze cloth painted with whitewash, and there was a gap in between the cloth and the roof where I sometimes saw snakes.

The rooms inside were vast, airy, but we spent most of our time outside on a wide veranda overlooking the lawns.

As soon as it could be arranged, Rose Anna adopted me and Thomas Garden and his wife Marcella became my guardians. They all felt it was best that way so that responsibility for my care was spread across three pairs of shoulders.

'Just in case anything should happen,' said Thomas. In time I came to understand that 'just in case anything should happen' referred to incidents such as snake bite, cholera, and a host of other deadly things that flourished in the heat of India.

They kept a mongoose in the compound for the purpose of eating any snakes that might get in. Munshi showed me the side-winding marks of a krait in the dust, so I could see with my own eyes the signs.

Munshi was the resident teacher; his real name was Jagachandra. The name means Moon of the Universe, but he was always referred to as Munshi.

With so many people to help, Walderon was made redundant and turned into a keen little bookworm! The Indians thought she must be a goddess because they had never seen a white woman so old.

As for myself, I did not take to my new elevated position naturally, confidence was something I had to learn. And the first time the family sat down at one great table to eat together, I wondered where I should sit.

Perhaps there was another table for me, around a corner, hidden from view? But Rose Anna could read my deference very well, and she pulled out the chair next to hers. 'This is where you sit,' she said.

In the India of my imagination elephants wandered tamely in the garden, with hand-painted gold saddles and flower garlands round their ears. This of course was not the reality, where wandering elephants were more carefully avoided, at least by the British. But to my surprise, in the India of the world, the elephants really did wear bracelets, and they really took baths, and they really were obliging enough to wear face paint, or any kind of garland you liked. Now tell me, which is the dream?

Sue

I came back to Egham this morning, to break the exciting news of my engagement to Aunt Coral.

Unfortunately, Quiz had to go straight to the university to take a lecture after he dropped me, and I went to find Aunt Coral to show her my ring. She was in the drawing room, so often the setting for the important scenes in my life. She looked so pleased to see me.

But I should have realized something was awry when she did not immediately crack open a bottle of champagne and call for the Admiral.

'Are you sure?' was all she said when I told her.

'You don't seem to be thriving, Sue. There are shadows under your eyes.'

'Of course I'm *sure*,' I said emphatically. 'Aren't you going to say congratulations?'

'Congratulations,' she said. 'Have you set a date yet?'

'No not yet,' I replied.

'Well that's good, there's no hurry,' she said.

I floundered for a comment, shocked at her response. When you consider how excitable she is, it was really under-whelming.

'You think he's too old for me, but it's only nine years, that's nothing.'

'No darling, it isn't that, it's just, perhaps at 18, perhaps you don't have to *marry* him, you could just see how you feel. And you don't need to choose between Quiz and Joe either – maybe you should . . . get a third?'

All the porcelain and pearls in the world cannot hide a true hippy.

'And are you sure that it's *love*?' she continued. 'If it isn't making you thrive then it might be . . . love's poor cousin,' she whispered in her *code*.

'And infatuation has little or nothing to do with love, does it? It has to do with *intoxication*,' went on Aunt C. 'I was infatuated with Professor Podger when I was at university, because I loved the *image* of being a Professor's wife, spending all my time in cosy studies with arch windows and all that sort of thing . . . but I saw very quickly that it was only a projection . . . of a life I had not *lived*,' she said anxiously.

'I see you've given that a lot of thought,' I said bitterly.

'I'm sorry darling, all I mean is I'm glad you're not rushing into it,' Aunt C floundered. 'I didn't mean to hurt your feelings.'

But I am totally bewildered and shocked. Surely this isn't the way *that* scene was supposed to go?

Tues August 16th 1988

Things are spiralling. This morning I received a *note* from Joe. I am mortified that he has heard my news already.

Dear Sue
I heard your news from Glenn the builder, who heard it from
Mrs Bunion, who heard it from Aunt Coral. I am sorry, but I
felt I just had to speak.

I don't understand why you feel you have to get *married* when you haven't even known Quiz a year. I must tell you that I think he is an opportunist and I'm angry with Aunt Coral for being so public about her will and turning you into a target for gold diggers.

I hope that you will see sense, I don't want you to get hurt, in spite of everything.

If I make myself sound like a saint, I don't feel like one. It is very hard for me to write this, let alone to keep seeing you with him.

Glenn also said that Aunt Coral is guessing that I will jack in doing the garden. Please will you tell her that I am still absolutely determined not to let her down. And so I expect I will see you around.

Joe

After Quiz got back from lectures, we went up to my suite for an urgent summit.

'Aunt Coral would be very upset if she knew about this,' I said, referring to Joe's note. 'I can't bear the thought of them falling out. Joe and Aunt Coral truly love each other.'

'You'd better tear it up so that she'll never find it,' said Quiz, shredding Joe's note.

'I think it would be better for everyone if we had a sabbatical for a few weeks at Greylands,' he went on, 'just until things die down and everyone has a chance to deal with their feelings. *C'est la goutte d'eau qui fait deborder le vase* – this is the drop of water that made the vase overflow. And what we must do is take a little water out.'

Sun Sept 18 1988

Here at Greylands, Sunday mornings begin with the church bells ringing out from the bottom of Cinder Street. The first eight peels of the bells come down a scale in a perfect fall, and then the last two chimes flow quicker and closer together, as though whoever is ringing the bells got tired and the effort is too great to keep time. I suspect I must have been a little bored here to pay such close attention.

I have all my books and notepads about me and Quiz has set me up at his fabulous old escritoire. It's a nice place to take extracts and try and get motivated again to take another look at my dissertation. Since my Jenny mauling, though I dream of that raspberry farm and of the simple life just digging, there is still a flicker inside me, that won't allow me to *quite* give up.

And if I don't ever fulfil my ambition to work around writing, I do believe I will die trying.

And now, I have the time to try, try again, because Quiz is away during the week at the university. So I must make an *effort* to get back to work.

But on a positive note, getting out of bed in the mornings, I notice I am walking on an uphill floorboard. It makes me pine for Green Place. Not that it isn't nice here.

Mrs Wilson has been very strange, though. She treats me as if I am just one of a succession of girls who have come to stay in the attic. I might even say she ignores me, but occasionally she has said hello if I pass her, or try and crack a little joke on the landing. She is very busy with her art. And on the rare occasion that she *does* talk to me, she doesn't talk to my *face*, she talks to my clothes.

But Quiz loves the idea of having a muse in his attic . . . he says that he looks forward all week to seeing me. But . . .

How lonely the life of the muse. I wait for my youth to be devoured
and slaughtered by the one who would never come.
A pensee by Susannah Parkes

Pensees: *A polite titter is the joker's despair.* SB

Since Joe said what he said about Quiz being an opportunist, I have reflected, that Quiz left Di *after* I became an heiress . . . and that he moved into Green Place *after* he saw 'Make will' on Aunt Coral's To Do. I may be putting together a paranoid argument. But in the light of Joe's warning and Aunt Coral's unexpected, joyless reaction to my engagement, I'm worried that there might be a little Colonel of truth in what Joe suggests. Things occur to me retrospectively, in this way; I think perhaps I am a bit slow. I wish I was more like Helen. And I think of her out there somewhere being common sense and no nonsense.

> *If autumn is the evening of the year, then winter is the night, and spring is high noon. But summer is six o'clock drinks, when the martinis are on ice.*
> *Oh home.*
> *Another pensee by Susannah Parkes.*

Pensees: *October, when the nights draw in and the grass sparkles.* SB

I'm sitting at the old escritoire trying to write, but I'm tired of Jenny and I can't even be bothered with 'The Emperor's Slippers'. I can't see the point today, when it has become clear to me that I am a bit of a ham.

Cars swish by on the roads outside and Pilgrim chews his

nails in the mornings. He has started coming up to my room at night. It is as though he knows I am lonely.

Sometimes I can't get out of my little dark place, and Joe was able to help with that. He could cast a beam of light into the darkest day, with a walk down the high street and a takeaway coffee. He could build a day around anything, around getting a specific kind of chewing gum. Once we made a great day out of running Aunt Coral around to buy some new summer vests.

But being with Quiz appears to drive me further into my dark place (or maybe I should say *not* being with Quiz seems to drive me further into it, because of course he's hardly ever here). But . . . in a whole-life context, I don't really know how I got here from there, this has all happened so *fast*.

FOR THE CONCERN OF THE RICH AND THE POOR

Master Benedict's brother, Thomas Garden, was something called a Collector Magistrate, an elite member of the Indian Civil Service (ICS). It was also called the 'Imperial Civil Service of the British Empire'.

I knew he must have been very important, because visitors always took off their hats to him, and when he left the compound of Svarga Ghara, the locals ran after his tonga waving through the trails of dust.

'He is here to keep law and order for India for Queen and for Empire,' said Rose Anna. 'He is in a position of great privilege.'

'To think, I was worried about finding a decent wage!' I said.

'Shh,' she said as we sat on the veranda, 'we might be overheard.'

'I thought you might have to sell your pearls,' I whispered.

'I see the walls of Edenthorpe had ears,' she replied.

'I'm sorry, we weren't eavesdropping.'

'I see,' she said, raising an eyebrow.

'We were worried about you – Master Benedict threatened you.'

'He is not the Master here.'

'But have you got your treasure with you, if we should ever need funds?'

'I would certainly have brought my treasure, as you call it! I was very fond of it, it had many happy memories attached, but due to our hasty departure, I did not have time to go and retrieve it,' she replied.

'Is it in your husband's grave?' I asked with horrified curiosity.

'Good grief no! I put it somewhere much safer. It is somewhere where I hope it might yet be of benefit to all. Anyway, you don't need to worry yourself about money again, London, we have the wealth of the Raj to support us. Though we must not be profligate.'

At the time I really had little comprehension of the type of wealth that she meant. My own treasure was still my niner, now laid amongst fine clothes inside a polished teak and silver drawer.

For just as suddenly as I had a fleet of parents, suddenly I had money, and not just enough of it, lots and lots and lots. I had so much money that I could throw some into the well. Pauper, vagrant, urchin, gardener, son and heir. My new family not only had their own beds to sleep in, but they had more than one house. During the very hot summer, they explained, we would travel to our second home in a hill station at the foot of the Himalayas, to escape the heat.

And almost a year to the day after we arrived in Jaunpur, we moved into our own quarters at Svarga Ghara, newly decorated and appointed and full of art and sculpture and gold. In 'Lakshmi' the floors were made of marble, and the building was made of brick, with elegant tiled arches and regal columns reminiscent of the Holy Roman Empire.

The first morning I woke up there the compound was full of raised voices because the children were quarrelling over why Vivien had something called dainty croissants in his picnic lunch and Patricia didn't.

'They are quarrelling over exotic delicacies, they do not know they are born,' I remember whispering to myself.

Sue

Thurs Oct 6 1988

Aunt Coral contacted all the local museums after I rang and read her the last extract! We agreed that one might deduce from what Rose Anna said that it does sound like she might have loaned the Shipwreck Pearl necklace to a private collection or put into other hands for safekeeping. But although Aunt C suspects that the jewels could be in a vault somewhere, she feels she will have a harder time persuading Jackie of that. Apparently the archaeologists are now on their third hole in the garden and are creeping nearer and nearer to the house, getting more and more excited. Aunt Coral says their cameras reveal spiders' webs mostly, like silver plankton in all the darkness.

Quiz told me on the phone last night that he has lots of ideas for how to make the house pay for itself when I inherit. But my doubts about his intentions have really taken root, and his suggestions only tinker with my inadequacy demons. Because there are, after all, still millions of people who marry for houses, not for love.

Word List

Profligate

Mid-evening Pensees of mid-autumn night:

Hindsight is a great critic. SB

So here I am in the world of Studio One and my notebooks lie cast aside at the bottom of the bed. My word lists overfloweth and within the pages of my jotters imagined people write imagined letters to imagined friends, and imagined hearts break and mend again over and over. Imagined doctors are called to imagined bedsides and shake their imagined heads. 'It's too late,' they say in imagined voices, pulling imagined sheets over imagined heads.

This month is crawling by, the days seem to last for weeks.

If I don't talk to somebody soon, I will forget how to do it. I used to love being on my own, having cereal at unseemly times of day, or cocktails in the bath and what have you. I don't know what has happened to me, I'm really not myself.

Because I have reflected that I had begun to feel at times *almost* happy, in spite of the loss of mum. But I go and break up with Joe and suddenly I miss so much her particular way of understanding, which no one, not even Aunt Coral, can mirror unfortunately. This is the sort of delicate thing that is known as irreplaceable, and without it loneliness has a new depth.

But if my mum were here now, and she asked me why I have broken everything, I would explain that Quiz and Joe are very different. I'd tell her that Quiz is terrifyingly masculine, a jaw-dropping alpha, that he is cultured, worldly, modern, magnificent, and supersonically confident with all the outer trappings of a gentleman. And that Joe is modest, poetic, loyal, sensitive and caring, with buckets of *inner* class. It comes naturally to Joe to be thoughtful. But Quiz, I have noticed, doesn't seem to notice anyone *else* very much. And Joe used to say he found *me* exciting. I suppose these things are all relative.

Of course it's easy to see all this now, all these weeks later, now that I have all this time to reflect. I had no idea I would miss Joe as much as I do. In all the giddiness I overlooked the fact that he was with me during the most difficult year of my life, and even at such times as we haven't been together Joe has been the small voice I look forward to hearing, somewhere on the end of a crackly phone. I'm sure Helen would find it terribly soupy of me to be pining after Joe, and then Quiz, and now again Joe. I must pull myself together.

Later 3am can't sleep

I have decided that tomorrow I am going to go to Green Place, to try and talk to Joe. Enough time has gone by now and I want to tell him how terribly sorry I am. And I want to let Aunt Coral know that I, and of course Quiz, would like to come back home.

We all make messes, it's what we do about them that matters. I know I have been very foolish, but I now feel absolutely determined to see Joe and talk it through. Of course there's the chance he may not be there and I may be absolutely determined on my own, but even so.

FOR THE CONCERN OF THE RICH AND THE POOR

Yet once again in my life came the problem of what to call myself. In Allahabad, in a land incongruously full of Montys and Tuppys and Teddys, the Colonial types had great trouble with the name London. It didn't quite match a person purporting to be a pucca Sahib (a real gentleman).

And so on Nov 16 1862, after a great deal of thought I might add (and at the age of twelve), I decided I should like to be known from then on as Lawrence Alfred Harold Garden. It is not difficult to hazard a guess as to some of my reasons. Lawrence means 'wearer of the laurel leaf', symbolic of the laurel I wear for Alfred. To have taken his name as my first would have cracked open my heart.

Every morning I woke to the sound of the brain fever bird singing his scales, which grew louder and louder in a crescendo. On free days, Ayah would come to wake us up and we would have some fruit under the shade of the veranda. And with the glory of my new name, I attended a Colonial School near Jaunpur, where I mixed with the children of the Police, Naval Officers and all ranks of forces families alike.

Marcella was very disapproving of Rose Anna's choice of school for me. Vivien was sent to Eton and Patricia was privately tutored. But having come so far, and through so much, in order to be united, Rose Anna was not about to send me to boarding school. And if Chaplain Cragg had neglected to teach his paupers how to write, the Colonial School saw to it that this matter was corrected.

And the day I signed my name to a letter was a day of great celebration. Lawrence Alfred Harold Garden, Esquire!

Farewell London Taylor, I wonder what Chaplain Cragg would have made of that? And how much sorrow and joy is alive in the story of my name.

That night Munshi told me a story about the magical white Guar (buffalo), whose colour was rinsed off by the Monsoon. He felt it was in keeping with the blessing of my evolution.

Sue

Finally I know who Lawrence Garden is! All this time I thought that possibly there was going to be a note at the back of the book explaining where Lawrence Garden found London Taylor's story!

I can't imagine my life without being able to write. I can understand why learning to write was such a *pinnacle* for Lawrence. Writing gives you the freedom to be able to express yourself in another way, and to remember what you expressed forever.

At 10 am

Pensees of a dog: *There is nothing finer*
than a piddle on a hillock. SB

I went out early to purchase a paper and decided to try the second of 3 hostilleries in Westover for my breakfast. Westover is much quainter than Egham. It's a place where vanilla-and-rose-scented ladies shop in the small boutiques and where even the graffiti behind the bike racks is quite restrained in that it just says 'F off'.

I walked back via the park, through the autumn cobwebs in the dew-drenched grass, getting wet trainers, wet socks and wet feet. When I got back I rang straight through to Aunt Coral. I thought of her by the phone in the hall, with the Admiral somewhere just off stage in the setting, chomping peacefully on his pipe, and Mrs Bunion clattering about helpfully somewhere . . . and Joe down in the walled garden.

'I wondered, do you think you might ask Joe for supper?' I asked Aunt Coral, casually, before we finished the call.

'What a good idea, of course I will and the Admiral and I will come and fetch you if you give a ring from the station,' she said.

She sounded like she was going to go straight into the kitchen and ask Mrs Bunion to rustle something up. I know her so well. I know each tone in her voice, and each change of pace and what it means. I can't wait to see her! It is a warmth so much the opposite of the polarized existences of the inhabitants of Greylands . . . where every man is an island, each in his *studio* den.

I had only just hung up when the phone rang again and it was Quiz calling from London to see how I was.

'I thought I would go to Green Place and visit Aunt Coral,' I said.

'I thought you were supposed to be writing?' he said.

'I'm reflecting,' I said.

'Are you sure it's wise to go? Won't Joe be there?'

'I'll be fine, and I do want to break the ice, I hate all this bad feeling. Maybe we've stayed away long enough now. Maybe we can all be friends. What are you up to?' I asked.

'I'm tied up in Bloomsbury again,' he said with a yawn.

'So you won't get back to Green Place tonight?' I asked.

'No, I'll need to stay at the flat again, it's such a bore. Shall I pick you up tomorrow evening and we can drive back to Westover together?' he asked.

'Yes lovely, thank you, that would make sense.'

I'm feeling much brighter at the thought of going home for a bit, and having a little break from Greylands. And also happy that it will soon be the weekend and I can actually *see* Quiz. I feel certain I've only to see him in the flesh and all my anxieties will melt away. It's being apart all the time that can't be helping.

FOR THE CONCERN OF THE RICH AND THE POOR

In what is optimistically called the cold weather, I sometimes accompanied Thomas on one of the tours he made of his district.

Everyone came, Munshi, Ayah and nine other members of staff. We took our little society with us wherever we went.

We made a meandering procession behind Thomas's horse, with our entire camp and every human being carried on the backs of elephants.

I never thought I would long to see the open arch of a dark wet umbrella, or a cool grey sky bursting with rain. The advance party from Svarga Ghara always travelled ahead of us and put up the tents and made camp, and we would follow in time for a cooked breakfast which would be waiting in the middle of a plain. The children played houses between the bridges of the banyan trees, which are said to be the resting place of Krishna.

Then after breakfast Thomas set up his 'office' for petitioners from the local villages to come.

It consisted of a wooden table, with a few chairs opposite his, under the shade of a tree. And people came from all over to discuss their problems, which Thomas said often resulted from disputes about bribes, women, gold or land.

At fourteen, I was halfway between playing soldiers between the tent pegs and wanting to help Thomas write up his reports ... reports on the states of the roads and the railways, where they had begun. And his thoughts on policing, tea gardens, accidents, it all went into his Officer's diary. A diary I thought, idealistically, which would contain the building bricks of my Utopian Empire of India, a far cry from the land of mutiny and dissent.

Sue

Pensees: *Aunt Coral's dream To Do: cheese knife, letter opener, clotted-cream jasmine, top hat, blueberries.* SB

I got into Egham at 4.04. It was a silvery grey day. When I got out of the train I was hit by the smell of smoke, and pasties, and cigarette butts on the wet platform. I passed by the station waiting room where grey-brown figures were huddled inside waiting to get on to warm trains.

As promised, the Admiral and Aunt Coral made a trip out to the station in the Bentley to collect me. It looked as though they had both got changed into their travelling clothes. Aunt Coral had a rug over her knees and her good woollen tights on, the Admiral was in his plus fours. They had taken the opportunity to potter into town a little earlier and there was a bottle-green carrier bag on the back seat next to me, with a packet of fudge and a new tablecloth in it. Aunt Coral must have had a little hit (at the shops). I am always relieved, when I haven't seen her for a while, to see her looking fit and well. My anxiety over her health can go from 0 to 60 very quickly.

'Any wintry problems on the trains?' asked the Admiral.

'All fine today, like clockwork,' I said.

'This time of year uncleared leaves on the tracks can cause major disruption. It's best to travel before autumn,' said the Admiral.

'I think you need to get out more Avery,' said Aunt Coral.

The Admiral grinned broadly, though in truth I don't think he understood what she meant.

When we arrived home I was most surprised to find that Mrs Bunion was away.

'Her daughter has not been very well,' said Aunt Coral. 'So she has gone to nurse her better. But the Admiral and I have been managing pretty well, haven't we Avery?'

'Laha,' replied the Admiral, looking up from his paper. 'I'm cooking the dinner tonight. I hope you've had your jabs.'

'Nonsense,' said Aunt C, as he rose to diddle with the drinks things. 'As a matter of fact I find the Admiral's porridge very fulfilling,' she explained. 'And of course one would never starve here, because when push comes to shove the house is crammed full of boxes of lingering chocolates.'

Later

They brought forward their cocktails to five o'clock because it had already been dark for over an hour and they couldn't wait. It was a blustering evening, spitting rain that couldn't quite get going.

'This wind is very disappointing,' said Aunt Coral.

'Quite,' said the Admiral. 'Aren't you going to take your coat off?'

'This is my indoor coat, Avery dear,' she replied. 'There were three little girls carrying umbrellas walking ahead of me in town,' continued Aunt C. 'They looked like they were going to do a number.'

'Is Joe coming to dinner?' I managed to cut in.

'I'm sorry darling, sadly no, he said he was busy.'

'Oh,' I said quietly. The words 'he said he was busy' conjured horrors within.

'But you'll be able to see him first thing in the morning. He's working on the surrounds for the sundial. He's making what he calls a "Gallant's Bower",' she said. 'And Jackie came over last night and we had another discussion about calling off the digging of any more little holes in the garden.'

'And are you going to stop?'

'Yes, but I have agreed to just one more investigation towards the kitchen, in the hopes of finding the you know what! They're coming to dig a little hole on Saturday, in a targetted area to the side.'

'Mmm-hmm,' I said.

'Just think, if we found the Shipwreck Pearls that could set you up with a start-up fund for running Green Place as and when you might need it.'

'Mmm-hmm,' I said again. But I was drifting, imagining myself as an old lady, alone in Green Place, lying on the drawing-room sofa covered in cats. I would stitch myself into my hat and coat and never bathe or put the heating on. I would recover from my frequent bouts of pneumonia and stare out of the window for hours. I would only eat bread and jam, and pine for the balmy days of duaphinois by the heater in the club. Interesting to note that I did not foresee Quiz in the picture.

'Can I freshen your glasses?' asked the Admiral, attending to our drinks.

'Ah, my favourite verb,' said Aunt Coral, 'especially in this context. On a chummy note, Avery, tell me, do you prefer male company to female company?' she added apropos of flirting.

'I prefer good company,' replied the Admiral.

'So do I,' I said. 'It is very good to be back. I hope things feel a little less *awkward* with Joe now so that I, and of course Quiz, can come home.'

Word List
Gallant's Bower

9.00pm

Pensees: *To say you are hopeless in the kitchen is the best way to get out of making dinner.* SB

I have just been lying in the bath in the Avocado bathroom, toying with some more concerns over my inheritance. Such as, what if at the time of inheriting, I should inherit some elderly residents along with the house? For example, what if I inherit the Admiral? I simply couldn't ever want to ask him to leave.

And he is suddenly looking older. Maybe his age is a number now that could well begin with an eight? I noticed he is not filling his pullover in the same way as he used to, his shape has turned softer, the way cushions go when they don't fill their linings flush.

But whether he was with me or not, obviously he'd be too elderly to help much, and he'd probably have to give up driving. So I'd have to work from dawn till dusk, with six different jobs just to be able to afford for us to camp in one room.

And I'd never be out of my wellies, as with great futility I'd pull up one or two weeds every month, till the garden became like a jungle that swallowed up Green Place, just like it did the walled garden and cottages. And one day Joe might come looking for me because no one had seen me for months and he'd find my body mummified by spiders after a full-scale search for the house.

Again, interesting to note that I fantasize Joe finding me not Quiz. And interesting to note that in my vision there was no hint of a forthcoming wedding.

But I am here to remind myself that Aunt Coral's wealth lasted for fifty years before she got down to holey pockets. Maybe I can eek out my £4.11. At least I have to retrain my thoughts to be more pragmatic, diplomatic, and less problematic.

And as regards becoming a chatelaine, I intend to step up to the mark, even in the face of enormous odds. And you never know, we may yet find the Shipwreck Pearls and their show-stopping clasp.

And anyway none of these concerns apply, and hopefully may not do for a long time. Aunt C is downstairs playing draughts with the Admiral and is very much alive and kicking.

FOR THE CONCERN OF THE RICH AND THE POOR

After I finished school, I got a job as a clerk to the Assistant Deputy Collector in Allahabad. Our office was near a meeting point of three rivers in Allahabad: first, Ma Ganga (Mother Ganges, the sublime wine of immortality), second, the river Jumna, and the third river is invisible, the Saraswati.

The meeting point of all three rivers is called the Sangam. It is believed to be a place of great sin-washing powers, which I hoped might go some way to alleviate my guilt about getting into this position through the back door. My family connections accounted for my position, I must have been the only English man in the Indian Civil Service who had not come through the hallowed halls of Haileybury, even to such a lowly position.

I suffered a good deal from my conscience about this. Sometimes I believe family connections account for everything except merit. I felt 'the machine' was an unjust thing . . . because by the time I joined the ICS, there were only 4 Indian Officers in the entire service, and yet I, who could have been anybody, got in through the back door. Pauper, vagrant, urchin, son, gentleman, coat-tailer.

Around the same time, Rose Anna began encouraging what she called a firm friendship with a convivial Major Turner. The poor fellow was desperate to marry her, still she said she couldn't bear 'to go through it all again'. Even so, her affection for him was heartfelt, if not yet outwardly acknowledged.

She never quite gave up wearing black, although she was no longer buttoned up to the elbows with her weeper's cuffs or shrouded behind her weeping veil, as she was before we left England.

But when the Indian sun had faded even the darkest of her gowns, she procured a deep grey heather mixed tweed from the box-wallah, which would not show dust or mud stains, yet could not lose its colour under the sun's glare. She was ever the determined widow.

As for me, unlike most of my peers, I was a late starter with girls. The only one I ever really found I could talk to was Patricia, and as she was six years younger than me and virtually my sister, so at the time I never thought twice.

We lost Walderon in the year of 1867. She was seventy-five, and probably the oldest white woman in India. She certainly made it past two Monsoons, which at the time was the grisly average for settlers. And though life is short, I have only to look at Walderon to know that it can also be long. The Doctor said it was due to the bite of the Naja Naj, the spectacled cobra, which is often the snake of the charmer.

I remember I thought that Walderon was terribly old when I first ever saw her outside Edenthorpe, but she must have just had one of those faces that was born old and then stayed the same.

Her grave is in Jaunpur, a long, long way from England. I felt ashamed when I saw her headstone.

The beloved
Agnes Walderon.
1792–1867
At peace

I had never known her first name.

Sue

Dawn Pensees:

Imagine being born in a year beginning with 17! What an adventure Walderon must have had, and what a blessing to have seen India, when it was still so *unknown*. I don't know many people, myself included, who wouldn't wish for a similar thing. But I wonder is there anywhere left where I could still *pioneer*? Where one can still go and be a traveller, not a tourist? But enough early pensees – I could go on and on, but I have a task today, to talk to *Joe*, and I'm nervous, and I feel like I've eaten something that hasn't quite *agreed*.

All day yesterday the Admiral had a joint of pork defrosting in a pool of blood on the boiler. Long after it had thawed it still lay there, unintentionally slow cooking. But at dinner, it was burnt on the outside and not cooked on the inside. I don't quite understand how he did it. And . . . I ate some out of solidarity, with plenty of apple sauce. Heading back to most distant and most private bathroom at the far end of East Wing passage.

*

A little later, after best efforts made with appearance, and feeling rather empty and fragile, I went down to the walled garden and took Joe a hot beverage.

'Hello stranger,' I said, boldly, on my approach. I didn't feel like taking any prisoners, especially if they were doubts.

'Hello, what are you doing here?' replied Joe, as if I really were a stranger.

'I just thought I'd pop down for a mid-week visit,' I said, inhaling the icy air.

Half the ground was covered in a sharp frost, and the other half was melting. He was working on a sort of surround for the sundial, and underneath it he has retained the swathes of Town Clock. Obviously they are just little promises at the moment.

He has sculpted curved terraced steps behind the sundial, which embrace it at the back and flow up in three tiers to a bench like a throne at the top. It is all decorated with climbers, and has a roof over its head. This I guessed must be what Aunt Coral referred to as the Gallant's Bower.

'How are you?' Joe asked politely.

'OK,' I said.

I expected he might put down his hoe and sit down to have a talk with me, but he carried on hoeing a bit of soil that already looked perfectly hoed. I sat on the bench at the top of the bower and held on to the wood either side of me.

'Joe,' I began cautiously with a pre-prepared inner speech. 'I'm so terribly sorry I've made such a mess of everything.'

'How do you mean?' he asked.

'With Quiz.'

'Oh,' he said, 'oh well, I don't know what to say.' He hoed on.

'I'm truly sorry. Do you think you can ever forgive me?'

'Sue, I don't know actually.'

'But I wanted to tell you I'm sorry and . . .'

'It's OK, I know you are,' he said, finally putting his hoe down. 'It isn't that. Of course I can forgive you. It's just that things have moved on for me as well. I've been seeing Charlie.' He said it very urgently.

The next two rotations of the earth went double speed. I gripped on to the bench. I wished that I could just drop off the earth.

'Congratulations,' I said. 'I'm so glad.'

'Thanks,' said Joe. 'I guess it was always on the cards.'

'When did you, when did it . . . ?'

'It didn't start in Sicily.'

'Mmm-hmm,' I said, and I felt the pressure of humiliated tears.

'So anyway, even if you feel you've made a mess, it looks like you haven't,' said Joe. 'I think you did the right thing.'

'Thanks Joe, I'll see you later then,' I said, and I turned and walked away, trying to give the impression of an ordinary stroll, trying to project from my back that I have this sort of talk *all* the time. But I desperately needed to get to a place of privacy, because if I'd stayed a moment longer I would have exposed myself just too much.

The robin that lives in the Admiral's bathroom landed on the sundial as I retreated, his breast brilliant raging red against the chilly white and silver in the air. Could it be possible that he might have taken off a hundred and twenty years ago from the same spot and landed here in 1988? I wished I could go back in time.

I walked back through the wintry garden, the frost a forgotten whisper in the low winter sun. I passed by a leaf caught in a cobweb; it looked like it was suspended in mid-air. It's funny the silly things you latch on to when your heart is breaking.

Later, back in the drawing room, the Admiral made a hasty exit during a discussion about 'feelings'.

'What have I done? What have I *done*?' I sobbed.

'It's all right darling,' said Aunt Coral. 'It'll be all right.'

'How could I have done this?' I said. 'I can't believe it. If only I hadn't fallen for Quiz, I'd still have Joe, and now I can never be with Joe again.'

'These sorts of things are never irrevocable,' said Aunt Coral.

'Yes they are. I've broken my own heart, how stupid is that? I wish Joe had broken it for me and then at least I could blame him.'

'Listen,' said Aunt Coral, 'whenever I have split up with anyone in the past, I always found it helpful to think of it like this. Imagine that you and Joe were two dolphins who meet in the big wide ocean, and for a while you frolicked together, jumping out of the water and swimming along in perfect sync, and parallel like synchronized swimmers, you know?'

'Yes.'

'Well, over however long a time you are frolicking, it's easy to get out of sync, one dolphin jumps higher, and therefore slower than the other, she finds herself in other waters, and gets swept another way. It's natural, it's life, everything changes, nothing stays the same, nothing lasts,' she said. 'Does that help?'

I collapsed into spasms of grief.

'You make it sound like he's *dead*,' I sobbed.

'He's not dead, for goodness sake, and he's going to go on and on living. I can just see him as a very old man, crossing the Sahara with a swagger. You mustn't worry about him; it's you we need to worry about. Now come on, what are we going to do about you? I think that it's time you came home. You don't have to hide away in Westover. There's nothing for you to be ashamed of. You're a young woman and you fell in love, it's going to happen *all the time*,' she said, trying desperately to cheer me up and put it all into a manageable older person's context. 'I just hope you don't fall in love with everyone who comes to stay in the house, because I'm quite keen on getting back into B and B.'

I managed a smile, albeit through humiliated tears.

'Anyway, very soon it will only be light for about six hours a day, so Joe won't even be coming in to do the garden much longer,' Aunt C concluded. 'Would you like the Admiral and me to take you back to Westover in the Bentley? Pick up your things and bring you home for good?'

'It's all right,' I said. 'Quiz is collecting me tonight. I'll go back with him and get my things. I must tell him how I really feel. I'm not being fair to him.'

Fri Oct 14 1988

Pensees: *'Men are born free and everywhere they are in chains.' (Rousseau)*
I think what he means by this are the chains that we can't see. SB

Midnight

Shortly after Quiz and I arrived back at Greylands this evening, I went up to Studio One and started to put together my notepads etc., which I cleared off his escritoire and put into a carrier bag ready to go home. I didn't feel ready to talk about Joe as we drove back to Greylands, so I managed to keep Quiz on the subject of himself, which was easy.

Mrs Wilson was not at home today. She drives to London on Fridays to visit the Galleries. It makes me sad, because when she goes she leaves Pilgrim at home on his own all day and long into the evening too.

He padded around the studio, panting, and brushed passed me

with an opportunist lick of my shin. I gave him a biscuit, and he buried it in my slipper, which I was wearing! In the midst of turbulence there is always a bit of happiness somewhere, and the shock of finding wet nose in your slipper is one such surprising joy.

Quiz came up and brought a couple of glasses of champagne with him.

'You appear to be packing,' he said. 'How did it go with Joe?'

'It was fine,' I said.

'Are you sure?'

'Mmm. It was OK.'

I was quiet for another moment while I gathered myself.

'Quiz, I've been thinking – I don't feel very *sure* about things any more.'

'I see,' he said, 'and is this because of Joe?'

'I think it is. I'm so sorry, I didn't know how much I felt for him, or how much this would hurt. I've been so stupid.'

He put down his champagne glass and sat on the bed. His face changed, his tone was subdued.

'I broke up with Di for you,' he said quietly. He put his head in his hands, he rubbed his eyes, he shook his head in disbelief.

'But you told me that it was already finished,' I said.

'I mean my relationship with her finished *because* of you. If there had been no you, then it wouldn't have finished, would it? I was just being protective of you, in the way that I *put it*. Are you telling me that I have thrown it all away for *nothing*?'

'No, of course not,' I said. 'You're confusing me. I just mean that I still have feelings for Joe and so I don't know if it's right that we should get married.'

'So you're saying you want to be together, but you're just not ready to get married? Is that what you're saying?'

'Yes,' I said, beginning to feel extremely muddled.

'And you still want to be engaged?'

'Yes,' I answered, nervously.

'Look, I can understand you still have feelings for Joe,' he said. 'I still have feelings for Di. They don't just disappear conveniently because you have fallen in love with someone else.'

He sighed heavily, and then he took hold of my hand. 'I'm sorry. I don't mean to be sharp. I have rushed you, of course – we can wait till you're ready till we set the date. I should never have left you alone here to brood. It hurts when relationships end. I didn't think it was a good idea that you went home yesterday, but I didn't like to say. It's much too soon. But if you still want to go, then we can both go back on Sunday night, of course we can. But please, darling Sue, please let's say this is just plus tard, not au revoir.'

Now I understand what people mean when they say that they are in too deep.

FOR THE CONCERN OF THE RICH AND THE POOR

Just before the Monsoon was due to break in July of 1868, I would have been eighteen, Major Turner invited Rose Anna and myself to visit him at the Old Fort James, near Oghi in the Agror Valley, which is a little place that lies right on the edge of the North West Frontier. The Fort is of legendary beauty, standing like an eagle on the top of a hill.

The North West Frontier is also known as the Khyber Pass, but many of the locals I know still call it the Old Silk Road. (As such it is a territorial trade route, much fought over and divided.) Major Turner was due to be stationed at the Fort for some time, to make a report on the Military Police Post at Oghi.

Rose Anna was not persuaded to come herself, when the Military Police Post itself had been established to curb lawless behaviour in the area. This was in spite of her deep affection for Major Turner.

But, for my part, I so wanted to see the wonder of the Fort, and argued that, although the territory around the North West Frontier was the scene of almost constant skirmishes, so as long as I kept well away from the tribal areas my visit should be uneventful. I was, after all, a civilian not a soldier.

Rose Anna was a little reluctant at first, but eventually agreed I should go, because she didn't want me to crush my spirit of adventure. We agreed there would be no cause for concern as long as I stayed within the safety of the Fort and did not venture out.

Fort James was once a castle – and from the roof I could see the distant mountains where Munshi set all his stories. I loved all the tales of the tribes who stood guard over the Khyber Pass, armed only with sticks, who never succumbed to the rule of the Empire, but went their own way under brave leaders who were full of noble intolerance.

The Fort perched on the top of a hill, with Gothic windows and wooden carvings and a statue of Saint Sebastian, the patron saint of soldiers, depicted tied to a pillar, standing guard over the hills opposite the gates, a talisman for all homesick subalterns.

Old trails and pathways led down the hillside to travellers' bungalows and hide-outs. Major Turner's rooms were inside Fort James itself, with a fifty-foot veranda under jasmine and frangipani on which to sit and look out. It was magnificent.

It was about midnight when we first heard the news that a skirmish had broken out at the police post . . . and the next morning Major Turner received a message that the situation had escalated and the police post was under attack by all three tribes of the Thor Ghar. It was a situation without precedent.

He called for reinforcements to come and aid the Frontier Force against the belligerents, and then he himself hurried on to the scene. There was only a very small garrison stationed there who were naturally struggling to cope.

When he did not return for three days, I became quite ill with worry.

I wanted to go and see what had happened, but Major Turner's secretary, Sergeant Price, begged me to stay. And yet I felt torn, as I knew that Rose Anna would be devastated should anything happen to Major Turner. So, impulsively, I decided to take matters into my own hands, and for the second time in my life I was blinded by my good intentions.

So I stole away under the concealment of night, having made my own small arrangement with the syce at Fort James. He gave me a black horse (for good luck) and agreed he would tell no one I was gone till morning.

Word List
Garrison

Sue

A Pensee for Sue
'In your beauty rests both my life and my death'
Maurice Scève
With my love
from Quiz X

I overslept this morning and I woke when Quiz gently tiptoed in carrying a breakfast tray, with a pensee on it that made my heart sink. And I was surprised he managed it, because in the small hours of last night he had to get up with one of his tension headaches.

'I've rung through to the faculty and said I'm not available next week,' he said. 'We need to spend some time together. I thought we could stay on here a bit longer. I'm going to really spoil you.'

'Thank you, that's a lovely thought, but I'd rather go back home,' I said.

'Let's just stay until Tuesday, make it a long weekend. I've been dying to take some time off work and there's something I want to show you. I only realized it since I had a little look at your book. And I've booked a table at Chez Rez tonight, and I've got tickets for the theatre tomorrow.'

'Thank you,' I said.

But he seemed to have *ignored* everything that I'd said.

Sat Oct 15 eve

> **Pensees**: *If you cannot express your anger, act as if you're walking furiously into a hallway wearing jodphurs and carrying a whip.* SB

So we sat in that smart restaurant and Quiz drank a lot of wine and we both had lots of fancy little things to eat. (Mrs Bunion would have been *appalled* at the portions.) Our chat was as restrained as one of those couples who sit silently through dinners which are punctuated only by the sound of scraping cutlery.

My suspicions about everything were aroused and bubbling under the surface, so eventually it all came out.

'So, has Di sometimes been staying at the flat as well as staying at her mother's?' I asked.

'Of course.'

'Have you been there together then? While I have been at Greylands?'

'I think we overlapped once or twice, yes,' he said.

I fell silent.

'Oh dear, I see that you're still looking for a way out,' he said uncomfortably. 'Next you'll concoct a ridiculous theory about being my Mistress or something.'

'You're right! I am *not* your Mistress! I am eighteen, and I'm from Titford!'

'Well you said you wanted to be more Russian,' said Quiz.

I fell silent again.

'I was teasing,' he said. 'You're very funny when you're angry.'

'And you're really nasty when you are,' I said. 'And if you think you can pull the wool over my eyes, you'll be surprised to learn that I'm not just going to sit out at Greylands quietly at my sewing. It's 1988!'

'Stop embarrassing yourself,' said Quiz. 'Waiter?' he called to the Maître, and we settled up.

We went back to Greylands in silence. I wished it had been earlier in the evening and I might have had the chance to get on a train to Egham.

But Quiz made us a cup of tea and tried to patch things up a little. He said he didn't want to let the sun go down on an argument.

'You'll feel differently in the morning,' he said gently, before he turned out his lamp. We lay miles apart between his icy sheets.

'This is just a blip you know. I love you,' he said. 'And I can't wait to show you my surprise, so we'll have it to look forward to. I think you'll be amazed and inspired.'

I lay and read for a little while by torchlight, back in the world of great heroism. I do so admire people's courage. I hate feeling such a coward.

FOR THE CONCERN OF THE RICH AND THE POOR

It was eerily silent when I set out into the night from Fort James. I could not hear any fire, there was no rumble of the cannon and no flash fires to light up the dark lands in the foothills of the Tor Guar (the Black Mountains).

I waited and watched until daybreak, from what I considered to be a safe distance from Oghi, and at the sound of the first bugle I could see distant figures, lining up for exercise. Major Turner really wasn't joking when he said he would call for reinforcements: there must have been hundreds, perhaps even thousands of troops on the ground.

As the sun rose, I decided to approach a little nearer to the M Police Post, to see if I might meet someone who could give me any news of what was happening, and the whereabouts of my friend Major Turner. My horse walked on, the sound of his hooves echoing in the wilderness.

I am not skilled in trick-riding, and so I proceeded slowly along the perilous trails with sheer drops from their edge. I had that horrible feeling that there were eyes watching me from dark hiding places between the rocks, but I put it down to my imagination, battling fears of being captured and ransomed.

I hadn't got very far, when through a heat haze that was like steam coming off the rock, I noticed a rifle lying on the ground.

Sensing that it may not be wise to leave it for the enemy to find, I dismounted in order to pick it up. It was still smoking. But the snap of a branch, somewhere, suddenly, frightened my horse and he reared and bolted. I could do nothing to stop him as he galloped away.

And so with all my instincts sharpening their knives in the sultry heat of the morning, I crept up to the rifle on foot. The same instincts that came to the fore the day I ran away from the Mead.

Slowly, I picked it up. It was a Martini-Henry with a silver trigger.

This was a weapon used on our side. And unusually it was the genuine article, and not a Khyber rifle copy, such as I had seen on my tours all over the District with Thomas. The gun was heavy and there was no strap, so that I could not sling it across my shoulder, and so greatly encumbered by the Martini Henry I crept forward in search of the soldier to whom I thought it must have belonged. Loss of a rifle was considered an offence punishable by Court Martial, which was all the more reason to find and return it to its owner.

After several paces, revealed through clouds of dust set in motion by my runaway horse, I saw a man lying face down in the dirt just ahead of me. He looked like a trooper. I rushed forward and stooped down to touch him, to see if he was still breathing. Then I heard a step behind me and I turned my cheek, to find I was looking straight into the eyes of a tribesman. He brandished his spear and drew it back in preparation. I thought that I faced my murderer, but as I swung round fully towards him, suddenly he ducked behind the cover of a rock, and then like lightning he fled.

I had forgotten I was still holding the Martini-Henry, yet the warrior could not have known that my aim at that moment was not to use it to shoot him, but to give it back to the man on the ground.

So in haste I turned back to the wounded man. His injuries were shocking. But an even greater shock lay in store for me when I rolled him over and saw his face. Even through the years and the blood and the dust and the dirt, I recognized Harry Benson.

Sue

I don't usually wake up at that sort of time, usually I'm a straight-through sleeper, but in the middle of the night my eyes opened like a doll held upside down, bright, alert and sudden. Perhaps it was the image of Harry Benson.

Or perhaps it was because I *knew* if I waited till the morning and Quiz and I talked again that I wouldn't leave Westover. I knew he would play on the regret and shame I felt for all I have done.

But as I lay there, staring at the ceiling in Studio One, the solution to the situation came clear to me. If Quiz wouldn't listen to me or let me go without a struggle, then I must leave *without him knowing*. Simple. Maybe I caught some of Lawrence Garden's courage.

I will always remember the sound of the rain as it slowly gathered momentum, falling heavier and heavier on the sky lights. I never knew a persistent rain could sound so much like fire. And when I sat up to look out, I caught sight of the dots of orange lamplight blurred into reflected splodges from the row of street lamps stretching diagonally down the hill and *away* from Cinder Street.

No sooner had the word *away* suggested itself than my body was acting on the suggestion. I rose swiftly.

I crept down to Studio Two to collect some of the things I'd already put into piles for packing, but Pilgrim must have heard my step on the creaky boards and he started to bark, so I bolted downstairs to quiet him before anyone else woke up.

But he wouldn't stop, he was so excited to see me, and I didn't have much time to think, my impulse to get out was so strong.

I opened the front door in the hope that that would stop him barking. He stepped outside as if he was going for a walk . . . and looked back at me in joyful expectation. I hesitated in the open doorway. The sounds of the weir came crashing in, as did the rain. I was terrified of going back upstairs to get my things in case somebody woke up, and, glancing down at my friend waiting patiently on the doorstep, neither did I have the heart to abandon him.

So I slipped on my pumps, grabbed my coat and Pilgrim's lead from the coat rack and, clipping it on to his collar, *we* fled. I had nothing in my hand but his lead, no money, nothing. When your instinct tells you to run . . . you run.

The wind was whistling across the dark fields behind Trevanin, the last house on Cinder Street, and somewhere in the distance I could hear turbines spinning. Spots of rain like leopard markings fell on the pavement, and as I walked down the street I could hear the screech of foxes coming from the woods.

I longed to get to a lamplit predictable road. Every bang, crash and bump made me jump. But I forged ahead in my nightie and coat with Pilgrim walking steadily beside me. Turning back was never an option.

We reached Westover, where a few late-night revellers were

still wandering about the streets. I passed the pub with the resident hermit-in-the-corner; his seat in the window was empty and distorted by the rain.

We walked on. I hoped to find the bypass just beyond the town, which would then lead to the road to London . . . but we came up to a sign that said Bristol 8 miles and I realized I was going the wrong way. I was just about to cross to the other side of the street when something stopped me.

It was a white sign, with curly pale blue writing, and it flashed up out of the darkness. *The St Edward's Mead Retirement Home.*

Could it have been what Quiz wanted to show me?

A group of buildings wrapped around the central courtyard I had read about and visited in my imagination. The courtyard was now adorned with a water feature in the middle, with a statue of Queen Victoria in it, holding the sceptre and the orb. Through the windows, inside the rooms I could see tinsel on the picture frames, empty rocking chairs casting their shadows, and amber wall lights glowing in a distant passage.

Surely this must be where London Taylor began his life, and from where he took flight, all those decades before! Maybe it was a sign that I was doing the right thing. For didn't London say running away was too big and too scary a thing for his mind to have been able to do, and so his legs made the decision for him? Perhaps this was one of the rare occasions when fear is a rational thing.

I crossed the road and walked back the other way, to find the bypass and follow it all night if I had to. Maybe I was re-tracing London Taylor's steps, steps that would lead me back to Green Place, just as they had led him there . . . treading the same path, making the same journey.

Car headlights flashed past me, lighting up my face,

searching. I wondered if Quiz was awake. If he realized I was gone he might jump in the car and come looking for me. I turned my collar up for protection.

In the pitch winter darkness people passed me in their cars, strangers sweeping by in the night, each the hero or heroine of a hundred million stories.

We were somewhere near the beginning of the bypass and either side of the road were fields and sweeps of dark downs. I stood at the edge of the road with Pilgrim, the rain by this time lashing at us, whipping us.

I stuck my thumb out, the tiny human signal that beckons the aid of strangers, and I waited. A few minutes later a juggernaut pulled over. It was such a relief to be out of the rain.

'Where are you going to, love?' asked the driver.

'I'm going to Egham in Surrey,' I said. 'I hope you don't mind my dog.'

'There's a towel up on the shelf,' he said.

I found an oily towel and dried Pilgrim's wet coat a little, expressing my thanks.

'I can take you as far as Stonehenge,' he said. 'I turn off to Salisbury after that.'

'Thank you,' I said.

'What's your name, love?' he asked.

'I'm Sue,' I replied.

'Brian,' he said.

He was a Margate man. He left school and went straight out to work and ended up in haulage. He had a family of six to support with his driving . . . a hero, passing by in the night.

I guess it must have been about 4.30 in the morning as I stood facing the stone circle at Stone Henge with Pilgrim. Was it courage, curiosity, or ancient forces that drew me to walk over the fields and enter within the stone ring? I knew full well that you are not even supposed to go *near* the sacred ground. Yet concealed by the night, it was a once-in-a-lifetime opportunity.

The wind danced into a hollow gatepost at the edge of the plain, because it had found a hole in it where it could get in and sing. I climbed over the gate and shivered with excitement. Pilgrim made his way between the bars, his hackles up, poised and ready for freedom and adventure.

All around us was pitch, the graves of Neolithic man lying in wait for the dawn's gentle light. I leant against a sacred stone. The wind made the stone pillars *chime*.

In the last scene in *Tess of the d'Urbervilles* (I read it at school) Tess and her love Angel also find themselves at Stone Henge. Tess has committed a crime, the consequences of which are inescapable, so they await in the ancient temple for the hand of justice to come down. Thomas Hardy says 'Tess, really tired by this time, flung herself upon an oblong slab' and a little later Angel says 'Sleepy are you, dear? I think you are lying on an altar.'

I looked up at the glowering sky, holding back its next downpour. I wonder when Thomas Hardy wrote *Tess* if he ever thought that when people come to Stone Henge they would think of her, his tragic, beautiful fiction. She has become in the world as real and familiar as these ancient stones, yet she is *not real*.

I dried my face with my coat sleeve. I couldn't stay very long, I needed to move on, to concentrate.

I heard a car door slam and I started off quickly, putting Pilgrim in front of me so that if it was Quiz hunting us, he wouldn't recognize our unmistakable panicky shadows.

By seven am the night was beginning to grow pale. I had

availed myself of two more lifts. As I got out of Harry's pie van in Egham my eyes were stinging and my feet were cold as ice. I walked through the empty market until finally I joined with the B4532.

There was hardly anybody about, just the odd early trader arriving to set out their stall. They must have thought I was a tramp.

The dawn rose on the horizon between the dark empty branches on the trees. I never really noticed before that dawn *rises*. The street lamps were burning, warming the air and buzzing, giving off a small heat, and the B4532 became Clockhouse Lane as the night became the morning.

I reached the lion gateposts at the entrance to Green Place and turned gratefully up the drive. The first sweet, shrill chirrups rang out from the birds in the feathery new light. Pilgrim's nails clipped as we walked through the orchard and up through the woods. I let him off his lead and he boldly skipped off. Out of the corner of my eye I saw an old woman, a witch crouching down in hiding. She metamorphosized into a folded trestle table with a waterproof cover on it as she came into clearer view. Darkness is just a liar.

I looked down the hill over the meadows where the grey-brown remains of the walled garden stood like a burnt-out castle in the dawn. I imagined London seeing it for the first time when it was alive with colour and glory. And when I looked back to the front of Green Place, there was another surprise: Joe's bike. I gasped at the thought that Quiz might have woken and found me gone and rung Aunt Coral, and that Aunt C must have called Joe.

The blood started to rise in my veins again, just when I thought it was all over. I felt as London must have felt when he arrived after his long journey and found the gates were closed. But I had no other wish than to conceal myself. I didn't want Joe to see me red nosed and blue limbed having been out all night in the rain. Surely at such moments one should be entitled to a little privacy. So I went around the side of the house, planning to get in through the kitchen window, my pulse drumming, my blood shot with adrenalin. I crept slowly to the side of the kitchen, over the wet grass. Pilgrim appeared out of the shadows and suddenly started towards me, as just as suddenly the ground beneath my feet gave way and I screamed.

In a flash the men came running. *Joe* and the Admiral, clearly straight from his bed. They stopped opposite each other, with me in a pit between them, clinging to a tuft of grass with my legs dangling in a gulf beneath.

'Help!' I cried out.

'Don't move!' shouted Joe.

Aunt Coral arrived, as desperately I clung on to the edge of the drop.

'Sue! Are you all right?' yelled Joe.

'I'm all right. I've lost a pump but I'm all right,' I replied.

Pilgrim lunged forward to reach me.

'Hold him back,' I shouted.

'Stand back, Joe, the ground's not stable,' said Aunt C, grabbing Pilgrim's lead. 'Hold on Sue. Avery, run and get a ladder.'

But my hands began to yield their grip and I slid down a few inches further, hanging on now by a prayer. Joe knelt down on the ground to try and reach me better, stretching out his hands to take mine.

'Hold on to me,' he said. 'I won't let you go.'

'I don't want to take you down with me,' I said.

But the ground began to crack and spit and open like there

was an earthquake. Joe tried to hold on to me, but he lost his balance and Aunt Coral screamed as I fell.

The ground caved in, the earth spilt apart, and then it was dark.

'Sue!' cried Joe. 'I'm coming for you!'

He leapt into the pit after me . . . there was a great commotion. Pilgrim barked, I could hear shouts and cries.

'Hurry, bring a ladder.'

Pilgrim wouldn't stop barking. But gradually his barks grew fainter and more muted in all the darkness and I realized I had landed with a hard knock at the bottom of the partially excavated tunnel . . . They're coming to dig another little hole on Saturday – I had quite forgotten. I didn't even see a cordon.

It was so dark that I could barely see my hand in front of me. I turned it the wrong way round when I landed. The noise it made didn't sound too good.

'Sue, where are you? Can you hear me?' said Joe. 'Don't worry, I'm here. I'll find you.'

'I'm here,' I croaked. 'Joe, I'm over here.'

I groaned and reached my hand out, but it fell weakly down to my side. With my good hand, I touched something hard and grasped it. It was cold, well made, yet still and deathly. It felt like a fine, small bone. I picked it up to try and see it better, and I shuddered. It *was* a bone, I'm sure of it. I told myself it was an animal bone, pushing away thoughts of Frittie.

'Sue, Sue, are you all right?' said Joe, finding me in the lost darkness.

'I think so, my wrist hurts. Are you all right Joe?'

'Hang on to me. I'm going to try and climb back up to the top,' he said. He groped around in the darkness. 'I can't find anything to get any purchase on.'

'Thank you for coming after me,' I said.

'Are you kidding? I wouldn't leave you down here alone.'

'I'm so sorry, it was so stupid of me not to remember the digging,' I said.

'You mustn't kick yourself, because you can't always see the slippery bits ahead,' Joe whispered. 'As long as you're all right that's the main thing.' He reached out and his hand found my cheek.

'Joe I'm so sorry I've made such a mess of everything. I don't know who I am. It spoils everything,' I said.

'It's OK,' said Joe. 'It's not that bad, is it? I think you'll just be one of those people who has lots of phases . . . your Group phase, your Russian phase . . . you know?' he said kindly.

'I know, I am sorry, I am flawed,' I gulped.

'No, it makes life much more interesting,' he replied tenderly. 'You're a true artist.'

The ground above us began thundering again, this time in threatening clumps, spewing down rocks and storms of soil which landed in great sprays over us.

We crouched down and I began to shiver. Joe wrapped his jacket round me.

'It's all right, I'm sure we'll be out of trouble in a minute,' he said.

I felt my eyelids grow thick and heavy, and I began to feel quite drained.

'I feel so sleepy,' I said.

'It's OK, I've got you,' said Joe.

Eventually I saw the bottom of a ladder coming down and then the Admiral's slippers appeared.

'Thank God,' said Joe.

'Good God,' said the Admiral. 'I'll get the Bentley.'

'Are you insane Miss Bowl? Has there been an insanity plea entered in case B4532?'

'There has been no plea, your Honour. It seems the family are willing to keep her at home, pending bail,' said Daphne.

'Thank you, Daphne, please put some clothes on.'

'Is it time for a Martini Henry?'

'One minute to six, would you like an umbrella?'

'Ooh go on, I'll have the pink.'

'But your Honour, a Martini Henry is not a cocktail, it is a gun!' I cried out.

'No! A Martini Henry is a drink! How dare yo' argue with me!'

'How do you know what it is anyway?' asked Daphne Snydley.

'I read about them in For the Concern of the Rich and the Poor.'

'Show me!' said the judge. 'I would like to see Exhibit A . . . For the Concern of the Rich and the Poor. If you are submitting this as evidence. I need to see it!

'But your Honour! I left it behind me when I ran!'

'You RAN?'

'My boyfriend wouldn't let me go!'

'Your . . . BOYFRIEND?'

'Youre Honore, he was my fiancée.'

'HE WAS?'

'I ended it by removing myself from the situation.'

'Have you been charged with ruining his life?'

'It is pending appeal.'

'Pah! I haven't come to hear todaye to talk about your feelings. Daphne, would you get the definitions book. Now please turn to the page where it clarifies what a Martini Henry is, thank you Daphne.'

'Yes your Honour, um, rifle rifle, scrummage, rustle.' Daphne flips big legal book. 'A Martini Henry Your Worship can be anything that gives a person a lift. It is the thing that you give back to a person when they are down on the ground, mentally or physically. As such it is the thing that provides solace and hope. Some people comfort and protect themselves with a gun, some with a song or a book, but others do it with their dogs and still others with their . . . boyfriends.'

'So, it is clarified as a symbol you say? Then make mine a Banana Daquiri with chippies! Bail is denied. That's all. Judgement for the plaintiff in the amount of £4.11.'

PART SIX

Firewater

Sue

Sun Nov 27th

Pense es: *Never trust a cross-eyed surgeon.* SB

I haven't felt able to write until today, when the need to purge myself drove me to it.

I broke my wrist on the night of my fall and sod's law it was my right hand. So the only writing I have been able to do has been with my left hand or with the help of my secretary, Aunt Coral. When I come to read back these entries in the future, I'll have to forgive the catch-up nature of the bulletins which, due to the passage of time, are bound to be somewhat salient-pointesque.

I'm typing this with one finger on my left hand, so it's rather arduous, for example any double letters, ouch, seem to pain my right side rather, due to the repetitive motion, such as the double ee in pense es, so I can't always do them. This is just a reminder to myself in future as to the reason I might have written, pens.

Pens: *November, time to bring the garden furniture in.* SB

I've had many thoughts slip out of my head. Jackie County is right, 'only the pen makes our days im mortal'. She was mortified about my fall into the hole and came straight through with copious insurance policies for repair work.

A halt has been cal led to the digging. The garden still lo oks a mes s though, but not so much of a mes s as my arm. And when it throbs, I hold on to Aunt Coral's promise that while it's awful now, in a few months' time it will become just an after din ner story.

Joe was so wonderful jumping into that pit after me, I am so incredibly grateful. And I wish I was the sort of person who awards medals for gal lantry, because he truly deserves one. He risked his life for me. Aunt Coral says those five words speak volumes, and I know I am not alone in feeling so very proud of him. Joe said he would jump down any hole I ever fell down, and he would do it again tomorrow, and yet on the other hand he seems quite serious about Charlie. I feel forlorn. I think that's the best way to put it.

As to the memory of what I grasped in my hands a few moments after I fell in the tun nel, that is very disturbing, the stillness of it, the smallness of it, the deadness . . . maybe I'm just being ghoulish . . . but I do know that they never actually *found* Frittie's remains.

In the past year I have come to realize that in my life I to o am searching for something. The trouble is I don't know what it is till I find it.

As far as my relationship with Joe is concerned, my wor ry is that maybe I found it and didn't realize, or maybe I found it and wasn't ready, or worse, maybe I found it and I threw it away.

Because after all that drama, there is no going back. Joe is still seeing Charlie, Quiz isn't speaking to me, Diane is still devastated, it's a mes s. But if all life is suffering as Buddha once said, then it's far better for me to suffer at Green Place with my tribal elders Aunt Coral and the Admiral than to suffer alone in a far-away attic.

I haven't seen Joe for weeks because obviously he has no need to come in and do the garden at this time of year. And obviously he wouldn't come and visit now for . . . any other reason.

Plus, I left *everything* behind me when I ran away from West-over, and so I have not been able to continue with Lawrence Garden's story. I am building myself up to get in touch with Quiz and arrange collection and what have you, but am not quite ready to do that, yet. It's to o big, to o scary and to o mes sy.

There has been no word from him al l this time which still is a great relief to me. Perhaps a bit of radio silence either side is the best thing for both of us at the moment.

Aunt Coral and Jackie are very frustrated with me for leaving the book and my extraction pad behind. They have not given up searching for the Shipwreck necklace; they are just exploring other avenues, rather than digging holes.

So here I am in the mid dle of everything.

Twelve hours ago, we celebrated my letting my arm down out of my sling, low key style with modest alcoholic cocos. My arm feels very *other*. And I still remain in my plaster.

Thurs Dec 1

Pense es: *We begin life by drinking milk, and by the end we have moved on to coco.* SB

It was a month and a half ago now that Mrs Wilson came to Green Place to get Quiz's things, including, unfortunately, Pilgrim.

She was heavily persuaded not to press charges for my theft of her dog. But I don't really understand why she wouldn't let me keep him when I offered.

Yet, I have had to remind myself that I am not Heidi and *my* life is not a novel. (Italics intend tone of bitterness.)

Pilgrim was such a joy to have around, such gentle and light-hearted company. He taught me all I wil l ever need to know about begging, *look at the hand, look at the plate, look at the hand, look at the plate, sigh, collapse . . .*

'I can't find the words to expres s how sad I was to see him go. I had barely be en to the toilet on my own since I met him,' I was explaining to Aunt Coral at lunchtime.

'Are you talking about Quiz dear?' she asked me.

Tuesday Dec 6 1988

Forlorn Pense es: *I have a spot on my cheek that is so bad today that I actually wish it would get dark earlier than 4 o'clock.* SB

I am under a rug in the drawing room, as per my fiscal concern fantasy – waiting for the spiders to mummify me. But my left arm is bravely sticking out of the cover idly pressing the keys of my type-writer which sits on the floor. I look like a profligate toff. I feel haunted by a persistent mental torture that asks why did I go to all the trouble of run ning away in the middle of the night and upset ting everybody and breaking my arm, when Joe wasn't even *available*. It seems rather sil ly.

And I can't seem to get Joe out of my head, even for a moment. Maybe it's a punishment.

Ad ded to which, I am plagued by a curse that only allows me to remember the good things about Quiz and so I mourn him to o, which is awful ly confusing. And as I sit here all I notice is that there are showers grazing the ro of. That's all. Judgement for the plaintiff in the amount of £4.11.

Pense es: *A big-head is someone who believes he looks out the window and melts the frost.* SB

Quiz would have been very happy in India because you had to wear a dinner jacket for dinner. I was reminded of this because the Admiral's veteran friend, Admiral Ranger, came round for dinner tonight, and he and the Admiral both wore dickie bows. Talking of India, I had a pens . . . that the likelihood of Lawrence Garden having rediscovered Har ry Benson after all those years was on a par with trying to make an alien believe that tobac co is something you put in your mouth and set fire to. What am I trying to say? Not sure, but I am aware that I am get ting a bit rusty at the pense es.

I'm having to start from scratch again with all my written work, which was also left behind when I ran. So as my arm gets stronger I intend to rework my revisions to 'Jen ny gets a Chance' and try and recal l the smal l improvements I made to 'The Emperor's Slippers'. (By way of trying to get my ambition back and by way of trying not to think about Joe.)

There were copious notes, and the other pieces I wrote while I was Quiz's muse, which I left abandoned, along with my word lists. These pieces now seem to me like bridges between two distinct sections of my life. Pieces such as a tale called 'Sanctimonia' which is all about a character called Sanctimonia Perfect, based on Mrs Wilson. She so seldom smiled that when she did I thought it was wind.

I revamped and reclaimed 'Sanctimonia' with the help of Aunt Coral last night and sent it off to Gordoney George at the *Echo* on a punt this morning. It's almost Christmas, and putting out fe elers is ter ribly Decemberesque.

Nothing ventured nothing gained, at least Quiz gave me that

ethos. And I am still seeking employment, and I can't help being hopeful that next year, it wil l be of the Plan A type rather than the Plan B. Aunt C says I *mustn't* give up.

She has persuaded me to drop my new pen name and revert to the name I was born with. She said she couldn't understand why I would want to assume a name when I was blessed with such a super name in real life. In signing 'Sanctimonia' I did how-ever make sure Gordoney knows that Susannah Parkes and Sue Bowl are the same person.

As for my word lists as and when I retrieve them, maybe I can put them to good use and save them for Pierre? Like a map to his big sister's life? I think I would call it 'A Thesaurus for Naughty Pierre' because he so loves dinosaurs.

The Titford thre e have been in Denmark again, and sent pho-tos of Pierre in national costume. When he grows up he will definitely be able to say '*I was adored once to o*'. Lo oking forward to seeing him again and how much he has changed and come on. (Babies are like little plants, it occurs to me, blob like until one day they suddenly *flower.*)

This morning Aunt Coral asked if she could read in my jour-nal about the night I walked from Westover to Egham (which I completed very slowly on the typewriter, just by the end of last month, having painstakingly worked on it all through Novem-ber). And after dinner she said that she thinks it reads like a short story in itself and that I should send it to Profes sor Mushrooms, *instead* of a revised 'Jenny Gets a Chance'. Provocative!

But surely she is right. Wandering the country in a nightie and coat is terribly Russian. I'm going to tinker with it tonight in bed as my revised dis sertation and then send it straight off and await Profes sor Mushro oms' response. I feel inspired again, and at a time when I least expected.

Pense es of an Admiral: *In the whole history of the world, it is my opinion that the weather has never been exactly the same twice.*
(Rear Admiral Avery Little)

The verb *bouder* in French actual ly means to sulk . . . therefore according to Di, the word *boudoir* actual ly means the 'sulking room'. I remember her telling me she did a whole essay on this for Timothy Magdalena's Decorative Furniture Collection at the British Library and had some very nice comments.

I fe el so terrible about the way I behaved to everybody. I need to make amends.

And so I have broken the radio silence and sent a card to Quiz to apologize and also get a few things off my chest. I did not however keep a copy of it for two reasons: A, I'm not really up to typing it twice, and B, I don't want to cringe and squirm and regret the way I put things on re-reading, because it's to o late now. It's gone. And I know that it's possible to arrive at the same point by *not* saying something, as by saying it. But it just takes longer, and then it still needs to be said. That's why Aunt C says she is more a fan of the angry word over the simmering resentment, or the heartfelt apology over the frosty hush.

Days can pass here at Green Place and we keep no company other than the weather people. In the winter the Admiral and Aunt Coral like to tune in to four bulletins a day, in the constant negotiation of when it is safe to travel and what woolly should be worn. But I love the brightness of the weather people, with their first-class presentational grooming and the handy little rain clouds that stick, and can be removed and replaced with sun. Apart from that, we don't watch much telly, though Aunt Coral loves *Starsky and Hutch*.

But within this small quiet calmness, there is a lot of time to reflect, and in spite of al l the bad things, as I said, I find that I only remember the go od things about Quiz.

But Aunt Coral suggested, apropos her brilliant anti-dotes to regret, that Quiz is a narcissist, and she came up with the following *Pense e*:

> '*No woman can ever be content with the man who is happiest of all with a mirror.*' CG.

In trying to unravel it all and ask myself what on earth was I thinking by ever getting involved with Quiz – I believe what got me in the first place was that he made the days se em so exciting, when much of my life, as I said, has been private and ordinary and small. I'm not making excuses but I think that's why I fel l for him, I thought he could make *every* day like that and I'd forget about al l my troubles. I know I was greedy to want Quiz when I already had Joe, but I do think I am susceptible to falling in love because it makes me forget how much I miss mum, at least for a while. But one can't go about having affairs all over the place and blaming it on someone who has died, that is really the inky bottom.

Weds Dec 14, 10am

Pense es: *Two least attractive qualities of men: Impatience and amour-propre.* SB

Jackie County rang, to say she has been meticulously researching into every private collection of jewellery and artefacts listed for local museums since 1859! Today she is heading to London for a private appointment with a Mr Theo Lousteau, an expert in tracing diamonds.

During Happy Hour (which takes place somewhat earlier at Green Place than elsewhere), Aunt Coral and I settled ourselves by the heater in the Orangery and Aunt C typed up a dictation for me so I could rest. It's a bit chil ly in there at the moment but it seems such a shame when Aunt C went to all that trouble not to use it al l year round.

'Quiz called my writing style Chinoisery,' Sue dictates, 'after the architects and artists who had never been to China in the seventeenth century, but yet who drew images of China on their palace walls. They painted terrifying dragons and fiery golden serpents and Chinese men with long moustaches and embroidered coats, even though they had never actually *seen* them. Chinoisery means *like* China, but it is not the *real* China.'

'Not the real China,' types Aunt C.

'I think Quiz likened my writing to Chinoisery because I nearly always write about things I have never experienced, things perhaps that I long for: One might call it, the style of *Linoisery*-meaning, *like* life. For example, when London Taylor longed for India so much he saw it in every tree and flower, the raindrops of his mind were sapphires, the pointed buds in the frostbitten garden the domes of his Taj Mahal. But as far as my writing goes,' Sue moves to conclusion, 'I've realized that in the books I love there's always an Aunt and there's always a gardener, always broken hearts, buried treasure, orphans. There are always creaky old houses that beckon you in the depths of winter to sit by a blazing fire, always fields, penury, stews boiling on the stove, loyal dogs, good and bad men, flibberty gibbets, rascals, heiresses, forgiveness, anger, love. I am part of their stories and so their stories are part of me. It's just that fiction is *like* life, and fact is *real* life. But sometimes there seems very little difference.'

Radio Silence over Westover has now been broken, this morning
I received a reply from Quiz.

Greylands
Cinder Street
Westover

Dear Sue

Since the moment you left I have also wanted to make an
apology.

In answer to the burning questions in your card I want
to say that it is true, I admit I was a little bewitched by your
circumstances at first. But even if that was the case to begin
with, it didn't take me long to transfer my affections. That is
the whole truth. No, I didn't want your house, and no I
wasn't still seeing Di. I don't know if this makes things worse
or better?

I know you are sorry, of course I forgive you. Di is all
right – and I'm sure as I can be that she can forgive you.
She's trying to forgive me, so I am sure that she'll manage it
with you. I'm not saying she is completely holy about
everything but don't forget that she has read every one of a
million books on the subject of loving more than one
person, so at least she is going to understand, even if she
can't transcend her personal feelings quite yet.

I don't regret it, neither am I sorry that it happened.
Since knowing you I am reunited with a part of myself that
had somehow come adrift. Perhaps you have recalled my
romance, I mean with life.

I believe that one day you might look back and
remember that man you met in Crete to whom you were

briefly engaged, now what was his name? You'll have odd memories such as the way my hair looked from the back, perhaps with the River Thames sweeping past it. But you will laugh about it and be untroubled as though it happened to a completely different person, and only then will you realize that you too have more than one forever. And as you said yourself, a gap of nine years in age would be nothing to Jane Austen or Charles Dickens.

I'm so sorry I was cruel to you, I'm not very good at being thrown over.

But remember I told you what Tolstoy once said? 'The best stories don't come from good versus bad, they come from good versus good.'

So please don't doubt that I truly loved you. It wasn't that kind of story.

Love

Quiz Xx

He returned my book and papers to me, and they smelt of his house. The objects of giddier days become like shrapnel fired back. I wasn't expecting that. And I wasn't expecting the tone in his letter, I was expecting, I hate you, you have spoilt everything.

Aunt Coral says she thinks Quiz has something called a sense of entitlement, but that we all have our fatal flaws.

> **Word List**
> *Sense of entitlement*
> *Fatal flaws*

FOR THE CONCERN OF THE RICH AND THE POOR

I put the Martini-Henry back into Harry's hands and I set him half upright with his back resting up against a tree in the shade, close to where I found him. His head was lolling forward, his fingers draped round the gun like an infant, my water flask at his side.

From my vantage point on the ridge, I could see several figures on horseback moving about on the plain below me; they looked like the Cavalry Lines or the Corps of Guides, so I hoped. I heard the mournful cry of the trumpet, but I couldn't identify if it was a watering order, Boot and Saddle or, God forbid, the call for the troops to ride. I decided I must take my chances in going to get help and so I stepped out into the sun's glare.

And an hour later I returned to find Harry unconscious in the same position as I left him. He had lost a great deal of blood from a gushing wound on his leg. The soldier who took me back to him was a trooper by the name of Baines. He arranged for Harry to be evacuated by the stretcher bearers and I accompanied them back to their camp and then on to a base hospital close to the border.

There I loitered for the remainder of that day, listening to many a barrack-room tale. But Harry Benson remained in a deep sleep and the Doctor said it would not be prudent for me to wait any longer.

So I set back forth to Fort James, leaving Harry a note with my address at Svarga Ghara, extending him an invitation to visit as soon as he was able. I signed it in my name Lawrence Garden, but at the bottom I added a post script: 'You might remember me as London Taylor.'

Sue

It is wonderful to be reunited with my book and with al l this time to kill, while my arm is out of action, I simply *must* get to the end of it. I'm ashamed to say it is now coming up to a year since I first discovered it. But in my defence I can only point out that life truly does get in the way.

Aunt Coral has had the brain wave that I should turn my extracts into a more formal abridgment to offer up on my CV. I can just see it in the future on some creaky old shelf in a corner of the British Library. *For the Concern: Rags to Riches*, abridged by Sue Bowl. Maybe . . .

But one more year and, if God spares me, we wil l be into the nineties!! It's 11am and I am sitting here shivering in the Orangery with Aunt C. We are bundled up in hats and coats and I have just paused mid pense e to put my hands under my rug to warm up; now back to recording our chat. The noise of the typewriter echoes in here and I can see my breath when I speak. I have it balanced on my languid kne e now, still like a relative profligate.

I expect that we will spend much of the winter like this, in the icy *thinking* room. And when I remember these days in the future,

I will see them from the perspective of a bird at the top of the tre es.

'Won't it be nice when Ec cles gets back,' says Aunt Coral. 'He cruises over the winter, you know.'

'Yes it will be lovely, but we'll have to watch him, he's a ter rible flirt,' I say.

'Do you *think* so?' asks Aunt Coral, shocked.

'Is *that* Joe?' I say, equal ly shocked, as I look out of the long windows down over the meadows to the wal led garden.

'I wasn't expecting to see flesh and blo od and a flash of pacific-blue t-shirt in the winter white-out,' I add.

'Yes, he's come to do something or other,' says Aunt C.

'In December?' I ask, panic-stricken.

'Yes, he seems very ke en,' she says. 'Where's the Admiral?' she adds impatiently.

'He's sitting by the heater in the Club.'

'Run and tell him I'm in here would you. He's missing the vista,' says Aunt Coral. 'Oh, and would you ask him to bring me my reading gloves?'

Typing suspended, profligate toff rises to run errand.

Later

Pense es: *When you feel lumpen wear*
something wafty SB

I pined for Joe in blissful secret, for a moment, from behind the window as I went past on my way to fetch the Admiral. It was *such* a shock to sud denly see him like that. But I had no desire to bump into him today, as it would take hours of personal gro oming for me to return to a person he might actually recognize. And I'd be devastated if he spotted I have written his initials in three places on my plaster, in between drawings of Pilgrim and love and peace. Actually, my plaster lo oks like the cave art of the last two months.

At any rate, I'd much rather Joe remembered me as I was, and not as I have *become*. So I retreated back upstairs for a lie down before lunch and tortured myself with thoughts of him and Charlie.

I can't believe that I used to be able to see Joe, or ring Joe any time I liked, and now here I am *hiding* from him, like he is some sort of *acquaintance*.

When I first got back from Westover I used to think of Joe every minute, sometimes every second; his face would be blazed across my soul like a backdrop, constantly *there*. But now it seems to have gone down to once an hour, on a good day, with bad days where I return to thinking about him every second.

Perhaps by the spring I will catch myself thinking, 'I haven't yet thought of him *today*.' Perhaps by then even the *thinking of him* will be a memory. Time really is a gentle and constant healer. So I'll just keep washing and putting one fo ot in front of the other, just keep picking up after myself and remembering the important birthdays. You don't notice the medicine, but it works.

FOR THE CONCERN OF THE RICH AND THE POOR

Three months later I received a letter from Harry's Commanding Officer:

1869

Dear Mr Garden,

I write with the sad news of the death of Sergeant Farrier Harold Benson. Benson was one of the finest sergeant farriers in his brigade and his loss is keenly felt. He was just twenty-four years of age.

In piecing together what led to Benson's attack, he managed to impart the following. A small group of troopers, highly skilled in riding, had set off on a reconnaissance mission on that fateful morning; it was their regular drill. But when they did not return as expected, Sergeant Benson and one of his shoeing smiths, Corporal Best, were the only men left equally skilled enough to go up to the ridge and search for them.

I would like it to be known that they were not given orders, but bravely volunteered and left without hesitation. But tragically, shortly after, Sergeant Benson was ambushed, attacked and left for dead, he believed it was by a lone warrior. His horse was so brutally injured that Sergeant Benson had to use his rifle to shoot the creature to put him out of his misery. I can only say that loving his horse as he did, this was truly a brave and heroic act.

And afterwards, in anguish and pain over his action, he threw off his gun and crawled away from the scene by some few feet . . . and that is when you found him.

I have set in motion an enquiry as to how Benson became separated from his cover. Corporal Best, who returned to the fold mercifully with the rest of our men who had been lost for some hours in the mountains.

I am now charged with the task of searching for Sergeant Benson's relatives. I believe he is survived by no direct family members, except for an infant daughter, who is in Canada and does not yet know she has been so lately orphaned. Her mother it seems passed away two years ago, as a result of the child's birth. And so, if you

are able to shed any light on whom I may contact, I
would be most grateful.

I am indebted to you for your valiant effort in trying
to save Sergeant Benson. I read out your note to him at
his hospital bedside and he managed a smile in
remembrance of your name.

Cordial best wishes and my deepest regrets,
Yours sincerely,
Farrier Quarter Master Sergeant Victor Webb
On behalf of the Regimental Veterinary Surgeon,
Royal Horse Artillery

The night I received the letter, I got drunk on a bottle
of firewater I had set aside for the joyful reunion I had
anticipated, when Cheeser and I would reminisce and
give thanks for the preservation of our lives.

I had polished the niner all ready for the long dreamt-of
ceremony of returning it to him, a decade after I chased
after it. So solemnly I returned it to its drawer, my one-
time ticket to life.

I only knew Harry for such a short time, and it's clear
that in the intervening years he had not changed from
the same fearless Cheeser, the same valiant Star of the
North.

I wonder what he would have thought had he ever
known that his example could have such far-reaching
effects on another man?

Because he may not have even remembered standing up
to Chaplain Cragg or cheering me into that field to take
flight from the workhouse, and yet for me these are seminal
moments. And so our paths crossed again for the briefest of
hours, yet his life crosses mine every day.

I might have retreated into myself after that, if
it weren't for Patricia. She dragged me by my boot

straps from the misty land of my dead and into the radiant sun.

> **Word List**
> *Trick riding*
> *Firewater (Indian phrase for alcohol)*

Sue

Pens e es: *Sometimes I do not want to join in the cultural pressure to be jolly.* SB

Aunt Coral announced yesterday, apro po the festive season, that there are times when I have been better company. I found Christmas a rag gedy state of affairs this year, what with one thing and another. Punt. It's lucky it takes very little to make Aunt C happy. She's very taken with a knitted tea cosy from Georgette and a quilted wash-bag from Taffeta, which are by far her most favourite presents.

I'm in bed again now, typewriter on floor, typing with left, profligate style, still scared to use right.

Christmas Day felt like one of those holidays where you arrive and get ill straight away. And this wasn't because it was Christmas itself, but I had my plaster taken off on Christmas Eve. And I was *so* looking forward to having my plaster off, but now that I have, it feels like a terrible anti-climax. I feel very naked without my plaster. I miss it.

But Aunt Coral is determined that I stop mopsie-ing. She says

I've done enough resting and gazing at the rain. It's time to get back in the saddle. This morning she was so brisk and business like when she threw open my curtains I felt as though I'd been bossed out of bed by a matron.

Downstairs in the kitchen at this precise moment Aunt Coral's Calendar reads thus:

Hair Monday
Face Tuesday
Toes Thursday
Arrival tights Fri
Event tights Sat

I wonder what she needs to do on Wednesday?

I spied on her from the upstairs landing while she was in the hall this afternoon. I was hovering at the top of the stairs.

Aunt C was looking at the number of calls displayed on her new telephone and answering machine. She takes great delight in not answering it when it rings and then standing mesmerized by the voice of the person leaving the message. This time it was Jackie to say she was in talks with Mr Theo Lousteau about a private collector in Hyde Park who has in her collection a stone called the Star of the Sea. 'I am hoping it might be the Star of the South's sister,' said the voice of Jackie.

Shortly after the message had clicked off, I went and joined Aunt Coral in the kitchen and we sat next to the stove to get warm. Boxing Day this year is very much about the basics.

'Isn't it wonderful you never have to answer the phone any more,' I said.

'Did you hear Jackie's message?' she asked me.

'Yes,' I replied, 'it sounds hopeful.'

'I think she's grasping at straws,' said Aunt Coral. 'She just doesn't know when to give up. I've never heard of diamonds having brothers and sisters.'

She flicked idly through *For the Concern of the Rich and the Poor* which I had left on the table after my last harrowing extract.

'Is a Martini-Henry similar to a Hooray Henry?' she asked.

'No a Martini-Henry is a rifle,' I explained, 'but I dreamt a Martini Henry is a symbolic thing that you use to help a person when they are struck down physically or mentally.'

'Do you mean a symbol such as a dog or a cat, or a handbag?' she asked plaintively.

'Yes, anything that offers a little solace.'

'I see,' she said, 'well then this is mine!' She poured herself a glass of Bombay Sapphire, even though it was only 2.30 in the afternoon. She is very opportunistic.

'I feel unfortunately that my Martini Henry was Joe,' I said sadly.

'Well I think your theory about that is all wrong, if you don't mind my saying,' said Aunt Coral briskly. 'And you shouldn't make your symbolic Martini Henry a person, because that's far too risky. No, I believe *this* is *your* Martini Henry' she said, and she handed me a pen. 'You have spent the last few weeks writing all over the house, with only one arm, with only one finger. You'd hang upside from a tree and write if you had to – you write everywhere. Remember what I said to you when you told me you'd become engaged to Quiz?' she asked.

'You said that I shouldn't choose between Joe and Quiz. You said I should get a third,' I answered.

'Exactly,' she went on, 'and men may come and go, but you shall *always* have your writing, as long as there is ink in the sea, as long as there is chalk in the quarry.'

'I thought you meant I should get a third boyfriend,' I said, somewhat perplexed.

'I think I did mean that, at the time,' said Aunt Coral.

I love the way she can adapt her advice!

HISTORICAL FACTLET

I'm told Martini-Henry has a hyphen when being referred to as a rifle if one wants to be correct. Punt.

Sat Dec 31 1988

And I can hand write again . . . in a wibbley wobbly way . . . !

I was just standing at the top of the stairs in my spying position and I heard the voice of Delia echoing around the hall on the answering machine. Aunt C was of course standing right by it listening in.

'We wondered if you might consider us coming for our Easter visit a little sooner than planned?' crackled Delia down the line. 'Admiral Gordon and I were thinking possibly in February? And Loudolle will be with us on an extended visit at Eaglehurst soon, so would it be OK with yourself if we all come to you? You can reach me on the usual number, I will be back by the phone from 6pm. Bye for now and lots of love to all.'

'Oh Sue, I wonder what is their hurry?' called Aunt C.

'How did you know I was here?' I replied.

She has ears like a fruit bat *and* eyes in the back of her head.

Tonight, to see the New Year in, we are having Tequila Slammers and a game hosted by the Admiral in the drawing room. The Nanas are coming, and Admiral Ranger and also George Buchanan the dentist. I am really looking forward to it.

Fri Jan 6 1989 (I can't get used to writing the 9!)

Miracle postbag!

How bizarre, but how wonderful! An invitation arrived in the post this morning. It was from Gordoney George's secretary *inviting* me to apply for the *Echo*'s new Winter-Spring Internship! Now there is a turn round for the books! The piece I sent him about 'Sanctimonia' must have done the trick! Putting together new cv for submission as I write!

Sat Jan 7 1989

Double whammy. It must be in the stars!

Professor Mushrooms' notes arrived back this morning, on 'Night On the Henge'! His critique says:

> *This is good work Sue! Not only more Russian but also more French and yet so British. It is an homage, Sue, a true fusion. I can see the beginnings of development of your own style and you have developed a more realistic heart to things.*

And there was a separate envelope with his notes, which contained my certificate from the Taverna!

Susan Olivia Bowl
Pass with distinction
Creative Writing Module One
Professor John Mushrooms

It was quite a moment, particularly when you consider I sent it in at a time when I had lost the ability to write!

Extract ahoy! (Please God, no more dying.)

FOR THE CONCERN OF THE RICH AND THE POOR

After some months of arduous correspondence, Thomas managed to trace Harry's young daughter, Mirenne. I was relieved to know she was in the care of her maternal uncle in Montreal.

When he was fourteen Harry left the Mead, it must have been two or so years after I did. He qualified for emigration to Canada, and there he met and married Mirenne Brady, the child's mother. Sadly Mirenne died in childbirth, which is why little Mirenne was taken in by her uncle. (Perhaps Harry returned home to join up in order to make ends meet, prior to his regiment being posted to India? Perhaps he was recruited in Canada? I don't know.)

Our lives followed different paths to different corners of the globe and yet, when I think of us both out there on the ridge, the world seems very small.

The skirmishes on the Frontier went on until the October of 1869 when peace was made, at least for a while. 12,000 troops marched from all over India and took part in ensuring that the territorial lines of the Empire were maintained.

Villages were burned and there was some defiant fighting, but the sheer numbers of the Frontier Force made it impossible for the tribesmen to continue with their assault. They retreated again to the mountains, to rise up again another day. And as they still do even now on the North West Frontier.

It was nothing as bloody as the Mutiny, but the first and last lesson I hope I will ever learn about war. Munshi said that the only school for war is war itself, and the only school for survival is survival.

There is a photograph in my study today, some fifty years later, of a group of people, all very much alive in 1870, and I at the age of twenty-one, with Munshi and

Rose Anna at the opening of the Harry Benson Bursary Foundation. It is a charitable organization I began that year, in memory of Harry, in an attempt to do something, anything, to balance the rule of the Empire.

The tribesman's face is still etched on my memory. I know he would have killed me too if he hadn't been scared off by the rifle. But I can never forget that the man was armed only with a spear, and it was after all his country, not mine.

I struggle to tolerate injustice, even in the setting of war. Harry Benson was the first person I knew in the world who ever stood up to the darkness that lies in supremacy. It is a bitter irony to me that he should end his days, in this cause at least, fighting for the other side.

But the money raised in the Bursary was intended to pay for more Indians to complete their training for the Indian Civil Service. In the hope that, as more men qualified, it would establish more equilibrium, till eventually the numbers of Indian Officers in the ICS might even equal the numbers of British. This was something that was promised back in the very early days of the Raj, but it was not acknowledged in action.

And in facing my critics, I can only say I do not wish to preach in sanctimonious hypocrisy from the dazzling wealth of my home, but if there is no point in doing anything, there is even less point in doing nothing at all. I did it because I felt strongly about the matter and I did it because I was able. And I did it because I wanted the world to know Harry Benson's name.

Sue

**Post extract pensees, pondering inclusion into
my notes at the end of abridgement:**

Over the course of his adulthood, Lawrence Garden's wealth
increased to dazzling proportions, he says he never had to tie his
own shoelaces and he had only to hold out his hand and someone
would put a gin in it, a far cry from his days of starvation at the
Mead.

But, due to his character, he never took it for granted. He
writes on page 2,365 that at every point in his life he has been
aware that 'the oppression of many creates the supremacy of the
few'. At the Mead it was the Masters who ruled over the inmates,
at Edenthorpe it was the Masters who ruled over the servants, and
in India it was the British who ruled over the Indians. But always,
he says in conclusion, always it was the rich over the poor.

> **Word list**
> *Equilibrium*

Today is my nineteenth birthday. Aunt Coral has a big meal planned, just for the three of us. I explained I was still feeling just the tiniest bit low key. But I wonder if Joe has remembered? It seems really, really important that he does. I don't want to go and look at the doormat in case I feel disappointed.

One hour later

Dear Sue,
Happy Birthday.
Looking forward to seeing you very soon!
With much love always from
Dad Ivana and Pierre
XXX

Dear Sue,
Happy Birthday!
Bet you thought I'd forgotten!
Thinking of you and happy days at home.
Lots of love
Aileen
X X X

Dear Sue,
Happy Birthday dear Granddaughter,
Out of sight but not out of mind.
Can't wait to see you when I get back.
Johnny
Xx

Dear Sue,
I hope your arm is on the mend. Wishing you a Happy
Birthday.
With love from
Joe
x

I don't know which is the more heartfelt wonder, Johnny's card from Australia, or Joe's from just down the road.

Mon Jan 16 1989

Dawn Pensees: *A true surprise is like seeing*
Brigitte Bardot in the hardware store
looking for a light bulb. SB

I woke with a jump because I thought it was Friday, and time for my internship interview. I was very relieved when I calmed down and realized there are still a full six days to go.

So I am now horizontal in bed with a cup of tea and *David Copperfield*. Aunt C said last night that we could wake up to a touch of frost. I often think that at this time of year it is almost worth waking yourself up an hour before you need to get up, and then relishing in the fact that you don't have to move yet, but linger and pensee and read and relax in all that darkness and warmth.

Poor Joe, in spite of the cold hard ground he seems determined not to neglect his work in the garden. He does not know I can spy on him. I find that quite delicious.

I just got up to open the curtain slightly and from my safe place behind it, I felt the same as I did when I was little and dressed in a raincoat and ten-pence plastic tiara. In the days when

I'd go with my mum to feed the geese by the river and I'd stand behind her legs, and dare to peek as I offered up some bread in my outstretched hand.

10 am

After breakfast I came into the White Room again, drawn like a magnet to the dedicated space for the past. But I was surprised to find all the paintings down on the floor, and Aunt Coral at the end of them methodically turning one over and giving it a little shake and a feel and a dust.

'What are you doing?' I asked her.

'I can't quite give up looking for the Shipwreck Pearls,' she said. 'I thought I'd better check that maybe the necklace could be hidden behind one of these canvases.'

'You've read too much Agatha Christie,' I said.

But Aunt Coral is an expert looker for things. Once she spent ten months looking for the spare keys to the Bentley and eventually she found them.

'I have decided to begin a series of notes on each character in the paintings and piece together their stories,' I said. 'I've made a list.'

'A list of what?' asked Aunt Coral, man handling Benedict's portrait.

'Of stories about all the dead relatives I want to write about. I thought I might offer the idea up to Gordoney at my interview, have it up my sleeve – you know. He might want to run it in conjunction with the Echoes of Egham festival that's coming up in the autumn.'

'Is that a Jackie lead?' she asked.

'Yes, she's kicking off with a piece about genealogy.'

'Goodness, that's a terrific idea.'

Fri Jan 20, 11.00 am

The Shilling Street Hotel, Egham

'At first I thought the table might be bugged,' said Gordoney. 'Then as time went on and more and more articles got through to me, I realized it must be an inside job. The reason I asked you to come in today was because I thought anyone who is prepared to make such, shall we say, creative overtures to an editor has got to be worth a second chance. Maybe I under-estimated you, Miss Bowl as in pudding.'

'Thank you,' I said.

'So, what I am going to ask you is, what do you think sets you apart from the other ten candidates sitting out there?' He sat back to wait for my answer.

A maid creaked through between the tables with a trolley laden with cakes. I was aware of a beautiful arrangement of flowers in the middle of the room, and aware of all things hotelly, the porter's lodge, concierge, bell boys, sparkling floors around me, a tinkly bell at reception, of the white tablecloths, silver cutlery and plush hotel air . . . a far cry from the smallness of recent days . . . and a far cry from this time last year.

'Because,' I began slowly, 'because all my life all I have ever wanted to do is write.'

'Why?' asked Gordoney. 'Why do you think that is?'

'Because I see things and I want to remember what I see – and to find expression for . . . how it feels to be part of things, to be a person. Even now as I sit here I have ten thousand ideas in my head, ideas for articles and for stories, and if I don't get them out I will get a blockage.'

'Can you tell me some of your ideas for articles?' he said.

'Well . . . just busking . . . what about a piece about a hotel as a capsule society, for example, something about the *real* hotel? "Behind the Service Lift Doors", maybe? I could get all the good gossip from that maid,' I embellished.

'Anything else?'

'In my spare time at the moment I am working on a collection of historical narratives. It's going to be a series about all my dead relatives, from the Victorian era going back . . . It could probably tie in quite well with the Echoes of Egham coming up,' I said. 'I've also been working on an abridgement of a 3,000-page novel. It is a rags to riches tale that crosses the path of our very house.'

'Fingers in lots of pies,' said Gordoney. 'That's what I like to see. And so tell me,' he continued, 'how are your social skills, Miss Bowl? Do you feel you would be able to cope with parties and drinks, and looking after strangers, and making them feel at ease?'

He sat back in his creaky leather chair again to study me, with his hands in the shape of a diamond up to his face.

'I have had some small experience of shmutzing at my Aunt's salons and parties. This year she is planning a whirlwind calendar of gatherings. She is extremely social and as a result I have learnt to be sociably skilled. But it's not difficult, because I'm genuinely *interested* in other people, and I can usually think of nice queries for openers, and after that, unless you're stuck with a lumpen, I find that conversation's very much a two-way thing,' I said knowledgeably.

'And finally, what is your preferred category would you say? Human interest, history, politics, cookery, gardening?'

'Oh I'm definitely between human interest and history, but in truth I have a scatter gun approach to interest,' I said. 'I might even go so far as to say I am the most interested person I know.'

'I like your style, Miss Bowl and . . . I'll let you know,' he said.

Mon Feb 6 1989

The *Egham Echo* is housed in an old warehouse by the river. It boasts fifteen rooms and brags a readership of three thousand.

In Features, there are five in an open-plan office: editor in chief, second in command, two hacks and an underdog. Gordoney George, Rueben York, Barry Arabian, Overcoat Home, and me!

We work in an airy room covering the entire top floor, with lots of windows on every side. Gordoney and Rueben's desks are partitioned off behind clear panels at the end, where you can watch them making important decisions.

There's a small desk for me by the lift. It is opposite the kitchenette, and near to the beverage-making facilities. And when I look at my new desk I feel such a buzz.

Each morning, there's a meeting and everyone pulls their chairs into a circle and talks articles. I do a beverage run, and I also contribute to ideas. And I'm learning the dynamics between them all, the friendships and rivalries. Overcoat Home and Barry Arabian are fiercely competitive – Gordoney says it's good for the paper. Overcoat says that I mustn't believe a word Barry Arabian says, and I mustn't fall for his slimy sales wink. And Barry Arabian accuses Overcoat of being too much of an aperchic in his approach to journalism. So every day I go back to Green Place with new words for the list!

And all in all, in a funny way, I think the ups and downs of last year have played a big part in helping me achieve my goal at long last. I was thinking about it earlier, when I went out with Features photographer Larry Sanger to carry his equipment, and we went into the town and got a couple of 'misty bike shots' for the weather page. It was so utterly glamorous, I had to pinch myself. Heaven can be lots of things: it can be sitting next to the toilet on a train when you're travelling with a small child, it can be standing in the drizzle holding the lens bag.

And the best analogy I can come up with, if anyone were to ask me what took me so long to be here living the dream, is that *now* the whole of last year seems to me . . . like a band playing four bars in, with each bar increasing in anticipation of the song that is to come.

Word List

Aperchic
Slimy sales wink

Here are some early *Hack Pensees* on working at the *Echo*.

I can't *wait* to get into the swing of writing in this kind of way, which is more edgy and punchy than my classical work.

And I really want to try and be no-nonsense in my writing, as well as more Russian and more French. I want to mix words, and mince them, I want to bend them and be provocative. I've already submitted an article, entitled 'Is going to someone's house for dinner a form of begging?'

Because I wanted to show Gordoney I can *argue*.

In my articles I plan to ask the questions that nobody else will ask for fear of looking foolish or uninformed. Such as what *is* the difference between pragmatic and phlegmatic? *Is* it something to do with having a cold? And . . . Why do we put a ship after anything we want to promote? For example, flagship, dealership, *readership*? Working with words will be a huge joy. And I want to turn the tables on what is expected. I'll say things are 'robust' and 'muscular' when I'm talking about legislation, and Dickensian and out of date when I'm talking about people's thighs.

I will wear Michael Cane glasses for reading, like I hear Cinema Nixon did, even though I don't actually need them. And who knows, maybe someday I will be hard-hitting enough to become referred to as just plain Bowl. For to be referred to by your surname only truly elevates your status . . . Bowl was born in Titford and began writing at the age of . . . Bowl has written a series of hard-hitting pensees . . . Bowl bagged the bypass scoop . . .

I'm going to have to attend on panels and bandy words like 'punitive' and 'retribution'. I'll have men friends called things like Maximo who have highlighted hair and do lunch. I'm going to have to enter into competitive rhetoric with such colleagues over fine wines and cigars, in the libraries of all kinds of lovely hotels.

And I have burnt my Russian coat on Joe's garden bonfire and in its place I have been wearing a man's pin stripe suite jacket (it belonged to the Admiral). Aunt Coral calls it my 'nearly Friday jacket' because it makes her think of city gents at the weekend. Like London and just as unexpectedly and intensely, I feel that I have *evolved*. And I remember what Di said about walled gardens being believed to have been transformative, and I had a poignant moment when I burnt my coat.

By 1876 Lawrence Garden had spent 15 years in India, and during that time he fell in love with Patricia. I must admit, in all his adventures I didn't see that coming!

FOR THE CONCERN OF THE RICH AND THE POOR

The rains were over, there was a divine freshness in the air driving over the plains into the sunset. We watched from the shade of the tonga as a line of smoke and dust collected on the horizon.

'The beginning of autumn,' said Patricia. The sunlight lit up the brim of her hat like a halo, still strong enough to burn through the straw it was made of.

The scene was so beautiful that we asked the tongawallah to stop for a moment, so we could see the very start of a new season, marked by the watery dust rising through the air like enchanted mist, the scents of jasmine, rain and wet branches reminded me of Edenthorpe.

I remember thinking how many days were behind us in order that we could arrive there in that particular moment, and yet the distant past seemed as near as yesterday morning. I felt as though I might turn around and suddenly see Patricia dancing about in Ayah's sari when she was a child, or I myself waking up from a dream and finding myself back at Edenthorpe, watching a solitary bee working the swaying branches of a blossom tree, overlapping each other like the masts of ships. Or basking in the glow of an English September sunset on a golden field of hay.

All the boys, all the young men I had ever been, seemed present simultaneously, materializing in the line of swaying dust on the horizon, so close I could almost reach out and take the hands of the pauper, the urchin, Alfred's orphan and Rose Anna's son. It seemed so hard to believe that such incarnations could be from just one life. And all because, once upon a time, I ran into a field after a conker.

I tapped my fingers on my knee, along to the rhythm of the insects in the long wet grass, and we listened to the trees, alive with all kinds of birds singing. The dying Monsoon wind whispered through the trees as she departed and we gazed at the hypnotic plumes of smoke coming from the village fires, laced with the dust of a thousand lives.

Patricia rested her hand gently upon mine, and spoke in the language of touch. And a mystical Swarmi materialized and whispered three little words to me, 'There she is.'

We married in 1878, the same year we adopted Mirenne Benson, who made a great voyage to join our family. Her uncle died and she was left at the tender age of nine to fend for herself.

A year later Jill and Judith were born. Two years after that Dorothy followed, and five years later came Dulcima. And I, the son, became the father.

Judith came into the world adoring animals; she never looked twice at her dollies. And Jill loved music and had a talent for painting. Dorothy was always sporty, and seems determined to sail single-handed around the Arabian Gulf!

Dulcie always maintained that she was going to have five children. Maybe it's because she grew up in a busy family of five sisters. Mirenne being the fifth and the eldest.

Patricia told me that at the Martiniere School in Lucknow, the children were asked what nationality they were, during a lecture on the flags of the British Empire. When it was Mirenne's turn to answer she said that she was a Canadian. Miss Scott, of course, who was ignorant of the story of Mirenne's past at the time, marvelled how British parents living in Jaunpur could have given birth to a Canadian. I shall have to tell her that stranger tales have been told!

The Bursary rolled on steadily, gathering momentum. I am proud of my own small contribution to changes in the system. After all, I am the man who came into the world with no name, I am one of the 'nameless millions'. And I passionately believe that education is the food of life.

But perhaps the writing was on the wall for me the minute the niner burned in my hand when I ran into that forbidden field after it. And hopes to leave the world a better place blew across the earth and into the future when Alfred stopped Chaplain Cragg from beating me because it would not be right.

And here I am, safely delivered to the other end of my life. Dust to dust, ashes to ashes, rags to riches, riches to rags, the same beginning, the same end, and we must fight for our story in the middle.

Sue

Sun Feb 12

Pensees: *'The pursuit of knowledge is better
than the pursuit of gold.'*
(Sanskrit)

Pierre is now nearly a year old! He runs Ivana ragged. He was
born just before tea time which may explain why he is always
hungry. And he has to wear special correcting glasses at the
moment because his eyes sometimes drift when he tries to focus.
The frames hook round his ears in an attempt to get them to
stay on.

Ivana says he is like an indoor tornado. When it's been tidied
the living room has a turnround time of ten minutes from looking
nice to looking destroyed, on Pierre's entrance. He covers the furniture in boiled egg and soldiers and puts his plate in his mouth.
He roars like a lion, he tries to climb out of windows, he is like a
tiny hectic alien with the brain of a bird and the brawn of a bear.
The air is alive with the cries of 'Naughty Pierre!', and Dad and
Ivana have both given up sleep. Gone are their film trips and their
spontaneous bubble baths; these things are now consigned to the

past and prefaced by 'Do you remember when?' I don't know where the elderly Buddha Pierre resembled when he was a new born has *gone*.

My old bedroom doesn't even seem like my old bedroom any more, it is very much Pierre's kingdom now. It's an empire of animals and colours and numbers, and sheep flying across the ceiling. An elephant, a pig and a stuffed planet stand together at attention, his own Anglo-Indian universe, waiting at the end of his bed.

Next weekend we are babysitting when Pierre will make his first ever visit to Green Place. And for all the years he was not part of my life, that constitutes a whole lifetime actually. It is curious now that when I think of him it seems as if he has always been there.

> **Word List**
> *Swarmi*
> *Tongawallah*

Mon Feb 13

Pensees of a hack. *I write therefore I am (and vice verser)*. SB

Delia, Admiral Gordon and Loudolle have arrived for Easter, somewhat earlier than anticipated. They would have come even sooner but for a nasty weather front that has been lingering over Aberdeenshire. Admiral Gordon said it was God's way of saying, 'Everybody stay where you are!'

Loudolle has her hair in an amazing shape these days. It is sort of poker straight but flicked out on the ends, like poop scoops. I have tried very hard not to be too avoidant and complimented her on her new look. She said she'd forgotten her hairbrush and asked me if I had anything she could borrow. I had to work very hard to hold back from saying, well, I do, I have a *broom*. She managed to congratulate me on my internship. Maybe she is on medication?

But the big news is . . . the reason for their special visit . . . Delia has a ring on her courtship finger! She brandishes it at every opportunity. It is a sapphire and diamond band of three stones that belonged to Admiral Gordon's mother. They have set the wedding date for next autumn, as they don't want to rush. And you can imagine how much Delia and Aunt C want to *linger* over the arrangements. They are perfect companions, the two of them. Aunt Coral was born with a cup of tea in her hand and Delia was born with a sandwich. Delia has been behaving giddily. She hung fairy lights all over the hall and the grand staircase. It must be love, because she used to be on the lazy side and found it an effort just to get up and switch on a light.

And when Admiral Gordon and Delia do marry, apparently Admiral G is going to make Loudolle Heiress to Eaglehurst! She pointed this out to me, almost before she had finished her unpacking. She is very competitive. She added that she is sickey-happy about it. I think she should have just stopped after sickey.

But, she can't compete with the burgeoning glorious gardens here, when I imagine in Aberdeenshire all she will have to lord it over are damp sweeps of heather and scrub.

But here at Green Place the smell of peaches and coconut waft from the gorse in the Meadows and the swaying trees grow so full in summer they make a roof over our heads along the drive, and most recently since a small pond at the bottom of the orchard has been rediscovered and reinstated, we have attracted a newt.

Joe broke off his work yesterday to come up to the house to tell us – oh it was so good to see him. Since I saw him I have been trying not to break into a soupy mutiny, keep myself busy and side-tracked . . . It must be extract o'clock.

FOR THE CONCERN OF THE RICH AND THE POOR

When Rose Anna became an old lady, she moved back into Gunyah to allow our tearaway girls more space. And there she faded from the scene very slowly, like the reluctant sun in autumn. And when she eventually sickened and took full time to her bed, I went to Gunyah every day so we would have as much time as possible together.

On what turned out to be the very last night of her life, I visited as usual. She was lying in her bed, too weak to do much more than whisper to me.

'Do you know, I thought I would never rest in my rocking chair and watch the young generation and come to wonder how they made everything new. But you came along and saved me from all that. I was resurrected within life.'

'I can't answer you, my tears prevent me,' I said. 'Thank you for wanting to be my mother. I could not love anyone more.'

I got up on to her bed beside her and lay down gently with my head against her shoulder. She was so brittle and shrunken, I thought she would break like a shell.

She fell asleep after that and when I came back in the morning, she was gone.

Nearly a hundred people turned out to say farewell to the woman who at forty would have cloistered herself away for ever.

Rose Anna was always so understated, so perfectly in keeping with tradition. She remained shrouded for years, before she would occasionally wear a little grey. Her half-mourning clothes were the same, even in the heat of

India. When I married Patricia, Rose Anna wore mauve, with just a tiniest trim of lilac, but still she refused all other colour, to brighten her misty widow's days. But as I was in charge of such decisions after she was no longer, when they laid her to rest in her coffin, by God she was dressed in white.

Sue

At last! Pierre made his grand entrance! Earlier today he was carried in from the car by Ivana, as she issued a million specific instructions particular to him: mind his hair, he likes his sleeves rolled back once, there are banana sandwiches in the Tupperware . . . he bangs his fist when he wants more food.

Everyone hovered around him, smitten and enchanted. For the residents of Green Place there can be nothing so delightful as a visit from a baby.

'He's so cute,' said Loudolle. 'I love his little specs. You don't really looky like though,' she added.

'That must be due to our different mothers,' I said.

Pierre unhooked his glasses, waved them in a bouncing arm and then dropped them on to the floor.

'Naughty Pierre!' said Ivana, putting them back on him. He tried to take them off again. 'No, Naughty Pierre!' she said.

'Look at his chubby leg rolls!' said Delia.

'But he's getting away with it!' said Aunt Coral.

'Look at his little shoes, look at his little buckles!' I said.

I followed him about as he explored. And I love seeing things through his eyes. He notices the most peculiar things and fixates on them – for example, a toilet roll, or a brass door handle.

Pierre spent some time pinching various noses . . . the larger the nose the more tempting. 'Naughty Pierre!' said Delia. 'Naughty Pierre!' said Admiral G.

After lunch I took a sandwich down to the garden for Joe the grafter, and Pierre came along. Today was mild for February, the sky was high and the air was light.

I carried Pierre down through the boulevard of trees, to the meadows, very, very slowly. He likes to take pit stops so he can climb down and crawl. And I remembered being in exactly the same spot, in the autumn last year, because at the time the spiky green sweet-chestnut casings lay on the grass, like the fallen stars of Mars. And I remember wondering, how could I feel sad at such a time, when the leaves curl and the trees are dripping with *gold*? But today the sight of Pierre makes me think of Frittie. How intense his moments in the sun must have been, how bright the green, green garden. How he must have drunk it all in, all the colour and the life.

As we came near to the walled garden, the only sounds apart from the gentle scrape from Joe's trowel were the crackling of a bonfire and a woodpecker pecking in a nearby tree. The garden is about to burst into bloom, and the tiny blades of grass underfoot appear to be sprinkled with stardust. Aunt Coral says she likes a blousy garden, not too perfectly manicured, and the wind moves through the weeds and time flowers and blows their delicate fluff away, as if it is scattering the dust of time.

'Hello there,' called Joe, putting down his trowel. He was a little way further down the garden.

'He's getting so big!' he said.

I put Pierre down and he crawled off in the direction of the sundial.

The familiar words 'For the Concern of the Rich and the Poor' lay in clear italic writing, facing the sun, with the shadow of the dial falling at one o'clock and the swathes of Town Clock underneath it, rustling.

'The Admiral made you a sandwich,' I said, walking over to where Joe was working, and offering him the dog-eared little bap.

He looked doubtful.

'The fish paste was within its sell by,' I said, before changing the subject. 'The Gallant's Bower looks wonderful.'

'Yes, I'm pleased with it,' said Joe.

'What's that on the roof of the bench?' I asked, referring to a glass shade Joe had constructed on the top of a long pole.

'It's a lantern,' said Joe. 'I thought Aunt Coral might like to light a candle in the summer.'

'She'll be thrilled with that. She thinks it's such a romantic idea anyway.'

'I don't think I built it because it was romantic, although I admit that it is,' said Joe. 'No, the Gallant's Bower is actually a fort. I spent time there one holiday in Devon.'

'Oh, I, we . . . thought you might have built it for romantic reasons,' I said.

'Maybe I built it because I wanted to protect you, and of course Aunt Coral,' said Joe. 'Some sort of unconscious thing I expect,' he added casually.

Pierre lay underneath the sundial, thrashing about and babbling.

'I'm training jasmine and tuberose on the roof over the bower, maybe he's knocked out by the smell!' said Joe.

'London Taylor's bench outside Edenthorpe was covered with

jasmine,' I said somewhat wistfully. 'Are you coming to the Sunday night salon tomorrow?' I added. 'Aunt Coral is planning a grand kick-off for the new year in the Orangery, and they are going to announce Admiral Gordon and Delia's engagement.'

'Are you kidding, of course I'm coming. When I heard it was happening, I went straight to John Anthony Gordon and bought a new tank top.'

'And obviously, do bring Charlie,' I said.

'Cheers a lot,' he said. I noted his language of cool, and we came to an awkward halt.

'What's Pierre doing?' asked Joe, breaking the silence.

'He looks like he's trying to dig up the Town Clock,' I said. 'Naughty Pierre!' I called out. I rushed to scoop him up before he did too much damage. 'Naughty Pierre!' I repeated.

And as I approached Pierre, I heard the sound of scraping.

'I think he's found something,' I said, crouching down in the shadow of the sundial. 'He's scratching at something – he's got a pebble.'

'What is it?' asked Joe as he joined me.

'I'm not sure,' I said. 'Maybe a stone.'

He ran over and launched into the dig with a special pointy spade he took from his technical tool belt. Pierre had already dug a tiny-fingered hole into the very damp soil underneath the Town Clock. Joe continued excavating, and eventually pulled out a small wooden box.

'Oh my God, shall I open it?' I said.

'Yes!' said Joe. 'Yes, yes, open it!' He passed it to me.

'I hope it's not full of insects!' I said.

A small creak emanated from the box as I opened it. It was all dark and fusty inside. And it had the same smell as old books and documents have, the smell of the *past*.

'It's lined with tin,' I said. 'Listen.' I tapped it. 'Funny.'

'Is there anything in there?' he asked.

'Some fabric I think.'

I peered in and there, revealed by the spring sunshine, were two raggedy long black muslin *cuffs*. And on the side of each one were long rows of partially concealed black *pearl* buttons!

'Oh my God!' I said. 'Rose Anna's weeper's cuffs! Of course, she had them on her all the time! She was wearing them all the time!'

I picked one cuff up very gently and, as I did, something fell out and lay on the ground *shimmering*. I scooped it up, like a star dropped from Heaven.

'The Star of the South!' I cried.

I started swiftly back up to the big house with the weeper's cuffs in the box and the Star of the South tumbling inside.

'Aunt Coral! We have found treasure!'

'We have found treasure!' cried Joe. He picked up Pierre and ran after me.

Sat Feb 25 1989

Hack Pensees: *And so, in conclusion to the answer to my titular question: '99 percent of people are morons, is that a bit harsh?' I would have to say that the answer is yes, and then sadly no.* SB *(Just a little reminder of the article that made it all* happen!)

So now the bank in Egham has taken receipt of the weeper's cuffs with their magnificent, cunningly concealed pearl buttons (more on the Star of the South in a moment).

Jackie is sourcing experts to value the items so they can one day be sold and turned into liquid in the hope that they will provide a decent fund with which to care for Green Place. Of course

it made sense that in order to hide the necklace Rose Anna dis-
banded it . . . It would be harder to find if it was in different pieces
and kept about her person. Clever lady. (But I believe that she
must have hidden her treasure in the ground beneath the sundial
quite some time *before* the night she had to leave Roselyne. Maybe
around the same sort of time that she stopped wearing the weeper's cuffs. But then she didn't have time to retrieve them on the
fateful night of the fire, and so there they have lain.)

I'm just looking out of the long windows in the Orangery, and
I can see the dark shapes of a couple seated on a bench beneath a
resplendent blossom. I think it is Admiral Gordon and Delia.

I had a sudden craving where years pass in an instant, and me
and Joe were together and living in the Croquet Hut. I saw myself
working away at a typewriter with a view, while Joe pottered
about with a row of strawberries facing south-east . . . and the
ferns in the meadows curl up at night as we do, and stretch out
again in the morning.

The evenings are getting lighter and lighter, and flowers and
bulbs alike are growing, waiting to burst with life, and the clouds
have, at last, finally lifted, and the peek-a-boo sun is trying to find
the gaps in between them. This is rapture. Now you see me, now
you don't.

'I, the sun, am truly egalitarian . . .'

Sun Feb 26 1989

Pensees: *Just because a person doesn't show their true feelings,*
doesn't mean they don't burn. SB

But I didn't feel particularly sparkling and witty when it came
time to get ready for the salon this evening. And I wasn't in the
mood for shmutzing. If I can't avoid the awkwardness of seeing

Joe and Charlie together, at least having some of my own friends coming too means I won't have to actually *talk* to them.

'Would you like a cocktail?' asked Aunt Coral, when I went up to her suite to pin her hair up. 'The Admiral said he would knock on my door at 5.30 and take orders.'

'Thank you. I'll have a Bellini,' I said.

'Oh?'

'It's what we drink in Features,' I said.

'In that case I'll have one too. You not getting spruced up?' she asked me.

'I don't feel like it,' I said.

She moved a hanger along on its rail.

'The pure sound of the *evening*,' she said.

It was around this time last year that I was concerned about her, because she looked so delicate when I got home from Greece. But I have since come to realize that this 'spectral alabaster' is just her winter colour, translucent and light-fingered.

'Would you help me put this on?' she asked me.

I clipped a strong chain around her neck from which dangled at her décolletage none other than the Star of the South.

'Just this once, eh?' said Aunt C. 'It seems fitting that I should just wear it once.'

The diamond shimmered and sparkled against the black of Aunt Coral's gown.

'Is it heavy?' I asked.

'Pleasantly,' replied Aunt C. 'Don't you think you should pop into something that would make more of a . . . visual impact on Joe?' she asked me.

'I can't be bothered, there's no point – he's coming with Charlie.'

'Oh do get dolled up, if not for him then for me,' said Aunt C.

So I succumbed to the heavy pressure and went down and put on a pretty dress, and heels, and make up . . . and jewellery . . . and perfume . . . the works by the time I had finished.

'Much better,' said Aunt C.

Later

Delia's trail of fairy lights had reached all around the Orangery, and she and Aunt Coral had gone to the trouble of hanging several wind chimes in the trees outside. The Admiral did caution against this, in case we come in for some bad weather, but the ladies were not for turning!

Eccles was back at the piano. And Aunt C had gone beyond herself and invited half of Egham! She greeted her guests at the door before they went in, a bit like the Queen. I stood in line next to her, practising my social skills. So there we hosted, as the Admiral, Delia, Admiral Gordon and Loudolle trooped in; then Dad, Ivana and Pierre; and then a welcome back to Mrs Bunion. Then Posiedon arrived, dressed till the nines for vamping, followed by William and Helen from Zola. William was wearing a cape and eyeliner. Helen says he thinks he's it.

The team from the *Echo* arrived about half an hour later, and Mr and Mrs Rodriguez came too (Posiedon's parents), closely followed by the Nanas, and then Icarus arrived, who Loudolle had asked along. And last but by no means least, fresh from the garden, Joe . . . and his girlfriend Charlie.

There was some chatter for a short while, and some voller vongs were handed out, small talk exchanged and forgotten.

'Where are you staying?' asked Posiedon.

'Effingham,' said William.

'That sounds quite rude,' said Helen.

I introduced them to Aunt Coral. William declined a cocktail because he has very recently declared that he is an alcoholic. (Helen thinks it's just affectation.)

'My name's William and I'm an alcoholic,' said William as he shook Aunt C's hand.

'Hello, you're the first alcoholic I've ever met,' beamed Aunt C.

'I like your tank top,' I said to Joe, launching in.

'Cheers a lot,' said Joe. He did look so, winning.

'Hi Sue, I like your frock,' Charlie followed.

I took the comment on the chin, because I don't believe she meant it to be pointy.

'Jackie County told me that the box we found the weeper's cuffs in was probably some sort of Victorian ice box,' I pattered. 'Oh hello, Mr Rodriguez, can I get you a napkin?' I asked, and after that, mercifully, Joe and Charlie moved away into the Orangery to shmutz.

A few minutes later Aunt Coral stepped into the middle of the dance floor, while the Admiral tinkled his spoon against his glass and the room fell silent.

'Welcome everybody and . . . it's so lovely to have you all here,' exclaimed Aunt Coral. 'Now before we kick off again tonight, while Eccles is just taking five minutes, I have a very important announcement to make, so please without further ado, would you all charge your glasses.'

The Admiral went around with the trolley making sure everyone had some champagne.

'It is my great pleasure to propose a toast to my dear friend Delia, and to draw your attention to Friday's *Times* announcing her forthcoming wedding to Admiral Gordon. The clipping is up on the noticeboard in the kitchen if anyone wants to see,' said Aunt C.

Delia and Admiral Gordon gave a little wave as if they were royalty. Delia had Disney eyes.

'To Delia and Admiral Gordon,' said the Admiral, raising his glass.

'To Admiral Gordon and Delia.'

'Now everybody please get ready to take your partners as Eccles will soon be kicking off again with a waltz,' announced Aunt C.

The general burble mounted again as the Orangery warmed up.

I returned to sit down on the banquette near my hostess position by the door, in case any guest should need assistance. And soon after, Joe came over to talk to me. He left Charlie with Loudolle, Icarus and Posiedon, the girls somewhat draped around Icarus.

'Hello. Mind if I sit?' he asked me.

'Banquette?' I offered, patting it.

'Not in front of everyone,' Joe replied.

I blushed, but I was relieved to see that Joe was blushing too at the absolute daring of his own joke.

'You look lovely. I love that dress,' he said.

'This old thing?' I said, pausing for effect, while I examined a niggling snag in my nail, at the same time as slightly *displaying* the cut of my dress. 'Oh yes . . . I remember now you telling me you liked it the night we went to that party in Staines,' I said. 'I had forgotten.'

'I was just thinking about the Admiral and Aunt Coral,' Joe chatted. 'Do you think they'll ever tie the knot?'

'I shouldn't think so, it would spoil all the romance too much.'

'You've become cynical and sophisticated,' said Joe.

'Oh I know,' I said.

'I agree though, I think that's right, for them,' Joe said, tactfully.

'Did I tell you I'm doing a genealogy series on all my dead relatives?' I pattered.

'Nice,' he said.

'Would you like to dance?' he asked.

I glanced over at Charlie dubiously.

'It's OK, Charlie only dances at clubs,' said Joe. 'Besides, she believes in free love, so I'm sure she won't mind if we *dance*.'

'That's modern,' I said.

'No it isn't, it's old hat,' said Joe, 'and it's not really in keeping with my ethos.'

'Your ethos being the committed house with the old cat?'

'You've got a good memory,' said Joe. 'Do you think you might ever have a phase for something like that?' he asked. 'After your hack phase maybe?'

'I think it's possible I might, one day. I hope.'

'Hello, anything in the wind?' asked the Admiral as he passed us on his way round to top up glasses.

We surveyed the room and had a brief pause in our flow. I like to believe it was because there were things that weren't being *said*.

Then Eccles came back from his break and so we got up to dance, joined by a chorus of wind chimes. And as we spun around the floor, if my eyes didn't deceive me, there appeared to be a tiny light flickering in the night, just beyond the meadows, coming from the Gallant's Bower.

Mon Feb 27 1989, 4am in the morning
And now everyone has gone, it is a small and silent hour . . . I drifted around after the party had finished, collecting stray glasses and plumping cushions and now find myself sitting in the White Room. I can hear the distant purr of the drawing-room clock on

the other side of the hall, and I can see the frost tingling on the lawns outside, as if it had been thrown from the glitter pots of fairies.

Here amongst the portraits the past feels as near as yesterday, as close as my last heartbeat.

Earlier I asked Delia if she will work on a portrait of Madam Rose Anna and London Taylor for this room; she is a very good painter. In my mind's eye I picture Madam Rose Anna in her widow's weeds, wearing the Shipwreck Pearls, with little blonde London on her knee and a dear old spaniel at their feet, and not forgetting perhaps Walderon her maid should be there too . . . and maybe Alfred in the garden . . . how quickly it turns into a bigger picture, that's the wonderful thing about stories. (I added the spaniel, that's the wonderful thing about writing.) And it's so strange to think that what happened here so long ago, to those whose lives ended even in a different *country*, still has an impact on today. Somehow they have passed on their knowledge, wealth, love, to us *here* and *now* . . . *today*.

But the chain is very tightly linked . . . Aunt Coral's father was born in 1898! And her grandmother Carolina came from 1875! And within *her* memory Carolina walked on the earth with her mother Adelaide who came from 1820 . . . and so on and so on. And the procession goes back and back all the way to the beginning of time. And I am at the other end of the line, beside my mother from 1944, beside her mother from 1925, and maybe in my writing I can catch the hand of a relative, revive them, retrace their steps, move beside them in the line. Run to the past with open arms, walk in history. For one day we will all rest in the quiet earth as it spins into infinity.

But I always know that when I start to think existentially, that it's probably time to go to bed . . . definitely in a Rousseau mood tonight! He wanted to abandon civilization and live in the trees. I wonder if he ever tried it?

The moon has set over the partially restored walls of the old garden, bright and full and clear; there is always something going on at Green Place to lift your spirits.

Yet sometimes on summer afternoons, I don't even notice the velvet dark shadows of the trees on the sunny lawns, or stop to detect the smell of fresh-mown grass with the sun beating down on it . . . or pause to think *these are* my golden-tinted summer days. This is it. It is my turn to live.

I'm struck by the dashes on the family tree, laid out on the table underneath my notepad, that lead to spouses and to children. But if London Taylor has taught me anything about hope, then as far as being reunited with Joe is concerned, the sky is the limit.

Maybe one day we might reach that stage that some long-established couples do, where the husband remembers the wife's sweethearts better than she does, and talks of them fondly, as if they are long-lost children. Utterly Russian.

As soon as it's light, I think I will go and leave a note for him to find in the hollow of the oak tree years from now, telling him how very much I love him on this February night.

FOR THE CONCERN OF THE RICH AND THE POOR

Jaunpur 1919
One velocipede, one coach, one rag-and-bone cart, two trains, across oceans, one lifetime later, I sit and write. While the fan blows my papers around my office and the ink from my pen is smudged by occasional tears falling from my eyes.

On our fortieth wedding anniversary Patricia gave me

a solid-gold horseshoe paperweight, to hold the pages of my manuscript down. It is engraved with our names, but her card was addressed to London Taylor, in honour of his long journey.

And memory is such a wonderful thing. I can be here with Patricia in 1919 and also be a Class One pauper at the Mead in 1857, at exactly the same time, and at any time that I choose. I can even enjoy being at the Mead, knowing that I'm not there any more, I'm here.

The stars are beginning to smoulder through the fine dust that is burning into the hot air of the night. I was just looking up to a painting Rose Anna did of Edenthorpe, remembering the cold, remembering Alfred. I treasure the memory of his life, as I treasure the many others I have remembered here. And promise and memory are both in themselves divine reflections.

It is in the actions of my friends, I would say, that I finally believed in God's message. For above the names Harry Benson, Alfred, Rose Anna, He carves his slogan, 'God is Love', and there I finally can understand it. For I am living testimony that He was never once at the Mead.

Yet I believe it is true to say that in life we each have to find our throne. Whether it is under the table with a Labrador, or on a boat out in the Arabian Sea, or, in my case, in the chair in which I sit on the veranda beside Patricia's.

But before I go, like the elephant who never forgets, I shall pay my final respects to the small creature that is the jewel in my crown.

A few days after Mirenne disembarked from her long voyage from Canada, we went up to the solicitors in Allahabad to sign the paperwork formally identifying both of us as Mirenne's guardians. We had a celebratory lunch afterwards, and I made Mirenne a little gift.

'This belonged to your father,' I said. 'It was always my intention to give it back to him.'

I strung the old niner on to a new shoelace and I placed it around her neck, and as I did I remembered the words Harry Benson said to me on the day I ran into the field after it.

'Don't be afraid!'

Acknowledgements

Thank you firstly to my editor Bella Bosworth, who has been such a source of inspiration to me, for all her guidance, support and notes, not least how I should go about fusing two stories into one. And to Harriet Bourton, Naomi Mantin, Rebecca Hunter and everyone at Transworld, a wonderful publisher.

Many thanks are also due to my splendid literary agent Sophie Scard, for reading the various dinosaur drafts and offering emergency insight.

And a thousand thanks to my wonderful friend Lizzie Knight, who has been so steadily kind, helpful and generous, in reading drafts and offering feedback, support and inspiration, far beyond the call of duty.

Huge thanks to my dad, Allen Crowe, for having me to work in his house, and dip in to his collection of books, with titles from how to set up home in the Tropics in the 1950s, to old Sotheby's catalogues left casually lying about, which is a surprisingly inspirational ploy. And to my dear mum, Neta, still here in mind and word, so long after leaving the party.

Very special thanks to the friends who took the time to read drafts for me: Lizzie, my sister Jan, and my friend Sue Holderness, who all put in the hours.

Warmest thanks to Tamsin Leaf for reading and pondering

and responding RPR. To which I say thank you NHN (no high number), and thank you to Roxie, Jakob, Nat and Rick.

Especial thanks to Ian Hallard and Mark Gatiss for all their support and encouragement.

I am deeply grateful to the friends who kindly provided me with space in their homes to write in when I was in a state of flux moving house. To Robin, Siobhan, Guy, Mia, Roger and Michael McCallum for the writing room, and to Sue Holderness and Mark Piper for the writing flat. And to both families for being such a strong source of inspiration to me.

A huge thank you to my sister Deb and to Nick, Mikey, Julia and Ruby and to cousin Naughty Pierre who once ran away with the doll. You are a legend.

Thank you to Barbara, Mike and young Niko, a constant source of inspiration, and ditto to Allen and Katy, all the wonderful Anglo-Greeks.

To the Taylor-Michaels; Annie, Dora, Mamie, Rex, Fergus and Rory, and to Vanessa, Lisa, Joan and Tim, thank you for being my gang.

Finally, last but not least, very special thanks to my husband, Sean, aka Simon de Boo-vee-ay, as always for all his encouragement, company, support, inspiration and understanding.

And to all the friends and rellies who have been so supportive and helpful along the way.

Books that I read when researching:
Plain Tales of the Raj edited by Charles Allen
Kipling's Kingdom by Charles Allen
Curry and Rice by George Francklin Atkinson
Life in a Victorian Workhouse by Peter Higginbotham
The Morville Year by Katherine Swift

The English Year: Autumn and Winter by William Beach Thomas and Anthony Keeling Collett

The Charm of Gardens by Dion Clayton Calthrop

The Fishing Fleet by Anne de Courcy

The Confessions of Rousseau by Jean Jaques himself

Sara Crowe's Imaginary Bookshop

What would be the name of your Imaginary Bookshop?
'Squirrel Books'.

Where would it be located?
In a magical forest . . . high on a hill, with a few fairy lights in the trees, a cool breeze, distant sea views beyond the far amber lights of a town . . . in spite of which . . . thriving custom at the bookshop.

Any special features?
Tree houses, hideouts and magical platforms among the treetops (also known as balconies), under the stars. I'd offer special overnight stays in a fully furnished tree house (luxury and candle light, optional patchwork quilt) with the book of your choice – plus twenty per cent off a second book if you can read the first one before morning. Entrepreneurial?

What would make your bookshop different from the others?
The tree houses would be pre-bookable and yet there'd always be one available last minute. And perhaps some beautiful quotes carved in the trees like: '*Nobody has ever measured, not even poets, how much the heart can hold*', Zelda Fitzgerald.

What sections would you have? What would you ditch?

I think banning anything would make it more interesting, so I wouldn't ditch anything. I'd try to have a section on everything under the sun, Humble Insects of the Hebrides . . . The Hermit Who Never Went Out . . . Thoughts On Cement . . .

What would be on your display table and why?

My groaning display table would have, under 'Fiction', *David Copperfield*, *Jane Eyre* (this is a bit like a dinner party) by Charles Dickens and Charlotte Brontë, *Sense and Sensibility* by Jane Austen, *Perfume* by Patrick Suskind, *The Life of Pi* by Yann Martel, *Kim* by Rudyard Kipling, *Rebecca* by Daphne Du Maurier, *Tender is the Night* by F. Scott Fitzgerald, *The Woman in Black* by Susan Hill.

Under 'Reference' there would be: *The Book of Decorative Furniture* by Edwin Foley, *England's Lost Houses* by Giles Worsley, *Daily Rituals* by Mason Curry. And 'For Beauty Reasons': *The Country Diary of an Edwardian Lady* by Edith Holden.

For 'Autobiography and Biography' we would see: *Confessions of Rousseau*, *The Morville Year* by Katherine Swift, *West with the Night* by Beryl Markham; *C. S. Lewis: A Biography* by A. N. Wilson, *The Coming of the Fairies* by Arthur Conan Doyle, *Film Stars Don't Die in Liverpool* by Peter Turner, *Eat, Pray, Love* by Elizabeth Gilbert, plus an 'Unforgettable Sub Section' of *If This is A Man, The Truce* by Primo Levi, *Man's Search for Meaning* by Viktor Frankl.

Last but not least, under 'Children's' I'd place *The Cat in the Hat* by Dr Seuss, *The Tiger Who Came to Tea* by Judith Kerr, *Black Beauty* by Anna Sewell, *The Lion, the Witch and the Wardrobe* by C. S. Lewis, *The Jungle Book* by Rudyard Kipling. (Small chairs available under table for children's reading.)

If you could have one author living or dead for an author event who would it be?
Not surprisingly, C. S. Lewis. But this is a close call between himself and The Brontës Reunited For One Night Only.

What sort of event would it be?
C. S. Lewis . . . On the Other Side of the Wardrobe: an event for children in the afternoon, with a reading from towards the end of *The Lion, the Witch and the Wardrobe*, which is the beginning of everything else . . .

'All their life in this world and all their adventures in Narnia had only been the cover and the title page. Now at least they were beginning Chapter One of the Great Story which no one on earth has ever read: which goes on forever: in which every chapter is better than the one before.'

And in the evening, a talk for the adults in the main tree house, all decorated with moss and twig diorama forests displayed on biscuit tin lids, such as the ones A. N. Wilson says Lewis made as a boy. Could they have been the beginnings of Narnia I would ask him?

A customer asks why they should buy your novel?
May I prescribe a few hours of a little light escapism?

What cake would be served at the launch?
Hot chocolate fudge brownies.

Have you read Sara Crowe's first novel,
Campari for Breakfast?

Life is full of terrible things. Ghosts of dead relatives, heartbreak . . . burnt toast.

In 1987, Sue Bowl's world changes for ever. Her mother dies, leaving her feeling like she's lost a vital part of herself. And then her father shacks up with an awful man-eater called Ivana.

But Sue's mother always told her to make the most of what she's got – and what she's got is a love of writing and some eccentric relatives. So Sue moves to her Aunt Coral's crumbling ancestral home, where she fully intends to write a book and fall in love . . . and perhaps drink Campari for breakfast.

Campari for Breakfast is a heart-warming, eccentric novel that joins the ranks of great British coming-of-age novels such as Dodie Smith's *I Capture the Castle* and Nancy Mitford's *The Pursuit of Love*.